Surviving Well
is the
Best Revenge

Book Two

A Novel of Montreal: 1960

by

Patric Ryan

Sarawak Studios Press & M.L. Ryan Publishing

Fiction by Patric Ryan

The Fogo's War Trilogy
Book One
Summer Wars & Winter Schooners
Book Two
Schooners Are Black & U-Boats Are Grey
Book Three
The Final Acts of Fogo's War

The Paris Shooter's Union

The Burning Islands

Surviving Well is the Best Revenge: Cuba

Surviving Well is the Best Revenge: Montreal

Surviving Well is the Best Revenge: Newfoundland

Non-fiction

Closing The Newfoundland Circles

Screenplays

Winter Schooner, Fogo's War & Ellie's Boat

Short Stories
Rum Runners & River Rats, The Last Fisherman,
The Skipjack Wars
& The Man From Chicago

Surviving Well is the Best Revenge

A novel of Montreal: 1960.

by **Patric Ryan**

Author of *The Fogo's War Trilogy*, *The Paris Shooter's Union* & *The Burning Islands*

Sarawak Studios & ML Ryan Publishing
Bruce Rd #1974.
Lion's Head, Ontario Canada N0H 1W0

Email: patric@patricryan.com
www.patricryan.com

Cover design: Sophie Ryan

Canadian Cataloguing in Publication Data
Ryan, Patric D.M.

Surviving Well is the Best Revenge: Montreal
ISBN 978-0-9698003-3-0

1. Ryan, Patric D.M., 2. Montreal 1960, 3.The FLQ, 4. Montreal and the FLQ Revolution. Drama. Fiction

For Dorie who inspired many of the critical scenes in Book Two. The events may be found in our memoir *Closing the Newfoundland Circles*

A special thanks to Sophie for her cover creativity and to my patient editors: Sarina and Dorie

Surviving Well Is The Best Revenge

Book Two

Montreal 1960

Jean-Pierre

"June 1960. Ile Royale. Ile de Montreal. Ville-Marie. Whatever...I'm home. The train ride from New York was a blur of heat and sandwich wrappers. The woman in the seat ahead cried constantly, leaving me to entertain her children..."

Christian had become more angular since Cuba. The long journey home, aged by experience and life lived hard on the margins, took their measure. Christian felt used up, like Cuba. He only wanted to be near the cooling waters of the Great River.

He walked from Windsor Station along Rue St. Antoine toward the river, pulled down by gravity. Turning off St. Antoine he continued on Rue St. Denis passed the market, crossed below Bonsecours, then around the basin of Old Victoria Wharf to the embankment.

Even beside the rushing river the dead air was hot and moist, and his T-shirt clung to skin, skin to bones. The low sun, red and malevolent, torched its way through the heat haze, flattening the city like a hot iron but the humidity softened the hard lines of the Jacques Cartier Bridge, turning to fool's gold in the dying sun. Below the bridge the scrap heaps of industrial Montreal were bronze pyramids. Opposite the basin the dark green trees of Ile Ste-Hélène, anchored in the lower rapids of the restless river, seemed a verdant refuge in the midst of commercial squalor. Further downriver the refineries of Montreal East and the low shore of suburban Longueuil and Boucherville, floated above the pewter coloured water. The smells coming from the St. Lawrence River were not like the clean fish smells of the beach at Los Espiritos. He wanted to remember only the good things but Cuba was a diffused memory of war and heat. And raw emotions.

There was a body lying too close to the edge of the broken concrete bulkhead. A slight young man, dark; dead too young, like Rosa and her young rebels. He remembered all the bodies, the friends and enemies, the young and the old. What did this one mean to his future and fortune? He should just walk away.

It had been a year and a half since the Revolution propelled Cuba into world consciousness. Fidel Castro strode the island like a caged lion as the Batista regime cringed and collapsed. Christian tasted the fear and smelled the death of revolution. Then he met Rosa and Esa, Renée arrived and Batista's soldiers attacked his village. The night of the first attack Miguel hid Christian in the cold cellar of his villa. There were American actors hiding in a cave beneath the villa. Ernesto Escobar was shot by a firing squad. And he had lost Renée, again.

Renée escaped with Ramon, the Fidel impersonator, sailing for Havana with the Louisiana fugitive, Mississippi Delta Maartyn. Tragically the beautiful revolutionary, Rosameralda Diez, had been killed during the final rebel march on Havana, and Christian was sleeping with her sister, Esameralda. Los Espiritos was a charred ruin. Life was a mess, but he had survived.

After the final battle Juanita brought him a bottle of rum and the news. *The bloody siege of Los Espiritos had been a grand deception and everybody was acting a part in a complicated drama to steal the revolution from Fidel Castro under the leadership of Ernesto Escobar.* Escobar was a fraud, a disgraced Spanish aristocrat living out his exile in a fishing village, hording fake Impressionist paintings, scheming to one day be the King of Cuba. Jocinto Diez, the jazz guitar master, died a natural death. One of many deaths, not natural, he considered, but that was subjective.

He still mourned Jocinto and the music. A pathological cop

named Yolondo Carnero, who ordered a twelve-year-old boy to shoot him with Rosameralda's pistol, had smashed his own saxophone. He longed for Rosa, Esa or Renée, or all three unequally. Cuba had been his lifeboat. The lifeboat ran aground on the Cuban Revolution and many friends were dead or missing.

In the spring of nineteen-sixty he decided to stop sleeping with Esameralda, said goodbye to his houseboy, Miguel, and his dog Wolf Pietro Marlon Brando and came home to Montreal by way of Louisiana.

Louisiana also smelled of dead fish. He prowled the Delta looking for Maartyn and the *Bayou Queen*. He wondered if the *Bayou Queen* still smelled of shrimp and dead Cubans...

The current fish smell came from the market near Victoria Wharf. Vieux Port reminded him of a gift of a long dead cod, an antique memory of Juanita.

To avoid the legion of memories he watched the Lachine Rapids tumbling like undisciplined children, boiling under the Jacques Cartier Bridge, and that made him think of Maartyn St. Jacques. Where was Maartyn? Jail probably, and Paulo in the next cell. He couldn't wonder about Maartyn without raising that dull ache in the center of his chest where Renée resided, or Esa. He tried summoning the warmth of Esameralda's brown body but only increased the ache. Renée had left him...for Ramon, the phony bastard, making out all the way to New York! And probably Paris! Damn! The image of them doing it in the first class passenger cabin of a French airliner didn't help. Why didn't he go with her? Imagined her crossing the Seine on the foot bridge to her flat on Ile St. Louis after a lingering lunch with some gigolo on the West Bank, in the shadow of Notre Dame, stopping to watch the black water flow sedately, the way a sophisticated French river should flow, not roaring like the St. Lawrence: wild and rambunctious, rude, vulgar. Renée thought of him as a rambunctious child.

Brown foam clung to the rocks. Not the way the ocean foams on rocks...fermenting wood chips and bleaching agents from the logging mills on the Ottawa River, the factories of the Lachine Canal, the toilets of LaSalle and Verdun. Industrial scum. Montreal treated her rivers like a sewer. Further down river Varennes, Trois-Riviéres and Québec City added their own, and so on, all the way to Tadoussac, and the Saguenay which carried the dross from Chicoutimi and Lac St. Jean and the aluminum plants of Arvida. A one way trip to the ocean where it mixed with the continental detritus from New York and Boston, riding the Gulf Stream, heading for Europe, to have coitus with the North Sea, where it picked up effluent from the Rhine and circled back on the mid-ocean drift to the West Indies and Cuba, and probably some junk from Montreal ended up on the beach below Escobar's Villa...and that made him think of the firing squad and the day he and Renée held each other while Rosameralda lined up her rebels in the court yard with their new rifles and shot the Batista spy, so that all the young rebels could taste blood. Escobar said it was necessary. It would get worse but at that moment Renée and Christian held each other tightly. It was the end of their self-indulgent Bohemian trip...trying not to think about Cuba was like trying to ignore vertigo.

Christian felt the familiar chill of foreboding. *Just walk away*, the voice said. Walk away...do not approach the body, but the body moved. What if it rolled into the river? He'd be responsible for another death. He wasn't responsible for the deaths of his Cuban friends, but he hadn't prevented them from dying. Not Rosameralda or the spy. He could have protested the execution of the spy, but it wasn't his war. Not Escobar. There was nothing he could do about Escobar, or maybe his presence in Los Espiritos put Escobar in danger. Jocinto died of old age. Maybe he pushed the old man to his death with the music...no, Jocinto was ready to go. This body, dressed in rough clothes: work boots, dirty jeans and T-shirt, looked frail and helpless. It moved again. What had drawn Christian to this place? Was it to intervene in the death of a vagrant? "Hello? Bonjour? Comment vous?"

Heavily rationalized nature photographers have a policy of not interfering with the subjects they stalk, only watching from a distance as hyenas taunt a lion cub or pull down a baby hippo as the mother hovers, helpless. Christian would not make a good by-stander at a mugging, which is why the thug-fugitive Maartyn was still his best friend. The young man on the rocks reminded him of Maartyn: dark, slim, disheveled, but not as muscular. Maartyn and Paulo were probably running drugs, one port ahead of the DEA. Or maybe they were happily shrimping along the Gulf Coast. Maartyn's old man had been chopped up by the propeller of his shrimp boat. Maartyn said Simon's body looked like it went through a meat grinder. Left in a freezer in Gulfport. Like Escobar and the spy. Too many visions. Too many bodies. The body at his feet moved in a spasm.

"Hey! You reasonably okay?"

"Quoi la?" The young man turned over. Dark eyes. Long lashes. He looked annoyed.

"Could you maybe, get away from the edge?"

"I'm fishing, for Christ's sake!" the young man said in good English.

"Oh, I thought, you were, you know, you looked..."

"Be still. Fish spook easy. See, they rest in the back eddies."

"Okay." His houseboy Miguel lectured him endlessly about fishing because Christian could never get up before sunrise, like a real fisherman. Well, he wasn't. He was a jazz musician who survived Batista's Secret Police, and all he had to show for the gig was Jocinto's bogus guitar. He missed his villa, in an ambiguous way, not fully removed from Cuba and Esameralda. The nun. How could she? He had guilt about cheating on Renée. That's a laugh, he said to himself. It's nighttime in Paris. Renée's probably tucked into bed with the flavour of the week. That's unfair, he thought. Renée's a free spirit. A child of Bohemian philosophies; free love, fuck-rather-than-fight, rationalized by the surety that we are all going to die tomorrow from nuclear annihilation, but not boredom. So jumping into bed was necessary. Often. And he had to admit that Renée and Esameralda were a quality substitute for death by angst. He could have gone to New York with Renée. He could have stayed in Cuba with Esa. He missed them both in conflicting waves of guilt. Who was he actually cheating on? Well, no one at the moment. He'd only been in town for three hours. Wandered down from Windsor Station with his knapsack and his guitar case instead of going home.

Home had been a walkup on Sherbrooke West, near Westmount, as if that did him any good. Didn't know if his mother still lived in the old apartment. Father left for Toronto with the 'other woman'. Sister might be living in Westmount with her banker, or still in Switzerland. Howie Martz might still be around. Fuck Howie! It was Howie who got them on heroin. Howie might be strung out, in jail, or married to a fading shiksa, living in a mansion below Mount Royal. Privilege has its own rewards. No, fuck Howie with a big one!

"Why are you fishing like this?" The thin nylon filament was angling from the young man's hand. Angling. Maybe that's why they call it angling.

The young fisherman gave a gentle tug on the line, a slight flick of the wrist. "Merd! Sit down at least. You spook the obstinate bastards!"

"You don't like these fish?"

"I need the fish. They don't need me."

Behind a white chunk of concrete a pathetic looking silver fish gulped for air, eyes wide in terror, staring back at him. Why do fish and dead people always stare at you, like it's your fault? He remembered the eyes of the *Bayou Queen's* dead engineer; arms akimbo, standing on the bottom of Los Espiritos harbour. They dumped the body inside the reef, weighted by the feet. Christian had come face to face with the thing while swimming. Still gave him cold sweats at night. Esameralda had helped but Esameralda was training to be a nursing nun in Pinar del Rio.

She'd had plenty of practice at the Ché Guevera hospital in Los Espiritos and before the Revolution she was a prostitute in Havana. The dead engineer went into the freezer at the Ché Guevera hospital, in residence even before the Batista spy and Escobar himself. The engineer looked like the dying fish. A cisco, a fresh water herring, about eight inches long, with stupid eyes, silver scales flaking off, attached to the rocks by the excellent fish glue; could stick there winter and summer for years. The fish flapped weakly again, whatever fight it once enjoyed, drained away with it's slimy fluids glistening on the broken concrete. "Why don't you either kill it or let it go?"

"It'll die."

"But, isn't that unnecessarily cruel?"

The young man nailed Christian with a hard look. "It will die in it's own time, just like you."

"Okay."

"We fish to eat. They stay fresh, if they aren't dead."

"You could string them and leave them in the water."

"Spook the other fish. Bad vibes, comrade."

Comrade? He didn't like the sound of that. "Well, I'll shove off. Good luck," said Christian, standing up to go, feeling a little dizzy. He shrugged it off. Sun. No food. Fatigue from being homeless.

"Where're you going?"

"Don't know."

"Where're you from?"

"Here, Montreal. Sherbrook West."

"Then how is it you don't know where you're going?"

"Long story. Been on the road."

"Where'd you just come from then?"

"Windsor Station..."

"Where before that, asshole?"

"Louisiana, and I spent an interesting year in Cuba."

"Cuba? No shit! Man!" The young man sat up. "Were you

7

there for the Revolution?"

"Yeah, I guess I was."

"Man, what was it like?" He scrambled to his feet and thrust his face at Christian. "Did you meet Castro?"

"Ah, sort of..." Christian didn't want to explain that he had been trapped in a cave with a crazed New York actor impersonating Fidel Castro, caught up in a goofy but dangerous plan to co-opt the revolution. The Cuban army trying to blow them out of the caves or fry them alive with gasoline, and having to fight their way out, Christian running down the mountain with Maartyn and Rosameralda's fighters covering their retreat. He and Maartyn escaped to the shrimp boat where the crew had been dead for two days and he had to row the bloated bodies ashore to Escobar's rebel hospital. The Cuban army retreated to Pinar del Rio. Renée left that night with Maartyn and Ramon but he stayed behind, sleeping off the effects of the battle in a leaky rowboat. Then Miguel deserted him to march on Havana with Rosameralda...All that was left was the promise of Esameralda, and the real story of the battle for Los Espiritos...

"What do you mean, *sort of*? Did you see Castro or not?"

"What? Yes, only from a distance. Speech in Havana. Lasted three hours, which is short by Fidel's standards, but heavy on the socialist rhetoric. The Americans'll take him out if he tries to grab their casinos. There are already signs. Cuba Si! Yankee No! Even Hemingway's leaving, the papers say..." He was rambling.

"Merd! I'd give my fucking sainted mother's statue of the Virgin to meet Castro. You should have got closer to the guy."

"He was a little preoccupied."

"Could you get back into Cuba?"

"Maybe. I know some people, if they survived the reprisals...hey, the fish!"

He jerked the line and a silver fish shot out of the water and landed at Christian's feet. Three spasms almost put it back in the river. The young man stomped on it, securing the stunned fish

8

with one finger hooked in its gills. "I'll give you this fish if you take me to Cuba."

"Must be a pretty important fish."

"The seminal fish."

"You mean, meaty or pithy?"

"No! Central fish of three. One more and we eat." He dropped the fish behind the rock beside its mate. A final spasm and the fish lay defeated, mouth opening and closing, gills lifting weakly in a mime of breathing.

"What's your name?" Christian asked.

"Why do you want to know?" The dark eyes stared hard at Christian. The young man's too cautious, too intense, thought Christian. He had seen the look in Escobar. "You a pig?" the fisherman asked, spitting out the word.

Christian looked at his own bare arms. They were thin. "I'm not dinner, if that's what you mean." He hadn't heard that term in Cuba. Chicago to Miami, on the road, the truckers were using the term on the CB radios; also fuzz, cop, or Yogi if the truckers were from Wisconsin. Or California. The truckers were in a constant battle with the state troopers but they seldom used the terms with vitriol.

"I asked if you're a pig, a cop?"

The alarm bells were sounding. "Well, see you later alligator, whatever your name," Christian said and turned away from the touchy fisherman, but with nowhere to go his attention was drawn to an odd looking boat; a double ended, roughly planked bateau, looking anachronistic and vulnerable between the McAllister Towing Co. tug and a rusting barge. Christian remembered the histories of the boats that carried freight and European immigrants up the Ottawa River, returning with furs. The stories were apocryphal; European entrepreneurs, encouraged by the Church, fought their way into the hinterland, beat down aboriginal resistance, plundered the resources, left behind missionaries and disease and progressed from exploiting furs and trees to aluminum and iron ore. Québec had come a long way in two hundred years. He had fled from his roots to escape the inevitable clash of cultures in his hometown where a quiet revolution was going on behind the doors of corporate boardrooms, the new towers and old cathedrals, while a counter-revolution was breeding underground in dark, smoke-filled rooms where young dissidents watched events in Latin America and Eastern Europe. In the countryside the clergy had their beads in knots trying to find new demons to dangle in front of their flocks. At all levels les Anglais and the Jews were the enemy. Where did Christian fit in this old, raw, nervous city?

Montreal in the summer of 1960 was a schizophrenic amalgam of French hyperbole, Anglais paranoia and Jewish denial. The French Canadians were enough Old World French to be difficult as well as paranoid. The English existed in colonial apathy and pretended the Empire still prevented sunsets. The Jews in their enclaves tried to forget Auschwitz and strove to achieve Zion in the shadow of Westmount. The Scots ran the banks with the Americans lurking in the background. Aggressive Jews became lawyers and doctors, opened corner stores or unionized, dreaming of Babylon. The French Canadians fumed in secular exile, wedged resolutely between their politicians and the clergy, the black robes wading through rural Québec with their cassocks hiked to their loins, herding their parishioners like sheep plodding along to confusion, and the politicians still searching for a style of their own, unsure whether to play up to their Anglais masters or drive them out. On the fringe of the cultural quilt the Polish and Ukrainian diaspora and a polyglot of Island immigrants edged in for their share, joining the displaced of Europe, sliding downhill to the New World. And at the bottom of the cultural barrel, the youth roamed the grey corridors of power kicking at locked doors. The impatient rebels and restive anarchists searching for a cause, or at least a focus for their new found anger while learning how to build bombs. But in the meantime there was the open talk of the

Quiet Revolution.

"Hey! Comrade, wait. I meant nothing," said the young man, jumping up, thrusting a wet hand. "I'm Jean. Jean-Pierre August Dumont. You know about Gabriel Dumont? Descendant of buffalo hunters and guerrilla fighters!"

Christian felt the chill again because he did know some of Gabriel Dumont's sordid history. Should have just moved on, he thought. "Hi, Jean-Pierre...I'm Chris…"

"Come'ere, Anglais." Jean-Pierre said in English, tugging Christian's arm. Christian followed Jean-Pierre to the shadow of the old clock tower. It was cooler in the shade. A desultory and useless land breeze wandered down from Bonsecours, smelling of diesel fumes from the McAllister salvage tug. It's mutter dissolving into the general din of commercial Montreal. A smaller tug, an older version of the McAllister tug, added it's oily fumes to the mix, panting easily with a low flame under its oil-fired boiler. Yellow steam and sooty smoke escaped from the black funnel like spirits tumbling from an undertaker's top hat, the fumes heavy and noxious. The dirty black hull worried its dock lines as if impatient to get away. Christian was old enough to remember the giant black trains and the canal freight boats with their heady smell of hot steam and burned train oil. He and his pals played dangerous games along the CNR rail yards. When they tired of dodging trains and yard cops they scrambled over rue Notre-Dame to the Lachine Ship Canal. They weren't concerned about the odd colours flushing into the canal and whirling in the wake of the boats or the stench of tanneries. There was a steady parade of small freighters carrying grain and general cargo. They would wave at the boats sliding silently by and cheer if the captain blew the whistle, or throw rocks if they were ignored. Just street urchins, swearing in English and French.

Christian sat uneasily on the crumbling foundation of the clock tower and watched Jean-Pierre produce a tooled leather pouch and cigarette papers, rolling dusty marijuana tops into doubled Chanticleers; the arrogant black rooster a symbol for hard-core dope heads. Christian experienced the familiar cold rush of fear that said, *stay clear of the pusher-man*. It's too soon. The picture on the blue packet reminded him of the house below his villa and the old woman chasing the black rooster out of her winter garden, and the walk-down jazz clubs of Chicago. They seldom got flower tops in the jazz clubs but there was no shortage of adulterated junk. Jean-Pierre must be connected.

Christian looked beyond the ugliness of the rusting bridge and shut his ears to the traffic, imagining the clear waters and peace of Los Espiritos before the battles. The revolution burned its way through Cuba and the reprisals began in Santiago even as the celebrations were going on in Havana. He was in Montreal, safe from rebels, imposters and dictators. Jean Lesage and the Quiet Revolution, the only change on the horizon. The stink was familiar though; the slow decay of the industrial city: the refineries, the salt piles and sand hills, scrap heaps, the broken concrete retaining walls and the rusted chain-link fences. Used up and worn down, the way Chicago and New York looked, everything stained brown and the edges chipped from too much humanity. The way all big American cities had aged too quickly. Carl Sandburg's America, once optimistic and big hearted, young by European standards, already decaying from hard use and the rush to open the West. The St. Lawrence River, which drained the rust belt of heavy industry around the Great Lakes, boiled past Montreal carrying the filth of two adolescent nations. He longed for the colours of the Caribbean and Cuba. Sweet, dying Cuba.

Jean-Pierre struck a wooden match and lit the fat joint, disappearing momentarily in the smoke, drawing the smoke into his lungs, his nose, his ears, his hair it seemed, choking it down. He handed the joint to Christian who was instantly thrilled by the proximity of clean cannabis and the smell of good grass. Should he accept a small toke as a ritual offering or just get good and stoned; forget hunger and heat, forget Cuba? He thought with some regret of Major Marti who made a ritual of lighting his cigars. He didn't choke on the smoke. Jean-Pierre was about the same build as Marti: lean, sinewy, with intense dark eyes, and that same edge of toughness. But Jean-Pierre was a bottom dweller. Christian sucked the joint expertly, drawing every particle deep into his soul, or so it seemed. Again, then passed the joint back to Jean-Pierre. And hours later it was back and he absorbed the chemicals into every pore of his body, filling in the gaps, but waking up his paranoia. "So, Anglais, are you going to tell me about Cuba?" Sometime later Christian returned from a cartoon adventure and answered... "What about Cuba?"

Red and green navigation lights came out of the haze: a saltwater freighter, trailing rust and diesel fumes, working up the harbour close to the grey industrial shore, angling for St. Lambert, the first lock on the St. Lawrence Seaway, destined for Detroit, Chicago or Duluth. Duluth. The name had a flat, thudding sound, like a door at the end of a long corridor shut in anger. Not like Strasbourg or Cherbourg. La Rochelle, Venice or Florence. Christian wondered if the sailors on the foreign vessels felt trapped on the narrow rock-strewn, lock-infested waterways, heading deeper into North America, as far as their sailing distance across the ocean to the English Channel; La Manche to the French, and the rivers that penetrated the heart of Europe. One could travel by boat to Rotterdam, Hamburg, and even Strasbourg. Even to Renée on her island in the center of Paris. Her family maintained a flat on Ile St. Louis so her father could be close to the government buildings on Ile de la Cité, *and his mistresses*, Renée had said bitterly. Perhaps Renée used the flat for her own trysts; young men picked up in a bistro on the Left Bank, ready for another Bohemian tumble. But the Bohemian trip was finished in Cuba even if Sartre and Hemingway did anoint the revolution by their presence. Still Hemingway was an American so he had to leave too. Bohemia died in the ashes of Los Espiritos and the reality of a firing squad. All that remained was experience. Christian dreamed of Montmartre. The cafés, the jazz clubs, and Renée on her island. Her mother stayed in their large manor house outside of Paris, not quite a chateau, Renée assured him, and pretended to be the dutiful Madame, or whatever French women are called with husbands in high places who live part of their time in the low places of Paris, returning home only to dine with the family. Renée exorcised her bitterness by finding some low places of her own. That's unfair, thought Christian. He was happy to wallow with Renée on the beaches of Andros. That was the summer of '58, before the Revolution. And Esameralda. Esameralda was safe in a convent in Pinar del Rio, devoting her dark warm body to the cause of the Blessed Virgin. Rosa was dead. So was Escobar. How could one miss bloodied revolutionaries who were as far from Christian's ken as the backside of the moon? Who did he miss the most? Miguel, Maartyn or even Juanita? He regretted the tragic death of Rosameralda. Maartyn would take her death badly. Escobar's death was also tragic, but in a different way. He missed Esa and Renée, but not equally. There was some anger and therefore some pain. He may still be in love with Renée, but right now he resented her more than he missed her. Resented that she left him that night on the beach below Escobar's villa to escape on the *Bayou Queen*. Renée with her cool, Gaulic sense of herself and the easy knowledge that all she had to do was arrive at the Havana airport and flash her diplomatic passport. First stop New York, for a shopping trip layover, before she flew home to Paris, with Ramon! Probably more laying-over Ramon than shopping. Damnit!

The haze had congealed into fog. The navigation lights of the deep laden freighter winked out behind the trees of Ile Ste.-Hélène...

"Okay, wake up! We can go now, Anglais," announced Jean-Pierre, feet still dangling over the edge of the quay. "You can tell me about Cuba over dinner." The roach was flattened and stained brown, the size of a fish scale. Jean-Pierre held it like the delicate

14

wing of a butterfly and sucked the last wisp of smoke out of the air. Roach clips not yet in the parlance of paraphernalia. This was pioneering. Then he crushed the roach between his hands and made a circle on his forehead with the ashes, rubbing the rest on his jeans. The worn denim polished to a sheen from dirt. The poorest guajiros in Cuba kept themselves clean at least, thought Christian.

"Go? Where?" He'd forgotten his place in the world, not ready to leave Cuba or Paris even if the scenes were hallucinations.

"Home. We must eat these fish while they are still fresh," he said picking up four sad fish that had expired among the rocks of the bulkhead, threading them on a shoelace. Four. He must have caught the last one while Christian was in Cuba. The copper sun dodged the warehouses of Old Montreal, casting the long shadow of the Dome of Bonsecours beyond Quay Jacques Cartier. The dome spilled into the green river and disappeared.

"I doubt those fish are fresh," Christian opined, brushing away a pair of copulating flies the size of hummingbirds. "Miguel would have kept them in a cold bag of salted water."

"Miguel was your servant?"

"Houseboy." Cuba and Los Espiritos, sweet and sour, poor and innocent, the way it was before Batista's soldiers blew up his villa.

"Listen, Anglais, it's enough I offer to share our supper, but don't get ideas."

"Sorry, I didn't mean..."

"That's okay, comrade. For your penance you can clean the fish."

"I've never cleaned a fish."

"I suppose you're going to tell me your houseboy did that also?"

"Actually, he did."

"You bourgeois bastard! Tonight you learn about cleaning

fish."

"Miguel threw the guts in the harbour."

"Don't throw away the guts. Feed them to the fucking cats. There are more cats than rats. And dogs. We should get a dog."

And he remembered Wolf Pietro Marlon Brando...

Jean-Pierre weaved ahead, the fish dangling from his belt like jewelry, like the ridiculous watch chains of the aging, post war Zoot Suiters still sulking on the sidewalks of Rue St. Denis, the chains of office adopted by truckers, toughs and bikers. Christian followed along the wharf to the concrete stairs leading up from the Victoria Basin to Vieux Port. Jean-Pierre had to use the iron rail to pull himself up the steps. It was a painfully slow ascent. Christian believed he was on an escalator and forgot to move his feet, and yet he was at the top. "Good stuff," Christian offered in Jean-Pierre's wake.

"What?" he asked, turning slowly, as if in pain.

"Nothing."

They followed railway tracks toward the warehouse district and the old fish market, toward the smells of his youth.

Montreal is a city of odours. He remembered the fish market. He thought about it often in Cuba and somehow fishing with Miguel made a connection. A surprising connection, not of experience, not of fishing, but of Old Montreal and the political puzzle that is Canada. Christian was part of a complex society crowding together from ocean to ocean along a border of lakes, rivers and streams. Fishing is important to the citizens of a landmass vast in scope, miniscule in world affairs. Christian had to explain Canada to his Cuban friends. It was not a problem Renée and Maartyn shared. The French and Americans carried no baggage of inferiority. The Cubans saw little beyond their flamboyant, sad little island and had no views about Canada, or Montreal and the emerging culture or political bitchiness that Christian had once called home.

Christian followed Jean-Pierre over unusually high railway tracks to a warehouse behind the fish market, stumbling over cracked concrete sloughing off rough walls. To Christian the jagged chunks were blocks of Arctic ice that had to be negotiated carefully. Avoiding the untidy scatters of waste hugging the margins, kicked aside by shuffling feet of drunks and drug addicts, almost hidden by the mélange of paper debris, restless in the hot wind. Winter remains roiled up. Gritty. Dirt and sweat, hard on the middle class office workers walking on lunch breaks. Ring around the collar a growing urban problem, competing with those nasty moulds in the Sani-boy. The first TV commercial he remembered was a woman smiling pleasantly while spraying a fog of chemicals into a metal bin beside the kitchen counter. There was no litter in Cuba, Christian remembered. No drive-in restaurants. There *was* poverty and shabbiness, but Cubans had some pride, or maybe they didn't have enough to litter. There are benefits to a marginal existence. He loved that about Cuba. Life had a certain sparse dignity, a delicate urgency of deprivation on the thin edge of survival. In Montreal he felt gritty and wasted in a land of plenty. There were stores above Bonsecours filled with goods from the world's food larder but his friends in Los Espiritos seemed to grub about endlessly in the dirt, or fish from battered boats to jig a meal. In Los Espiritos it became a comforting routine; fishing, scrounging for food, but taking some responsibility for one's survival. A ground-level existence at best. It made him think of Jean-Paul Sartre and, of course, Renée. What would Sartre say about these Montreal streets that you could taste as a proof of existence? Was there a reason for this littered street, this scruffy harbour and this desperate alley? And why was Christian following this odd young man home, with four fish to clean and no free will to object, always swept along by circumstances? Life, beyond hunger, was a constant search for freedom and a lament for missed opportunities. Then isn't the regret for opportunities a form of tyranny? And what about Renée? She is freely back home

17

on the country estate, or in Paris humping earnest young Communists in the family's island flat. Damn her!

Christian was pulled along in the dusty wake of his new friend as if in a dream. Montreal was also a dream. Cuba was real. Was he reasoning well into the age of reason? Fuck Sartre! The future had to be experienced, not determined by words in a god-damned book, even if they were the words of the venerated Jean-Paul, the man, though still alive, had become a god-myth. Where are the Nazis when you need them? Christian had grown to loath the whole idea of Existentialism. Too effete, and too necessary. He barely understood what the hell Sartre was talking about, and wondered if the others really got the essential message. Groaked the jist, as the newest New Age novel said. He was a stranger even in his homeland and Sartre was no help as a guide. He could understand the message in Nausea; the repulsion a free thinker could feel for the cloying existence forced on the still functioning mind not demented by drugs, disease, or dumbness. Intellectuals have a responsibility to rage against injustice and the shackles of anti-liberalism. But where was he at that moment? Nowhere. More precisely; in dirty, hot Montreal, nowhere. In the Islands he was almost an intellectual, at least on the beach, under clear stars, half tanked on tequila or rum; or stoned, with his hand in Renée's panties, attempting to get her to stop talking philosophy long enough to screw. A discussion of Sartre's latest pronouncement was the price of admission, *pardon the pun*, he sniggered, and the talk usually revolved to free love, Bohemian style, which meant: wine, dope, talking bullshit, and laying the most available member of the opposite sex, or otherwise, depending... "Jesus, what a screwed up life!"

Jean-Pierre turned and said, "Why do you criticize? You came to us, my Cuban revolutionary friend."

"No, I mean before..." Then he wondered how before was more screwed up than being back in Montreal with no home, no family and no prospects. He did have some money left from the

Moosehead stash; singed tens and twenties that raised eyebrows at banks. The odd burnt-meat smell. Store clerks in the Southern States refused to take his money and at the banks he had to answer questions. One delicate teller at the Louisiana State Mortgage and Trust almost tossed her lunch. Christian could only wonder how pragmatic would an old guajiro be fingering tainted money. No questions, for sure. He missed the place desperately. Leaving Cuba was another mistake, like arriving. It had been a mistake to leave Montreal for Paris, then Paris for Chicago and a bigger mistake to leave his going-nowhere-band in Chicago for the uncertainties of the road, and a huge mistake to land in Cuba at the climax of the goddamned revolution and end up trading gunfire with Batista's soldiers in a cave filling with gasoline, but then...hadn't he felt really alive for the first time? The high-octane adrenaline purer than any adulterated heroin rush. So, was leaving Cuba, which he had fought for and suffered for, and coming home the biggest mistake ever? What would Sartre say about the rationale for homecoming? "Fuck Sartre!!"

"You're right, comrade. Fuck all phony bourgeois intellectuals." Jean-Pierre stopped at a door in the deep shadow of the run-down warehouse. The service entrance was barely discernible from the crates of rotting garbage, waiting for the City collectors who seldom visit the fish market alley. The fish market was dead, but the smell remained because some of the residents of the boarded up building fished in the river for mercury polluted junk fish or stole over-ripe white fish and carp from the bins behind the Jewish smokehouse on Dorchester. "Sartre should be fucked, avec un grand chou, up the ass!"

"It was un grand erreur to leave Cuba."

"Comettre une bévue."

"Precisely!" Christian said, laughing, stumbling forward into Jean-Pierre.

"Tu m'adore si vite?"

"Peut etre, la odour. C'est dur."

"And so are you. Can you stand?"

"Si, I mean, oui. Yes."

"Bon, we entré ici au bas la, carefully. It's dark so watch your step. Follow me closely."

Christian froze. He was back in the cave and Renée was leading him through the darkness to escape the soldiers. Dizzy and weak, the roaring noise in his head deafening. Later the gunfire.

"Coming, Anglais?"

"Yes, yes..." He almost reached for Jean-Pierre slipping away into darkness like a scribbled drawing disappearing into an inkwell.

The smell was different inside, in the cool dark, but no better. Urine, acrid and musty, the smell that goes with poverty and anarchy. He prayed Jean-Pierre didn't live in the basement. He shuffled along after the dim figure, ducking when told, stepping over whatever Jean-Pierre indicated. One was either human or just a discarded trench coat. They seemed to be in a narrow corridor of rusting pipes and dripping water. At least there was running water.

Suddenly a light bulb flashed. Christian was staring at the wooden slats of a freight elevator. "We go up now," said Jean-Pierre.

"Thank Christ!" offered Christian.

"Thank the Mayor of Montreal who is too distracted by politics and preparations for his fucking big show to impress les Capitalists. Exposition des Francophoné. See how clever we are, just like you Anglais capitalists on West-Fucking-Mount your daughter's ass before the Kikes and the Frogs get to her."

Whew, thought Christian, this man is angry about something, and it starts on the English side of the mountain. He felt very uncomfortable, being an obvious Anglais from Sherbrooke Street, and too near Westmount for comfort, although Irish Catholic, and therefore on the opposite side of the privacy hedge, but close enough to the English that one would have to identify one's IRA roots to hang out with the anarchists in Old Montreal. Politics of anarchy as complicated as the higher orders, he thought. "Oh, shit," he whispered. "I've only been here a day..."

"Come-on. There's someone I want badly for you to be introduced to."

"Your syntax is slipping."

"It happens when I'm hungry. I speak English for practice, so that when we take over Québec we can tell the English to fuck off in their own language, that is, just before we ban it from Québec forever!" Jean-Paul kicked the wooden gate; dislodging whatever was holding it closed, and motioned for Christian.

"And us too?" asked Christian stepping reluctantly over a steel sill into the small cage with rough planked floor that seemed to have no walls. The cage was suspended from old steel cables that were probably rusting through, strands popping out, a thread left, one fish too many...a final *twang* sending them crashing into a basement full of foul black water with things swimming...

"Depends, Anglais. You've been through a revolution. You read some philosophy, even though it's that sop Sartre, who can't get a hard-on without analyzing the usefulness of his tiny dick that Simone must bathe with absinthe before she sucks it! Maybe you understand what we're doing in Québec. It's your home. You can't help your genes, but maybe your brain isn't potatoes."

"Or French fries?" He remembered he too was hungry.

Jean-Pierre punched a dark button, too filthy to be green. Five floors above them, in the euphemistically named penthouse, an ancient electric motor ground to life. Arthritic gears turned, unserviced since Mayor Drapeau took control and sent Montreal reeling into the Twentieth Century with the promise of his Big Show. The old parts of the city that didn't get on board the spending wagon languished in neglect. Christian winced, unsure of the origin of a new fear. Jean-Pierre looked up, grinning. "The inspectors were too busy taking bribes." It would usher in a new era of political wheel greasing on the bumpy road to paradise, Québécois style. "The unions and government flunkies finger each other every night and slip out of bed before dawn. It's a Quiet Revolution for a good reason. Professional whores and politicians don't like baggage, so travel light." A practiced assessment, delivered with some passion, Christian analyzed.

Christian remembered Québec politics as the usual us-against-them cliché, with lines clearly drawn; French versus English. Not the popular Two Solitudes, but adversaries toeing up to the line, waiting for the real fight to begin. There was talk of Separation. The English ruled the financial districts and everything west of rue St. Denis. French politicians wrung their hands, trying to decide which side of the line their loyalties lay: federalists, separatists, nationalists; while the clergy fought to keep the souls, and the minds of the faithful focused on God and giving. Mostly giving. Rural churches in Québec rivaled cathedrals in rural France, all to the glory of God, but the new French Canadian middle class were slowly, stutteringly, emerging as a third element. The Church would suffer.

The cage shook and lurched upwards when the slack came out of the greasy wire. They rose in screeches and halts, leaving the worst of the odours behind.

Down a dark service corridor awash in the amorphous clutter of Bohemia, they stopped at a double door that had been chopped at and scrawled on until it resembled modern art. There was a sign crudely done with red lettering that said 'Vive Québec Libre'.

Jean-Pierre knuckled the door in a rapid code. Footsteps sounded. Locks were thrown. The door opened hesitantly and a short person, back-lit by large windows so that the thick body was in silhouette, peered at them myopically. Christian could see only a female figure clad in a long dress. The short person returned to a stuffed chair and resumed working on a hoop with a needle.

"Come in, Chris…she won't bite." The industrial slum warehouse had high ceilings and high windows, mullioned panels so dirty that the poor light spilled in dusty shafts over a littered plank floor, as if several careless people had abused the room and left in a hurry. The most prominent feature was a sleeping loft made of old utility poles. The space under the loft was the food preparation area identified by a liberated ornate store counter of some breeding and fish boxes for shelving. Three people sat around a Victorian table flanked by chrome chairs with red vinyl seats bleeding stuffing. The utility poles dripped creosote, which helped mask the ubiquitous smell of anarchy. In the new era, thought Christian, Beat Generation rebellion in North America was giving rise to slovenly habits, which ultimately diminish freedom. Freedom was happening in Cuba at that moment but he couldn't imagine his poorest friends living in such squalor.

"That piece of work," said Jean-Pierre pointing the string of fish, "is Gargoire, our Métis-Montanais co-production. Québec's cultural apogee, self-proclaimed." Gargoire ignored Christian and eyed Jean-Pierre coldly.

Gargoire, a male of medium height, with shifting dark eyes, could pass for a West Coast Indian about the time European photographers invaded the Queen Charlotte Islands. Missing was the bowler hat. He too was lean and dark, with long greasy hair pulled back and tied with a leather thong. With moustache and chin beard he could pass for Métis or Montanais, but there was something Waspish about his profile. His red tam with crow feather and dark suit jacket and pants made him look like a character out of a Remington sketch; a frontiersman caught between the town drunk and a potlatch gone sour. The tam O'Shanter, though out of context, did add some class and the Voyageur sash under the Sally Ann vest was just so Québécois. "And this little flower, his tiny, impudent girlfriend, calls herself Princess Sprudence Ironfeather."

"You can call me Spru," said the whiney voice of the short person loosely resembling a female.

"She's a missionary school escapee and our token French convert." Sprudence smiled and adjusted her badly fitting false teeth. Christian stepped forward and extended his hand, first to Ironfeather. Her hand was rough and hard. Gargoire shook Christian's hand quickly and indifferently, as if shunning human contact. Christian wanted to like them instantly for their oddity and singular appearance.

"Hi. Good to meet you," he tried, holding the smile.

"Sprudence claims to be a Haida Princess from British Columbia by way of Northern Québec, among other things," continued Jean-Pierre, as if proud to display his acquisition of a rare species.

Sprudence, a shade over five feet, was wearing a sweat-stained suede dress with overdone beadwork. Without prompting she began chattering in a language that might have been native. Christian decided the language was gibberish. Sprudence shifted to broken French, explaining that she had made the dress after her man, (not Gargoire), killed the deer with his bare hands. "I chewed the leather myself." With or without teeth, Christian wondered? She was very proud, grinning a punctuation at the end of each sentence, pinching her beady eyes almost closed so that he couldn't tell what colour they were. He usually judged people by their eyes. The tiny glasses didn't help. There was nothing there to give her away. Christian was fascinated. How they must suffer, the two characters in costume, in the Montreal humidity, Christian reasoned, comparing his own attire of T-shirt, cut off jeans and sandals. He decided that the pair of misfits were simply *poseurs* who never outgrew Halloween or Mardi Gras but there was something attractive about their complete lack of grace and surfeit of pretension.

Gargoire edged back into the shadows and sat on a packing crate, arms folded, still glaring at Jean-Pierre.

"Me and Petit Jacques rescued these two from the river, adrift in a stolen boat," explained Jean-Pierre. Sprudence grinned and adjusted her teeth with her tongue.

Gargoire looked uncomfortable. "We didn't need rescuing,"

he protested.

"No? They came down les chutes sideways, and their funny York boat half full of scummy water..."

"Durham boat!...and it wasn't stolen! I was building it. Government grant. They wouldn't pay. We left on our own."

"York, Durham. Anglais bateau. You know, in the old days, les Anglais, they carried bad whiskey and disease to the natives and brought out stolen furs," said Jean-Pierre.

"The French were first," protested Gargoire.

"Would that be their boat in the harbour?"

"Obviously, comrade. We pulled them out of the rapids into Victoria Basin. Stoned on something, I can tell you. I talked to them for hours just to keep them from doing something foolish. The Princess thought she could swim to Nova Scotia. Kept putting her leg over the side and saying things about Micmac and Haida ancestors. Big dream to reunite the Confederacy. Gargoire was on his way to Newfoundland to find the last Beothic woman living on Tops'le Mountain. Wanted to mate with her, rebuild the clan and establish a colony."

"I could have made it, if you hadn't stopped us, and the goddamned Mounties weren't after us."

"Well, you did steal their boat."

"Didn't. They owed us four month's wages."

"Bien sur! Don't let the motherfucker Ottawa dogs short you, like they do we true Québécois, every chance."

"I'm going back to British Columbia," interjected Sprudence. "My grandmother was a Haida Princess."

"And my grandfather was King Louis-fucking-Fourteen!" said Jean-Pierre. He had heard the story many times. The argument spun away in French and English. Three people talking, but not necessarily to each other.

Christian was losing the fabric of the conversation, noting that British Columbia was in the opposite direction from their intended destination. And the West Coast Indians seldom wore leather, being a woven goods and wood culture. The Princess seemed very confused about her identity. It was then he noticed another person in the form of a long bare leg hanging over the edge of the loft. The leg moved in a spasm, that sudden twitch, perhaps a lingering feeling of violation and vulnerability. The disturbed mind swarming with dangerous images. At least that's how it affected Christian. And lately when he awoke from one of those post-Revolution dreams he noticed a buzzing, or ringing in his ears and there was the problem of slight tone distortion when he played the bogus guitar...but blamed it on the guitar.

"No, it's true," Sprudence protested. "I have this letter from a gyna-collegy society..."

"Genealogy!" corrected Gargoire irritably.

"Yes, it cost me twenty dollars and it says, 'Princess Spru, direct descendent of First Lodge Princess Kwakuluta'. I'm an Osprey."

Christian's sense of historical imperatives reacted to the term 'lodge'. As far as he knew West Coast native cultures didn't use the term for dwellings, but 'house'. "Ah, what village group did your grandmother belong to?" he probed.

"Oh, village? Ah, the Nanaimos. The Nanaimos of Queen Charlotte."

"Nanaimo? That's a long way from the Queen Charlotte Islands."

"No, that was before. Kitimat. The Kitimats from Nanaimo."

Kitimat, Christian remembered, is an industrial town on the mainland, opposite the Queen Charlotte Islands. Obviously Princess Spru knew almost nothing about the geography of the Haida Indians.

It was a nice leg, the one dangling from the loft, and more interesting. Mediterranean dark, a shapely foot, perfect toes with sandal marks. Then it twitched rhythmically, as if there was music. Jean-Pierre noticed Christian's fascination with the dangling appendage. "Careful, comrade. One could fall in love with that leg."

It was true. The leg was exquisite. Christian's heart beat oddly, imagining the rest of the body. A hand fell over the edge of the loft, fingers opening slowly, dropping a heavy porcelain mug. Jean-Pierre lunged for the falling cup, missed and kicked it across the floor; the indestructible cup skipping off the uneven planking like a stone on a pond. It came to rest with a clink against a leather cowboy boot belonging to an emaciated young man slouched in a crumbling easy chair. The chalk-white face was banded by a black beard and dark spikey hair, with a long nose sticking up like a church spire from a forest. The person in the chair was dressed in dirty jeans, grey sweatshirt and black leather jacket that blended with the age-abused chair fabric. Another inappropriate ensemble for the conditions of heat and humidity, he thought. An orange tabby cat slept on the back of the chair beside his head. The young man didn't move, appeared not to breathe. Just another body, not as interesting as the leg.

"This's Dominique." Jean-Pierre stroked the leg proprietarily. "Our resident bourgeois bitch. Parents live in Outremont. She comes down on the Métro, the long way around so she can be close to her Jewish boyfriend who lives in Westmount. His parents won't let them cohabit. Nice Jewish boy complies or loses his place in daddy's business. Dominique's in mourning. Been stoned about three weeks now. Suns in the nude on the roof to drive the traffic guys in the helicopters crazy. I tell her she is a hazard and may cause an accident. I sometimes lay on top of her to protect them."

Christian exhaled. Jean-Pierre said quickly, "Dominique won't sleep with anyone but me. I like to keep her around, like a pet cat, you know? Une chatte tres cher, a fait bonne chère."

"Expensive pet."

"Ah, yes, but like purebreds, she gives the place some class, eh?"

A second leg appeared over the edge of the loft, a match for the first. The legs turned, feet searching for the ladder. The rest of

Dominique came into view gracefully. The ensemble was perfection and not spoiled by clothing. The long legs and impossibly rounded derriere reminded Christian of Renée, but the resemblance ended there. Large, firm breasts and short, dark hair, tosseled but elegantly so. Dominique arrived at the floor level scrutinizing the newcomer, slipped into a pair of sandals and, carrying a Japanese silk kimono, walked demurely to the door.

"I am neither bourgeois nor your bitch," she said to Jean-Pierre, but was looking at Christian with those green eyes with gold flecks. He received the message while noting the dusky complexion; definitely Mediterranean, the full lips with hint of pout. No makeup. None necessary. The profile, however, was more European, with the high cheekbones of an aristocrat, good hybrid breeding with the resources to maintain the effect, he decided.

"Sure. Dominique's a wonderful studio model," offered Jean-Pierre.

"I can see that," breathed Christian.

"Artists and fashion photographers. Does it just to annoy her parents. They're nouveau riche. Father's Syrian. Mother's a social climbing Parisienne. The worst kind of bourgeoisie. She also poses for nude magazines, the raunchy stuff. You know, the ones that show pretend sex with blacked out tits. Gives the money to charity, so she says."

"I'm hungry," announced Gargoire.

"So, what did you find in the bins?" asked Jean-Pierre.

"Didn't go out."

"Then how do you plan to eat?"

"You fished," stated Sprudence as if he had been sent on a mission.

"The great mariners," said Jean-Pierre. "He claims to have built a canoe up in La Vérendrye and paddled down the Gatineau to Hull, living off the river. I think he was diving into tourist's trash. And Sprudence Princess, daughter of a great bird renowned

28

for fishing?" Jean-Pierre said it as a joke.

Gargoire clenched his fists. Christian felt the tension between the frontier wanderers and their host. Sprudence and Gargoire were tolerated, like guests who have overstayed their welcome. He vowed to run and stay free of obligations. No firm rules to keep or break. Keep moving on...

Christian left Cuba on the ferry to Key West, just days before the service was suspended, with no plans other than to find Maartyn then make his way home to Montreal. The Louisiana refugee was his only family and they had shared an adventure; two young people who came of age on the run and Maartyn and Paulo had a year to get lost on the Gulf Coast. It was hot in the Florida Keys so he hitchhiked to St. Petersburg, cashed in Canadian money at the First National Bank of Dade County and hopped a bus to Mobile, Alabama. Then, checking out the backwater fishing ports, he caught a ride on a shrimper heading for Bayou La Batre, the *Bayou Queen's* homeport. He walked the docks in Gulfport asking questions and receiving only warnings. He decided to try La Hache on the Delta and as a last resort, Port Eades, Maartyn's hometown.

The trek around the Gulf to Port Eades was a puzzling experience of red neck suspicion and hostility. But once there, awash in heat and humidity worse than the Keys, he found an ancient black woman who remembered Maartyn's mother and the story of Simon, but would not say about Maartyn's whereabouts.

A shrimp boat skipper in La Hache told him there could be a dozen *Bayou Queens* working the Gulf. He knew of two out of Bayou La Batre, owned by brothers, who refused to give in and choose the alternate designation *Bayou Queen Two* or *Three*. The brothers fought it out on the wharf. One brother drowned and the other just sailed away and disappeared into the bayous. There are lots of places to hide a shrimper on the Gulf, he said. Fishing, surviving, smuggling and poaching are considered free enterprise and the fugitives guard their territory ruthlessly. He also told Christian he had better stop asking questions. Things were hot and steamy on the Delta but the trail was cold. Christian reasoned that if Maartyn was staying out of sight in his milieu then he might as well go home.

Montreal was just another island of dirt and humidity. If he were ever to escape the underworld and the squalor he would have to get out of Old Montreal, and soon.

Jean-Pierre lectured on about the bourgeoisie and les Anglais. Gargoire retreated further into shadows, as if the present company was beneath his station. Christian had seen the attitude many times in his travels. The wall of paranoia and silence, the imagined guardian. Seldom was the wall enclosing anything but a pathetically insecure individual. He puzzled over the frontier-boat builder, and about the boat itself. It reminded him of the working boats of the Caribbean and Mediterranean and spoke eloquently of old world ways. It had that rough, unfinished quality associated with the edge of civilization that Québec City and Ile Royale had been in their pioneer phase, when Canada was the raw idea of society, the browning fringe on a rich green wilderness, poised to spread it's values of greed and disease on the unsuspecting aboriginals. The replica boat was a symbol of European commerce; the means of opening up that wilderness to the flood tide of avarice and rapine. Interesting that the bureaucrats in Ottawa chose to further insult the native groups by funding replicas of the wedge that drove between the aboriginals and their land. So, where did Gargoire and Sprudence fit into this picture? They had stolen the boat and powered it with an ancient one-cylinder diesel engine. Probably stolen also. Liberated in the parlance. That was a good indicator. What did Jean-Pierre see in them? And could they be trusted? Christian was becoming cynical since leaving home, travelling on the rough road of life, the drugs and the Cuban Revolution. But wait, this was Montreal, not Havana. There was no blood in the streets or firing squads. He was home. All he had to do was find a place...

"Hey, Anglais! Stop dreaming and clean the fish," Jean-Pierre said, holding up the string. His tone was not menacing, but there was an element of command.

Christian cleared a space on the counter beside an enamel pan of greasy dishes in cold water. There was no sink. He held his Swiss Army knife trying to remember how Miguel dispatched and cleaned their fish. The dispatched part seemed to be solved; the fish appeared very dead. Miguel kept their fish in an evaporation bag and they never smelled bad. How much did he miss Miguel? Should he start with the head?

Sprudence, without leave, opened his battered guitar case with a squeal of delight and ripped the besotted thing from its crushed velvet lair. Christian could never decide if the mal-adjusted instrument was male, female or hermaphrodite. The temperamental guitar displayed gender traits depending on cosmic forces, or perhaps it was just the changing humidity. Christian was unable to cajole a tune from the thing since leaving Cuba. Karmic Santeria soul left behind? Culture shock? He suspected Jocinto's spirit was unable to leave the island...The Princess strummed a screeching chord. There was only one guitar in the world that looked that good but sounded that bad. He wanted to tell her to put the sacred instrument away but he was intrigued. She pretended to tune the instrument, nodding in satisfaction. "This is a song I wrote on the train from Winnipeg. Crossing the Red River was my inspiration. It's called the Lament of Louis Riel."

Sprudence sang as badly as the guitar sounded, as if the guitar and the bogus Haida Princess were soul mates. He decided to give her the guitar and didn't notice Gargoire riffling through the case. The fish squirmed at the touch of the knife...

The severed head rested near the body, silver scales flecking the grimy counter top, surprised eyes watching Christian's clumsy attempts to slice open the soft belly with the dull Swiss Army knife. Fish guts splayed across the counter, unraveling in untidy loops. The slimy thing next in line jerked again. He chopped at it, feeling like an executioner.

"You leave the head on," said Gargoire, his arrogant tone expressive.

Of course, he should have remembered. Miguel never removed the head while gutting their fish on the bow of the skiff in one swift motion: the bloody entrails arching away into the clear lagoon. Christian tried to concentrate on the job, distracted by a calico cat and a nearly blind tabby brushing the back of his bare legs, snarling and purring loud enough to be heard between verses of the song. Louis Riel languishing in a prison cell, eaten by big rats, about to be hanged. French Canada condemned English Canada. Louis Riel howled on as the course rope, was it manila or hemp? dangled 'round his neck, angled into Canadian history by Ontario Orangemen who failed to consider the consequences of killing a scruffy Métis madman who only wanted to raise awareness of western identity as distinct from the east, an issue that would plague Canada's sense of self until the French of Québec carved out their own identity. English verdict? Death by hanging for murdering Thomas Scott. The real issue was the uneasy association between two language groups, two religions; separate cultures sharing the same ground, the new Dominion of Canada. So, the deaths of an obscure frontiersmen and a Métis malcontent, the former an Irish Protestant, were the wedges that drove between French and English, not just the loss of French Canada. Wars and defeat in battle can be forgiven, but not cultural assimilation. It seemed inevitable. Despite the cultural divide, Canada progressed, but so did the confrontations. Christian was gutting industrially poisoned fish in Montreal at the very cusp of the new crisis, unaware. Dead fish and groveling cats and a vision of Dominique, were the issues of the moment.

The song ground on, seemingly without end. Princess Spru

had a flawed but folksy grasp of the situation, but then, the myth of Louis Riel was more romance than reality. If the spongy flat-lands of the new territories, swarming with mosquitos and black flies, stinking of bear grease and castor funk could be considered romantic. The buffalo hunt from horseback was another matter and the Métis excelled at gunning down bison on the run; a fact that may have inspired the Canadian Parliament to negotiate with Riel and spring for the creation of a new province called Manito-ba. Louis was a decent guy, if self possessed, who happened to believe that all souls inhabiting the raw frontier of Canada should be represented under the laws of the realm, in equal doses, not ig-nored and patronized like troublesome children. The government sent surveyors to the Red River to stake out their vision of an or-derly landscape in the image of dissected and bisected Ontario, which happened to counter the Métis practice of carving out long narrow plots along the river, as was the habit of their cousins along the St. Lawrence. When Louis objected to the off hand treatment of the Métis settlements on the Red River he was dis-missed by the Orange-dominated clique who controlled parlia-ment. Louis, with the help of his pal, Gabriel Dumont, as intense and demented as the Mad Monk Rasputin, caused a small ruckus to get attention. They seized Fort Gary and forced the new gov-ernment of Canada to negotiate. That was the ruckus of 1870. There was the other ruckus in 1885 that involved the Métis and the Indians against the still intransigent government of John A. McDonald. The American solution would have been to simply wipe out the Métis along with the Natives. But in the 1870 pre-rebellion atmosphere the Canadian government demurred and sent a show of force, not an army bent on slaughter. Gabriel Dumont was there.

"Gabriel Dumont!" shouted Jean-Pierre proudly over the la-ment, "he was my Great Grandfather. A fighter. A rebel patriot, just like me."

The original disagreement of 1870, staged by Louis' ragged

but disciplined Métis buffalo hunters, was blown into a full scale rebellion by the Orange power elite in Ottawa when Louis' followers convened a military style court martial and shot Thomas Scott, an Irish Protestant who happened to be passing Fort Gary with an armed band of settlers on their way home to Portage la Prairie. A big mistake. The murder of Thomas Scott, who would have been hanged himself in Ontario perhaps, became a cause célebre for the Protestants and an embarrassment to the Canadian government who really wanted to do right by the Métis. The press roared and the Orange members of Parliament pontificated, playing to the anti-French sentiment in Ontario. A militia force of British and colonial troops, wearing bright red tunics, was dispatched to put down the insurrection.

Louis was convicted of murder and banished to Montana. Gabriel Dumont wisely faded into the hinterland after failing to free his leader from jail. English settlers continued to encroach on the frontier. In the meantime the Métis and Gabriel Dumont were forced further west into the fastness of the Saskatchewan Territories. The buffalo were gone and the Métis did not take to large-scale grain farming but still there was the land question. The Métis wished to homestead, and have their plots in the long, narrow river-lots. "Dumont, est vivre la."

The fish ordeal was finished. The abused carcasses lay on the counter side by side, represented by eight ragged fillets, neatly arranged. Christian felt obliged to present well to compensate.

"Not so bad, for a rookie. You might become some use after all," Jean-Pierre said scooping the guts into his hand and flinging them into the far corner for the cats. Jean-Pierre produced a rusted out pressure gas stove and began pumping furiously. Christian remembered the cranky Coleman stove from their only attempt at a family outing: a fateful camping trip north of Montreal in a provincial park that resembled an Amazon rain forest. His father performed a similar act of wilderness craft and succeeded in setting the picnic table on fire, their only real campfire of the entire rain-washed weekend.

Jean-Pierre obviously had greater survival skills and after the usual frightening orange fireball that reached up to the boards of the loft, the stove settled down to the miraculous blue halo. Little jets of promise. Miguel could do that.

The fish disappeared into a bag with flour, salt and pepper and a spice that looked like red pepper dust. The skillet sizzled with butter. Hot enough to kill bacteria Christian hoped. When the butter began to turn brown Jean-Pierre carefully arranged the fillets in the pan, whistling as he moved them about with a wooden implement that looked like a lopsided spatula. The fish began to curl around the edges, becoming golden brown. Christian's stomach reacted to his marijuana-heightened hunger. There were six people, counting Dominique. There were four fish. Sprudence continued singing, repeating her favourite phrases from the Lament but kept a covetous eye on the progress of the frying fish. Gargoire, moving to the table, pretending to be preoccupied with a pipe and a small tinfoil package, turned his back as if uninterested in dinner.

Christian decided to give Sprudence the guitar *and* his fish.

The dining table was a large cable spool, the kind left behind at construction sites. It had a hole in the center for an axel but the centerpiece was a plastic skull on a broom handle with a hand-lettered sign in French that said, 'The last bourgeois pig to challenge the New Left.' Candles drooping from wine bottles ringed the message, casting shadows in the hollow eye sockets. Christian had seen the real thing in Juanita's Santeria shrine in the cave, and that brought back memories far more disturbing than Jean-Pierre's attempt at menacing humour. Still, the reference to the New Left was unsettling. Comrades. Bourgeoisie. The familiar squalor of anarchy, wine, drugs, promiscuous sex...when would the rhetoric begin...?

"Let's eat, comrades."

Gargoire and Sprudence had already taken up station, prepositioning on the excuse of space for cutting hash for Gargoire's pipe, which he didn't offer to share, and Sprudence needed to write down a new verse for the Lament.

Dominique had not reappeared and the Biker may have died, so the numbers were not immediately a problem, still Christian felt uncomfortable and begged off. "I'm not hungry."

"What? Not hungry? You arrive like a beggar, smoke my dope, prepare the ritual sacrifice and then you decline to partake?"

"I, ah, had a bite on the train." Partially true. He was out of American money by the time the train left Louisiana. The Dinning Car would not exchange old smelly Canadian money. He was exhausted, weak and starving, about to lapse into one of those unexplained states that had become more frequent since Cuba. One of the wonderfully sweet, but rambunctious children of the wailing woman shared her dried cheese sandwich and warm coke. Christian was deeply touched. The mother's problems, and they seemed profound, had obviously not affected her kids. They carried on as if taking care of dysfunctional adults was their mission. He could imagine them in Biafra or Ethiopia, wherever people suffered want of food or just needed a hand up. And that made him think about Esameralda in the convent, and that made him think of Renée...Dominique entered the room, this time wearing the Japanese kimono...and Christian forgot about the two girls who's light was rapidly fading in the glow of this tall, dark, beautiful and oddly placed creature of man's dreams or worst nightmares.

"As usual it stinks of fish in here," she pronounced. Dominique climbed the ladder to the loft. The kimono sailed down like a colourful kite suddenly deprived of wind, arranging itself lightly on the floor. The calico cat took possession, curling into a ball, and disappeared into the camouflage of orchids, cherry blossoms and Samurai warriors. Contradictions only the Japanese could justify with grace. Or Monet. The thought gave him a moment's pleasure.

"Did the cops come?" asked Jean-Pierre.

"Which context?" came the voice from above.

"Did they hover?"

"They hovered, so I presented my best sides. They went away satisfied. I, however, am not."

"She wants me," said Jean-Pierre absently. It was not a boast. "She'll eat later. And he won't wake up for hours," said Jean-Pierre, indicating the dead man in the dissolving chair. So, we eat the fish, eh?" Jean-Pierre produced a can of lima beans. Christian had a survival experience with canned lima beans mixed with canned mushroom soup, a last resort. The mixture made him sick. Jean-Pierre opened the can of lima beans. The smell turned Christian's stomach and he bolted for the doors on the opposite side of the big room.

"Going for a walk...check out the building."

"Careful where you go," warned Jean-Pierre. "There's a skin head group next door who stomp on anyone." Jean-Pierre pointed to the east side of their building. Christian did not see the gesture.

"Thanks." He opened one of the double doors and was met with a different set of smells, not better, just different. And the ever present smell of urine. At least there was no trace of lima beans. There was a wide corridor with a large window at one end. The filthy windows let in enough light to make out debris associated with careless habitation, cans of garbage, and rats. "Must be why they have cats." But the rats were almost as large as the cats so Christian reasoned it was more of a territorial standoff. The rats did garbage outside and the cats did fish guts in house. The rats stayed in the corridors and the basement and the cats mooched off the humans. Ecological equilibrium.

Half way along the corridor was another set of double doors and angry voices spilling out. Christian moved carefully toward the door, avoiding anything higher than the warped floor planks. The roof leaked. He cautiously looked in. There was a broad back and a shaved head with no neck. The back was clothed in some dark uniform with the sleeves cut off revealing thick arms and a tattoo: skull and crossed bones. How original. But below the skull a curved dagger and the words, 'Kill niggers!' Christian's heart sank. Not here too? This is Montreal. Polyglot, tolerant Montreal. Beyond the door-guardian, Christian could see an older man in military style uniform complete with Sam Brown belt, a dead-give-away, talking to a crowd of shaved heads in similar uniform. The cropped hair of the speaker, with a slant of bang looked theatrical, but deadly serious. The Nazi arm patch said more. All that was missing was the smudge of a moustache. The room was dim except for reflected light on a dozen shaved heads, and a stage light focused on the speaker that spilled over the blood-red swastika flag. Neo-Nazis are skinheads with a cause. Christian felt sick for another reason, real fear, but not for himself as much as for his city. The politics of French and English, the awkward but workable dichotomy of two restless cultures and the friction between Catholic and Protestant or Christian and Jew was decades long; an undercurrent of discontent, but it was manageable, predictable and even showed signs of movement, at least of a mutual standoff, like the rats and cats. But this!?...

Christian retreated, backing into a garbage container, knocking the lid to the floor with a hollow clang. He turned to run but the door swung open. Christian plastered himself against the brick wall in the shadow of a support column and held his breath.

The guardian looked up and down the deserted corridor and spit. "Fucking rats!" The door closed with an echoing, metallic boom.

Christian retreated to what had recently become his haven, in the bosom of some other, less dangerous misfits. The real skinheads Jean-Pierre warned about must be in the other direction, behind door number three. Life isn't a game show.

"Aryan Nations," explained Jean-Pierre. "They're okay, a bit up tight, keep to themselves. But they might try to put the grabs on you, dress you in black shirts and feed you all the Hitler Mein Kampf bullshit. But really, they're not a bad bunch. Just bored and pampered kids, some from upper middle class homes in the suburbs. They dress up and come down here on the Metro, just like Dominique, to slum and get all that Aryan angst out about losing the Second World War."

"They're not even German, most of them," said Dominique from the loft. "One of them lives in my neighbourhood."

"What nationality?" asked Jean-Pierre.

"Syrian. Like me. Parents are opening a Persian rug company in Place Ville-Marie."

"Not exactly Aryan stock," said Christian.

"There, see? They target the Jews and niggers, but they miss the point. They don't know a thing about the real issues. I mean, the whole fucked up world order thing. The capitalist pigs, led by the Jews, yeah, who conspire to control the entire world economy. They're right here in Montreal, comrades. They won't stomp on you with jackboots, or stick a knife in your guts. No, they do it in a way you don't know until it's happened. They do it from banks and office buildings and the fucking National Assembly. And those Anglais wanks in Ottawa, man! They can eviscerate you, pick your pocket and pat you on the head all at the same time and have a few hands left over to feed you bullshit, grease your palm at election time and steal your life's savings. Taxation is a candy store. The good ol' boys network can suck your blood through a pen. No, comrades, in the streets it's a simple blood battle. The Aryans sound tough. We even have a chapter of the KKK one floor down. No one can figure out whom they hate. No, it's the skinheads you must watch for. They hate everyone, even themselves. If they get you alone, look out. Stomp! Just for the hell of it. Dig?"

"Yeah," Christian sighed. What happened to the relaxed, indolent Beat Generation in the three years since he left Montreal? Paris had hints of a communist movement, but it was still Paris.

Cool, arrogant Paris. In Paris Beatniks just sit around drinking wine, reading poetry and talking about esoteric things to do with poetry and philosophy between episodes of jumping into the sack. He should get out of Old Montreal without hesitation. But where? He couldn't live in the Beat cafés. There were no youth hostels as in Europe and the downtown hotels were fleece joints, flophouses or brothels, or shooting galleries for the new breed of addicts. There were missions for street bums and there was the Norwegian Seaman's Mission but he wasn't shipping out again. Maybe he should. Europe. Paris again. Renée was in Paris. Renée had told him to come to Paris. No! Too easy. He had about a thousand bucks in the guitar case and he was free, but there wasn't going to be another money moose spewing cash.

The meal was over with no casualties. Dominique also declined dinner, choosing to dangle a seductive leg over the edge of the loft, reading. The Princess was hammering away on the guitar again. Gargoire smoked hash, not offering to share the pipe, even with The Princess who accepted a sympathetic toke from Jean-Pierre's roach. Biker slept on. The cats ate the last fish then went to sleep. He should too...

When was the last time he had actually slept in a bed of his own? In the crumbling villa, the night before he left Los Espiritos. Esameralda was warm and inventive. He had stayed a year longer, after the Revolution, unable to tear himself away from his shattered villa and Esa, but they were leaving the next day on the back of a military supply truck for Pinar del Rio, she to enter the convent because the Ché Guevara Hospital was closing down. His own villa had much structural damage from the tank shell. Miguel left for Havana to join the Castro government. Juanita was still in mourning, sitting in the ashes of her cantina drinking warm beer and sobbing for her husband or the moose. His part in the Cuban experiment was unclear and he was out of reasons to stay.

The Past: That last day Christian rode on the truck with

Esameralda and the last of the casualties, said goodbye at the convent gate and hopped the next bus for Havana, attended a Fidel Castro rally, slept in a park and caught the last ferry for Key West. Castro had shut down the remaining airline service to Florida as a protest against the Americans. He slept badly on the beach under the boardwalk, slept badly in cars to St. Petersburg. He made the trip to St. Petersburg just to see the Everglades. The Everglades were endless, green and wet. One dead alligator beside the highway, the pathetic beast not versed in the mad rush of the new mechanized tourist. Slept hardly at all on the bus from St. Petersburg to Panama City. Above St. Petersburg, near the Zephyr Hills, he saw two armadillos. One was flat and the other, the mate, dragging it's smashed shell off the pavement.

The Present: Late evening in Montreal. It was hot and dense with humidity in the warehouse; the copper sun dropping behind the downtown office towers, struggling through the haze. The St. Lawrence ran like molten lead into the crucible of Lac St. Pierre. Christian wanted only to lie down and close his eyes. There were other chairs and couches fading into the gloom of the large room; more chairs and couches than necessary, and all had that abused, liberated from second hand stores look. He didn't care...

"Hey, Anglais!" Jean-Pierre said. "If you want to sack out go over there, but make it quick."

Christian had been nodding where he sat at the round table. "Why?"

"Some comrades dropping by later."

Revisiting the Past: After Panama City and Mobile, the trek along the Gulf Coast to La Hache and Pilottown looking for Maartyn was an endurance test. Swamps and mosquitos. Beaches with sand fleas, cheap motels with cockroaches the size of small birds, and an odd assortment of 'new friends', who wanted to take something or give something...most wanted to steal his money or his mind. He was learning to protect himself, but still in the novice stage. If one learns anything it is that one has limits to understanding, because every time a door of thought opens the result is a larger room filled with more things, but the accumulation of facts dilutes the ability to understand...fortunate is the happy idiot locked in a room with a few familiar artifacts, content to know them fully. Still, it was freedom of sorts. He could choose to move or stay. To talk or remain silent. To ask questions or give up the search for Maartyn. If he had chosen to remain adrift he could have caromed around the Southern States in a limbo of poverty. Or, using Juanita's money, return to the islands to continue the pursuit of indolence. But the tyranny of home and roots pulled him north.

Home in the present, almost: The couch by the window overlooking the harbour was soft, with horse hair and springs protruding, reminding him of the American couch in the villa, dissolving like the Biker's chair, its mate, and smelled of dust and mould. Old food lodged in the crevasses.

When he woke the light had gone from the windows. The river was a dark ribbon between lines of dock lights, navigation buoys and ships moored safely to quaysides. Around him people were talking earnestly and the air was thick with the smoke of candles, tobacco, marijuana, and hash; a stew of carbon particles and chemicals swirling with the ancient industrial dust. The voices mingled and crashed around him...faces of anarchists without bodies who swirled and bobbed. All young and intense. The comrades. The Biker, Henri, was sitting on the spool table talking, waving a wine bottle in the air, and the people smoked and some argued with The Biker. Where was Dominique? He needed to anchor the room in reality. There was a female beside him, in the ubiquitous uniform of the street; dirty jeans, hand painted T-shirt with the words Libre-Vivre-Morté, hair chopped and spikey, like Hans the Hedgehog. Animated by what Henri was saying she kept shouting, 'yes, yes, right fucking on!' each time Henri stabbed the air with the wine bottle. It was political hysteria and the arguments were driven by drugs and alcohal. Those smoking marijuana nodded agreement. If all decisions were made under the influence of marijuana it would be a different world. It is always a mistake to make decisions when drunk on Scotch. One regrets deeply. Decisions made when drunk on beer are meaningless, but decisions made when under the influence of wine are often brilliant or impractical promises to oneself; impractical because the heightened sense of self is not found in the same zone of the brain the next morning...Christian had that problem...during the time he was 'away' on wine or in one of 'those times' he would have visions and make affirmations of the creative urges that kept nudging the surface of awareness without breaking through unless the semi-permeable membrane was dissolved by red wine. He struggled on the surface, unable to submerse himself in the destructive element of creativity, the way he struggled with relationships. If life was an ocean he had always been afraid of the water, deep and dark. Things hidden, unseen. But he was more afraid on the surface...Damn Conrad! Christian believed in the principle of confronting one's challenges, and tried, but, like the impoverished deep-sea diver forced to submerge with faulty equipment, he lacked the means to fully commit. He was struggling on the surface now, the room a murky lagoon filled with dangers. He turned to the window for a different perspective and noticed a familiar dark-hulled boat, just under the Jacques Cartier Bridge, drifting down with the current, keeping to the center of the stream. In the loom of a red buoy he thought he recognized the odd craft.

"Comrades...the time will come, very soon, when we throw off the yoke of the English capitalist's occupation..." Affirmations bubbled up from the group. Henri waited for silence, weaving, holding the wine bottle aloft. "Québec will be free!"

"Yes, yes, yes!" shouted the woman beside him. Christian recoiled to his end of the couch. Sure, Christian thought, vivre fucking Québec libre, and then what?

"Hey, you, doll," said Chopped and Spikey, "Jean-Pierre says you were in Cuba!" coming closer, hand on his leg, thrusting her bottle in his face. "Tell me about it..."

Later: "You're from Montreal, and political," Jean-Pierre answered when Christian asked him why he was included in the separatist group. The meeting had spun to a climax and quickly broke up when Henri lead the primed group into the streets to protest at a Jean Lesage rally.

Jean-Pierre remained behind. Dominique lounged in The Biker's chair and stroked the cats. She looked like a Japanese geisha in her colourful kimono, legs tucked up, showing one tantalizing tanned foot that moved with the rhythm of the purring cats. Dominique was a sensuous animal, protected by an icy calm. The effect confused Christian, but then women in general confused him. Esameralda was the exception. He melted into Esameralda's fire willingly and never felt threatened. Not so with Renée who held him like an indentured slave, at service, called on when needed, but she was at least predictable and he had loved her deeply, which complicated things even more. Dominique was just a puzzle.

Dominique's cool green and gold eyes kept pulling his attention back to her face. She was doing it on purpose. If she was Syrian, how could her eyes be green and gold...?

The Princess and Gargoire were conspicuous by their absence. Jean-Pierre said they were supposed to have a mission later but obviously they had slipped away. They didn't seem the type to be passionate about a cause greater than their own. If they lied and escaped, well, that was their business. He was relieved to be free of their presence, often drawn to but seldom comfortable with aberrant behaviour, recalling his life on the road and the continual exposure to the oddities of humanity.

"So they're gone? Gargoire and the Haida Princess?"

"Apparently."

"Was that their boat on the river?"

"Yes, gone."

"Gone? Where?"

"Why should you care, other than they took your retched guitar?"

"What?" Christian looked around the untidy room. Maybe it got shuffled out of the way. He searched the area. Nothing.

"Your guitar was just worthless but they took our stash of hashish," said Jean-Pierre, resigned, unfazed, as if he expected nothing more of people he dragged out of the river.

The guitar was indeed gone. "And my knapsack?" He looked at Dominique. She shrugged. "Jesus!" he said softly, in awe of such dishonesty. "Why would they do that?"

"It was just a lousy guitar," said Jean-Pierre.

"I know that. I was going to give it to her, but all my money was in the case."

"You had money? Why didn't you say so?"

"Would that have made a difference?"

"We wouldn't have to eat fucking poisoned fish!"

"You sound like a friend of mine...Jesus Christ! Now what?"

"Was it a lot of money?"

"Depends what you mean by a lot. It was my ticket back to university."

"Did you work hard for this money?"

"Yes and no."

"Could you make more?"

"It's not just the money." All his worldly possessions: black beret, poetry books, journal. Shit, the journal! The record of his existence since leaving home at eighteen. The sum total of his experience. "And, no. I don't have any skills, other than music, and I don't have an instrument." He had his Swiss Army knife. Life could not be simpler.

Christian threw himself on the couch, hands massaging his

temples, slowly dragging his fingers down his face as if testing to see if he was really in there and not some other place where nice people lived, people he could trust. He knew nothing about his current friends, except that the Métis Faker and the Princess Imposter were common thieves. But who or what had he recently left behind in Cuba? No one was who they seemed either, but then, no one actually stole from him directly. He scanned the faces of his Cuban characters. Con artists all, but not one of them simply stole from a friend. Was he friends with G. and S.? He had shared his fish, and was going to give S. his guitar. Wasn't that a bond? Would a long-term relationship with them have made any difference? He decided not. The end would have been the same, only the loss greater. He suddenly knew who they were. They were the worst kind of bottom feeders: survivors *and* liars. Dishonest among friends. The very worst kind.

"Damnit! How could I be so...so...?" The correct, descriptive accusation would not form.

"Naive?" offered Jean-Pierre.

"Stupid! Three years of dealing with people on the run and I haven't learned a thing."

Dominique spoke up. "Some, with certain hearts, never do." Her tone was soft, sympathetic yet prophetic. The icy barrier relaxed, the natural animal warmth flowing, or was he just wishing in that direction? It was a sympathetic balm or a word of caution. Like an old grade school teacher, a nun who summed him up too accurately, 'You have potential, Christian, but you are not hard enough on yourself'. What? Wasn't he running hard? Out there in the world taking the knocks and living rough? Apparently that was just running from reality. It is harder to stay and face the bastards who try to breach the walls. He was not a fortress; he was a beat up John Steinbeck caravan careening down a rocky mountain trail out of control... "Go on with your confession," she purred.

"I'm too...I don't want to talk about it."

"For me it is more problematical," said Jean-Pierre flatly.

"We fed them and housed them and they made certain promises. And just now that I need them they bugger off."

"Maybe they're just out sailing," Christian said hopefully, knowing they were not. He had seen the boat heading down river in a strong current, the escapees crouched in the bottom.

"No, they've fled the scene and have taken the stash. Gargoire's been pinching it in small amounts, which I tolerated because we needed him. This time it was the whole kilo."

"Kilo? Jesus Christ, that's worth a fortune...and, and you claim to be broke and have nothing but fish and lima beans to eat?"

"I was holding it for a the revolution, just easing off a little for storage fees. It came in from Panama by boat and a runner dropped it to me as they were tying up. As soon as he got ashore the cops grab him, but, he's clean and I'm sampling the goods before he's even out of the cruiser."

"Hold on! Revolution? Dope smuggling? What have I got myself into here?"

"What do you want to be into, Anglais?"

"Nothing!"

"Then you are free to go."

"Fine! I'm going..." He started to get up.

"But first we have to cut your tongue out." Jean-Pierre's features shifted subtly. He was smiling but it was the most threatening smile Christian had ever seen. The psychotic Cuban cop Yolando Carnero was openly dangerous but predictable. Jean-Pierre was a harlequin, or worse: two, maybe three people hiding behind that dark, changeable façade. "The tongue? Get it out, now!"

Christian chuckled nervously. He looked to Dominique for help. Jean-Pierre was just kidding? Her now cool green eyes seemed to shift to ice blue. Nothing there. "I, ah, don't know...anything. I'll just go..." Getting to his feet he felt heavy, as if all the comrades were pulling him down. He felt dizzy. No! Not now! Jean-Pierre was holding a long, thin fishing knife. He felt the pain a fish might feel when the filleting knife slides in at the throat and out at the anus.

"Sit down, Christian. I want to tell you something."

Christian sat, shrinking into the couch. It could be his last resting place. "Really, I am not interested in your group, politics, anything."

"You've seen Cuba. Fidel's Revolution. I brought you into our circle because you are an expert in Castro's vision and tactics. You will teach us. You will lead the political wing."

"I can't. I don't lead anything. Never wanted to..."

"You will. You have chosen us this day. You came to us just as the Prophet said you would."

Now prophets. Jesus! Next it'll be tablets from God. This is getting serious. It isn't just politics and some urban socialism, they're fanatical religious zealots; anarchists playing at politics, the worst possible combination. If they could only stick to spirit worship and alien visits.

"You know about our plans."

"I was asleep!"

"I think you knew about us before you found me at the river, just like Jesus when he came upon the despondent apostles in their boat, and said, 'cast your nets...'"

"Or a police undercover agent," interjected Dominique.

"I'm not like Jesus, even close!"

"Then you are an agent."

"No, for God's sake! Do I look like an agent?"

"Under cover cops seldom look like cops, obviously," said Dominique. There was a strange tone to her voice, as if she was being ironic.

"I'll accept Jesus."

"Christian and Christ. See? It's not just a coincidence. Delivered straight from Lord Castro as if from the right hand of God. He was sent by God to deliver the Cubans from evil. Did you really come by train, or were you transported from Havana by angels? Havana, sounds like heaven, right?"

"Train. I assure you. I have the marks to prove it."

"Will you baptize us? We want to marry, but Dominique's parents won't allow her to marry anyone who isn't baptized, especially Jews." Jean-Pierre sheathed the knife and ran around the kitchen area looking for water and a bowl. "You are the highest authority on earth, even greater than Castro or the fucking Pope!"

"Don't say fuck and Pope in the same sentence," cautioned Dominique.

Completely nuts, concluded Christian. Capable of anything. He began to sweat.

"A ritual slaughter then! Better! The cats. Slit their throats and you can anoint us with their blood!" Jean-Pierre grabbed the blind tabby from Dominique. He held the terrified cat up by the back legs and drew out the fishing knife, holding both high above his head. "A blessing. You first have to bless the animal and the knife. Say some words!"

"I don't know any."

"Say some fucking words or I'll just cut off the head and a spell will come down and smite thee, oh Christian, oh brother of God."

"Jean, please, take it easy...God doesn't have a brother."

"How do we know that?"

"Because..."

"Because you were there! See? I knew."

"Dominique?" he appealed. She just shrugged.

"First we kill the cat then bless it later."

"Wait. In the Old Testament they blessed the sacrifice by sprinkling rice," he offered desperately.

"No rice. Only lima beans."

"Fine. I'll get the lima beans, just don't do anything."

"Do anything stupid? Is that what you were going to say?"

"No."

"You pretend to go along with us but you think we're stupid?

Want to know how stupid? Suppose I sacrifice Dominique? She's just a useless bitch from Outremont."

"No, Jean, please...calm down." Christian put himself between Jean-Pierre and Dominique.

"Oh, now that's touching. Chivalry in the modern era. You want me to sacrifice you? Even better!" He dropped the cat and advanced on Christian.

"Don't!" Christian said with more force than he thought he could summon. He was dissolving inside at the prospect of being eviscerated like a fish. Regretted gutting the fish earlier. Felt this may be his punishment. Now he knew the fish was still alive at the moment he cut its throat.

Jean-Pierre advanced another step, raised the knife above his head and stared into Christian's eyes. Christian willed himself not to blink. He thought of Ernesto Escobar facing the firing squad. What is it at the penultimate moment that makes a person want not to flinch?

"Okay, that's enough," said Dominique softly.

"You're right." Jean said, grinning like it was all a joke. "This man can take it." He put his arm around Christian's shoulder. "Let's have a drink and a toke. Shit, there's no hash. Check the ashtrays."

Christian, both relieved and terrified, submitted to being lead to a chair opposite Dominique and eased down. A bottle of wine was placed in his hand. Jean-Pierre and Dominique each held bottles. "To the Revolution!" shouted Jean-Pierre. Christian looked at him blankly, then at the bottle. His bottle had recently been shared by the disciples, remembering that Carnero had spit in his last bottle of good wine and held it out to him. How many comrades had swigged from this bottle? Still, he hadn't seen it happen and this was no time to be queasy. "To the Revolution." He meant the Cuban Revolution; the one that had been a doubtful rebellion first and succeeded to become a clear, clean revolution. The last real revolution from the heart, but Cubans were still killing each other in the reprisals, the outcome yet to be determined. He wished he was back in Cuba where he understood the situation; Miguel coordinated the food and did the fish cleaning. "I wish I was back in Cuba," he said.

"So?" asked Jean-Pierre.

"Why?" asked Dominique.

"Oh, well, Cuba feels more like home than Montreal."

A door opened and a person walked out of the shadows; a tall, big boned young man who was very black. "Cuba, mawn? I heard you are recently from the Islands." His French was very cultured and hard to place, but Christian took him for a Jamaican. The whole Caribbean could be his neighbourhood.

Relieved to have an ally or perhaps neutral at least, Christian relaxed. "I was in Cuba recently."

"I too was in Cuba. I joined Fidel in the Sierra Maestra in '58, and was with Fidel when he took Santiago. That was some celebration, mawn. Then it turned ugly with the beatings and killings, so I came away to Montreal."

"A Castro Brigade fighter. Jesus!" Christian almost whispered in awe. His small, and at times comical role in the Revolution suddenly seemed irrelevant, a sideshow, although to those who died or lost their homes it was serious enough. And he had been under fire, still, he only knew a Castro impersonator and the bastard had stole his girl. Not true. He gave her away. And then there was Esameralda; a serious reason to stay behind when Renée left for Paris with Ramon. The bastard! "You speak French, but you sound Jamaican."

"No, mawn. I'm from Haiti."

"This gentleman is our military strategist," said Jean-Pierre proudly. "Meet Gerard Déslumé. He'll assist you in the planning of the take over."

"What take over?"

Jean-Pierre puffed up, gesticulating in that way. "Of the government! You know, the classic; we intellectuals foment disen-

51

chantment in the common classes and escalate by degrees until we have the masses enflamed to march against the government. Henri is leading a small group as we speak, agitating for the press and television. Tomorrow we will have a headline, 'Civil unrest in Montreal', but it's only the beginning. We'll start with City Hall, and then move on the National Assembly because they are in bed with the Federalists, and then..."

"Whoa, wait! Gerard, are you going along with this?"

"I left Haiti in '57 to escape Papa Doc Duvalier. I was an actor. The Ton ton broke into our theatre during a rehearsal of The Chalk Circle. I saw most of my friends machine-gunned and hacked to death. I fled Haiti to learn to fight. Castro was in the Sierra Maestra making an army to move on Batista. I learned much. My brother fled Port-au-Prince and came to Montreal an' I come here to find him. He was a doctor in Haiti, but he is a big disappointment. Now he's driving a taxicab and married a French girl. They have a baby on the way. He's become very domesticated and weak. First I will help Jean-Pierre and Henri overthrow the English and then I will go back to Haiti and free my people of Duvalier."

"Phew. That's a heavy agenda."

"Well, we should get started," said Jean-Pierre. "I appoint you the Political Provo. Gerard is the Military Provo. Dominique is the Financial Provo. Henri is the President, and will be the figurehead of the country. I am the Secretary General and the head of the party. There. Everyone has a job."

"I don't want a job!"

"You want to live to see another day?"

There seemed little point in arguing. Just because he didn't want to be involved did not mean that he could not be involved, but there were complications. "I'm now broke, thanks to your friends, and I want to go back to university."

"Fine. Go to school, it's perfect. A hotbed of dissent. Organize the students to the cause."

"And the matter of money?"

"Dominique will arrange something. All her friends are millionaires."

"Not all," she protested.

"Enough of them."

"Thanks. I'll get a job," said Christian.

"So fucking noble! You're perfect for the Political Provo. Incorruptible."

Gerard shook Christian's hand. The grip was warm and firm. "Welcome to the Front." Someone to trust at least, thought Christian, especially at the 'Front'. A friend perhaps. If only the situation wasn't so...so, fucked up, as Maartyn would say. What *would* Maartyn say about this turn?

"Okay, we've had a small setback in the plans with the defection of Gargoire, but that can be remedied. There's Petit Jacques and the *Elloise*."

Christian instantly felt ill at ease again. "What did that Métis impersonator have to do with this, this madness?"

"We needed his boat to make a run, perfect cover. Who would suspect a crazy frontiersman?"

"Run? What kind of run?" The alarm bells were going off again.

"Can't tell you. You're the political wing. You aren't supposed to know what the military wing is doing, in case they capture you and torture you. You don't seem the type who can stand interrogation."

Christian didn't know whether to laugh, be insulted, or scared. He chose scared.

The River Run

In the alley Jean-Pierre and Christian waited for Gerard to return. Then Jean-Pierre and Gerard consulted, animated but whispering harshly so Christian could not follow the argument. Jean-Pierre turned to him and said, "It's arranged. Petit Jacques is waiting in the Basin."

"Why do I have to go?"

"Because, I've decide the Political Provo needs to prove himself, under fire."

"Fire? I don't want to...you know, be implicated."

"You aren't. I'm talking metaphorically. It's just that I can't leave you behind."

"Why?"

"Reasons." Jean-Pierre moved along the alley like a commando in the shadows of the warehouses, skirting the yellow pool of light from a security lamp.

Christian followed Jean-Pierre with Gerard behind to cover the rear, or prevent Christian from bolting. The night was a thick blanket of humidity as dense as fog, hanging over the waterfront, muffling sounds. Even the ever-present road traffic seemed drawn back and muted. A patrol car crawled silently along Rue de la Commune and turned up St. Hubert. Christian had the feeling the cops were looking for him. They were creeping in the shadows, wearing dark clothes and blackened faces. His uniform was a mouldy pair of mechanic's coveralls, the name *Fred*, stenciled in red on a white ground over the left pocket. Wondered who Fred was. The carbon black on his face was running with the sweat into his eyes. Gerard was feeling smug about not having to wear the stuff, Christian decided.

"Cross slowly and be nonchalant. We're just some dock workers out for a walk. Gerard first. Then you. I'll join you at the Basin."

The city exhaled, breathed in and rustled to a steady beat. An invisible ship's engine throbbed. A small freighter was working upstream to the warehouse quays opposite Old Montreal. The river, alive with currents, was an undulating, heaving black beast, speckled with a confusion of barely visible lights. A deck winch clattered at the grain elevators on Alexandra Quay where a tramp steamer topped up a load of Canadian grain for Europe. Christian had embarked from that old quay on his trip to Holland and France. The same sparrows darted in and out of the girders chirping warnings. No, couldn't be the same sparrows. The flock had stayed with the ship for the entire crossing, being knocked off one by one, day by day, by a hawk who had joined the voyage somewhere in the Gulf of St. Lawrence. The hawk and one sparrow made it to Holland. It had been an early lesson in survival for Christian. Far to the east, down the Great River, was the ocean and freedom from the land. And somewhere down stream were his guitar and his recorded life, not to mention his entire financial assets. Damn them! It may be necessary, pushed to the limit, to kill to survive but one should not steal from friends.

Gerard ambled over rue Commune, body graceful and controlled, slowly stepping across the tracks toward the river and Victoria Wharf, down the embankment to the quay level then down the stairs to the dock. When he disappeared under the shadow of a rusting coastal freighter Jean-Pierre nudged Christian. Christian felt silly pretending to be a casual stroller. He was tempted to just run away, but where would he go? He knew there was danger but felt at least protected between Jean-Pierre and Gerard, choosing to be beside Gerard if the skinheads showed up. That was one of the warnings from Jean-Pierre, besides not talking to strangers. That's funny, he thought, in the circumstances: never go out alone, especially at night, tie up your shoes, eat broccoli. He was under protective custody. But there were deeper warnings, not verbal, but hints about Dominique. Not being a traitor and not defecting, the consequences only imagined, but somehow it seemed less dangerous to just submit to this odd collection of people who were deluded about anarchy. He had seen anarchy close up in Cuba, studied anarchy and anarchists in school, was fascinated by the psychology of dissent. He had no heroes when it came to anarchists and political dissidents, but he did understand rebels like Michael Collins, Castro and Major Marti, Mao, Jefferson, Wolf Tone, and even Louis Riel. A disparate and desperate lot but with a common thread...

"Go! Go...!" Jean-Pierre snarled.

Christian crossed the road and stopped to watch the river, rooted by a reverie, one foot on the railway track, speculating about the next step. All he was allowed to know was that they were making a run by that black boat, in the Victoria Basin which sizzled and hissed, dwarfed by the bulk and throaty mutter of the diesel generator on the McAllister Company tug.

"Go!"

The deep voice in the darkened wheelhouse startled Christian. "Seaway, this is the *Elloise*, in Market Basin. Permission to lock up?" "Tug *Elloise*, this is Seaway Beauharnois. Affirmative. You'll lock through with *Fort Chambly*. The *Edmund Fitzgerald's* down at Lambert and should be clear of the canal by O three-thirty."

"Seaway, *Elloise*. Roger that. Can I get in ahead of the *Chambly*?"

"*Elloise*, Seaway. Affirmative. *Chambly's* anchored below Sainte Hélèna, you can pass her to port when *Fitzgerald* has cleared M191."

"Roger, Seaway. *Elloise* gone." He hung up the VHF microphone and said sarcastically, "Nous affirmative zat, you Anglais loving asshole!"

"Meet Petit Jacques. He's one of us."

Christian could see only a dark form that seemed as wide as it was tall. Petit Jacques, at five-five and three hundred pounds, just about filled the wheelhouse of the tug. Christian wondered if there was a Gros Jacques. Petit Jacques, from French Guinea, wearing coveralls with the arms cut off and no shirt, seemed to be all beard and hair every where except on top of his head. He smoked a cigar that, Christian speculated, was about the size of

Gerard's dick. That unfortunate faux pas of racial typing resulted from his year in the Caribbean with Renée, who constantly speculated about the length and girth of the handsome native boys. Christian felt intimidated and small, even though Renée never did, as far as he knew, go further than to covet the bulge in their swim trunks. And Esameralda never complained or even hinted she was anything but sweetly satisfied by Christian. But Renée could tear him apart with her frank, Bohemian-inspired take on the new philosophy of free love. He was always one cult philosopher or new Beat poet behind her. Christian was just catching up when he left Cubaa and Esameralda was a wonderful therapist...

"Welcome 'board, sonny!" Petit Jacques grabbed Christian's hand and dragged him, almost lifted him, up the metal steps into the wheelhouse where the air was a dense soup of cigar smoke, body odour, grease, burned oil, curried chicken, marijuana smoke, damp hash pipes, rancid coveralls, mould, rotting charts, and bad breath exuding expensive Madeira, Fine Old Malmsey, twelve-years old, at least. There were bottles stashed around the wheelhouse. This was not meant to instill confidence, but fortunately Christian knew little about the dangers of commercial shipping and the fine art of boat handling when your little tug is an eight ounce piglet trying to bully an eight-hundred pound momma into a corner. Gerard disappeared below into the engine room. Jean-Pierre and Petit Jacques passed a bottle and exchanged news about the river. "Drink?" It was not a question. He thrust a half empty bottle of Madeira into Christian's hand.

"Ah, thanks..." His stomach turned at the thought of what else was in the bottle. A recently acquired phobia: sharing a bottle of wine, having shared with a Cuban cop who could have easily beat Christian with the blunt end. Madeira was a new experience for Christian: heavy, smooth, but edgy, with a sweet aftertaste, and strong. The first obligatory swig bypassed his stomach and went straight to his brain. At least that's how it felt. He was ready for anything.

"Get the fucking bow line!"

'Anything' was being enlisted as deckhand apparently. His most recent boating experience consisted of rowing a waterlogged skiff around the Los Espiritos waterfront as far as the reef and one night helping Maartyn load the bodies of the *Bayou Queen's* crew into the skiff and rowing them ashore.

Jean-Pierre was hauling in the heavy stern mooring line. Petit Jacques was using the big prop's transverse thrust and the taught bow line to spring the tug's stern away from the dock. The sideways motion of the tug disoriented Christian, causing him to seek handholds. Everything on the tug was sticky or hot. Door handles, railings and vents. The deck was coated with some kind of tar.

"Bow line! Fucking now!"

Since Jean-Pierre was at the stern, Christian concluded correctly that the bow line must be at the front end of the ship so he started in that direction. It was uphill and tough going because his sandals stuck to the deck. The dock lights were moving away at an odd angle. The engine pounded. The hull vibrated. Oily soot fumes flowed over him. He felt sick to his stomach. Would not be a good impression to be seasick before the boat left the dock. Christian had once been violently ill over the side of the ferry to Prince Edward Island, on a flat calm day. It turned out to be the flu but at the time the passengers were amused, sort of.

"Hey, Rookie! Are ya gonna get the Jesus bow line today or what!?"

"Okay!"

"When I cut the power toss the line up on the dock!"

Christian made it to the bow but not without tripping over a metal object securely fastened to the steel deck. He could feel the blood oozing under his foot, making the leather slippery. But there were greater concerns than personal injury. He found what must be the bow line, a filthy nylon hawser about the thickness of his leg, solidly attached to the bow mooring bitt. The line to the dock was bar tight and groaning with the strain. Suddenly Petit

Jacques cut the power and the boat almost leapt forward, the nylon hawser acting like a giant spring. Christian was thrown backward, falling over the metal object that had so recently assaulted his big toe. The tug meanwhile, was drifting forward, bow-on to the dock. Lying there on the deck, waiting for Petit Jacques to yell at him, Christian summarized his life since leaving Cuba. The Cuban Revolution was a vacation experience by comparison, and things did not seem to be improving. Then he heard laughter. That was enough. He got up and seized the hawser, unwound it from the bitt, prepared to give it his best effort. The hawser was much heavier than he imagined, the weight pulling him forward until one arm was through the hawse pipe. He had to reach over the bulwark cap to get at the hawser. Jean-Pierre's hand on his shoulder prevented him from going over the bow as Jean-Pierre reached over him and got a hold of the line. Christian grabbed the line from Jean-Pierre, saying, "Thanks. I can do it!"

"All right, comrade."

Christian gathered a few feet of hawser in a loop, swung it back and forth and gave it his best. The eye and the line arched up and landed on the dock with a loop hanging over the edge. Christian dared the line to move. It did. Slowly, like a sleepy snake, it slid off the concrete and the eye winked at him as it hopped over the edge and disappeared. The splash was final and he waited for the reprimand. The steam engine wheezed again, the big prop thumped. Petit Jacques scared the daylights out of Christian by sounding three sharp blasts on the ship's whistle. Christian stood at the bow watching the dock retreat, the damned hawser pointing straight down into the water.

"Never mind, man. Good try."

"Yeah. How is it I had to throw mine away?"

"The man say do it...the man's in charge."

Christian made his way aft, passing the open door of the wheelhouse. A New York City radio station splashed out late night rhythm and blues. James Brown, 'I'll Go Crazy.' "Sorry," he said to Petit Jacques who was looking forward, despite the fact they were still going astern, fairly quickly, Christian thought.

"Okay, sonny. Isn't the first time a rookie fucks up."

"Is it a problem?"

"No, no, when we get back, you jump in water, climb that line an' throw it back on board."

Jesus, was he serious, Christian wondered? He continued aft, working his way along the deckhouse using the handrail, almost falling into the engine room when he reached for the rail that was an open door. The music followed. The blast of heat and the sound of the steam engine should have warned him, but there was so much unfamiliar in the darkness: the motion, the music, the unseen objects to avoid. He should just find a safe place and stay low until they were safely back at their dock. Then he remembered they were on an illegal run, or something. It certainly wasn't a pleasure cruise. Wondered how people found midnight excursions on the water remotely interesting. Still when he looked around there was a mysterious, if dangerous, beauty. The heavy tug suspended in blackness, and to Christian the only evidence of water was the dancing shore lights and buoys. The only recognizable landmark the Sailors Memorial clock tower on the end of Victoria Wharf where he and Jean-Pierre had fished sharing a toke, just like old fishing pals. And they were quickly leaving it behind, or ahead, since the boat was still going backwards, faster and faster. Petit Jacques must know what he's doing, he reasoned. He focused on the clock tower. Only a few hours ago he had approached a body near that tower, and now...it was all going too fast, the events of his life, maybe the boat too. The engine had gone dormant again, but the boat seemed to be picking up speed, and yet, there was no sensation of the hull moving through the water. He felt the nausea, verging on irrational panic. What if the others had all jumped overboard leaving him adrift, heading downstream to destruction at the foot of the Jacques Cartier Bridge? He remembered that earlier, from the warehouse window, he had seen the stolen Durham boat with his guitar and money approaching the Jacques Cartier Bridge, heading down hill, toward the ocean, maybe.

"That's Grand Jacques."

"Jesus! What?"

"Jacques Cartier Bridge."

"Oh, Jean, you scared the daylights out of me."

"Grand Jacques," he said, pointing up. "The bridge. Petit Jacques drives the boat. That's his bridge, he says."

"Okay, I get it."

"Good. Compliment him on his nice bridge. He likes that."

"Sure. Ah, the motor stopped." The steam engine was idling, but still breathing, steam escaping from the condenser and blow off valves and the boiler draft drawing like an asthmatic vacuum cleaner. "But we're going so fast. Is everything okay?"

"Very good...the current."

That seemed like an explanation of everything until, beyond the protection of Victoria Basin the boat began to turn, the stern pushed toward shore by the current. When the tug was broadside to the flow Petit Jacques rang for 'Full Ahead' and they turned and slipped away downstream. Once on course the skipper eased back to 'Half Ahead'. They were going faster than the current but matching the breeze so the world became calm and a more orderly place.

Jean-Pierre sat on the rail, perilously close to death by drowning, Christian thought, and put a match to a thick joint. Never find a body in that dark water. The match hardly wavered in the dead air. The smoke hung with them, curling provocatively around Jean-Pierre's head. Jean-Pierre took several deep drags, building one on top of the other without exhaling, jerking in spasms. He wanted to sit down also but there was nothing except the narrow rail cap. The damp deck, which smelled like hot asphalt, was out of the question. There was a big towing bitt aft of the deckhouse. It would probably be strong enough to hold him, but...He chose to stand and hold on, waiting for Jean-Pierre to share and he to politely refuse, for many reasons.

"Where are we going? Can you tell me now?" He envisioned Varennes, Trois-Riviéres or Québec City, which he knew were down river.

Jean-Pierre exhaled loudly, gasping. He held the joint out to Christian. "Cau-ghna-waga," he managed to get out.

Christian wasn't sure if he said Caughnawaga or was just choking to death. "Did you say Caughnawaga?"

"You got it, Sherlock. You want this fucking joint or what?"

"Ah, no, thanks. Caughnawaga. The Indian Reserve?"

"That's right."

"We're going to the Indian Reserve?"

"With Indians. Yes. Redskins. Natives. Native Americans to be precise."

"And, isn't it that way?" Christian thumbed vaguely astern, to the south of their course, which was about northeast.

"Right again."

"So, why are we going *that* way?"

"Can't go up the rapids. Run Seaway...to Lac St. Louis."

"Oh. What will we do when we get there?"

"Trade dope."

"Okay, I should have guessed."

"Why?"

"Figures. But I thought they took your hash supply?"

"Did. But Petit Jacques got a shipment recently. He keeps one for emergencies."

"Is this an emergency?"

"We made an order from our Native brothers. Have to buy or big shit happens."

"What? Order, what?"

"Guns, explosives..."

"Great." Christian had considered the possible scenarios and at the top of his list were narcotics or contraband of some description; since smoking dope and doing drugs seemed to be a serious preoccupation with Jean-Pierre and his friends. And Caughnawaga was a special place where certain of the residence, who do not consider themselves citizens of either Canada or the United States, do things a little differently. One of their specialties, like their brethren near Cornwall, is passing goods back and forth across the merely inconvenient boarders and boundaries without being bothered by customs agents or taxes. Shopping for groceries, dry goods, cigarettes and alcohol duty free on the reserve is one thing, but some items are strictly illegal to buy, sell or transport.

"Why do you need guns?"

"Bank robberies."

"Jesus, you're bank robbers too?"

"For a greater cause. We liberate only the Capitalist's banks run by Jews. Arm the proletariat! Once we have liberated Québec and New Brunswick from the Oppressors we will take the revolution to our comrades in America and join up with the Cubans and Mexicans driving into the capitalist heart of Yankee imperialism, New York and Washington D.C. But first we need their guns."

Christian had faced the reality of revolutionary smuggling in Cuba. His own villa, built by a New York businessman, Señor Frank the Butcher Bartuchi, was the center of a narcotics trade before Juanita's Cantina became the conduit for smuggling weapons and people for the phony Cuban Revolution. One tunnel to the cave ran under his house. There was another entrance in a shed on the property, so he wasn't about to be shocked by Jean-Pierre's revelations. Given the events of the day, the rhetoric, and the politics, he would have been surprised by anything less, but bank robbery? He was caught up in another bizarre episode of his young life, hoping that he could survive this latest turn of events and escape without more bloodshed. His toe was beginning to ache badly, and the blood made little pools in his sandals.

His new friends were nice enough, aside from the thieves

who made off with his entire life's holdings, but they were playing a dangerous game. Guns, explosives, narcotics, banks. Night runs. Smuggling and rum running were a national heritage. Tales of Jamaican Inn and all that. He had read fascinating stories of the prohibition era in Canada. Well known families, some from Montreal, had done very well in the dark trade, supplying the goods for the new breed of privateers in sleek, fast speedboats with special mufflers, and fishing schooners with silent sails. The coastline of Eastern Canada from Rainy River to Black's Harbour, New Brunswick and even Newfoundland, was a porous boundary, a pipeline, an aqueduct of illegal alcohol. The runners using every means to spirit contraband across the water under the nose of the authorities, but always stealth was the secret to success. "So, why this huge, noisy tug boat?"

"Because," answered Jean-Pierre, choking down another draft, "they took off with the fucking bateau!"

Meaning, of course, the Poseur and The Princess. But he didn't see how a rickety wooden, Eighteenth Century replica could be less obvious than a fuming, smoke belching, yellow and black steel tug.

"Because," Jean-Pierre explained patiently, starting to nod, "there's to be a historical pageant at Ste. Anne de Bellevue. Canoes, bateaux, costumes, shit like that. Who'd know?"

"This old steam boat may be a floating relic but hardly qualifies as a historic vessel."

Jean-Pierre resurfaced. "You fucking Anglais moron...!" Then he remembered where they were, and why. "Oh, sorry, man, I didn't mean...it's just that we had to move tonight so couldn't be too choosey."

"Okay, but how, why tonight?"

"There's a Salty aground in Lac St. Louis." Jean-Pierre offered no further explanation.

A Salty must be a foreign ship of some kind, he reasoned. Christian decided to just relax and try to enjoy the ride. He was developing a certain fatalism because life wasn't predictable. Sure, he could stop putting himself in harm's way, or could he? What choices could he make? He had nothing to use for leverage. No skills to drive a wedge into the thin cracks of society. No future mountain to claw up to gain the summit of power and success. No money, savings, or real estate. Nothing. No hand up either, except for Jean-Pierre and Gerard, and all of them were now in the clutches of some crazed tugboat skipper from West Africa. Montreal did look nice from the river though, all lights and colours, and it was cooler on the water, the air soft, but freshening, between drafts of sooty oil smoke. And it was noticeably windier. In fact it was becoming a little gusty, crested wavelets keeping pace. The dark sky to the southwest was a shade darker and the distant lights of the south shore were fading.

"Petit Jacques says dirty weather coming."

"What kind of dirty weather?"

"Tornado, maybe." Petit Jacques had the benefit of marine weather forecasts but even they could not predict the severity of the wild systems that crash around Eastern Canada on hot summer nights. Summer heat, high humidity, a swollen low-pressure mass, and a flow of moist air from the Gulf of Mexico. All weather breeders, but tornado warnings in the middle of the night?

Christian could feel the change in the air. At that moment a cold front tracking along the lower Great Lakes Basin, overtaking the warm front and swinging northeast to follow the St. Lawrence River valley, was sweeping across Lac St. Louis into Montreal Harbour.

"Is it going to be bad?"

"Could be bad."

"How bad?"

"Tornado? Blow you to Rimouski. Want a toke?"

"Ah, no, well, okay..." He thought, what the hell? They were doomed. "Why...did we leave...the dock then?"

"If you wait for good weather you never leave. Besides, bad

weather is good. River patrols stay home." Jean-Pierre closed his eyes.

Christian toyed with the roach. River patrols could not be a good thing if one is involved in smuggling. Christian didn't consider himself a criminal but tried to imagine explaining to the police that he was forced against his will aboard a tugboat carrying illegal weapons, drugs, explosives, toking up to relax. Right...The Jacques Cartier Bridge, now astern, was swallowed up by a mass of rolling clouds. But only Christian noticed. Radio station WABC New York blasted a new sound from California, The Deltones, 'Let's Go Trippin'.'

The tug, rockin' and rollin' to the tunes, with Petit Jacques doing the Twist to Surfin' music, cut toward the fairway buoy off the north end of Ile Stainte-Hélène, the shortcut approach to the Seaway Canal. They escaped the current, rolling in long easy arcs from their own wake, the air going suddenly, ominously, from gusty to a heavy calm. The calm did not last long.

Christian was adjusting to the new motion when the leading edge of the storm hit, a microburst; a local but intense system of violent winds that sweep in unannounced and go off like a bomb. The clash of Surfin' guitars and wind, then nothing...

He remembered later that he had the sensation of being unable to breathe, as if the furies sucked the air out of his lungs. In reality he was facing the storm, mouth open in awe and he could not exhale. The tug lurched first to starboard and as she came up the full fury of the wind caught the flat superstructure. The tug snap-rolled to port. In a dream Christian turned to call to Jean-Pierre who had been sitting on the rail. He was gone. Then the cold driving rain blinded him. The tug heeled further to port. Large hail began pinging on steel. Then the hail became a hammer. Christian dropped to the deck, which was coming up to meet him, hard and unyielding.

How much trouble could a sturdy little tug get into close to shore? A furious wind could not build up much of a sea in the short reach between riverbanks, broken by buildings, bridges and islands. But waves were not the problem. Petit Jacques had been blasting along at full speed, as was his custom. Vessels approaching the Seaway canals are expected to proceed with caution. There are speed limits. In open waters it is as conditions dictate. In the Harbour of Montreal it is, as far as Petit Jacques was concerned, what you could get away with. Below the Victoria Bridge the river is considered International Waters for the purposes of shipping regulations. There are rules, and vessels move about like vehicles, in traffic lanes. But ships on the water do not react the same as trucks on highways. They tend to slew about and drift and do odd things, usually at the worst time, such as when a big salt water freighter is making a tight bend in a narrow channel and the helmsman, who may be from Sri Lanka, obeys an order from his captain who may be from Newcastle or Barcelona, who just received a steering command from the river pilot who is resolutely Québecois, speaking his version of English. If there is a slight misinterpretation of the intent, and in the ensuing confusion, the engineer misreads the telegraph indicator that flips madly from slow ahead to full astern, and at the same moment the steering motor in the stern packs up, then chaos happens. Which was why there was a Liberian freighter, owned by a French company with Spanish officers and an Asian crew, stuck in the mud on Lac St. Louis at the moment the storm hit. Petit Jacques knew about the Liberian.

When the storm swept across Lac St. Louis a seven hundred foot American Great Lakes bulk carrier, the *Edmund Fitzgerald*, was clearing the St. Lambert Lock, powering out of the South River Canal. Seaway Beauharnois decided to let the bulk carrier proceed down, despite the high wind warnings, thinking there was enough time for the big freighter to clear the Canal and for the tug *Elloise* to squeeze into the lock to cycle up with the *Fort Chambly*, a three hundred and fifty foot packet freighter of the Canada Steamship Lines, and then deal with the *Mer d'Oiseau*, which was stuck in the mud as the captain and the river pilot fought it out in the wheelhouse, each blaming the other for the mishap. The wheelsman had vanished below and was getting drunk on strong Spanish wine.

Petit Jacques knew all this before they left the dock. Seaway Control had the *Mer d'Oiseau* approaching Cote-St. Catherine Lock, when she went aground, had plotted her image on the big ship movement board with a little ship model since the *Mer d'Oiseau* reported in at the Sault Locks, Cape Vincent at the beginning of the St. Lawrence River and at Cornwall and Valleyfield and when she cleared the Beauharnois Lock and again at Pte de Moulin entering Lac St. Louis. There they lost her, so to speak. But other eyes were watching and listening.

The *Mer d'Oiseau* left Duluth with a thud; her rudder striking a submerged piling. The third engineer, a surly Scot who hated his chief engineer, didn't bother to report another odd noise because it might delay their departure. He was up to there with his arrogant Chief who was a cultured Indian from Goa and a great friend of the captain who was from Bilbao. So, *Mer d'Oiseau* had sailed from Duluth with a damaged rudder looking for a place to fail. There had been many opportunities for disaster and Lac St. Louis was a good choice. The limestone ledges of the lake bottom are covered with alluvial silt mixed with rotting bark: a smooth, wonderfully sticky goo. The *Mer d'Oiseau* was only one of many vessels to find the bottom at the bend in the lake. Great Lakes skippers routinely pilot their own big boats on narrow canals but saltwater skippers are directed by pilots every step of the way.

Accidents mean big salvage jobs. Petit Jacques and his *Elloise* specialized in getting to a casualty. If it doesn't budge he simply throws off the line, leaving the derelict to a McAllister tug, and waits for another late night call from his network of 'observers'. Observers are river rats or independents in the waterfront community who monitor ship radio traffic for hints of situations, engine troubles or disasters. The captain of the stranded *Mer d'Oiseau* dispatched the pilot and made a call to his company's agent in Montreal. He would wait for instructions from the owners in France before he called the Coast Guard. The ship was in no danger and was well off the channel when it came to rest with its bow aground and its stern hanging over a deep spot. The next large vessel down-bound, the bulk carrier *Gleneagles* was still in the Beauharnois Lock. The *Gleneagles*, following them since Port Arthur, was going to the scrap yard after the run to Québec City and the skipper had been chatting with other ships for three days enjoying his farewell tour and commenting about the odd behaviour of the ship ahead of him.

That's why Petit Jacques knew about the embarrassment of the *Mer d'Oiseau*. Earlier that night, before the big storm, Petit Jacques had been joking in the wheelhouse that his observer had changed the name of their casualty to *Oiseux du Mer*, which means useless or unemployed.

When the storm front swept the Montreal Harbour most people still out and about were blinded by wind, dust, rain and hail. Ship's officer's adjusted radar sets, and marked their targets because every vessel was now a potential enemy. Petit Jacques, who was not fond of his own radar device, noted the stern light of the *Fort Chambly* a mile ahead, anchored outside the holding area on the west side of the entry to the South River Canal. Petit Jacques took the usual short cut across the shoal waters off the northern tip of Ile Sainte-Hélène, well inside the fairway buoy. He had a *go slow* order from Seaway Control and was about to actually slow down when the storm took him broadside, wrenching the wheel from his hands and sending him sprawling out the wheelhouse door. Jean-Pierre stumbled to his aid. Gerard rushed up from the engine room and took the wheel as the tug lurched from side to side. Jean-Pierre held on to Petit Jacques to keep him from pitching over the side while Gerard, clutching a voodoo icon on a leather thong around his neck, moaning incantations to his dead grandmother, tried to figure out their position. "Where the fuck are we, mawn?"

"South Canal!" yelled Petit Jacques. Gerard had to leave the wheel to look at the radar and immediately the tug began a wild turn to starboard, heeling over deeply again, sending Petit Jacques down hard on Jean-Pierre, knocking the wind out of him.

"Throttle back! Throttle back!" Petit Jacques yelled.

"Get off me!" croaked Jean-Pierre.

The wheelhouse was in darkness; the only light was the green glow from the radar hood. Gerard peered into the radar and chanted his mantra. The wheel spun again and again as the tug lurched from side to side. He hugged the radar console like a lover, the glow lighting his face from below like a campfire.

The tug kept turning, which was a good thing, considering the *Fort Chambly* was dragging her anchor. The packet ship was blown away from *Elloise* but into the path of the charging freighter.

The skipper of the *Fitzgerald* had increased power for steerage. Striking the wall or the bank and ending up sideways in the canal would mean shutting down the recently opened Seaway. He knew the *Fort Chambly* was anchored below the entrance to the South River Canal, just outside the holding area below buoy M191. He could 'see' the *Fort Chambly* on his radar, and three other small targets in the vicinity; one would be the buoy, another appeared to be swinging out of harm's way. The third appeared to be entering the anchorage area. The small targets had to be rationalized, that is, left to their own devices. His second radar could also 'see' the big container ship leaving her berth below the Vickers Company shipyard, two and a half miles downstream. He had been advised of the big ship's manoeuvrer. The container ship was told to proceed dead slow upstream, under the control of the tugs, until the *Fitzgerald* passed downstream. Normally the British registered ship would have been told to wait for the freighter to clear down before leaving the dock but the container ship was already two days behind schedule and the agent was pacing the dock, pleading with the harbour supervisor; old friends who wanted to get to the bar before it closed. And dock time meant money. It was agreed that the Laker could be down river and clear by the time the bigger salt-water ship was half way up to the turning point below the three quays that jut out into the harbour fairway. It was a nice call, and would have worked out beautifully on a clear night.

On a clear night the ancient, wooden, passenger vessel cruising blissfully along the eastern shore of Montreal Harbour, hugging the green, as they say, would have been in no danger. The *Honore France Villard* was a goélette, a former Lower St. Lawrence coaster, converted to a party boat; her equally ancient captain had been lured out of retirement by the promise of easy money and short cruises. The guests and the crew enjoyed the music and free beer, supplied by a local brewery. The air was thick with legal smoke and the new diversion, Mary Jane, la Marie Blessé, a joke on Mother Church. The brewery representative had just delivered the captain another cold beer. The night was warm and sultry and the atmosphere right for strolling on deck. But the *Villard* was rebuilt to function like a Texas roadhouse. The forward work deck was closed in by glass; a floating tavern with a dance floor and a place for the band on the fo'c'sle. The bar in the cargo hold had tables packed with guests who knew nothing about boats or weather forecasts. The windows were steamed over, but with the flashing party lights and the noise, they could have been moored in a Longueuil strip mall.

"Oh, Jesus, Mary an' Joseph. Wind's like da hurricane!" said the old skipper, peering through the suddenly opaque windows.

"Just a summer storm, isn't it? It'll blow over, right? My guests..." The brewery representative was cut off by a sharper gust of wind.

The captain, blinded and confused by the lights on Route 3, and suburban Longueuil, and the goélette's own flashing billboard, was grimly holding the wheel with one hand and clutching the cold beer with the other. The brewery man knew about beer, nothing about boats. The old skipper knew about boats and beer and almost nothing about the WWII vintage Westinghouse radar glowing in the corner of the wheelhouse. When the storm hit, his instincts told him to increase power and turn into the wind. "Oh, yes. Bless me. Blow over, yes. Dese storms don' last."

"But how can you see?"

"Radar, la." He looked into the screen that showed only the ghost of the Jacques Cartier Bridge and the tops of office towers in downtown Montreal.

In the murk of the furies the goélette was now also headed across the entrance to the South River Canal. The *Elloise* was again turning into the line of the *Fitzgerald*, herself altering to avoid the *Chambly*. Downstream, and still out of danger, the container ship and her tugs were being blown steadily into mid channel.

The only vessels of record not yet in harm's way that night were the *Mer d'Oiseau* and the *Gleneagles*.

At 3:25 a.m. the *Gleneagles*, released from the lock despite the weather warning, was passing the anchorage area below the Beauharnois Lock, approaching Pte de Moulin. The current was strong from the outflow of the Beauharnois power dam so *Gleneagles* was forced to keep going into Lac St. Louis, the skipper hoping to make the wall at Cote-Ste. Catherine, an industrial site with large bollards, before the bad weather worsened. But Seaway Control advised the *Gleneagles* there was a problem ahead. Just what exactly was the nature and location of the problem was not yet known, just 'Be advised'.

The nature of the problem was *Mer d'Oiseau*, blown off the mud when the wind and the falling barometric pressure raised the water level of the shallow lake. During the fight with the pilot the captain had neglected to drop his anchors. The aging steam turbine had been allowed to power down while the captain waited for instructions from his agent. Now the errant *Oiseau* was temporarily back in the channel, but out of control. The captain ordered the bow anchors dropped. The crew reacted uncharacteristically quickly, letting go both anchors together. The anchors fouled each other and dragged impotently over the mud. This time the frantic salt-water skipper was forced to report his ship's plight. *Mer d'Oiseau* was now reported aground, in or near the channel above Cote-Ste Catherine Lock. The Spanish skipper wasn't sure. Seaway Control was blind as well as confused. The *Mer d'Oiseau* was in fact well stranded half way across the channel at the spoil ground three miles above the Mercier Bridge.

The captain of the *Gleneagles* could clearly 'see' on his radar the channel buoys and the shoreline of Lac St. Louis. He was approaching the tricky turn that would put the wind, now gusting to eighty knots, on his stern. He could also 'see' the *Mer d'Oiseau* lying across the channel between his ship and the safety of the Cote-Ste Catherine Dock. The captain reported his concerns to Seaway Control and was asked to 'Standby' as the controllers scrambled to understand the situation. At the moment the stern of the *Honore Villard* was crushed by the *Edmund Fitzgerald*, the seasoned skipper of *Gleneagles* decided on a bold manoeuvrer. He dropped the stern anchor, reversed power to slow down, and ordered the wheelsman to hold his course, intending to enter the deep spot off the channel recently vacated by the *Oiseau* with the expectation of going aground. It worked. The bow of the *Gleneagles* nosed out of the bend, crossed the deep hole and mushed into the mud bank so gently that, in the dark, it was hard to tell that the hull had stopped moving.

The engine room and wheelhouse of the *Honore France Villard* crumpled under the bow of the *Edmund Fitzgerald*. The skipper died with a beer in his hand. The brewery representative's body was found at Ile aux Rats, below Verchères. The forward section of the *Villard* spun away and was blown back into the holding area, fetching up on the mud a hundred yards from the Longueuil Yacht Club. The stunned passengers were rescued by incredulous club members in the morning, assuming an explosion had blown the stern off the old *Villard*. (It was only weeks later, at the marine inquiry into the rash of groundings and near misses, that the fate of the *Villard* was connected to the wild events of that dark night but it was never concluded or recorded that the *Edmund Fitzgerald* had been involved).

The bow wave of the *Fitzgerald* came on board the *Elloise*, washed around Christian, picked him up and nearly floated him over the side. Survival instincts caused him to hang on to something, anything; the cleat that had wrecked his big toe, that meant he was at the bow, not the stern, how...what? Christian got to his feet, knee deep in water, dazed and confused because he was staring at the solid wall of steel, glowing red from their port running light. Symbols and numbers flashed by. He didn't know it was a ship. He thought they were in a tunnel. He wondered how they got into a tunnel and why the tug was sinking. He tried to focus on something familiar, like a book. Spain...'37, Madrid, he said to himself. I've been through the Cuban Revolution. I would have gone to Spain to join the International Brigades. I don't want to die in another tunnel...

The Hurricane

The old shrimper, *Bayou Queen,* laboured in confused seas southeast of Miami. Green water mounted the foredeck and squirted through the bullet holes in the wheelhouse. Paulo was busy locating the holes and stuffing them with rags. "We're going to die!" whined Paulo.

"Y'all can stop moanin' about it," snapped Maartyn.

"I told you this shit box was a death trap."

"It was your idea to run the dope!"

About the time Christian was contemplating his own death by drowning, Maartyn St. Jacques and his reluctant crewman, Paulo the Basque Drug King, were facing their own trial by water. A massive cyclone was plodding through the Bahamas, laying waste to whole islands in its ponderous track. The Miami Hurricane Centre had named the rapidly intensifying tropical storm, Rose; in its formative phase near the Cape Verde Islands, endearingly referred to by weather watchers as TS Rosie.

Maartyn was running with the Gulf Stream into the fringe of the northwest quadrant of the hurricane, bucking a wave phenomenon known as tide lop. Maartyn and Paulo were also running from the law ahead of the storm whose eye was destined to pursue the *Bayou Queen* all the way to Savannah, Georgia. Maartyn wasn't concerned about making Savannah; he was concerned with keeping his ailing Gulf shrimper afloat. They had been on the run for a year without the means to properly refit the aging vessel after Maartyn had delivered Renée and Ramon safely to Havana in time for Castro's arrival.

Maartyn then escaped Havana Harbour and Castro's Revolution, headed home for the Mississippi Delta. While crossing the Gulf in perfect weather Paulo convinced Maartyn to divert west and trade marijuana from Mexico to the Gulf Coast. But Paulo misjudged the pirates who controlled the coast between Galveston, Texas and Mobile, Alabama. Guns, alcohol and immigrants, high jacked oil, and toxic waste dumping were okay but the good ol' boys drew the line at narcotics. It just wasn't the American way in the bible-enriched Deep South. Maartyn tried to warn him. The boatload of Mexican marijuana they attempted to land in Gulfport brought down the wrath of the good ol' boys. A year later the Coast Guard, the FBI, the DEA and their Mexican benefactors were still after them. Maartyn had wisely slipped his lines one night and disappeared from their last sanctuary on the Gulf Coast.

They had found a temporary haven in a small port called Cedar Key in an isolated group of islands of the same name, stuck out in the Gulf of Mexico ninety miles north of Tampa Bay, bathed by the turbid but nutrient rich waters of the Suwannee

River. Cedar Key had been a busy Civil War era railhead where Eberhard and Faber made their famous yellow pencils; the real ones with that wonderful smell of cedar and graphite. Cedar Key fishermen still shipped mullet, blue crabs and oysters but Cedar Key had fallen on hard times. Road travel killed water commerce. Hurricanes wrecked wharfs and warehouses and rendered Cedar Key redundant. Idling in southern indolence and Charleston-charming, Cedar Key was slowly filling up with beer cans and whiskey bottles, waiting for tourism to detour from its mad rush to Key West.

Paulo decided it would be a perfect headquarters for his smuggling empire. Maartyn wisely waited for things to settle down, and began making repairs to the boat. But a shrimp boat that doesn't go shrimping is bound to attract attention and being docked in the center of homey Cedar Key was like being parked too long in a drive-in restaurant with a barely street legal drag racer. In the local fisherman's bar Maartyn overheard comments about Paulo who didn't quite fit with the Gulf watermen. Then Paulo tried to entice the teenage wife of one of the local fishermen aboard the *Bayou Queen*. The scene on the dock was ugly and the *Bayou Queen* left port in disarray. Maartyn was forced to navigate the torturous channels through the islands, against a foul tide, to the relative safety of the Gulf; on the run again.

Like Christian, Maartyn didn't have a life plan. He had an ailing shrimp boat and a cargo of marijuana. The marijuana was on loan from a Mexican drug lord who assured Paulo that they would track the shipment through their network, and if anything went wrong...Well, plenty was going wrong. Maartyn wanted to dump the marijuana but Paulo threatened him at gunpoint. Paulo's logic: they could sell the marijuana and pay off the cartel or if the Mexicans did find them first they could simply return the stuff and bargain for their lives. Maartyn's logic: the Mexicans would kill them anyway. Options: they could fish and dump the marijuana, or they could fish, land the marijuana, sell it cheap, pay off the cartel and run. A small complication arose. There were several bales of dry marijuana in the fish hold. They would have to put ice and wet shrimp in the same hold. In the meantime Maartyn headed south to round Florida, seeking the Gulf Stream, reasoning that they could drift on the Stream to save fuel, working north to the Carolina's. A working shrimp boat would not be noticed between Florida and Chesapeake Bay. After that? Maartyn wanted to find his friend Christian in Canada. Montreal was on a big River.

Now the *Bayou Queen*, running from a tropical storm, was caught in the deep abyss of the Florida Straits, between Miami Beach and the Great Bahamas Bank. Maartyn wrestled with the decision to put into Miami despite the DEA but remembered his previous Gulf shrimper experience, caught in port during a hurricane. On that occasion the crew and Maartyn survived the blow in a local bar but their boat was reduced to storm wrack. All that was left was the engine on a sandbar that hadn't been there before the storm. The *Bayou Queen* staggered on toward the Carolinas. The eye of the hurricane came ashore behind them and veered back out to sea.

Late in the evening of the same night of the storms on the St. Lawrence River, two people dressed as Salvation Army refugees fled the warehouse in old Montreal carrying knapsacks and a stolen guitar case. They threw their belongings into the replica of an old wooden boat, slipped the lines and stole silently like thieves in the night, out of the basin in the shadow of the *Elloise*, and a tug of the McAllister Towing Company, ghosting past a rusting, ice-damaged coastal freighter loading canoes and cases of Coca Cola for isolated Arctic communities. By the time Gargoire had the motor operating they were in the grip of the current, spinning out of control. Gargoire and the Princess were leaving Montreal and their new friends, heading for a mythical civilization that existed only in their confused minds.

They had left in such a hurry they had no time to fill their water bottles. Sprudence, the dutiful provider, rather than risk the wrath of her mate, dipped a bucket of river water and shared a mug with Gargoire. It wasn't exactly like sharing the apple of Paradise. By the time the gale reached them that night they were both prostrate in the bilge of their sinking boat while the ferocity of the wind drove their boat down stream, finding its own way between the islands and sand bars. The escapees huddled under a tarp for protection from the rain, bailing between bouts of vomiting. Christian would have been glad to know that his guitar, at least, was safe from the elements.

The stern of the big ship passed on and Christian was released from his vision of death by drowning in a tunnel. Released but not relieved, trying to focus on a new reality: the moment, but the tug was still sinking. What should I do with the rest of my life? Christian wondered. He would never get back to Paris. Ireland? What did it matter? He mused on the immediate crisis. He might not have much of a life left but Christian was relieved to see Jean-Pierre rise above the water, alive...

"Christian! Help us!"

Jean-Pierre surfaced holding the unconscious Petit Jacques. Jean-Pierre and Petit Jacques appeared to rise and fall like swimmers frolicking in the waves at the beach. He saw Gerard through the streaming windows of the wheelhouse; his bulging eyes made him look like a blowfish in an aquarium. Christian might have laughed but a green buoy flashed at the same moment the tug ran it down, the clang sounding like a death knell. Christian took in the scene in snap shots as the stern lights of the *Edmund Fitzgerald* slipped away. The freighter was travelling at twelve knots. The tug was making eight in the opposite direction.

"Christian, take the wheel!" screamed Gerard.

Why was Jean-Pierre holding Petit Jacques? Why was Gerard

yelling at him, and what did he mean by 'take the wheel'? Did he mean steer? Where? Gerard didn't know either, but he had to get back to the engine room.

The tug, out of control, had made a full circle, sweeping back into the anchorage barely missing the dragging *Fort Chambly*. Gerard was able to veer aside just in time to prevent disaster but had no idea what direction they were going. Christian saw yellow circles of light, then the slab of black steel. The ship beside them was one danger. Land was another. The buoy they had just run over was gone before Gerard could see the number. It wouldn't have mattered. There was no time to consult a chart. An open door with a man outlined by the engine room light, staring down at him, flashed by.

Then *Fort Chambly* was gone in a blur of thumping, jumping water. The huge ship reduced to spectral lights against the haze of the city slowly emerging from the storm front. Christian was sure the thumping was in his brain.

"Christian! God-damn! Christian!"

Jean-Pierre and Gerard were yelling at him. Spurred to move, Christian let go of the deck cleat, and stumbled through the receding water toward the deckhouse. The tug was rocking from side to side and still rocketing ahead. He stopped to help Jean-Pierre, that is, to try to move Petit Jacques, but Petit Jacques was hairy and slippery and heavy.

"Take the fucking wheel, mawn!" yelled Gerard.

Christian climbed to the wheelhouse. "What?" The radio was still blaring rock music. Christian's brain was doing loops.

"Steer!"

"Where?"

"I don't know, just don' hit anything."

Christian gingerly touched the spokes on the big wooden wheel as Gerard disappeared down a ladder at the back of the wheelhouse. "I can't see anything!"

"Just keep on, mawn"

Christian held the wheel, peering into blackness. The canal was calm, only the backwash of *Fitzgerald's* wake from the slopping sides of the bank rocked them gently. He began to make out lights ahead that seemed to be in parallel lines, like streetlights on a broad avenue. At least the *Edmund Fitzgerald* had given them a direction; the canal leading to the St. Lambert Lock. Christian didn't know this of course but at least there was nothing immediately ahead so he steered between the lights as Gerard slowed the tug's engine.

The *Fitzgerald* meanwhile had cleared the canal, having missed the *Fort Chambly* by the smallest of margins and, after running down the *Villard*, was entering the harbour proper, where the British container ship and four harbour tugs were in a battle with the wind to keep the vessel from going aground on the east side of Montreal Harbour. The *Fitzgerald* was forced to the western side, where the three quays jutted out from the shore. The skipper knew his loaded Great Lakes freighter, with a following wind and three knots of current, was not going to stop in the distance between his ship and the container vessel's turn, now almost sideways in the fairway, so he did a rare thing. In a calm and steady voice he told the helmsman to just steer her through.

The *Elloise* glided silently in the protective confines of the canal. The wind had died away and the tug, with no steerageway was drifting, turning slowly, bow nuzzling the armour stone of the east bank, just below the Jacques Cartier Bridge. The transistor radio wept...'I'm sorry. So sorry.' Brenda Lee...Christian still held the wheel in a death grip.

"You can let go now," said Gerard, a hint of sarcasm sounding odd in the circumstance. Gerard was standing on the engine room ladder wiping his hands with a rag. Steam from the safety blow off hissed below him and wafted up the hatchway. Gerard seemed to float in a cloud, uplifted by ethereal spirits of the underworld. Petit Jacques was sitting up, back against the rail while Jean-Pierre assessed the damages. Blood seeped from a deep gash

80

on Petit Jacques' forehead, running down around his right eye, getting lost in the black mass of beard. "You put a big dent in the rail, old man."

No one seemed concerned about the fate of the tug so Christian let go of the wheel. He wanted to turn the radio off.

"Well, my little mawn, you did very good."

"Thanks," said Christian, just beginning to feel the effects of the tension. The episode had lasted about ten minutes from the first blast of wind to dead calm in the approach canal. It seemed to Christian that the nightmare was endless, and that he was merely a voyeur in a confusing tableau of horror moments, interspersed with blackouts, highlighted by strobe lights, and accompanied by rock and roll music. "What was that? That man in the doorway..."

"What was what?"

"Bottle!" demanded Petit Jacques.

"The boss needs a drink."

"A man was standing in an open door, just looking down at me."

"Oh, that would be the engineer," responded Gerard, handing a bottle of Madeira to Jean-Pierre.

"Then, it *was* a train?" he asked, forgetting all he had learned about engines and engineers in Cuba.

"No, mawn, big boat, *Chambly*, in a hurry. Engineer's the man who makes 'er go. Engineers never know what's going on topside, so they watch the world out their little gang door."

In Chicago Christian rode the elevated trains and watched people in third floor apartment windows, wondering about their singular lives: their loves, their hopes, and their problems. Some buildings were whorehouses and the ladies would wave at the trains while servicing a client. It was a big moving picture show, like a kinescope in a human museum. Chicago was a vast museum of human endeavor and frailty, side by side in display cases. But, wasn't he part of the show? Going past in his own window and the whores wondering who the pretty boy was staring back at them, puzzled by the inequities, the vagaries, and the deep mysteries of life. Come in boy, they seemed to say, and sample some real life, that smells bad by the end of the night and the ladies stop douching and wiping up because the drunks at 3:00 a.m. don't care. More often throw up and make a worse mess. It's hard money. By 4:00 a.m. the jazz clubs are shutting down and the city takes a break. The trains, mostly empty, flash by windows now vacant. Each pain dulled by booze or drugs, then sleep. The morning shift begins to trickle in and the windows are blank with the rising sun on them, driving the night crawlers deeper underground. Christian was always left in limbo, neither one nor the other, a poseur himself, playing at the game of life in the slums, hoping someday he could shake out the needle. He always knew it would be the Caribbean but was unprepared for Cuba and now Montreal, with a revolution behind him, on a slow tug boat to nowhere...Seaway Control was calling *Elloise* to ask what the hell she was doing? The song on the radio was 'Stay.' Maurice Williams whining and moaning, 'tella me yer gonna, *stay!*' But the beat was good and the tug stayed, as ordered.

The *Edmund Fitzgerald's* helmsman had dutifully steered his ship between the quays and the container ship and the rock steady skipper was slowing down for the turn at M173, happy to have escaped, still unaware of the fate of the *Honore France Villard*. Shore controllers, and port captains attempted to sort out the brief flurry of near disasters. And the captain and the chief engineer of the *Mer d'Oiseau* compared notes and doctored the log to put the best face on their own situation while waiting for the marine surveyors, the police, their agent, the insurance investigators, and the Coast Guard. The first vulture on the scene would be the tug *Elloise*.

The skipper of the *Gleneagles* had a quiet drink in the chartroom with his chief officer, speculating on the events of the rogue storm. They had little information other than what they could see and radio traffic, but considered they were fortunate to be securely aground while *Mer d'Oiseau* was safely sideways across the channel at the spoil ground, one and a half miles to the east of their position.

Into the Eye of the Storm

The northeast quadrant wind was still blowing the tops off confused waves in a carpet of white froth from horizon to horizon. A rogue wave loomed out of the murk and took the *Bayou Queen* squarely on the starboard bow. The shrimp boat shuddered and pitched her bow high in the air. Anything movable came adrift and crashed to leeward. Paulo was thrown down the sloping deck to fetch up hard against the aft bulkhead. Maartyn, instinctively grasping for the wheel, became momentarily vertical then lost his grip and slid to the bulkhead beside Paulo. Punched aside like a toy, the labouring boat came down hard in the trough and the top-heavy shrimper continued down, rolled deep, and Maartyn and Paulo were thrown back across the wheelhouse.

"Oh sweet Jesus!" breathed Maartyn, trying desperately to get back to the wheel. "She'll go this time!" Another big wave lifted the *Bayou Queen* like a mighty hand, the crest towering higher and higher, ready to break. There was a moment of calm as the huge wave blanked the wind, but the spume rained down on them in a torrent. Maartyn dove at the controls, slammed the throttle full open and spun the wheel to port. It was a risk but they had to turn away. Maartyn was attempting to send the boat back down the face of the wave before the wall of water collapsed. It was a calculated risk; they could pitch forward, dive like a submarine and flip end for end. Too late. The boat was sliding sideways down the face of the wave, slow at first, then faster and faster. The prop spun and the rudder stalled. They were surfing out of control.

"Do something, for God's sake," screamed Paulo, clutching at Maartyn's legs.

"You sure ain't helpin'!"

"I don't want to die on this miserable piece of shit boat!"

"You won't. This ol' boat can take it." He wasn't convinced. His boat was at the mercy of the elements and Maartyn knew this wave was going to break on top of them. The ocean roared and hissed, rolled down the slope and tumbled aboard. White water rose up and over the bulwarks. The *Bayou Queen* disappeared in a welter of foam, sinking with the weight, green water poured over the rails, forcing her further down until only her mast remained above the confusion of falling water. Paulo swore he saw a school of fish, swimming desperately to save themselves, cross by the wheelhouse windows. Maartyn was too busy to notice. His new concern was the amount of water pouring into the engine room. If it reached the blower...

The wheelhouse doors bulged inward and water shot in around the frame. Water squirted through the bullet holes, driving out Paulo's rag plugs. Engine gauges began shorting out; the oil gauge first. The water temperature gauge went next in a brief but spectacular flare. Then the tachometer died. But the *Bayou Queen* struggled up like a cork, shook off the water running about her deck gear and floated sluggishly in the strange roiling calm after a rogue wave.

"Okay, see? She's up."

Paulo buried his face in Maartyn's legs, simpering. "What about the next wave?"

Maartyn waited for the right moment and turned the *Queen* to face the waves once more. The noise returned. Rain and spume slashed the wheelhouse windows and water gushed in the cracks and bullet holes.

"Plug those god-damned holes an' shut the fuck up!"

The bow pitched high again but this time the *Queen* slipped over the crest and plunged into a deep trough as if she had learned a lesson. Maartyn powered up to climb the face of the next wave, confident that they, together, had this storm-wave issue figured out. Then the engine faltered with a heart-stopping drop in revolutions. The violent action had stirred up crud in the fuel tanks or air was sucked into a fuel lines. Maartyn throttled back and the engine resumed its comforting rhythm. He vowed to purge the tanks, first chance, and cursed the foreign-born diesel engine, not for the first time. Why wasn't it a Jimmie, or a Cat at least? The battle went on into the gloom of a hurricane dusk.

With most of the gauges out the wheelhouse was in darkness now except for the red glow behind the numbers on the marine radio. The weather channel announcer droned on with up dates and alarming numbers. But what use was a weather report, or a radio? There was no one to call. Maartyn and Paulo were very much alone on the ocean, somewhere off the coast of Florida. On a clear night the lights of Miami and Fort Lauderdale would look like Las Vegas and they could have been in the desert. During the Battle of the Atlantic, German submarines surfaced in this same area to listen to the music from the dancehalls and wait for the silhouette of a lone ship to blank out the shore lights. A fat tanker from Galveston or Baton Rogue trying to sneak up the coast close to the edge of the Strait. But on this night of Rosie there was nothing to be seen except shredded, tumbling water and torn up clouds. Then another steep wave roared over them out of the darkness and the boat was thrown on its side. The *Queen* gamely staggered up again but above the wind and the engine noise there was a new banging and thumping.

"Gear's come loose. Check it out," Maartyn said to Paulo.

"No way. I'm not going out there."

"Then steer!"

"I can't steer! What if..."

His question was answered by another huge wave that stopped the *Queen* and drove her backwards. Maartyn fought the wheel, trying to feel the weight of the water to determine their direction because there was nothing to see. The tired *Bayou Queen* was overwhelmed, pushed aside and fell over at the top of the crest, rolling too deep to recover. She went over on her starboard side, burying her railings at the base of the next wave and the wheelhouse door burst open. Warm salt water flowed around them and it should have been the end but half way through the roll the wave spun the *Queen* upright and spit her out the back. They were suddenly in dead air and a calm spot, sheltering in a deep trough. "Oh, Jesus! Not another one!" Maartyn knew what the eerie calm meant. The next wave was very big.

Somehow the engine kept running. Maartyn untangled himself from Paulo who was now screaming as well as whimpering, convinced he was drowning in the water swirling around the small wheelhouse. His yelling stopped finally when he took a mouthful of salt water.

Maartyn stared hard out the window, at first not seeing the wave that filled the view. Up and up they rose from the foot to the crest of the monster wall. A dolphin jumped clear of the wave and sailed over the bow. Maartyn could just make it out in the gloom but it told him what he needed to know. There was no use turning away. The *Queen* would make it over or die trying.

The *Bayou Queen* survived another near capsize and Maartyn turned to face the seas once more. Paulo fell into an exhausted sleep and left Maartyn to drive his boat into the future.

It was two hours before dawn when Paulo mercifully fell asleep, or drowned. It was all the same to Maartyn who would continue the manoeuvre for another six hours, feeling his way from wave to wave, sensing the size of the wave by the calms, the angle of lift, sound of the wind. Life was simplified to a narrow horizon: the size of the next wave. There was nothing more. They were at the mercy of the Gulf Stream fighting for their lives on the maelstrom known as the Florida Straits.

Rockin' the Seaway

The tug *Elloise*: Fourteen hundred miles to the north Christian sat at the back of the wheelhouse, out of the way. The transistor radio continued to pound out the mesmerizing music from WABC. The New York disc jockey babbling on between raucous numbers with song titles he had never heard, except for Jerry Lee Lewis, thanks to Maartyn. But the disc jockey said Jerry Lee was 'no-where's-ville' man. The Coasters were, 'solid Maxwell'. The latest song was Charlie Brown, a follow up to their smash wax, 'Ya-kity Yak.' Dig it, baby? What was the man talking about? And what was that sax player doing? King Curtis, wow! That's no place for a sax man. Who is Lloyd Price? Never heard of Clyde McPhatter. The Coasters. The Crests. Bo Diddley? Sounds of the new music, rock 'n' roll, fighting it out with rhythm and blues. Little Anthony and the Imperials. Rockabilly? What happened to big band jazz? Glen Miller? Kenton? He accepted that his own jazz was to remain on the fringe and liked it that way, but the new sounds were an assault on the senses. No Dexter Gordon on stage at the Apollo. Man, he really had been living on the moon for the past three years. Petit Jacques, still bleeding from his assault on the steel railing, was at the wheel. Jean-Pierre was beside him, talking under the music. Gerard, nerves recovered from the storm, jived in the engine room tending the wheezing baby. The tug idled placidly along the South River Canal between the shore lights toward the St. Lambert Lock. They could have been on a suburban highway, approaching a small town with sights focused on the new mall. Red lights turned green. Stop lights, he thought. Why are there stoplights on a canal?

It was cooler after the storm. Gerard came on deck for a breather and a toke. The night strangely passive, as if contrite, ashamed of the chaos it caused an hour before. They didn't realize there had been deaths. Petit Jacques and Jean-Pierre discussed the events and concluded they were very lucky to be alive. The medicinal bottle of Madeira passed back and forth, and then another. Gerard declined and went below to be ready with engine controls. Christian drank to calm his nerves.

"Never been that close to a ship without I wanted to hit it," said Petit Jacques, "for a reason." He felt expansive. "Once had to hit a ship hard and drive her quick to keep her from hitting the end of a pier. It was a close thing. Damaged my boat but saved the company a lot of money. Do you think the captain would compensate? He chew me out good for scratching his rusting hulk of a ship. No god-damn way! So next time same thing happen I lay back an'...*wham*!" He slammed a ham-sized fist into his palm. "She hit the end of that pier bow on an' the captain fell down an' broke his nose. He come out yelling at me, the blood running down. I said, 'that'll teach you, you cheap ol' bastard! Next time you let Petit Jacques do it his way an' compensate!'"

Work lights from the pier flooded the tug. They were approaching St. Lambert and a narrow steel gate rose up in the center of the lock area that was all grey steel and concrete, industrial and deserted.

"On deck, rookie. Time to earn your keep," said Petit Jacques. The bandage on his head made him look like a Turk, thought Christian. Or Buda. Gautama Buda cruising along at the wheel of a big truck...

"C'mon, Chris. I'll show you."

"What? Show me what?" He followed Jean-Pierre reluctantly out of the wheelhouse. The small space, smelling of booze, steam and hot grease, had been at least comforting, like his mother's kitchen on a winter day with the cook stove rumbling and a pot boiling tough old chicken bought from The Kosher Meat Market, but the memory was better than the smell. Then there were the cookies. He could smell them as he climbed the icy stairs from the alley after school. There would be hot cocoa and the world was calm and he could talk to his mother before his father returned...often drunk, to pick a fight.

They made their way along the deck to the bow. Christian remembered to avoid the deck cleats and fo'c'sle hatch combing. "When we get in the lock the dock hand will drop a line. Port side, there," he said because Christian looked puzzled. "You tie his line on this eye." Jean-Pierre held up a heavy hawser with a spliced loop. The hawser came out of the hawse pipe and back over the rail. It reminded Christian of his goof up a couple hours before as they left the dock in the Basin. He showed him the knot, a quick bowline with a slip. "Then you jerk the line when it's tied on."

"Okay. Then what?"

"Then the fucking guy up above will jerk your line...Get it? Jerk you off?"

"No, I don't get it. Why do we have to do this?"

"In the lock, you have to tie up."

"Lock?"

"Lift us. Up river, we're going up."

"Oh. Right..."

"Okay?"

"Why can't you do it?"

"I'm going aft. To do the same...It's a rule. Why else do you think we brought you along?"

"I thought it was for other reasons, like political, or..."

"To keep you away from Dominique?"

"Well, yeah."

"Don't get excited. I told you she only sleeps with me."

"Sure, okay."

"And when the guy says, 'Okay Froggie', she's yours, or tie off, you say, 'Fuck you Anglais asshole', but you tie off this big line to that bit." He pointed to the double bitt at the bow.

"What if he isn't Anglais."

"They're Anglais alright, this bunch, at night. French aren't smart enough to do lines yet. And if he's French you say *mange moi* anyway, just don't be polite or they'll forget to untie the line

89

when it's time to go. Sometimes they ask for money."

"Bullshit! This isn't the Panama Canal."

"You're right. Jacques knows them all. He pays them off with booze and cigarettes, or other things, and they forget to record his trips so he doesn't have to pay lockage."

"So, it is like the Panama Canal."

"You can get anything on the canals."

"Anything? Like what?"

"There's a Madame up on Lac Francois who runs girls out to the ships. The girls get off at Iroquois. Maybe catch a down bound. Know who gets off first?"

"No. The Madame?"

"The captain!"

Christian looked blank. "Why would the captain?...Oh, yeah, I get it."

"You dumb, Anglais fuck head," Jean-Pierre said, laughing. "And up by Cornwall there's boats come right alongside at night and send up cases of booze from the American side, while the ship's moving."

"Christ, aren't there laws?"

"Not at night. If the pilots see they don't say. They get their baksheesh. They go up and down the river too. And people? The Asian boats, man, it's like the Marines landing. Net over the side and the monkeys scrambling down, into a fast boat and zippo, they're in New York. Women. Children. They lose a few. Nobody knows, but Jacques has pulled some bodies for the police."

"Why don't they stop it?"

"Who? The police? Not their business 'til they're ashore. Coast Guard? They'd have to stop and search every fucking ship coming into the Gulf. Since the container ports opened the Asian population of New York has probably doubled. Okay, Anglais, we're almost there."

"Where?"

"The lock."

Christian looked ahead of the tug. The doors were open and there were lights and steelwork rising on both sides of a big, dark, dripping concrete box. The tug glided into the wet cavern. Every sound echoed and bounced around the space. The water looked thick and black. At the other end of the box a cascade of water tumbled from under a huge set of doors, splashing into the lock like a tropical waterfall. And above them along the edge of the box he could see faces peering down.

"Hey, Jacques, we heard the Big Guy tried to run you over. Bet you shit your pants!"

"Fuck you, Melvin! You didn't get wet hiding in your little shithouse, did you?"

Word of the series of near misses down river had spread quickly along the system. The workers could joke but management's britches were in knots trying to figure out who did what to whom.

"What's with the fucking turban? You get religion?"

"I got big message for you, dickhead."

"You gonna pull the Paki off the mud?" He meant *Mer d'Oiseau* but any vessel of foreign registry was a Paki to the dockies.

"You gonna pull off at coffee break like you always do?"

Christian was listening to the infantile repartee when a manila line smacked him on the head, the rest of the coil falling onto the deck. He could hear the laughter above but didn't have a clever comeback other than, "Hey, you. Watchit!" His voice sounded too high and the echo mocked him.

"New deck hand, Jacques? You gotta stop drownin' your boys, or is this one a girl?"

Christian untangled himself from the dirty manila, found the end of the light line and attempted to tie a bowline on the loop of the hawser. The line jerked out of his hand before he could make the first turn. "What the...Hey, dickhead! I wasn't ready!" Anonymous laughter rippled around the cavern. "Dickheads!!" He felt better.

"Oh, sorry, Francine."

The line dropped down again but this time Christian was ready, jumping back, grabbing the line before it hit the deck. Boy Scout bowline thrown on in record time, he jerked the line hard and heard a satisfying curse above. The line shot upwards hauling the heavy hawser with it. Christian prayed the knot would hold. The loop of the hawser curled over the edge of the lock wall and walked along the edge, keeping pace with the tug still moving ahead toward the waterfall. Christian was mesmerized by the sights and sounds of the concrete canyon and didn't notice that although the hawser had stopped rising it hadn't stop running out the hawse pipe. A bell jangled in the engine room and Petit Jacques was half way out the door.

"Hey, for Christ's sake, stop the fucking line!"

"Jesus!" He jumped at the escaping hawser. "Sorry..."

"That line gets in the prop, we're here for the night! Fucking kids!"

"Hey, Jacques. What union hall'd you find that one in!?"

"Fuck you, Melvin. Our union wouldn't let you assholes pick up cigarette butts!"

"Everyone feels badly about not going to Madrid," said Jean-Pierre, "even Melvin, who sees himself stuck on this dock, in a foreign country. He's a Communist but being Anglais, he has no cause worth fighting for. We on the other hand have nothing to regret, but our freedom."

"You've read Sartre?"

"Of course, hasn't everyone who thinks?"

They were tied up, the lines angling steeply to the invisible bollards on the top of the wall. There were no dock hands to be seen, gone back to their shelter after admonishing Christian to keep a strain on the line. The lock chamber continued to drip, hollow splashes of invisible water and the wheezing of the steam engine the only sounds.

They were waiting for the *Fort Chambly* to enter the lock so Jean-Pierre came forward to show Christian how to take up the slack as the water rose in the lock. "Watch the current. Don't let the boat be driven away from the wall."

Gerard sat in the engine room door cooling off. Petit Jacques spent his time on the VHF radio talking to his 'Observers' getting the latest news. The *Mer d'Oiseau* was still hard aground, broadside, at the spoil bank, they said. *Gleneagles* was an easy tow with her bow in soft mud, deep water under her stern and they had the jump on the McAllister tug. Jacques could pass on *Mer d'Oiseau* or get her first. Yes, there was just enough water off *Oiseau's* stern. Next he talked to someone near Caughnawaga sitting in a dark vehicle parked in the shadow of the Mercier Bridge. They talked in code. Christian could hear the words but they made no sense. Jean-Pierre watched his new comrade's consternation. "Don't worry about it. It's not your business."

"Some how I doubt that," Christian said fatalistically.

"At Madrid the Brigades didn't know the treachery about to fall on them. They were betrayed by the generals."

"Besides being bombed by the Germans and Italians," said Christian sadly.

"Sold out, but they happily marched along to defeat, singing the brave songs in many languages, to agony and destruction, but happy."

"How happy?" Christian asked. This was a part of Sartre Renée never talked about.

"Happy to know they were there and the others, like Mathieu, weren't."

"Mathieu wasn't a coward," responded Christian defensively. He identified with Mathieu but wondered if it were true.

"No. But he wasn't there. He lacked the balls. The cojones as fucking Hemingway insists, and when the great one insists we fall in line, eh? And he regretted it all his life, Mathieu did."

"He was fictional," began Christian, surprised to learn that Jean-Pierre reads Hemingway.

"Maybe. Maybe he was a just symbol."

"Sartre's Everyman," offered Christian.

"Or maybe Sartre himself didn't recognize the importance of the moment."

Ah, yes, the moment, thought Christian, wondering if he was in it. When we are young we think it's going to last forever, so there's time, for Madrid and Havana. "It's too late for Havana," pronounced Christian.

"Santiago was the moment," countered Jean-Pierre. "Ask Gerard, he knows. Santiago de Cuba and Moncada. Did you know, Christian, that Fidel's compadres were murdered, after they surrendered at Moncada?"

"Yes, I know...I was lectured by one of his..." Christian stopped the train of thought, realizing Rosameralda was not one of Castro's loyal comrades, but a traitor to the Revolution. A self-serving she-devil in the skin of an angel. How could she?

"And it's not too late for Havana, but maybe Cuba would not have been delivered if Batista had shown some mercy, some intelligence at least and not made martyrs of Castro's followers. The worst thing a dictator can do is to create martyrs. They're all so stupid. If they only knew that a few words and a few coins to the peasants, maybe a hospital bed, and a visit, a little education, would win their hearts. Look what Eva Peron did in Argentina. What does a sewing machine cost, wholesale, compared to a machine gun to keep the rabble in line?"

"Castro knows how to win hearts," argued Christian. "He sent Ché to administer the sick and they built clinics, and they never stole from the poor."

"Exactly!" shouted Gerard. "An' look what he got in return, a whole fucking revolution, handed to him, free for the taking. If the stupid politicians only knew how to really seduce the masses, mawn."

Jean-Pierre jumped back in. "Hitler knew. He might have been mad, but he played to all the worst fears and hatreds of the Germans. He rescued millions from the Depression."

"And killed millions in the process," said Christian, to keep a balance.

"Yes, but it is the consequence of being a great leader."

"Not all great leaders cause great evil," countered Christian, for argument's sake, trying hard to remember one who hadn't.

"Yes, they all do. Think of all the great men of history. Genghis Khan, Hannibal, Maximilian, Alexander, Hitler, Churchill, Roosevelt, Stalin, Mao. And half of them in this century."

Admitting defeat Christian added, "Okay, and Nero, Napoleon, even Mackenzie King." King in his turn committed thousands of young Canadians to their fate.

"Ah, another fucked up Anglais. But in the 1800's there was a religious war in China that killed twenty million because some asshole with a few pages out of a bible decided all Chinese should be Christians. You have never heard of this leader."

"I've heard of this leader..." There was a young Senator from Massachusetts who had promise in the American elections just heating up to the South. Christian wondered how it would relate to Cuba, or affect the Revolution, his friends.

"We are out of great leaders," pronounced Jean-Pierre. "Now-a-days the limp politicians think a few clichés and slogans, and a few promises that they always break, are enough, and the threats...no, you must give the prols something to chew on."

"Like bread?"

"Bread is good, but not cake."

They both laughed. The debate was over and the moment was seized. Christian felt a new kinship with Jean-Pierre, even though he knew it was dangerous and would probably end badly, as with Maartyn he feared. But it didn't end badly with Maartyn. The Delta refugee had character, if rough-edged, and a loyalty not always available from the elite. He missed Maartyn almost as much as he missed Renée and Esa, maybe Esa more than Renée. He worried about his friends but Renée was safe in Paris, even if she was being fucked blue by Ramon. Or maybe Ramon was gay. That would be funny, but maybe it wouldn't matter to Renée. Esameralda is safe in the convent in Pinar. How safe? She is Rosameralda's sister. If Rosa's treachery is found out the reprisals would not stop until all of Los Espiritos is punished. Juanita foremost. He had a vision of all his friends lined up outside Escobar's villa for the firing squad. The new rag tag army lounging about in the shade of Royal palms to watch the spectacle of fresh blood splattered over the white-washed stones...they shot Escobar in his own garden. No, that was Batista's soldiers who killed Escobar and he had it coming. But Fidel's too busy pulling together his revolution. The several factions are vying for Havana and the Americans are upset about Castro's growing socialist rhetoric. Surely the little misdemeanor acted out in Los Espiritos would not get much play in the greater scenario of revolution and retribution. There were plenty of Batistianos to go around. Major Marti was the key. But were did Marti's loyalties lie? With Cuba? The Revolution? To his people? Not to Castro and surely he wouldn't see Juanita and Miguel as conspirators against Castro. But, what if he used them to gain favour with the new regime? Jesus! Couldn't he just forget Cuba? Wasn't he in enough trouble already in Canada? His own Montreal. He'd only been in town a day. Less than a day. About twelve hours, and life, his own mortality, had been dangled in front of him and they were 'locking up' into more trouble.

The storm had blown away to the northeast, leaving Montreal under a broken sky, with stars, the temperature cool but comfortable. The forward half of the *Honore France Villard* was safely aground with only two deaths and a Durham boat replica ghosting downstream, out of control, in the main channel below Varennes as the two occupants alternately retched and slept in dirty bilge water, unaware that the *Edmund Fitzgerald* was bearing down on them.

"I don't keep a diary," said Jean-Pierre, out of the blue. "I should record everything so one day I can write my memoirs, of my own revolution."

Christian, feeling instantly guilty, though he couldn't say why, said, "The journal, is not about myself so much..."

"I don't have anything about myself important enough to say, yet. But some day I will be a great leader, then maybe."

Christian went from feeling guilty to rejecting shame, as if he was a spy. "About people...events."

"About people you meet? Did you keep a journal about Cuba and Castro?"

"Yeah, sort of," he hedged, felt relieved. Jean-Pierre was interested in the Revolution, but he could not hold that against him.

"If I was president of Cuba the first thing I'd do is forgive all my enemies, and invite them to join my Revolution, except for Batista's generals and closest cronies. Those bastards I'd throw in jail and shoot the worst!"

"Where would you stop? I mean how would you decide?" Christian asked, knowing that even as they spoke the new dawn meant more trials and reprisal killings. How deep would the reprisals go before Castro relented? Or the Americans intervened? Christian was convinced the United States would simply invade Cuba the moment Castro tried to move on his idea of liberal socialism; the new dawn of Caribbean politics. The paranoid Americans translated anything with the name socialism as communism, in no mood for the Red Menace on their doorstep, egged on by the Mafia bosses not amused by Castro's pledges to clean up Cuban society.

The *Fort Chambly* entered the St. Lambert lock slowly and silently like a big cat stalking a mouse. Christian and Jean-Pierre, deep in conversation, were unaware until the flared bow of the packet steamer loomed high over their stern. There was more shouting of orders and clanks and winches grinding, echoing about the concrete box. Christian was almost speechless, feeling humble and insignificant. The steel monster could crush the *El-loise* like a bug, if aberrant human behaviour turned on him at that moment; but no, the thing stopped, the twin anchors overhanging her stern. The huge hydraulic doors closed with a soft whoosh, shutting out the lights of Montreal Harbour. The skyline, reflecting off the last of the storm clouds, glowed above the edge of the lock and almost immediately the water on *Elloise's* starboard side began to boil like a caldron over the fires of Hades.

"Just keep a strain on, take up around the bitt, like I showed you."

Jean-Pierre headed aft to tend his line. Christian was mesmerized by the towering nearness of the *Chambly* but the sudden rush of water slammed the tug, throwing *Elloise* rudely against the lock wall.

"Chris! The line!" Jean-Pierre was yelling at him and Petit Jacques' white turban and black eyes looming at him from the wheelhouse window. Gerard, his face shiny with sweat, was grinning maniacally from the engine room door. The bow line, no longer bar tight, was coiling on the deck like a giant Python. The hull, seized by unseen fingers, the bow canting outward, was thrust toward the lock sill, the cascade of water soaking him. Christian jumped for the line. Too late. The slack was gone and the strain came on before he could let off the turns. The bow angled sharply away from the wall then was being pushed back. Christian loosened the greasy, slimy coils and began hauling in the new slack. The tug slammed the lock wall with a shudder and screeching of rubber tires, then silence and apprehension, like a traffic accident at night. Christian was sent sprawling but he did not let go of his line. On his knees he gained line, determined to keep the tug from canting outward again. Puffing and sweating he hauled hand over hand, gaining more line. But this time when the current tried to sheer the bow away, Christian was ready with a turn on the bitt. The tug responded, obediently, subdued. He heard gratuitous clapping from Petit Jacques and Gerard, acting like patrons of the drama in a mezzanine loge.

The rest of the ascent went smoothly, at least the bumps were fewer and less severe in the boiling cauldron, but he noticed that Jean-Pierre was barely able to keep his own line tight and the stern under control. Christian had been admitted to the society of river rats.

Reprieve

Far to the south of the St. Lawrence River, in the Strait of Florida, hurricane Rose continued to churn the Gulf Stream into a cauldron of another kind. A witches' brew of tumbling, racing water while shredded clouds obliterated the dawn, but the worst was over.

Maartyn suddenly whooped. "We didn't die, Paulo. You owe me twenty bucks."

"That was a figure of speech."

The *Bayou Queen* lurched from confused wave tops to turbulent troughs, bucking the steep seas thrown up as the Gulf Stream battled the storm waves still spinning out of the massive low. Now it was a question of keeping the old boat afloat and the engine running. The spinning compass his only guide, Maartyn was heading away from the Florida coast, but they could be anywhere between Miami and Grand Bahamas Island. Maartyn considered putting into the Bahamas to make repairs but preferred to take his chances on the East coast, even if the FBI and the Mexican Syndicate were looking for them.

"Get me to land," pleaded Paulo who looked pale and pathetic, holding onto the chart table with a death grip. The charts were just lumps of pulp stuck to all surfaces, as were the contents of Paulo's stomach. The interior of the wheelhouse looked like a septic tank after a pump out.

Maartyn, black sockets and red pools for eyes, was energized by the challenge. "We're still afloat, you fuckin' weenie queen, and I figure we've got two day's worth of fuel. We can make Jacksonville easy, maybe Savannah."

"Two days? I'll die."

"See if there's any food."

"Who cares about food, man?"

"You've got a few choices. Find food or steer, or I break your fingers."

"I'll go."

The *Elloise* was level with the lock wall and the lock hands had changed shift so the patter reverted to joual. "Hey, Jacques, we bet you'd been run down by the big boat!"

"Yeah, boy, I lost ten bucks!"

"Whose the new deckie? Looks like a girl."

"Hey, Frenchie! Hear the one about the queer priest? Bend over I'll show ya!"

"How much for the new deck hand? She looks like a good go."

"Fuck you!" said Jean-Pierre.

"Leave 'er here 'til you gets back, an' maybe we won't say nuthin' about the trip up."

The upper lock doors opened and the hands slipped the eyes off the bollards, tossing them roughly aboard *Elloise*. Christian's hawser came over the rail too fast but he managed to catch the loop and wrestle the filthy, wet hawser aboard. On the signal from Petit Jacques, Gerard eased the gear lever and *Elloise* churned ahead. The canal lights running into the dark distance defined the long, curving canal above the St Lambert Lock and the low land on either side of the maze of locks, gates, and bridges looked industrial and coldly efficient.

"You goin' after that foreign job!?" a dockhand shouted.

"Hear 'es fucked t'ings up good."

"Just a pleasure cruise," answered Petit Jacques.

"Bye, bye, cutie!"

The VHF crackled to life. "*Elloise*, Seaway Beauharnois"

"Seaway, *Elloise* here."

"You're cleared to Cote-Ste Catherines and Lac St. Louis. Be advised, *Mer d'Oiseau* is aground at the spoil patch above Mercier. There's room to pass her astern, but you are not authorized to assist the *Mer d'Oiseau* at this time. Repeat, not authorized. The *Gleneagles* is aground at the Junction. Seaway out."

"Roger, Seaway. We'll make out okay. *Elloise* clear."

"*Fort Chambly*, Seaway Beauharnois..."

"Seaway, *Chambly*..."

"Captain, you may proceed to the wall at Cote St. Catherines. Be advised...the Harbour Authority and Coast Guard will meet you there."

"We're advised. Thank you, Seaway. *Chambly* out."

Petit Jacques knew that *Mer d'Oiseau* was a bad luck bird. Foreign vessels in difficulty or aground, although lucrative if the salvage succeeds, are trouble for salvage crews. The often ailing Salties had odd customs and protocols as well as language barriers. The rusted out ships were routinely deficient in safety equipment and impossibly short of seamanship in close waters. The crews tended to be sulky and disinterested, if they even stayed aboard long enough to help with the salvage. More often they were over the side in the darkness on their way to New York City. And there were inevitable delays in payoffs. Once free of the embarrassment, the victim's shipping company went to court to prove that their excellent ship was never in trouble and that all captains of salvage company tugs were no better than opportunistic pirates.

Petit Jacques was not unhappy about being warned off *Mer d'Oiseau* and had only a passing interest in the salvage job. The plan was a cobbled together alternative to using the missing Durham boat. The Gleneagles was a gift, but the events of the early morning storm added complications. The authorities would want to speak to anyone involved in the near disasters at the entrance to the Seaway and the investigators might question how the skipper of the *Elloise* knew about the stranding of *Mer d'Oiseau* even before the Seaway was informed?

Years of experience on the rivers of the world told Petit Jacques to stay clear of the authorities. There would be a protracted inquiry. Every officer and some surviving crewman of all the vessels involved would be called to answer endless questions. Blame would be laid as each agency of the different jurisdictions tried to cover their respective butts and the Coast Guard and Seaway Authority would be running hard to explain their actions that night. Montreal Harbour Authority would blame everyone, especially the Federal Government.

Petit Jacques had his eyes set on *Gleneagles* after a brief stop at the Mercier Bridge, which he didn't feel necessary to mention to Seaway Control. The skipper kept *Elloise* moving up the canal slowly, on her best behaviour, so as not to attract attention.

"So, what will your journal say about this night?"

The journal. "It was in my knapsack!" He would start over. So much had happened since he stepped off the train. Coming home. The buildings, the traffic, and the people looked the same, but the pace was faster. Obviously the politics had changed. A new regime was promising to bring Québec into the twentieth century but he had only been on the streets for as long as it took to walk from Windsor Station to Victoria Wharf. Not enough time to know if there was a new feeling. But then, he wasn't that aware of the streets, having been cloistered on the fringe of suburban Westmount, wasting a year at McGill University arguing about world disorder, retreating into a drug haze, escaping first to Paris and then to Chicago, to continue the illusions and delusion of youth transitioning from the curse of vapid existence to the uncertainties of adulthood. He was told to go to Paris, assured by the itinerant jazz musicians that Paris was where it's at. What exactly is 'it', he wondered? They meant the more tolerant drug and music scene. Nowhere else is Paris. Freedom in the City of Lights, but nothing is free.

A musician in Paris gave him a contact in Chicago and he left Paris reluctantly. Chicago was not the answer. Then he was told to go to the Bahamas. The Islands. Blue. Green. Turquois. Hot, but different than Montreal summers. Montreal went from hot to frigid with a brief, brilliant season to catch one's breath. The Caribbean is hot, warm and hot again, but softer about it. The seasons are subtle and without the anxiety. It takes weeks to come down, but he was just beginning to relax, even with Maartyn for a companion, when they met Renée on the beach on Nassau and things heated up again. But Maartyn was also from a warm place, Louisiana, a separate entity from Texas and Alabama. So Maartyn was already relaxed about seasons and didn't understand Christian's awe.

Christian had a theory. There is less crime in cold countries, not counting atrocities in war, because the natives spend so much time surviving the elements. And when there is a spell of nice weather they have to make use of it by laying in the sun crisping up, just to have something to talk about when winter returns. He wondered how people coped in places like St. Kilda, a storm-bashed rock west of the Outer Hebrides, a mere speck of wind-blown civilization in the North Atlantic that endured, even prospered, for a thousand years because birds nested in the crevices and sheep survived hurricane winds. Grass and gardens grew in isolation. But only when the children began to move away was St. Kilda condemned.

The Inuit flourished in the Arctic for ten thousand years. They didn't run away to The Bahamas. Why couldn't he endure Montreal? Fall would be splendid. Cool, with colour, then winter would be cold and dry. He could build an igloo on Mount Royal and forage in the trash bins, or snare squirrels beneath the pines, ranging the island of Montreal for survival.

Islands fascinated Christian. Islands define themselves with clean boundaries of rocks and water. Tropic islands had sand, and warm water, and the most interesting women. An island like Malta has all that and history. Cuba is an island. Esa is an island of calm...

"So, Chris, who was the most interesting politician you met on your travels?"

How long had Jean-Pierre been waiting for an answer? He had been thinking about his personal prostitute, Esameralda. Warm, soft, Esa who believed most politicians were whores. "A prostitute in Georgia," he said.

"I asked about political leaders."

"I didn't meet any political leaders, as such." Except for Escobar, he thought, but... "But the most interesting person I met was this woman who lived near a truck stop in Georgia. She had some experience with politics all right. The drivers would call her on their citizen's band radio. This woman has a radio too, and she calls herself 'Miss Devine on the Line, call anytime.' She'd meet them at truck stops on the Interstate and bring their favourite cookies or cakes, celebrate birthdays, anniversaries, their kids graduation, whatever..."

"Man! She also fucked them of course."

"Well, yeah, it was her job, but she also felt it was her duty to bring a little home comfort to the boys."

"A real slummin' Samaritan."

"This one driver I rode with called her from north of Chattanooga. Miss Devine met us outside of Macon. Our truck had a sleeper cab big enough for an apartment. Miss Devine arrived with a cake to celebrate my driver's wedding anniversary, wearing baby doll pajamas, just like his wife's, and a bottle of Champaign. She climbs into the sleeper and they party. Toasts and tears, like they were old friends, and I guess they were. She offered to do me free. Guess I looked like I needed one. Said she'd been addicted to heroin herself. The driver wanted to party on and asked me if I could drive the truck because he was getting a little behind. They got a huge laugh out of that one."

"So, did you let her do you, as a favour?"

"She was so nice, and pretty. But the interesting thing is, her father's a big shot politician, a Supreme Court judge and her husband's a senior partner in her father's law firm, and her brother's Chief of the Macon police force."

"Man, the power's on her side, Chris."

"Sure. Get this. She was twenty-eight, she said, but looked older, and had three kids and six abortions. The oldest kid was by her father. The next oldest by her brother. And the youngest by her lover, their chauffeur, who's black. The husband tried to make her have the abortion, she refused, and he tried to kill her."

"Man, that is some fucked up family."

"Yeah? There's more. Her lover, the chauffeur, was murdered by her brother and two other cops and the husband got them off on a plea of self defense. Then they try to take the black kid away from her so she split. She's living in a trailer near the Interstate with her mother, who has terminal something. The mother's also a part time hooker. She's retired now, the mother...looks after the kids while Miss Devine's working, you know, she's on the road a lot because the truckers can't always stick around to enjoy the homey comforts. Anyway, her mamma's specialty in her time was servicing the construction workers on the Interstate, and this was while she was living in a Georgia mansion with the judge. She did it as revenge for him abusing her daughter, and forcing her to have sex with his buddies after golf. He was running for Senate then and some reporter found out about the mom's day job. There goes the Senate gig. The judge hired some bikers to kill his wife in revenge but she was such a good trick they faked her death and sold her to a big time pimp in Atlanta who kept her in another mansion for five years servicing judges and politicians, until her husband was booked in as a client! He tried to kill her again, this time with his own hands. She escaped and lived on the streets under a different name, until her daughter, Miss Devine, found her in a mission."

"Man, if she had just waited..."

They both had a good laugh.

"But get this. In college Miss Devine was an 'A' student, cheerleader, runner up in the Miss Georgia Pageant and Homecoming Queen. Her real name is Cindy Lou Lovington, and she's so sweet, and nice...And now she's got some disease called multiple sclerosis and will soon have to give it up...the truck stop work. All she wants is a nice home and a good man. Can you believe that?"

"No! Chris, I think you either made it up or what she told you is complete bullshit. She's a con, but, whatever you do, don't tell that story to Noél, the girl you were sitting beside at the meeting tonight? She'll fly to Georgia to find Cindy Lou Lovey-dovey and rehabilitate her!"

"Rehabilitate? I don't get it. This woman's making the best of a bad life."

"Be warned, Anglais. The women are getting militant about being subservient. If this story of your Georgia beauty queen is true, and I don't believe a word of it, she's a candidate for reform. They call it woman's emancipation. If they get organized..."

Christian was unaware of a woman's movement. Montreal was not New York City. And Montreal women, especially French women, lacked nothing when it came to being assertive, even self-possessed. He had little knowledge of life in rural French Canada or the Southern United States, where it was still very much a man's domain. And the islands? Two years in paradise and a serious revolution had kept him occupied, but there was Renée. How emancipated could a woman be? But maybe Renée was not a good example. She had privilege. Diplomatic immunity. Money. But what about Esa, and Rosameralda? Two stronger women he could not imagine. Poor as dirt, but strong. And Juanita? Juanita did not seem to be in danger of exploitation by male chauvinism. However, she was a bit weepy about her lost husband...how she suffered. How do people suffer? Everything is about freedom and suffering. He thought of Lola, Sartre's aging nightclub chanteuse who sang about suffering. Took on the attitude, the pose, every gesture of suffering. But acting, even convincing acting, is not the same as suffering if the pain is only imagined. But Lola suffered in other ways. Her younger boyfriend, Boris, was ready to move on. Then there was Mathieu. 'I don't know how to suffer' said Mathieu, although he wanted to. Felt ashamed that he had not. Sought to suffer. Self-inflicted if necessary. Perhaps he would have suffered if he went to Spain to fight with the International Brigades. But he didn't go. Why? Because he was not committed. Perhaps he suffered for not going, but then other things got in the way, like the suffering he could inflict on Marcelle if he did not marry her. Marcelle was with child, if it was his child. Could he be sure...? In the end Mathieu let someone else resolve his dilemma about freedom and the self.

Christian had slipped far away into his mind's view of other lives. His own not yet rounded enough to poke above the clouds. What, he wondered, did he lack? He should go back to Paris. There were writers and artists migrating to the Bohemian life of Paris: deprivation and depravity. The jazz scene was hot. Some of the best, even the mediocre, became celebrities. The French women devoured them, and the audiences grooved. Some day he would go back, like Mathieu, maybe even to Madrid, but of course, it wouldn't be the same. Not going 'over' on purpose. You weren't supposed to say, 'I'm going to Paris to suffer for art'. What did one use for an excuse?...

Elloise ghosted along the canal, hissing steam, sending up muted, well oiled mechanical sounds. Christian could feel the throb of the steam engine through the steel deck; the push rods, and crankshaft and the big prop. He had no real knowledge of engines in general, but he was fascinated by their ability to make things go. He remembered the ferry to Bimini. A thundering converted Chris Craft sport fisherman, with automotive gas engines; twin V-8 Chevies, as Maartyn explained. Water-cooled exhausts, whatever that meant. The noise still deafening, the speed exhilarating and terrifying, the shattered waves flying away in sparkling plumes against the dark tropic clouds, as the hull leapt from crest to crest. He hung on, feeling sick. Maartyn, of course, stood erect, legs apart, showing off. Taunting the Bahamian crew. Spoiling for a fight, he drank and swaggered and the boys held back. But on the dock, their turf, one of the boys made a comment about Maartyn's crew cut. There was a scuffle; testing, sizing up, and later again in the bar where the black boys followed them because they knew it was coming. Maartyn was badly beaten up but did not get the worst of it. Suffering with a grin, shrugging it off with a laugh. Christian, swept along in Maartyn's wake, too scared to run, narrowly escaped a beating himself, rescued at the last moment by Maartyn. He wondered aloud if he should try to escape Bimini before Maartyn got them both tossed to the sharks. That only made a swaggering Maartyn laugh and flex his muscles and pat the bulge of the revolver in his right pocket. "Come on, boys." The Bahamians backed off. They only wanted some fun too, not to get killed by some crazed Yankee. Then there was the obvious interest some of the Bahamians took in Christian, making suggestions, even passes. Maartyn would get very angry and threatening, so proprietary that Christian felt it was safer to remain under Maartyn's protective wing, wondering if that's how women felt, as chattels. Biggest cock on the walk, isn't just a saying. Renée said that weak women love to be dominated; herself excluded of course, which was why she usually avoided other women, preferring the company of men. Then why had she chosen Christian? He was quiet, almost shy. Respectful of women, not demanding. At times she seemed to despise Christian for his lack of, what did she call it? machismo. Then why did she stay? She came to Cuba to find him, but she arrived with Paulo. Damn! Paulo's queer, so Renée was just having an experience, so casual in her love affairs that the idea of a contradiction never entered her mind. In the meantime their relationship was complicated by the Revolution and survival, but that didn't prevent Renée from putting Christian through hoops. Women are more complicated than revolutions, he concluded. And what did he accomplish in Cuba? He ended up in the middle of a deadly firefight with the Cuban army, friends killed or on the run, in love with two women who couldn't be more opposite than their skin colour. He had to laugh. Day and night, they were. Esa loved Renée, and Renée said she loved Esa, and Rosameralda, and that concept sent Christian into a spinning funk. His girlfriends loved each other, and what else? Okay, get used to it. Then he found himself thinking of Rosameralda again. But Rosa was dead. Try to forget Rosameralda. And now there's Dominique.

"Dominique's a mystery," he said aloud.

"Man...I told you, forget it. She won't sleep with you."

"Who is she, really?" He didn't believe the Syrian connection.

The tug glided through pools of light, like a big limo cruising a silent boulevard. Christian was restless with anticipation but Jean-Pierre seemed content to sit, legs splayed out, against the wheelhouse bulkhead smoking joint after joint.

"Cut your hair," he said to the smoke.

"What?"

"You do look like a girl."

"I don't want to get a haircut."

"And I don't want to have to fucking defend you all the time."

"Don't be ridiculous!" Christian said, but felt that Jean-Pierre was taking Maartyn's place.

"You don't understand the scene, man. Montreal will eat you alive. You want to hang out with us, then be with us."

"What makes you think I want to...?"

"You're here, aren't you?"

"You forced me to come on this boat ride."

"You can leave any time."

Jean-Pierre nodded off, dropping the roach in his crotch. Petit Jacques and Gerard were talking in the wheelhouse. The low tones and rhythmic, oil-fired life of the tug was comforting, like a good home with a wood stove in the kitchen. He drifted into thoughts of his childhood and his mother...Then one of the VHF radios crackled. The conversation was brief and muffled. Petit Jacques grunted, 'Champlain' and 'late'. They were passing under the Champlain Bridge and overhead the hum and rattle of early morning traffic heading into the city sounded surreal.

The first blush of the false dawn was showing over the scrub trees of the eastern shore and the sky had blown clear to the south and east. It would be another hot day. Even if he could leave where would he go? To the right was the steep embankment that separates the canal from the St. Lawrence River. He could hear the Lachine rapids boiling down to Montreal Harbour. To the left was a lower embankment, more spoil ground with gaps showing reedy, calm water and beyond the low, grassy shoreline, more scrub brush and the traffic on the AutoRoute. He couldn't go back to the imposing lock and the hostile dockworkers. Ahead the canal turned west in a long arc to Caughnawaga; The Reserve land. Nor could he just throw himself overboard and strike out across country. He had no identification. No money...

"Hey! Jean-Pierre!" Jacques called.

Jean-Pierre opened his eyes and struggled to his feet. He brushed past Christian with a sigh. "Still here, little man?" He leaned into the wheelhouse, one foot on the lower step, holding onto the handrails, looking wasted or ill.

"Vince says it's probably too late to make the pick up."

That seemed to jerk J.P. into the present. "Shit! What time will we be at Mercier?"

"Another hour before we clear Ste. Catherine, if they take us up right away. Twenty more if they piss about."

Jean-Pierre, looking at the eastern sky, was suddenly clear-headed and decisive. "Tell the chicken shit we'll be there. Give him an ETA and to get the stuff ready. Son of a bitch, fucking Gargoire! Fucking weather! Everybody on the god-damned river knows we're here."

Christian remembered the many possible reasons for the excursion: narcotics, guns, explosives, bank robberies. Damn! His mind doing loops, as it often did in tense situations, detoured into Sartre and The Age of Reason. Mathieu's dilemma. Delaying growing up. Struggling to survive in a tangle of involvements, like the reclusive Marcelle, who dwelt in her room, in a pink, perfumed haze. Marcelle was a baited trap that Mathieu sprung by getting her pregnant. The more Mathieu dwelt on freedom the deeper the entanglement. Freedom. Freedom...

The VHF radio crackled again. *"Elle?"* "Yeah...here," answered Jacques in a near whisper. The radio talk was perfunctory but Christian didn't want to hear anything, to be implicated. He wanted to hide but on a working salvage tug there are few places to hide. The wheelhouse, the small galley and engine room used up the deckhouse. There were spaces below deck, but no easy access. The rest of the sixty-five foot workboat was open decks with a bewildering array of salvage gear, tanks, towing bitts and a huge articulated hook behind the deckhouse. He was blissfully unaware of the purpose for the gear and marine complications.

They passed the sprawling town of La Prairie and Christian could hear the traffic on Route Three as the tug made the long sweeping curve to westward, and see that the shoreline was mostly spoil banks and gaps, with a view of shallow water and a few ducks foraging in the weeds for breakfast.

The lift at Cote-Ste. Catherine lock went smoothly enough. Christian handled his line reasonably well; the tug didn't slam the wall and there were no comments from the line handlers. A supervisor spoke to Petit Jacques when the tug's rail came level with the dock apron. Their conversation was brief, and a package passed between them. When the upper lock doors swung fully open the tug eased away, the supervisor returned to his Seaway vehicle and made a call on the mobile radio.

Jean-Pierre stowed his stern line and came forward to help Christian. "The white hat collects pornography."

"Oh?" Christian tried to shrug off the information.

"Petit Jacques has a little business on the side."

"I see."

"It's none of your business, Anglais."

"No, of course not. I didn't even see the, whatever..."

"You did and you wonder. You'll see many things today. You'll forget them all."

"Sure..."

Jean-Pierre walked to the ship's galley behind the wheel-house, saying something to Petit Jacques as he passed the wheel-house door. Jacques laughed. Christian was left staring ahead feeling uncomfortable because he felt out of sync with life and there was trouble on the horizon, like a black storm cloud. The scenery wasn't any better than the industrial bleakness of the Cote-Ste. Catherine dock. A grey-hulled bulk carrier hugged the wall, with it's gear swung out, disgorging cargo. Beyond the grey ship there were piles of sand and gravel and a vast open, flat area, the aftermath of the huge Seaway project that leveled and flooded the St. Lawrence River Valley from Montreal to the Iroquois control dam, leaving the landscape raw and bruised. Whole towns were moved and lakes formed where once cattle grazed. The rest of the long dock was vacant, the destination of the *Fort Chambly* to await the authorities and the inquisition. A bored deck hand on the bow of the unloader waved. Christian waved back. When the concrete dock ended the scrub began again and continued in two converging lines separated by calm, green water.

It was fully light now. Beyond the high embankment on his right Christian could see the dark outline of the Honore Mercier Bridge arching over the Lachine Rapids. Beyond the Mercier Bridge was the CP Rail Bridge, and beyond that, The Mount, its tall, slender cross, appearing to hold up the rail bridge, just catching the first rays of the sun.

Jean-Pierre was beside him again, looking tense. "Caughnawaga." He held a cup of coffee out to Christian.

"Thanks."

"I, ah, apologize for being rough. It's not your fault."

They stood in silence sipping the bitter black coffee.

Jean-Pierre scanned the shoreline on the left bank. There were more trees now on either side, then, as the *Elloise* made another curving turn to the west, they could see one foot of the Mercier Bridge. Jean-Pierre focused on the concrete abutment dropping into the water right at the edge of the shore. One half mile from the bridge the *Elloise* slowed to three knots. Birds sang in the trees on both sides. The water was very calm, the bridges reflecting perfectly as a contrast to the hiss and tumble of the rapids behind them, muted by distance and the higher land. There was no current or breeze in the canal and the tug seemed to glide on air, merely ruffling the water at her bow with a sound like a hand brushing silk.

The sharp crackle of the VHF startled Christian. *"Elle?"* Jean-Pierre never took his eyes off the spot beside the abutment. Petit Jacques keyed the microphone. "Vince?"

"Here."

"Ten minutes."

"Okey doke...I'll be there," said the too cheerful voice in French. The accent was not joual.

The big prop stopped turning. The only noises were the crickets, sound of traffic on the bridge and the soft hiss of steam. Christian could smell the hot oil, as if the tug herself were perspiring. He gripped the cap rail until his knuckles were white. Relax, he said. You've been in situations before. Yeah, and the Cuban army was shooting at us and Maartyn was riddled with fragments, then Maartyn was bleeding to death on the cot beside him and Paulo's knee was on the verge of gangrene from a dog bite. His own dog, Wolf Pietro Marlon Brando, badly burned. And the wounded being carried in from the cave entrance. He felt the ringing, a distant siren actually, high pitched. The silence of the canal dulling down, because silence has a level and he was hearing less of the little noises. He felt the nausea. No, no, no!

A big truck rolled out onto the bridge and shifted gears, backfiring. Everyone froze but the traffic noise on the Mercier Bridge continued and the tug ghosted toward the bridge.

"There's Vince," Jean-Pierre whispered, pointing to a gap in the scrub trees near the water's edge beside the wide base of the bridge abutment. Vince was easing a grey box down to the shore, skidding on the mud and loose gravel, using his body to keep the box from sliding into the canal. There were other boxes waiting at the edge of the water. Close enough now to see the packing crates, military supply boxes. God, how could he be mixed up in this? Bank robberies, and who knows what with explosives! "Jesus!" Christian breathed.

"Two hours late! It should be dark," said Jean-Pierre.

The tug angled for the shore, making just enough way to carry the remaining distance. No one spoke. Christian could see Vince clearly in the growing light, green rubber hunting boots ankle deep in the mud. An Indian, short and square, belly protruding from a hunting jacket with leather patches on the shoulders. A camouflage peak hat, flaps incongruously pulled down, even though it was warm. His black, collar-length hair fell in chunks framing a dark broad face, veined and pockmarked and once handsome. A rifle lay across one of the packing cases. Both Vince and Jean-Pierre looked nervously around, checking every bush. The pick-up spot was perfect, he supposed. The canal bent away in both directions and the bridge was directly overhead. There were no sight lines unless someone was watching from the trees on the spoil bank opposite.

The *Elloise* crunched into the sloping canal bank, the turn of the bilge scraping along the gravel until the tug came to a stop beside Vince. Jean-Pierre threw him a light line that was attached to both bow and stern. Vince pulled the line tight and secured it to a small tree.

Petit Jacques handed Jean-Pierre a package, like the one he handed to the Seaway supervisor. Jean-Pierre climbed over the rail and jumped across the gap to the mud. "Shit!" he whispered as his boots sank into the soft earth. He stumbled forward but Vince did not offer to help, only continued looking nervously across the canal, then up and down the canal. The brush-covered bank behind him was about twenty feet high. There was a path worn to the water's edge beside the abutment. A road ran along the top of the bank and under the bridge where an old Mercury pickup was parked and Christian could make out another man sitting in the driver's seat of the truck with the motor idling.

Vince clutched his rifle and edged back as Jean-Pierre opened the boxes. "Okay." He handed the package to Vince who immediately turned and began to scramble up the embankment. "You bastard! You could help us load!"

"I can't. You're late! Alphose an' Gilles see me coming…"

"Gerard, come up an' help Jean," ordered Petit Jacques. Gerard, shirtless, coveralls tied around his waist, climbed over the rail, his muscular body, graceful and deliberate, a contrast to the escaping Vince crashing through the undergrowth. Jean-Pierre and Gerard swung a box up to the rail. Petit Jacques made no move to leave the wheelhouse so Christian grabbed an end and did his best to ease the heavy box on board. It came off the rail too fast and slammed down on the deck with a resounding thump. The tug vibrated. Then the crack from a high-powered rifle shattered the silence and the bullet *whanged* into the pickup truck. Vince fired his rifle at something across the canal. In rapid succession there was another shot, a shriek from Vince, the truck door opened, a scramble near the top of the bank, and Vince came rolling back down the bank, breaking small trees, colliding with the packing crates as the pickup truck roared away throwing gravel and dust over the bank. Another shot caromed off the steel cap rail beside Christian. He hit the deck and instinctively sought shelter behind the deckhouse. Jean-Pierre and Gerard dropped to the mud.

A third shot splintered the corner of the wooden box on deck. "Come on!" yelled Petit Jacques. "Other side!" He indicated the direction of the shots, a stand of trees on the far shore, high up, almost under the bridge.

Jean-Pierre and Gerard were over the rail and on the deck beside Christian.

"Power!" yelled Petit Jacques, who was squatting beside the wheel, cigar clenched defiantly in his teeth.

Gerard bolted down the engine room ladder and immediately the steam lever was thrown and the prop began to turn. The tug moved ahead but with scant momentum the two lines ashore held. The tug lurched backwards and stopped, the prop still turning. Another shot *cranged* the deck near the box, ricocheted and went spinning away over Christian's head.

"Cut the god-damned lines!"

Jean-Pierre looked stricken. Christian thought he had been hit by a bullet. Jacques yelled again. Jean-Pierre gasped, "Shit! I need a knife," and scrambled for the galley door. Christian heard him rummaging about in the galley, cursing loudly. Then another shot took the end out of the box and Christian could see the dynamite sticks. He ran forward with his utility knife, keeping below the bulwarks, and began sawing madly at the bow line. The bar-tight rope parted with a crack as loud as the rifle fire. The tug swung her bow away from the shore as Christian started aft to cut the other line, colliding with Jean-Pierre coming out of the galley. The tug slowly gathered way, ripping the small tree out by its roots, the tree fouling Vince and a box of weapons, dragging them into the canal as well. The box sank away leaving Vince grasping at the sapling, attempting to pull himself up on the thin trunk which kept sinking under his weight. Christian grabbed Jean-Pierre's arm, pointing at the drowning man.

"The lousy bastard! I'd like to shoot him myself. He got a kilo of our hash and all we got is a box of dynamite!"

"Jean, the guy needs help."

"So, help him."

"Jacques?"

"I see'im," Jacques answered sardonically, but made no move to slow down.

Vince, floundering in the swirling wake of the tug on his short tether, was alternately lifted and dunked by the boiling prop wash. Each time he tried to get his head further out of the water the tree submerged under his weight.

"Let'im suffer," said Jean-Pierre.

Gerard had the oil burners on full and the steam was rising quickly. The tug increased speed, forcing Vince and his tree under for longer periods.

"Jesus! He's drowning!" protested Christian, feeling helpless. "Can he swim?"

"Probably not," answered Jacques. "Treaty Indian."

Christian didn't understand why that was an answer to his question. He started aft, leaving the protection of the deckhouse, grabbed the line that angled from the port quarter and pulled, but the drag was too great.

They were closing on Caughnawaga, Vince's home village. A ten-foot high, concrete retaining wall ran the length of the village right to the water's edge, and there were ladders every two hundred feet. Maybe Vince could get to one of those, Christian thought. He surprised himself by yelling at the captain. "Jacques, at least get him close!" And was more surprised when Jacques responded by angling the tug for the retaining wall.

"When we get in cut the fucking line!" Jacques ordered.

Jacques shaved the wall, the rubber tires screeching along the concrete, tires snapping off, the bilge scraping underwater rocks, but Vince wouldn't let go. They passed one ladder and still Vince wouldn't relinquish his porpoising tree. "Cut the line!"

Christian began hacking at the line with his dull utility knife. A bullet smacked the water beside Vince.

"Get down!" yelled Jean-Pierre.

Christian dropped behind the protection of the stern bulwark.

"That was from the church," said Jacques.

"Is everybody crazy?"

"There! Look!" Jean-Pierre pointed to the church steeple.

Christian could see the open cupola and the bell. What a beautiful church, he thought. The back of the stone church faced the river. One small Gothic window below the finial looked like a gun slit, but where was the shooter? The church's many outbuildings were enclosed by a high stone wall, like a fortress. His thoughts looped away to a movie he had seen before he left Montreal. Humphrey Bogart. Katherine Hepburn. The title? *Bayou Queen?* No, *African Queen*. World War One. Steamboat on a river in Africa, under the guns of a German fortress. What next? Waterfalls on the Seaway? Bogey got an Academy Award. He didn't feel like a Bogart. Another shot smacked the water beside Vince. Then he saw the dark form of the shooter in the cupola.

"They're shooting at Vince!"

"Get down, Anglais!"

"You told me to look!" He tried again to cut the line. "Let go," he shouted at Vince. Jean-Pierre also shouted at Vince. Another bullet *whanged* Vince's tree and Christian tucked himself under the curve of the tug's stern.

Then they heard Petit Jacques laughing.

When they were out of the line of fire Jacques slowed down enough for Christian and Jean-Pierre to haul Vince in like a winded beluga whale, scared white. Christian cut the tree away and watched it turning slowly in their wake then turned his attention to the stone village, wondering if the whole world was out to kill him. Vince was sprawled on the deck, bleeding from a shoulder wound. Jean-Pierre brought him a hot coffee laced with Madeira.

That should fix him, thought Christian, if he survived the coffee. Jean-Pierre set about stemming the blood with dirty rags from the engine room.

"Who was shooting at us?" he asked as he probed the wound.

"Who? Alphonse…an' Wacky Gilles," answered Vince, who seemed to be in shock.

"The hell!? I thought…God-damnit to hell, why!?"

Christian also began to shiver from the shock of the brief encounter. He pulled his gaze away from Caughnawaga, the cross of the church spire still visible over the trees, and went forward to the wheelhouse. This time he would request a stiff draft of Madeira for himself.

They were a mile above Caughnawaga and barely twenty minutes had gone by since the first shot. Many puzzling things had happened in those brief moments. He regretted his inability to think straight in an emergency. His mind seemed to fly away to some safe haven. It began as a defense against the rampages of his Irish father. His long-suffering mother was the target and there was nothing young Christian James could do about it except escape into his thoughts and his books. If life was going to keep dealing him low cards he had better start using his wits.

The tug was approaching the open waters of Lac St. Louis. Christian had a last look back at the church spire outlined by the rising sun. Wacky Gilles? How was it that a person with a name like that suddenly held his life in the cross hairs of a rifle?

In the distance Lac St. Louis looked like a shimmering parking lot, the far shore dulled by humidity haze. One mile ahead, her rust streaked stern glowing in the sunrise, the *Mer d'Oiseau* lay sullenly immobile against a spoil bank. And another mile and half beyond *Mer d'Oiseau* was the Great Lakes bulk freighter *Gleneagles*, safely stuck on the mud. Both vessels appeared to be on a collision course with land, in a few feet of water. Christian did not know this, had no knowledge of big ships, but he did think it odd.

"Should they be doing that?"

"What?" asked Jacques irritably.

"Coming that close to shore? Won't they be...?"

"Aground, yes, both."

"Oh."

"Maybe, we'll rescue them."

That question answered, Christian pointed at the splintered box of dynamite, the sticks flung about like a child's game come apart. "Dynamite?" he asked.

"Duds."

"Harmless?" he asked again, hopefully.

"Wet. No good. Vince probably knew that."

"So, that's why we're not..."

"Blown up? Shooter knew that too, is my guess."

"Vince says he knows who was shooting at us?"

"Not us. Vince."

"Cops?"

"Alphonse," Petit Jacques laughed.

"Alphonse, is...who?"

"Alphonse Desormeux, under the bridge. Wacky Gilles in the church tower."

"You know these guys?"

"Very well," answered Jacques, grinning too broadly, or maybe it was a grimace of pain.

"Then why were they shooting at us?"

"Like I said, Anglais, they were shooting at Vince."

"Couple shots came pretty close to me." Christian shivered again.

"Alphonse an' Gilles, very good shots. If they wanted to hit you, or Vince, they would."

"But...why? Jesus." Christian said under his breath. Nothing made sense. "Vince *was* shot."

"Wounded. Trade rivals. Alphonse's pissed off that Vince's trading with us. Wacky Gilles' just shooting for the hell of it. It's why we wanted to get in and out before dawn. By sun up they knew we were coming."

"How would they know?"

"River has eyes." He meant the Observers, for both sides.

"Now what do we do?"

"What, what? Too many questions, Rookie!"

"Shouldn't we get Vince to a hospital?"

"Tough Indian. He'll probably live."

"And if he dies?"

"Over the side."

"Jesus! We're not cut-throat pirates, are we?"

"Hospitals ask questions about bullet wounds, unless bodies found in river. Then they assume some trouble on the Reserve, and that's the end. One less Treaty Indian on welfare."

What is this thing about Treaty Indians? Christian couldn't believe he was hearing this in Montreal. What the hell had happened in three years? Or had he just not been paying attention? A wave of fatigue and nausea flowed over Christian as the sun cleared the shoreline trees and warmed his back. He wanted to lie down but the stern of the foreign ship loomed above them as Jacques slowed down to pass the stranded *Mer d'Oiseau*. Deck hands idling at the stern rail were chattering away and pointing down at the tiny tug. "They're laughing at us."

"Get rid of that stuff," ordered Jacques.

"Me?"

"Are you standing on my boat drinking my coffee?"

"Okay, where?"

"Over side."

Christian wondered aloud, "What if...?"

"Over!"

"Okay."

Christian approached the shattered box and the imagined danger circumspectly. The dynamite sticks were reddish orange, with black lettering; *Danger. High Explosives. Keep dry.* Some were split open with a yellowish, crystalline substance leaking out that looked harmless, like beach sand. His palms began to sweat. The red tubes reminded him of fireworks on Victoria Day or Guy Fawkes Day. The English in Montreal make a great show of celebrating anything that annoys the French. What if...? he wondered again.

Now, with Lac St. Louis for a backdrop he could not see a future, only the vapour wall, like a scrim cloth in a theatre of make-believe. Christian had a strange sense of detachment. Petit Jacques and Jean-Pierre controlled his future and his life could be altered, even ended, irrationally. Or, he wondered, is there a pre-ordained, cosmic force, an inevitable timeline at work that had been determined for him a million, billion years ago? Oh, for Christ's sake, thought Christian, not the cosmic imperative. Renée drove him crazy puzzling over imperatives. Esameralda never let the esoteric intrude on reality. Esy, a prostitute for practical reasons, met life as it was served, until it was time to embrace the Blessed Virgin. Christian had to laugh at that, as he contemplated Lac St. Louis, and the mist-shrouded shore. It was going to be another hot day but it was pleasant enough out on the lake, if one ignored the recent past, and the steam tug that was his current vehicle. Neptune's Car. And that made him think of Poseidon. Damnit to hell! Life isn't performed on a pile of rocks on some fucking paradise island in the Mediterranean. "Okay, I'll go to Malta," he vowed. The cradle of history, not of civilization, that was Mesopotamia, as the Tigris is the cradle of life; before Theatre Noir. Before Existential thought. Before Fascism. "I'll go, just to prove that it was nothing more than an opportunistic era."

Christian's reality avoidance thought path spiraled deeper. The Phoenicians had no opponents, at first. Sure, the Greeks had a leg up, because they were at it early. The Romans practically evolved from the Greeks. Any era would have come up with the Theory of Forms and Democracy, given half a chance. The Germans took a run at Existentialism, before the Nazis co-opted philosophy and turned it into an excuse for mass extinction. At least they had a plan. So, if life is pointless, how does one get out of it? To extinct one's self from this level, as some actualists say, because they cannot explain either the before or the after, then to what level do we aspire? Thinking selfishly of course, that there is a purpose. Maybe not. Descartes put the problem first, but many hit the wall before him. If I'm here, on this boat, on this lake, there must be some reason, so doesn't that prove existence? Not necessarily, says Sartre. Existence could be pure imagination. The hallucinations of a random collection of cells that simply interact in a salty medium under the influence of electrical stimuli. Really? So, let's start over. Yesterday I was on a train. Today I'm on a boat. The events in between are meaningless because they may or may not have happened. And yet, I feel that I was on the train for a reason. Then I was put aboard this boat. And there's Vince. He got here because of circumstances that have to do with crime and anarchy, and our crimes will probably lead to some new disaster, so doesn't that prove existence? I am in danger, therefore I am. If my life is threatened by their actions...no, wait...I was just contemplating suicide because, having lost control and purpose, this empty lake seems to prove existence.

So, how does one do it, creatively? The accepted methods are just too facile, is that the word? No, too plebian. Both are appropriate. The problem is to take the exit with class. To exit well is the best revenge. Forget, to be or not to be. To get out fast and facile and not be a plebian about it. Or bourgeois. Not conventional or humdrum. Get on with it, but get the job done in an existential way. Oh, get off it! Existentialism just means another way to be meaningless. There must be a purpose. The problem is to come up with an argument that refutes Sartre and his bunch, including Renée. Damn the baguette-eating bourgeois bitch! He didn't mean that...

Christian was under the influence of the Madeira. He would never say Renée and bitch in the same sentence. Even bourgeois. She was anything but middle class. Yes, she was infuriating, and yes, he was probably in love with her and he missed her, and was torn apart by jealousy. The Bohemian, low-life-impersonating broad was probably fucking Ramon at that moment! No, it was almost noon in Paris, well so what? In Paris they fuck all day and stop for baguettes and wine, with some of those clever Italian mushrooms thrown in to keep up the libido. Not really. Clinically the French are no different than the Italians or the Scots. What? Jesus, got to get a different mood or the day will be a total disaster. That's a joke. The day has been going on since I left New Orleans and there's no end in sight. What time is it? Who cares? The sun's up so that means daytime. What will Jacques do with that ship? Suicide is necessary. If life is Existential, suicide is the answer. Just being depressed is not good enough. Screwing up means having attempted something life-affirming so just get on with it. But for the Existentialist, suicide is the only answer. Or putting one's self into a situation where death is almost a certainty, like going to Madrid and letting the Fascist do the job. A direct hit from a Stuka would be final, and glorious. But then death would have some meaning, ergo, life would have some meaning, and, since Existentialism denies meaning...oh God! If life is meaningless then there is no great loss getting out. The contradiction is, if there is something to get out of then Existentialism is a lie. Okay, forget Existentialism. Descartesian thought says, 'thought proves existence, existence is meaningless and freedom of the self is everything'. So, be free to end a purposeless existence. Renée, I think I need you at this moment. Forget Renée. She's a million miles away in the center of some boisterous city of light eating baguettes...Fuck it! The problem is, how? Something classy and memorable. Memorable for who? Whom? Maartyn said his old man Simon went over the bow of the shrimper.

"Jacques, how big is the prop on this fine vessel?"

"What do you care, Anglais?"

"Curious, is all."

"Big enough to chop you up into bite sized pieces." Christ, is he reading my mind? "Big enough to tow that ship." He pointed to the stranded freighter serenely at rest on the leaden lake.

"Is that the *Gleneagles*?" The sun was hard on the flat side of the big ship making the black paint look grey, with streaks of gold, capped by white icebergs.

"Get on with it, rookie!"

Life reduced to the simplicity of dumping dynamite, one swollen stick at a time. *Plunk.* The ship ahead looked like a Rhine River barge, but bigger. *Plunk.* Like the big motor barges on the Danube. *Ker-plunk.* Like the canal boats he watched as a kid passing down the Lachine Canal into Montreal. He once tried to reach out and touch the side of one. Dumb, he thought. Kids are so dumb. How smart was it to be on the *Elloise* dumping dynamite? *Plunk.* But to return to the problem of his own demise. How to? When to? *Plunk. Plunk.* "To jump in the destructive element..."

Christian decided he was living in a vacuum, without the benefit of a past. I am a wasteland. Must die. How? "Could just fall off the front of this stupid boat," he muttered. *Plunk.* Suppose the prop wasn't really big enough and he was merely maimed. "What if one of these hits the prop?"

Jacques was talking on the radio to the captain of the *Mer d'Oiseau* who asked what the deckhand was throwing into the canal. "Dynamite. Blow you off the mud." Jacques wished the captain a good day. Next he called the *Gleneagles* to say he would be alongside in twenty minutes. Then he called Seaway Beauharnois and told them to inform Québec Surité that his deckhands heard gunfire from the village. It wasn't the first time. "His deckhands?" said Christian. "So, now I'm a deckhand, not just a troublesome rookie."

Being Ordinary Seaman Joyce at the time of death is a form of failure. Common deckhand. No, has to be something more creative. What if he swallowed the dynamite? Or beat himself to death with his guitar? But Jocinto's bogus guitar was somewhere down the St. Lawrence, in the hands of a peculiar person who thought she was related to West Coast Indians. At least she believes in something. To believe, to be absorbed so deeply where reality has no place to intrude into the bliss of ignorance. Ah, ignorance. Please make me a vegetable, Lord. I will be the best turnip ever. Just give me another chance. The 'Do Wa Ditty' of real life. Something to look forward to besides anarchy and bank robberies. Jesus! He was sliding downhill at a greater rate.

Christian slumped deeper into his growing pessimism with the gnawing sense that he would never be in control. Not trained for anything. Well, there was the music, but he wasn't playing his music. Hadn't since Carnero smashed his beloved saxophone. The music was fading. Not only fading, he sensed that his music was being invaded and compromised by the new sounds, Rock'n'Roll and Rhythm and Blues. Where would it end?

Christian, after escaping from Cuba, had slouched through the Latin Quarter of New Orleans, intimidated by the easy grace of the real jazz musicians in smoke filled jazz joints, alone, and out of context. Forced to the fringe by his own lethargy, he gravitated to the new clubs and the new sound. Raw and raunchy, crudely dragged chords on electrified guitars, backed up by brassy sax riffs, pounded into the floor by the volume. Jazz was changing and he was an alien in a strange land.

On the train heading for New York he met a black youth about his own age who had a transistor radio. They listened to rhythm and blues from New York. What struck him was a slow but driving song by a female trio, the Shirelles. The beat was hypnotic. Simple. Laced with violins driving a big sound, without subtlety or innovation. Then tune after tune, alternating between tortured laments and fun-crazed moments, interspersed with jive talk intended to keep the listeners focused. The boy was on his way to Detroit to look for a gig with a vocal group. Back up vocals at first, he said, but he wanted to start his own group like The Coasters. Did he know 'Yakety Yak'? He sang the whole thing, adding inflections, bass voice and rhythm by banging on the seat back until the woman ahead threatened to call the conductor. Black kid had a nerve even riding on the train with white people, she said. It was still there, the racial imperative, but the music was empowering. He thought of Maartyn and Jerry Lee.

The batteries died by Tennessee so they talked about music and life, slept and dreamed about food until they parted at Union Station. By then Christian had received an education about changing life in the Deep South, the prospects for blacks and the music. Music was the ticket out for blacks in the first years of the sixties. But what was in the music for Christian? He had a guitar that would be more at home in the Appalachians and he wasn't in tune with the Delta Blues. He couldn't sing well enough to sound black, or righteous. In other words, Christian was out of prospects.

The young man begged Christian to stay in New York. He had a friend in Harlem who could put them up for a few days but Christian, over-dosed in reality, continued north. He was transposed to Montreal in a heartbeat. To the St. Lawrence River in another.

Well, Christian, old boy, it could not have been any worse in Harlem, he concluded.

"Hey, Deckie!" Jacques yelled. "Get aft an' help Jean-Pierre with the tow wire!"

Lac St. Louis' version of reality was the morning sun burning off the mist, replaced by humidity haze. Behind him were snipers. Ahead was a ship to be salvaged. Christian moved aft automatically where Vince lay on the deck as if dead, but the blood still flowed toward the scuppers.

"Help me move him to the galley," said Jean-Pierre.

"Shouldn't we get him to a hospital?"

"No time. Jacques has a contract."

"Jesus! Doesn't this man's life mean anything?"

"He's not that bad. Just losing some blood."

"Well, doesn't that count? I mean, if he loses enough..."

"Take his feet."

Vince moaned and cursed them. In the small galley they stashed Vince on a bench behind the table. Jean-Pierre went out immediately, saying sarcastically, "Okay, Florence Nightingale, see what you can do with him."

The galley was hot and greasy. Not exactly filthy, but greasy from an accumulation of years of fried foods cooked on an oil stove, and the benign neglect of seamen who clean only what is absolutely necessary. "Do you want a drink of water?"

"Coffee," Vince answered so weakly Christian didn't hear the request.

There was one tap on the small sink. Christian turned the handle and a jet of steam shot out in coughing spasms until super heated water shot out. Hot water was not the problem. It came out of the tap straight from the boiler hot enough to scald bare skin. The tiny sink was filled with cups swimming in cold water that looked like a cesspool. He rinsed one with the hot water. "Can you drink it that hot?"

"Yeah, sure, if it's coffee. Never drink water. No good."

The table was covered by an ancient oilcloth, worn and peeling. Christian recognized the pattern. A tangle of faded cabbage rose clusters climbing a blue trellis on white garden wall. His mother lined her kitchen cupboards with the same stuff. The irony of the homecoming was not lost. Christian put the cup on the table and helped Vince sit up, using a heavy duffle coat from the locker as a pillow. He pushed the cup towards Vince's shaking hand. "Are you cold?"

"Yeah."

"Maybe the hot water will help."

"Coffee."

"I, ah, don't know how..."

"Cupboard." Vince pointed to another supply locker beside the sink.

Christian fumbled with the brass latch. The interior of the locker was a shambles; saltshaker on its side, an opened box of

Saltine crackers, a dish of rancid butter. And there was a jar of Maxwell House coffee, lid off, and an encrusted spoon blackened with age. He emptied the chipped cup, rinsed it again with the scalding water, careful to turn on the tap slowly. He looked dubiously at the spoon in the jar. "There," said Vince, pointing to an inconspicuous drawer beside the small sink. What would Miguel think of this pantry? he wondered as he refilled the cup.

"You've been on this boat?" Christian asked, spooning coffee lumps into the cup, watching it dissolve to the colour of dried blood, feeling uncomfortable in the silence.

"Maybe."

Hardly an answer so he tried, "Do you know if there's milk?"

"Sugar's good." Vince pointed to a Skippy peanut butter jar half full of sugar at the back of the cupboard, beside a wooden cigar box. Christian was just curious enough to lift the lid as he reached for the jar. The light was sufficient to show a hand gun partially wrapped in oily rags. He thought of Maartyn again, and even as the chill ran down his spine he laughed, as if to say, it figures. "Don't touch that," said Vince flatly.

"No way." Christian put the jar on the table. Vince looked at the sugar jar and then at Christian. "Sorry," Christian said. He opened the jar and slid it across the table. Vince struggled, pulling himself up with his good arm. Christian wanted to help but Vince waved him off.

"Okay. I can do it." Vince spooned sugar until the coffee was about to overflow. Christian was fixated. If it spilled he'd have to find a cloth. He listened to the thump of the engine and Gerard singing an island song in time to the beat. The transistor radio in the wheelhouse belched a news cast from WABC New York. A gangland style killing in Queens. He thought of his brief friend, the rock and roll singer from New Orleans, wishing he'd stayed in Cuba...distant, tidy, safe, Cuba...Esy; warm, soft, safe...The engine room telegraph jangled. The revolutions slowed to idle and the wheelhouse VHF crackled almost immediately, as if the Observers could see into the boat. He heard 'stern', Jacques grunted and then Jean-Pierre called to him. He'd wanted to ask Vince about the pickup truck and the shooters.

Christian stepped out of the galley into the cool of the shadow cast by the *Gleneagles'* stern towering high above them. Two deckhands peered over the rail; young, tough looking and unshaven, who appeared to have been drinking all night with nothing else to do on the mud of Lac St. Louis. Jacques backed the tug under the shapely counter of the Laker and immediately a heaving line snaked out. "Watch it," Jean-Pierre said as the monkey's fist thumped onto the deck beside Christian, bouncing into the scuppers. Jean-Pierre grabbed the line and started pulling the wire towline with a big loop that dropped out of the stern hawse pipe and dove for the lake. "Get a hold, Deckie!"

"Where?"

"Anywhere!"

Christian grabbed the manila heaving line in front of Jean-Pierre so that he was taking the weight, bracing himself against the rail cap. The wire rope ran out faster and faster.

"Jesus Christ!" shouted Jean-Pierre. "Hey! Slow it down you assholes!"

The deckhands laughed, but the winch brake squealed and the heavy wire stopped running out. The tug was gliding slowly ahead and the strain came on the wire. Grunting and sweating Christian and Jean-Pierre handed the wire loop aboard dripping and grease-smeared, full of broken strands called meat hooks. Jean-Pierre was wearing gloves. Christian was about to reach for the wire loop.

"Here, Rookie!" Jacques was behind him holding out a pair of work gloves. "Too fucking dumb to be on a towboat, Anglais. But I need you today."

"Thanks." He put the gloves on, took hold of the wire and turned to Jean-Pierre. "Why didn't you tell me?"

"You're not dumb. You just need to figure things out."

"Stop bullshitting and get the wire on," said Jacques. He grabbed the wire below the spliced loop and almost knocked the two down pulling the wire in.

They sweated the heavy towline up the deck and dropped the loop over the towing hook. The wire was running out through the Laker's hawse pipe again. Jacques grunted and padded up the deck to the wheelhouse muttering about foreign-born idiots. Foreign-born? Christian detected Newfoundland accents. The tug moved ahead, but not as fast as the wire was running off the winch. Jacques leaned out of the wheelhouse and shouted. "Stop the god-damned wire 'til I get the slack, you morons! Lazy, good for nothing, Anglais!"

"He really doesn't like the English."

"Some day he'll tell you why. Let's get forward. When that wire tightens up...maybe it'll break and cut you in half."

"Great. I just love this job."

Christian had been in town about eighteen hours and his life had been threatened, he'd been shot at, he'd received physical injury and racial insults. What he hadn't had was enough food. He felt weak, hollow and light headed. He remembered fondly the cheese sandwich and warm coke, the smell of the cooked fish.

The copper sun was beating the lake into a burnished plain and the engine room temperature touched one hundred and twenty-five degrees. The *Elloise*, with five hundred feet of steel cable behind her, shivered, strained and panted. The large prop of the *Gleneagles* flailed the water to a boiling froth. Black mud spread out from the two ships in a growing fan. The engineers on the *Gleneagles* pumped water from the bow tanks into the stern tanks while the deckhands worried the anchor winch keeping a strain on the ground tackle, doing everything that could be done, short of unloading the cargo.

Christian and Jean-Pierre sat on the railing forward suffering in the hot sun. Gerard stayed near the thumping engine, greasing and oiling his baby, happy in the heat while keeping an eye and a hand on bearings. Jean-Pierre rolled joint after joint for he and Gerard while Jacques drank Madeira. Christian, already deep into his psyche, declined to indulge but watched anxiously as his protectors consumed mind-altering substances. One hour into the 'tow' a Coast Guard boat arrived from the Seaway and pulled alongside the *Gleneagles*. Three men dressed in white coveralls, one carrying a brief case, climbed the accommodation ladder and were greeted by the captain. They moved forward, talking and gesticulating. Jacques, standing in the wheelhouse door, spit over the side. "Inspectors," he said. "One's Salvage Association. Tough bastard. He don't like me. The other one's insurance adjuster. Doesn't know a cargo hold from his bung hole. The fat one's Coast Guard. Big boss. Pilots a desk most time. They'll have a quick look to make sure she's not makin' water, and have a drink in the captain's cabin. They'll try to cheat me. Bastards! We do all the work, eh?"

"What's actually going on here?" Christian whispered to Jean-Pierre.

"We're towing, man. Salvage job."

"I can see that. But, nothing's happening. We've been sitting here like this for hours."

"One hour? Man, nothin'. *Whew*...takes time."

"How much time?"

"Seems like days...a week, man." Jean-Pierre laughed then giggled.

Petit Jacques came forward to sit with Jean-Pierre and Christian. Gerard came up out of his dark hole for a breather.

"Since you're so interested, bucko," Jacques said to Christian, "we're waiting for two things. The wind'll come from the Southwest and they're going to let some water out of the Beauharnois."

"Yeah, so?" shrugged Christian. Wind direction and more water meant nothing in his parlance.

"So, maybe you're dumber than I thought. Water comes up couple of inches. Off she comes and home we go."

Jacques went back to his wheelhouse and turned the radio up very loud: Jerry Butler, 'He Will Break Your Heart', smooth rhythm and blues drowning out the sound of the thumping propeller.

"Well, man, you managed to upset him again."

"I don't get it. What difference would two inches make?" he asked, looking at the huge bulk of the Great Lakes freighter.

"Doesn't take much. Just a big fat balloon." Jean-Pierre laughed and choked on a toke. "Maybe, like big airship just drift off into those clouds..."

"I'm going to check on Vince."

At ten-fifteen Christian climbed up to the wheelhouse with the latest news. "Vince's dead, I think." Jacques, looking tired, just shrugged. Blood was flowing from under his head bandage. The morning breeze was getting up from the Southwest, as he had predicted.

At ten thirty-three the *Gleneagles* shuddered and slid slowly, smoothly off the mud bank, the steady 'tow' finally overcoming the glue-like mud. *Elloise* eased ahead to keep *Gleneagles'* stern pointed up stream. Her captain got the stern anchor chain hove in short and the bow heading down the canal toward Cote-Ste. Catherine to wait for the McAllister tugs to free *Mer d'Oiseau* from the spoil bank. The recalcitrant Saltie was headed in the wrong direction and it was decided to take her down stern first. A slow process and the Seaway would be jammed up for a few hours. Jacques ordered his deck crew to cast off the wire and then collapsed in the wheelhouse from heat exhaustion and blood loss. Probably too much Madeira as well.

This was a new problem. There was a corpse in the overheated galley and the great bulk of their unconscious skipper was jammed against the wheel. And they were drifting with the current.

"I think we should call for help," said Christian as the three

133

of them strained and grunted to move Jacques out of the wheel-house.

"Are you crazy, man?" shouted Jean-Pierre. "Jacques probably jus' has concussion. Maybe fucking heat, man." He was weaving and unfocused.

"Too much blood gone," pronounced Gerard.

Elloise drifted beyond the stern of the *Gleneagles*, heading for the Lachine Canal, the old route to Montreal. The current from the Beauharnois dam did not follow the dredged channel to the Seaway Canal. Lac St. Louis was still part of the St. Lawrence River and the current followed the river bottom toward the lake's outflow pushing *Elloise* into the channel beyond the deep hole where the *Gleneagles* had found refuge. On either side of the narrow channel were spoil grounds.

Jean-Pierre wandered to the bow and stood looking across the placid lake toward Montreal. The jagged skyline, dominated by office towers cut off at the knees by trees, hovered in the haze. He spread his arms and embraced life.

"Jean?"

Gerard shook his head and sighed. "He's too stoned, man. Better you take the wheel an' I'll see to the engine."

"Me? Where are we going?"

"Just follow those buoys."

"Boys?"

"Those posts in the water."

"How do I follow them?"

"Stay in between. Red on right, green on left."

"But..."

"Move that handle to Slow Ahead." Gerard indicated the brass Chadburn beside the wheel. Christian gingerly took hold of the handle and moved the pointer, rewarded by a bell jangling in the engine room. Christian looked pleased. "Good," said Gerard, as if talking to a kindergarten student who had just made his first letter. "Now I'll go below and make it happen. When you want to go faster, or stop, move the handle."

"Then what do I do?"

"Steer."

Gerard disappeared into the engine room. *Elloise* began to move, very slowly at first, but not slowly enough for Christian. He gripped the spokes and gave the wheel a tentative turn. Almost immediately the bow began to swing towards mid-channel. Christian was encouraged but the bow kept moving until it was aiming at a red post and before Christian could react, hit it squarely. The stern followed, the big prop chopping the post into splinters. "Damn!"

"Mawn, what you just do?" asked Gerard from the darkness of his sanctum.

"Oh, hit something, I guess. One of those posts." Christian decided to let the tug make a full circle until it was back in the channel. And it would have worked had it not been for a mound of spoil ground just under the surface. The tug came to a mushy standstill. "Damn! Damn!! Okay. Stop the engine." He moved the handle to stop. The engine stopped. "Okay. Backup". He moved the handle to slow astern, Gerard answered and momentarily the prop was sending up great gouts of mud but nothing happened. Jean-Pierre, eyes wide, turned slowly to look at him, a stupid grin on his face. "Okay. More power." He moved the handle to Half Astern, rewarded by vibrations, even shudders. Christian took a lesson from the towing session. It takes time. Gerard's head appeared above the combing of the engine room, sweat steaming down his face. Christian shrugged. Gerard shook his head and sunk back into his lair. A few more minutes were chewed up, like the mud, before the tug came unstuck and almost leapt astern. Christian froze but Gerard was ready. He stopped the engine on his own. The tug glided stern first across the channel, narrowly missing a green post and promptly buried her skeg in another mud bank.

Gerard popped up again, eyes wide, like Jean-Pierre's who

was plastered against the wheelhouse window like a child eying toys in a department store. Christian couldn't tell if his expression was pain or amusement. But when he heard Jacques moan he was reminded that action was necessary. He moved the Chadburn handle to Half Ahead. The bell jangled and Gerard disappeared to do his duty. The prop dug into the mud and pushed the tug ahead, but this time Christian was ready. He spun the wheel in the direction he thought they should go and *Elloise* obeyed instantly. He had no idea why because he had never driven a car. Steering a powerful tug was an adaptation. Soon he was able to gauge the amount of 'wheel' necessary to achieve direction, but since the Chadburn had asked for Half Ahead instead of Slow Ahead, *Elloise* was galloping along the channel, caressing starboard hand buoys, knocking them aside like toy ducks in a carnival game, and straight ahead was the municipality of Lachine, the entrance to the defunct Lachine Canal. A dead-end.

The old Lachine Canal was designed to allow ships to bypass the rapids of the same name. There was a reason. The river, tumbling over the rock ledges, was moving too swiftly for even powerful steam ships to work their way upstream. The Lachine, and the Long Sault Rapids further upstream, were barriers to commerce so the Europeans built the first canals to move goods and people. The St. Lawrence Seaway is only the latest attempt to defy nature. The process began when Europeans scraped a ditch above Montreal to drag loaded skiffs upstream to calmer waters. The ditch was enlarged over time in a succession of clever canals and locks. Christian had no knowledge of the limited options and dangers ahead, he only remembered as a kid watching the big ships going in and out of Montreal Harbour. The immediate problem was direction.

To port was a sharp turn into another channel defined by a maze of buoys leading to St. Anne de Bellevue and the Ottawa River, but to starboard was the seemingly open water of the Great River and Montreal. He had no understanding of the buoyage system so he chose the open water of the St. Lawrence River.

Imagine the chagrin of the European explorers, Cartier and Champlain, stymied in their quest for the West by a watercourse that looked so promising, wide and inviting, a natural waterway to the Promised Land, the Orient. But the River was a beautiful deceiver. Channels that began well vanished in rocky cul-de-sacs. What appeared to be deep, open water masked gravel shoals and hidden sandbars. Rapids barred the way in several places; a quirk of geology, the legacy of glaciers and tectonic forces and perhaps even the whim of the Almighty, as superstitious French explorers concluded, so Christian's mistake was blameless. But Jean-Pierre's behaviour was not an aid to navigation either. Jean-Pierre, eyes wide and wild, gyrated around the bow pointing in several directions at once.

"Can't go that way, man, or that way," Jean-Pierre said, passing through the wheelhouse to grab another bottle of Madeira.

"Why?"

"Because...don't know."

Jean-Pierre seemed to lose interest in the game, stepped over Petit Jacques and wandered aft. Christian was left to wonder. Okay, where then? Should I turn around? All Christian could see was a broad expanse of sparkling water. "Why don't you run this thing?" Christian steered for the middle of the river where Lac St. Louis becomes the St. Lawrence again. "Gerard!" There was no answer.

In The Gulf Stream

The silver disc of a shy sun broke through shredded hurricane clouds, dazzling on a scene of watery chaos; the Gulf Stream in full rebellion. The Stream was a translucent green with gouts of white foam, waves jumping about, collapsing, undecided about direction now that the low pressure had moved on. The *Bayou*

Queen wallowed and rolled sluggishly; dirty bilge water sloshing about in her holds and engine room. The living quarters and galley forward a shambles of dissolving food, clothing and bedding, left too long in a giant washing machine.

"We're sinking!" whined Paulo.

"No we're not! I keep telling you! Get back out there and work that pump like your life depends on it!"

"I knew it. We're sinking."

They were sinking. The *Bayou Queen* had fought a good fight but deep in her bones the relentless ocean waves smashing against the hull had worked the joints between the heavy keel and the hull planks. A wooden boat is an evolutionary union of many parts with a collective strength, like a well-governed society: strong as long as the unity is preserved. With time, weakness in one vulnerable area threatens the whole. The *Bayou Queen* was an old girl, already past her prime when the Cuban smugglers bought her from an Alabama shrimper. Years of dragging huge seine nets and battling storms, running from the authorities and running aground on reefs and sand bars, as well as willful neglect at the hands of her Cuban crew, put her in jeopardy. A hurricane was almost the final insult. Maartyn knew her problems and had done a good job of nursing her through, but the water was coming in as fast as Paulo could pump. Exhausted, he had rebelled and gave up the business.

"You steer," he ordered Paulo.

"I don't know how."

"Just keep'er heading toward the waves."

Paulo had repeatedly refused to run the boat, condescending only to prepare food in self-defense, leaving Maartyn to pilot and maintain the engine. His constant contribution was to complain. But this time he felt it was not a good idea to push Maartyn too far.

Maartyn stepped out of the wheelhouse and stopped to take in the wild, dangerous beauty. The sun changed everything. He had never seen the ocean in such a confused state or as luminous, the translucent green of a normally dark blue Gulf Stream driven mad. The battle, fought to a stalemate, had been exhilarating and he wasn't about to give up his boat without a fight. He was also battling fatigue after hours standing at the wheel, bracing against the rolls and dives, clutching hand holds until his fingers ached, always with the fear that the next wave might put them under. He was fatalistic about their chances, had been since they escaped from the Cuban navy, but Maartyn had always been a fighter. Being on the run from the American authorities only sharpened his skills. His part in the Cuban Revolution was merely amusing. The hardest thing was getting over Rosameralda. At the height of the storm he could see her face in the waves. Maybe he was just hallucinating from lack of sleep, but Rosa was never far from his mind, awake or dreaming. She was the greatest loss of his life, even though she had barely been a part of it. The distant, unattainable beauty had teased him with her dark eyes and dusky body. The vision would torment him forever, so he thought. But then he was still young. No time for Rosa. He had to fix the engine pump.

As he feared, the engine room was a shambles, like the rest of the boat. Nothing was where it was supposed to be except the engine and the fuel tanks, and one tank had nearly broken loose. He secured the straps, hoping they would hold and knee deep in oily water he surveyed cans and rags drifting aimlessly about, threatening to tangle with pulley belts. A rooster tail of water was spinning off the tail shaft showering the engine space. A gas engine would not have tolerated the conditions. Maartyn's second main concern was water being sucked into the air intake, but the first job was getting the engine pump to operate. The link belt drive had slipped off, or was knocked off. He groped around in the black water feeling for the belt. He found tools, spare parts and assorted junk. Finally Maartyn's hand grazed the link belt as it drifted back and forth under the engine.

Maartyn prayed that one of the wrenches he had rescued was

the right size. The last wrench fit. In twenty minutes Maartyn had the belt back on, threw in the clutch and was rewarded by the sound of the pump drawing. But before he could rest he had to spend more time crawling about with his head barely above the water searching the bilge for loose items that could clog the pump. The changing motion of the boat alerted him that Paulo was not at the wheel, or worse, had gone overboard.

Maartyn clawed his way to the wheelhouse. "Oh, Jesus H, I knew it! Paulo!" The *Queen* was going in a big circle. Maartyn spun the wheel and put her bow into the waves. "Paulo!"

"Down here!"

Paulo's voice came from the hold aft of the deckhouse.

"What in hell's name are ya doin'!?"

Paulo appeared at the edge of the combing, his grey face stricken. "The stuff...man." Paulo's face contorted as if he was about to cry. "Oh, man, we're dead."

Their cargo, a dozen cotton-wrapped bales of marijuana that the Mexicans cared little about, being so over-supplied, was reduced to a thick pulp that surged back and forth in the hold like restless seaweed.

Into The Rapids Immerse

Christian heard the splash. Jean-Pierre filled the wheelhouse door looking pale but sober. "Turn around. Turn!"

"You dumped Vince?"

"Okay, yeah, you said he was gone...turn around!"

"Vince?"

"Rapids!" Jean-Pierre pointed down river. What had been a comforting, broad expanse of water showed only dimples at first and from Christian's view it was hard to see the full extent of the Lachine Rapids because the water was dropping away, the rocks and waves still invisible. And as the river became shallower the current was increasing. "Turn! Turn!"

The gods have funny ways of dealing with humans and emergencies. Christian froze, then panicked. He spun the wheel hard to starboard. Why starboard he wasn't sure. A natural tendency? Go to the right; when meeting pedestrian traffic go to the right. His mother told him that. He always turned right if he had to reverse direction for some reason, as in, walking along a beach absorbed in thought, and it was time to return, he turned right, but never turn against the sun a sailor had told him. In this moment of life affirming or life altering decisions, it made no difference. The slack steering chain had jumped off the quadrant.

"Turn!"

"I'm turning!"

"You're not!"

"You do it then!" Christian, breathless with adrenalin, stood back.

Jean-Pierre seized the big wheel which spun too easily. Spun until the chain shackles reached lock. He threw the wheel back the other way. Same thing. "What the…? Ah, man. Gerard!"

Elloise, left to her own devices, turned broadside to the current, but was still powering ahead, which meant that now they were heading for the Caughnawaga spoil bank.

"Shut it off!"

Gerard shut the engine down, opened the pressure relief valves and popped up the ladder. "Drop the anchor, mawn!"

There followed only silence and the absence of movement. Christian embraced the moment, imagining that he was not on the river, but in a quiet place where nothing had happened, nor was about to happen. That he was not on a strange steamboat drifting out of control. That a body was not floating behind them.

"Anchor!" said Gerard firmly.

Jean-Pierre and Christian bolted out either door, Christian stepping over Jacques.

The anchor, a rusted relic with one fluke nonchalantly hung

over the rail, was attached to a rusted chain that lead through a hawse pipe and disappeared through a hole in the deck. Without a word they seized the anchor and flung it over the bow. The chain rushed out, leaving a growing pile of rust on the deck. The noise was deafening but hopeful until the last link whipped out of the deck hole and disappeared through the hawse pipe. The dust lingered over the scene, keeping pace with the tug as *Elloise* continued to drift down river. The new silence was profound. Christian stared at the empty hole and then the spot where he was certain the anchor had joined Vince's body on the bottom of the St. Lawrence River. The body! Vince's body rose to the surface and waved. "Vince...!" Christian pointed.

"Oh Jesus, Mary an' Joseph," breathed Jean-Pierre. "He's still alive."

"I can't believe you threw him in."

"You said he was dead."

"I thought...didn't you check?"

"No, man."

Gerard ambled aft and crawled under the steel grating covering the stern hatch. He wiggled his large frame into darkness. Jean-Pierre and Christian continued to stare at Vince splashing about with one arm, keeping pace, but too far away.

"Do something!" Christian shouted. "Go after him!"

"I can't swim." Jean-Pierre turned to look at the rapids. They could hear them now and the tug was moving faster. So was Vince. Christian remembered a life ring on the wall behind the deckhouse and ran to the stern, colliding with Gerard heading for the wheelhouse. "Vince...drowning!"

"Mawn, I thought he was dead."

"No, in the water." Christian grabbed the life ring and attempted to toss it overboard. The ring was old and firmly attached to the bulkhead by a manila line. "Damn!"

"Never mind. Steering fixed. You steer," ordered Gerard. Gerard dropped down the ladder into the engine room. Christian

obediently climbed up and stood at the wheel. The indicator jangled and the inside pointer stopped at Full Ahead. Christian dutifully adjusted the wheelhouse indicator to agree, the opposite of
engine command procedure, but...the engine was throbbing and
Elloise gathered way and began a wide arc that would take her
above Vince's position. Christian corrected, guessing at the turn
to bring the tug closer to the floundering man.

"Turn up! Turn up!" shouted Jean-Pierre, pointing upstream.

Christian shook his head, indicating Vince.

"No time!" screamed Jean-Pierre. Jean-Pierre grabbed at the
wheel. They struggled for control.

Suddenly Jean-Pierre was wrenched away from the wheel.
Gerard had him in a bear hug. "Jean, be a good boy. You get the
boat hook and wait at the port side." And to Christian..."Can you
steer beside him?"

"I think so."

"Just tell me when we are close, an' if we need to back up.
Never mind the Chadburn."

"Okay." He didn't know what a Chadburn was, so it didn't
matter.

The river was moving faster now, rushing toward the first
over-fall of the Lachine Rapids. But two bodies in a mass of water,
move relative to each other as if the water was a calm lake, or a
big ocean. Christian focused on Vince. A hundred yards separated
them. Vince was weakening, thrashing more than swimming and
going under more often and staying under longer. "Come on,
come on, Gerard," he whispered, as if Gerard could force more
revolutions out of the old steam engine.

"Christian, mawn! Talk to me," said Gerard from the depths.

"Okay, okay, we're close." The revolutions instantly dropped
and *Elloise* lost way. "No, no! We're not that close. Oh, shit!"
When the revolutions dropped off, the course of the tug sagged
below the convergence line he had established by experimenting.
"Go faster!" The thumping increased and the tug rounded up, now

with her stern pointing downstream. The gap was closing again. Christian tried not to look at the shore. He felt vertigo, the sense of movement in a plain not predicted by the mind, going backward and forward at the same time. "Okay, slow down, a little!" The revolutions dropped. "Good, good. Now slow down a little more!"

Jean-Pierre was at the bow clutching a long red pole with a wicked looking pike and hook. It could kill as easily as save. Christian was thinking about the prop and Maartyn's father Simon. "Oh, Jesus, if we run over him..." He pictured Maartyn's old man going under the bow of the shrimper and coming up the other end as chopped liver, or was it steak? Didn't matter. "We don't have ice." Christian wanted to be sick but was too afraid. His mouth watered and he broke out in a cold sweat. "Oh, shit!" Vince disappeared from Christian's view. "Stop! Gerard!" The engine stopped. Jean-Pierre reached over the bow with the pole. He cursed and began working along the port rail, jabbing and stabbing. "You'll kill him! Where is he?"

"Under. Back up!"

"No!"

"Wait!" Jean-Pierre ran aft, stepping on Petit Jacques. At the stern Jean-Pierre flung the pole full length. "Got the bastard!" As if he had hooked a great fish. Christian ran aft to help. Two boys playing in the water with a long stick; rapids, tumbling and jumping, for a backdrop, the sound now a roar. Vince's death-white face appeared over the stern rail looking pained and beat up. Gerard who had been watching from the engine room hatch, threw open the throttle. "Chris! Steer, mawn!"

Christian left Vince with Jean-Pierre holding him, raced back to the wheelhouse, stumbled on the steps and sprawled across the deck. "Damnit!" On his feet again, throwing the wheel to starboard, to the right. *Elloise* obediently turned in her own length and was soon making better than six knots. Then seven. Eight. Nine. Better than her hull speed. Gerard had jammed the safety valve with a spanner. *Elloise*, obeying the physics of fluid motion, romped and bucked and threw water over her bow, keel banging on the rocks. The same rock. Going fast. Faster than she had ever gone, but she kept slamming the same rock. She had been stopped dead by the current, just as if she had run full tilt on a reef. Still she thumped and throbbed, straining to obey. The pressure gauge crept above safe working load. She was now in danger of exploding, blowing the house off the tug and the crew with it. Gerard eyed the shoreline. "C'mon, dear. C'mon, darlin', move. Jus' a little." Steam was escaping from unusual places. He imagined he could see the boiler expanding.

Petit Jacques' bloody visage appeared over the engine room combing like an apparition, eyes wild and wide. He opened his mouth to speak, the words surprisingly calm and gentle, "Gerard, shut her down, son. Please, before she blows up."

Gerard eased the throttle, smacked the spanner with a mallet and tugged on the steam whistle cord all in the same motion. Live steam screamed out of the safety valve. *Elloise* stopped struggling and fell sideways off the first rock over-fall, burying her rail in white water.

"What happened?" asked Christian, still clutching the wheel.

Gerard just stared at him. "Do what you can, mawn. Just steer."

"Where?'

Petit Jacques spoke again, as if the voice of God had interceded in the earthling's foolishness. "Down, you damned idiot! Just keep to the middle of the channel."

"Okay," Christian said doubtfully.

"Avoid the rock over-falls. Gerard, just keep enough power on for steerage." Gerard nodded and grinned.

"Right." What are over-falls? Christian wondered. He stood at the wheel, legs wide to fight the bucking and rolling motion of the hull, numbed by the roar of white water. He held the wheel with a death grip and tried to decide what was the middle of the leaping chaos around *Elloise* and which were the rock over-falls. *Elloise* did her part; buoyant and lively, she seemed to thrill at the speed, galloping along at a combined speed of fourteen knots. The shoreline and small islands flew by. Waves leapt and exploded under her forefoot like happy dolphins. Jacques cursed if Christian veered the slightest off line. Vince moaned, Gerard sweated over his controls and Jean-Pierre smoked another joint as if chaos was a separate reality.

The sun was high now and visibility good. Wave definition and rock formations clear, to Petit Jacques, who seemed oddly at ease.

"How we doin', mawn?" asked Gerard, his eyes and nose above the gangway combing. He looked like a troll in a book Christian's father read to him over and over. That was before home became a hell of snarls and broken mirrors. Hold her in the middle. Avoid the rock over-falls...how in the hell did he come to this? wishing Maartyn was along for the ride. What would Maartyn do? Maartyn, the delinquent psychopath, gangster and possibly murderer. But Maartyn was his best friend. Really? What does that say about my life? he wondered. "I don't know. Where are we going?" All he knew was that he felt more confident when Maartyn was around. Maartyn, his caretaker? He wasn't able to look after himself? The evidence was plentiful. He and his tug were cascading down a river of rapids. Cascading, the verb...is that the right term? No, the rapids were the cascades, a noun. Well, not exactly. Waterfalls are cascades. Even though some of these over-falls, as Jacques calls them, looked to him like waterfalls, they were just, well, rapids. The Niagara River has these huge waves even though the rocks are forty feet below. He'd read that somewhere. So what is there to worry about? Plenty, probably, he concluded in his waking delirium. Just keep *Elloise* in the middle of the channel Jacques said. Some channel...

The run away steam-tug *Elloise,* barely under control in the hands of a complete novice, shot under the CPR railway bridge and then the Mercier Bridge in quick succession. The narrow bridges were just brief shadows overhead as if a pair of giant birds swooped low mistaking *Elloise* for prey...if the shooter was still there what would he think of the target now, shooting the rapids?...shadows of winged doom. Christian cringed, thinking about the gun shots, just hours before...hours? Four, maybe five, since he was nearly killed by a sniper. "Jesus Christ! Does it ever end...?" He must have spoken aloud.

"It's okay," Jacques said. He had pulled himself up to the wheelhouse combing. With his turban bandage he looked like a cartoon troll. Christian was surrounded by trolls. Black trolls into whose hands his life has been cast. And there's a white guy getting stoned at the stern. What's his purpose? He wondered if Jean-Pierre remembered to pull Vince all the way over the rail or had he let him slip back into the river? Christian looked to see if Vince was swimming beside them. Don't be stupid! Never survive that. What would Maartyn think of this whole show? He'd laugh. And Miguel? Miguel would probably lecture him. And how could a fourteen-year old urchin, beach bum, junior revolutionary, lecture him? And Renée?

"Just keep'er in mid channel...cascades...they did it, lots of times. I talked to an old skipper who told me..." he trailed off as if distracted by a memory. What? Jacques was obviously delirious too, thought Christian, but he did say cascades. He doubted they would survive the mad voyage downhill, over-fall by over-fall. "There's islands right ahead, sonny. Steer to the right of the big island," said Jacques too calmly.

"What about the little one?"

"Keep to the left of that one; just stay in middle..." Then Jacques slid away again. Christian heard him hit the deck.

"Oh, great! Left, right, middle?"

Christian angled *Elloise* for mid channel again, surprised at how easily the tug answered the helm. They shot past a small island, maybe too close, then he had to turn again to miss the big island. They were moving much faster, diving over waves and into bottomless holes, then up again. Below the big island was a stretch of relatively calm water before the next over-fall. Feet planted wide apart, the wooden wheel solid in his sweating hands, he was getting the 'feel' as *Elloise* bucked and yawed into the troughs and over the crests. Spray lashed the windows and Christian expected any moment they would hit a rock and die. But they could survive, if...nothing else bad happened.

"She's runnin' low on fuel, mawn," announced Gerard.

"As if I could do anything about that!"

"Just to let you know we have to make the Market Basin or next stop's Trois-Rivières."

"We have to make it down this river first."

"No problem there, mawn. We're goin' down river, like it or not. Question is, how far?"

"Maybe far enough to catch up with my guitar." He actually laughed out loud. So did Gerard. He suddenly felt better. The knot in his stomach unwound. *Elloise* chugged on, flew on, and the next set of over-falls and jumping waves didn't look as menacing. A cool breeze passed through the wheelhouse. He reached for the whistle cord and gave a good tug, the shrill blast adding to the roar of the rapids, and laughed again.

"Don't do that, mawn! Wastin' steam."

"Oh, sorry." Damnit! Why was he always sorry for something? Fuck it! He blew the whistle again.

"Okay, I get it. You're the captain."

"No, I'm not. I haven't a clue what I'm doing."

"Well, mawn...you'd best just keep doing it."

"Right. What's that ahead?..."

Elloise had just cleared another set of rapids below the big island. The river opened up as it turned north. The water was calmer as they crossed Basin La Prairie.

"Champlain Bridge. Go under it," answered Gerard.

"Very funny! I mean the things in the water?"

Below the bridge there appeared to be a series of concrete islands stretching from shore to shore. White water boiled around the structures. Gerard climbed up to the wheelhouse for a better view. "Ice control structure."

"What does it do?"

"Controls ice."

"As in, stops it?"

"Breaks it up."

"Now what, Gerard?"

"Well, mawn, we can't go back," he said flatly. There was a fatality to Gerard's tone that scared Christian.

"Couldn't we just run aground, or something? Or go behind that island?"

The shoreline on either side was alive with white water jumping over boulders. There was another big island to port with what looked like calm, safe water behind. In between were rocks, like blackened teeth, jutting up above frothy gums. But before they could even contemplate making the mouth of the safe harbour they were carried beyond the opening.

"Jacques'll kill you if you run his *Elloise* into somethin'."

"But..."

"Steer, Captain!"

Ice control dams break ice flows into smaller chunks and let them proceed down river, protecting the bridges and shipping. There was not time to contemplate an alternative plan. "Oh, shit!" The gap was wide enough, but even at a distance of three hundred yards it was obvious the river was higher on their side of the structure. But what was the drop?

"Couldn't we at least slow down?"

"No, mawn, you got to steer through!"

Christian aimed at the nearest gap. *Elloise* was swept between the concrete piers, the keel struck hard once and *Elloise* was flung like a toy boat over the sill; her battered hull exposed from the forefoot to the wheelhouse before she dove into the maelstrom below. She continued downward until Christian was looking through solid water. Then *Elloise* floated free, decks awash with bodies floating about.

Free of the ice structures, with water gushing from her scuppers, the tug continued her voyage like a duck emerging from a dunking. Gerard shut off the engine. Jean-Pierre pursued Vince's body and trapped him against the stern bulwarks. Petit Jacques, lying face down, was wedged between the wheelhouse ladder and the fuel tank vent. The choking sounds meant he was still alive.

Elloise, bobbing and lurching, was carried sideways under the Champlain Bridge while overhead a large crowd of motorists gathered to watch the bizarre display of seamanship, to see what the funny little boat would do next as it spun into the last set of rapids before Montreal Harbour.

The dunking revived Petit Jacques and he crawled to the cap rail below the wheelhouse door, glowering at Christian who had wrapped himself around the wheel. "What are you doing to my boat?"

"Jesus, sorry. I, had nothing to do with that! The river..." explained Christian turning the wheel as if actually steering.

"Piece of cake," said Jacques, easing himself down on the rail, automatically feeling for a cigar as if it was break time. "Old days steamboats used to run these rapids all the time. Big steamers goin' down, faster than taking the Canal. The Indians showed them how to do it. Made up a big raft with poles sticking out the bottom an' sent the raft down river from the Galop Rapids, an' let 'er come down all the rapids. When they looked, none of the poles were broken so they knew a steamer could make it, if she stayed in mid channel."

"Now you tell me. But what about that?" He pointed astern to the Ice Dam.

"Oh, that. I forgot about that thing."

Gerard had the engine running again. Jacques made no move to take over so Christian steered *Elloise* back into mid channel.

The city spread out before them; normal river traffic, rush of commerce on bridges and seagulls gliding on the afternoon breeze. Everything was as usual except that they were rocking and rolling through another set of rapids, rocketing under Victoria Bridge like a racehorse and Christian was beginning to worry again. "She's out of oil now, mawn," pronounced Gerard in his deepest, gloomiest Haitian accent, "but she have jus' enough steam to make the Basin, only don't blow the Jesus whistle again."

Elloise leveled out opposite the quays of Old Montreal and Gerard told him how to steer on the clock tower, letting the current do the work. He turned toward the basin, lined up the clock tower and, when Gerard put on the power, eased out of the current into the slack water behind the embankment.

Jean-Pierre was still slumped beside Vince at the stern and Petit Jacques, dazed but awake, was sitting on the cap rail, humming an African tune. Gerard was needed in the engine room, so Christian steered for their dock, dead slow, calling the distances down to Gerard. There was the hawser still hanging over the edge of the pier, its eye in the filthy water. Christian summoned the courage, "Jacques, could you get the hawser, please."

"Aye, skipper," Jacques said, grinning. He worked along the rail to the bow and waited for the hawser to come to him. "Go astern, now," he called.

"Astern, now, Gerard!"

"I was waiting for that, mawn."

The steam engine paused, reversed and the tug shuddered as the big prop dug in, then the engine went silent. The rubber fenders thumped the pier and the bow glanced away, but not before Jacques reached over and seized the errant hawser. Gerard jumped ashore with the stern line. Secured. Finished With Engines. And a good thing. There was not a pound of steam pressure left in the boiler.

It was mid afternoon in Montreal. June-humid, and the ubiquitous copper-sun hot and heavy with portent. It was also just twenty-four hours since Christian had stepped off the train in Windsor Station, walked down to the Market Basin and met Jean-Pierre as if life had a destination. Their cruise adventure had taken up twelve of those hours. Gerard heard sirens and hastily disappeared across the tracks in the direction of the old Market Building. And Christian still had eaten nothing since the dry cheese sandwich on the train.

The watchman from the absent McAllister tug, which was still busy mothering *Mer d'Oiseau* through the locks, ambled to the edge of the pier and looked down on Jacques, who, though slowly, but carefully coiling down lines, was a bloodied, disheveled mess. The man eyed Vince, an Indian, slumped against the stern, still bleeding from an obvious gunshot wound. Jean-Pierre was sitting beside the towing winch holding a dead roach. He eyed the newcomer, Christian, in the wheelhouse drinking Madeira out of the bottle. WABC New York spewed rock'n'roll. 'Dizzy Miss Lizzie' slammed to a finish. He surveyed the shambles of the little tug, and jerked a thumb at the approaching ambulance. It was all connected in his mind, obviously.

"Rough trip, Skipper?"

"Had worse," answered Petit Jacques off handedly.

"Did you hear, Jacques? Somebody blew up that old goélette last night. You know the one, *Villard*? Probably runnin' booze or drugs, is my guess. Killed the captain. Old Antoine, eh? Should'a stayed in the home. They say it was the Mafia. An' there was some shooting over at Caughnawaga this morning. Mafia again, maybe?"

"Bad business," shrugged Jacques.

The siren speeding to the Market Basin drowned out the Shirelles, 'Tonight's the Night'...

Part Two

Dominique

Dominique, wearing a light summer dress that complimented her colour, lay back in the big chair, long tanned legs dangling over one arm. The Calico cat stretched out on the other, paws drawn up, like a Sphinx, purring in nasal bass. Dominique stroked the big cat slowly, trailing her long fingers over the fur from neck to tail, intensifying the cat's pleasure. Each time her fingers reached the base of the tail the cat's hind end rose. And each time the purring stopped in a croak of pleasure. Christian watched Dominique arousing the cat, his attention wavering from the lecture. Jean-Pierre was trying to explain to the group why the arms run, though foiled by enemies, was not a failure.

"We have succeeded in confusing the authorities, comrades. The pigs are chasing shadows in the night. They blame the Mafia. They think the old goélette was running contraband and the Mafia does not like competition. Next time we will succeed right under their noses!"

"But, comrade, how do you explain the actions of the boat and the wounded man, to the authorities?"

"That will be decided by the Political Provo. Obviously the military wing is not to be compromised or revealed yet."

Another voice of doubt spoke up. "But what about the hash? You lost the investment and now we have neither the arms nor hash, nor money to buy more."

"Simple. We'll rob a bank." Gasps and whispers of protest from the young rebels circled the room. This was a new direction. Dangerous and real. "But if they connect Caughnawaga to the boat?" asked another comrade.

"Our Political Provo, Christian, will find a way to turn the events of the glorious Fifteenth of June to our advantage. Christian?"

What was Jean talking about? Glorious Fifteenth? It was a disaster from the moment they left the dock. "Ah, I told the police inspector that we found the wounded man, Vince, in the water after the salvage job and we got caught in the rapids rescuing him when the engine failed and our captain was injured. We had no choice but to run the rapids, as the old steamers used to do, to get the injured to the hospital as fast as possible. And I told them that, yes, we had heard shots after we passed the Indian village...It might be connected to the wounded man, Vince." It sounded hollow, like something out of a bad gangster movie, even though there was some truth to the tale. The ambulance had taken away Vince and Petit Jacques, both pretending to be unconscious or incoherent. But so, it appeared, was Jean-Pierre. They assumed, correctly, that Christian was a rookie on the tug and Jean-Pierre was just a drunken deck hand. Gerard, in the country illegally, had wisely faded from the scene, leaving Christian to explain the events of the Glorious Fifteenth of June. What did he know about the *Honore France Villard*, the police had asked?

Nothing. Which was the truth, or close enough.

"I think you're lying," the Inspector had said. Obviously there was something suspicious about *Elloise's* movements on the night in question even though the old tug was well known on the Seaway and Montreal Harbour. But the inspector was Québec Surité, investigating gunshots and gunshot wounds, and not familiar with the harbour scene.

They were applauding. "Thank you, comrade, Christian."

Dominique moved to get comfortable, revealing the rest of her legs. She noticed Christian's gaze and moved again so that he had a better view. Christian, of course, averted his eyes, for a moment, and when he was drawn back Dominique was smiling. It was very hot in the old building but it wasn't the humid air that caused Christian to break out in a sweat. There was no mistaking her intent. Jean-Pierre droned on, now outlining plans for the bank job. "The Bank of Nova Scotia, the worst of the English clique, is owned by those bastards on Westmount, the dogs of Orange and Ulster. We will visit them and make a 'loan', comrades!" Calls of yes, yes and right on! Dominique pouted and crossed her lovely long legs but continued to hold Christian's eyes. He could have sworn she said, the loft. "We've been thrown too long into narrow provincialism by the English masters. We will strike them where it hurts and take back their plunder a little bit at a time until we are ready to rise up and strike them down!"

Cheers shocked Christian back to reality. Dominique was real enough, and her message was clear, unless she was just trying him out, gauging his loyalty to Jean-Pierre and the cause. What cause? He was only vaguely aware of what the people in the stuffy room were shouting about. Wine was circulating, enflaming the already hot passions. There always seemed to be enough wine and drugs, never enough food. He would settle for a half cooked little silver fish.

"Québec must throw off the yoke of British Imperialism and the New Jewish Colonialism. We'll send the Zionists all packing to Israel if that's what they want." Did he mean les Anglais also? Christian wondered. "We'll shame the British and the sons of Zion and force them out of their Westmount enclave, blow them out if necessary, and then we will invite the Americans to provide the goods while we enjoy the fruits of our own labours for a change."

"Jean never worked a day in his life," whispered Dominique.

"We will replace British Imperialism with Québec Nationalism. Our capital will be Montreal! We will close down their English university on the hill and reestablish our legislative assembly where it belongs, as it was in the days when New France was lord and master of a continent! Vive Montreal!"

"Vive Montreal! Vive liberté!"

"We will reject all attempts to accommodate the English, not like that traitor Bourassa, sucking up to the English, begging them to give us a little kingdom of our own within their walls. No, not one Imperialist left in Québec. The English and the English language will be extinguished for all time! Death to the Imperialist dogs!!" Cheers and oaths, then one young woman turned on Christian.

"What about him? He's Anglais!"

Silence. The eyes of the gang of young revolutionaries turned to Christian. Dominique playfully spread her legs again and quickly crossed them. Jean-Pierre saw the interplay.

"Christian is a friend of the movement...Irish descendant of the IRA," said Jean-Pierre in Christian's defense but looked angry. "He can explain his part in the Cuban Revolution and what he learned from comrade Castro. But first I want to read you something." Jean-Pierre held up a small, tattered hardcover book. "We must learn from those who have laid the foundation of rebellion. You all know Abbé Groulx, the father of modern Québec. He is our first nationalist, not a sympathizer with the English. Does not dine with them. He says, *'The future shall be theirs, who keep the past...Who keep their unremorseful memories whole...And stay near tombs of glory to the last...To mingle with the dead their living soul...The future shall be theirs whose proudest goal...Is the retention of their mother tongue'.*"

There was an uncomfortable silence. Few knew Abbé Groulx. Fewer understood what Jean-Pierre was saying. What do Abbé Groulx and Fidel Castro have in common? Sure, the young revolutionaries in training wanted a free Québec, but language wasn't a problem. They could shop in either tongue. And there are parts of Montreal, east of Rue St. Denis, that is all French. And out in the parishes, wasn't it 'rule by habitant'? There was a struggle going on within Québec, they knew, it was in the papers. One faction, the Groulx group, wanted to isolate Québec from the rest of North America. The other group, mostly the new and growing business elite, want some form of economic association with the English and Americans, to expand Québec's delicate economy and to break away from ruralism and regional nationalism. The small band of street radicals listening to Jean-Pierre that fetid night thought they wanted autonomy for Québec, yes, but they wanted it on their own terms. So what was Jean-Pierre talking about? And why quote Groulx, a fading cleric and academic?

Henri, the appointed president of Free Québec, who seemed to be asleep, got up and held a bottle of wine above his head. "I drink to Québec and our beautiful French language. What Jean-Pierre means is, our fathers carved out this nation from the wilderness. We should celebrate the Battle of Québec as our day of infamy the way the Americans celebrate their Pearl Harbour. We may have suffered a setback in seventeen fifty-nine, a temporary setback, but at that time our French ancestors ruled North America from the mouth of the St. Lawrence to the mouth of the Mississippi...there is a history that unites us...a culture."

Yes, thought Christian, jazz and blues. The continent is held together by African music from Montreal to Chicago to New Orleans. Black music, soul. Even rock and roll. And across the Gulf is Cuba; warm, exciting Cuba and all its Afro-Cuban music. Hot jazz. Salsa spice. He couldn't focus on the lecture. He had run from Montreal's narrowing provincialism and complicated climate of cold weather and over-heated politics. The more the young anarchists argued about freedom from the yoke of the establishment, the narrower became their arguments, until it all collapsed into the divided streets of their wonderfully complicated city, as St. Denis and St. Urban separated English Canada and French Canada with the Jews in the middle, never to be reconciled apparently. And now he is back, thrown into the argument as if he had never left, swamped by the increasing complexity, and just having survived a cruise from hell to trade for weapons and then to rob banks. His old friend Maartyn is just a common criminal and not at all complex. His new friends are terrorists.

"...And we shall rise up to smite our enemy in battle! Remember Louis Riel! The revolution of eighteen seventy-nine! Remember conscription!" Henri drank deeply from his bottle and collapsed back into his chair, dislodging the black cat.

Jean-Pierre regained the floor. "Thank you, Henri. And you all know of Gabriel Dumont, my great grandfather, a patriot fighter, serving only a Free French Canada! Dumonts have always defended our right to live with the land...within the French culture of our ancestors."

"Gabriel Dumont..." whispered Christian to Dominique, "the Metis buffalo hunter. He was such a patriot he stayed as far from Québec as he could and still be in reach of civilization."

"I know. He talks about Dumont all the time. Jean-Pierre says Dumont was a great leader."

"Really? He ended up as a trick rider in Buffalo Bill's Wild West show," said Christian. Dominique suppressed a giggle.

Jean-Pierre noticed Dominique and Christian whispering together. "And now Christian will tell us about another great patriot. The struggle also goes on in the Americas to throw off the yoke of English Imperialism. Christian?"

Christian considered his alternatives. He could go along with the charade or be beaten to a pulp and left in the alley, or the river. "Ah, Fidel Castro. Yes. I had a friend in Cuba who could explain Castro's politics better than I. Unfortunately she was killed in the last battle for Havana..." Christian immediately had the attention of the Montreal rebels, or bank robbers, whatever. "Latin America's in a mood to rebel. Bolivia. Guatemala. Cuba. Castro was a law student who studied repression and rebellion and saw his beloved country run into the ground by a succession of dictators. He is no head-in-the-clouds visionary, but a cold, calculating patriot, using every tactic available to bring his people out of colonial rule, first by the Spanish and recently by the Americans like Mayer Lansky and the Mob. Fulgencio Batista was just a puppet. Castro sees the weakness of Cuba being exploited by her own men like Machado and Batista after the overthrow of the Spanish Grandees." He paused to see if his audience was following his history lesson, or dozing off in the heat, like kids confined to school in June. They seemed fixated. "Castro sees Cuba's economy stolen in turn by the Americans and is determined to end the cycle of economic repression. Much the way we, I'm sorry to admit, les Anglais, have repressed Québec for two hundred years. The Cubans on the streets shout, Cuba si. Yankee no! with good reason."

There was applause and cheers. Apparently they were buying his line. Was he really saying this? Dominique stared at him, cutting into his heart with her eyes. Was she disapproving or surprised in turn by his eloquence?

It had to be the disturbing presence of Dominique, the effect of the wine and hunger, or the fatigue that lowered his defenses. Since leaving Cuba he had vowed to be more on guard. To avoid complications. Well, he was certainly swimming in the destructive element again, too quickly promoted from bum-on-the-run to Political Provo of a quasi military gang hours after stepping off the train. He thought of Vladimir Ilyich Lenin arriving back in Russia being immediately proclaimed leader of the Bolsheviks. They were just a rag tag gang of intellectuals and malcontents, fomenting rebellion in a chaotic Russia after the overthrow of the Czar. Montreal was not Moscow. "Go on, comrade Christian."

"...Castro studied socialism, but he is not a Socialist, per se." What? Did he really say that? He was back in a University of McGill classroom and a stout little man with a dark beard and intense but shifty eyes was lecturing on Bolshevism. He used the term 'per se' a lot. It annoyed the students who counted the number of times he used the phrase when dissecting the Russian Revolution, as if he was afraid to make a point or take a stance, always qualifying his statements. Castro would never say, 'per se'. "Remember, Lenin was originally a Social Democrat..."

"We don't care about democracy!" shouted the girl he had sat beside the night before. "We want freedom. The English jam their brand of democracy down our throats. We're fed up!" There was a rumble of agreement from the gang.

"What I mean is, Castro studied the Communist Manifesto and the Russian Revolution, only to further understand his country's dilemma and the solution. He didn't follow any one philosophy, or movement..."

"Don't give us philosophy! We want the truth. Straight!"

"Not going too well, Christian," whispered Dominique. "Better give them something to chew on."

"The first party to organize in Russia before the fall of the Czar was the Social Democratic Labour Party. And they studied the Communist Manifesto of Marx, a socialist. At that time it meant the Party of the People. Oppressed people. Marx said that..."

"We know what Marx said! Just tell us how Castro did it!"

"Okay...Castro...wrote his own manifesto while he was in jail, after his first rebellion failed. He went to Mexico and got together a gang of young idealists, bought some guns, and a boat and went back to Cuba. Things went wrong. Traitors. Ambush. He ended up on a mountain with a few guerrillas, twelve, like the disciples, and then he put his ideas to work." Christian paused to digest what he had just said, which sounded too close to what he had just done. The cruise for guns on the steam-tug *Elloise*, in which he was almost killed. And the *Bayou Queen*, Renée's escape vehicle. His guitar and all his money left Montreal on a bateau. His own skiff had bad memories of drowned engineers and rowing bodies ashore after the battle in the caves. There were too many boats in his life.

"What ideas? Tell us the way!"

"Okay. Castro knew that the only way to carry a revolution is with the peasants. It is a basic tenet of revolution. The intellectuals present their theories to an enslaved and embittered populace, give them a few slogans and get them on side by not doing what the tyrants do. That is, treat them well and they will respond with their lives on the barricades. Castro told his troops to be pure and not to drink, and never, never steal from the peasants. That's what tyrants do. Buy their food. Don't beat them up. Don't kill them. Don't rape their women. Don't take their children, let the peasants offer them up. They will. And they did. The Cuban farmers helped steal weapons from the military until Castro's army numbered over two thousand well armed fighters and he was ready to leave the protection of the Sierra Maestra and march on Santiago. Castro sent Ché, his trusted comandanté..." A loud cheer interrupted his primer on rebellion. "...he sent comandenté Ché, to set up clinics." More cheers and clapping, as if it was a show.

Encouraged by the cheering he continued... "The poor responded by giving Castro everything they could spare, plus their lives, to protect him when the soldiers came. Castro sent his comandentés with their brigades to capture the garrisons in Eastern Cuba. One by one the garrisons surrendered without much resistance, and the troops joined the revolution, or fled, leaving the weapons and supplies Castro needed to continue his march. This went on all during the late summer and fall of '58 until Batista had no one left in the countryside to resist Castro."

"Batista had kept the best of his army and air force close to Havana, afraid that his own commanders would turn on him before he could escape. He flew out of Camp Columbia on New Years Eve with some of his closest friends and as much wealth as he could steal from the Cubans. The weak resistance failed. Castro took Santiago and then made a triumphant road trip to Havana and began talking." It sounded too easy and his own disciples believed Québec was on the verge of a swift, sweet revolution.

"He's still talking." He stopped talking and sat down.

"That's it? It sounds too simple," said a skeptic.

Christian wearily got to his feet again. "No, it was more complicated than that. There were other factions also waiting to take over Cuba. The Communists. The Labour Party. The Democrats. Then there was..." Yes, there was his own bunch of revolutionaries. The fakes. The frauds. The poseurs. The actors, literally, like Ramon. And there was Escobar, who wanted to steal the revolution and be king. Everyone was posing. He looked at Dominique. Who is she? he wondered. Dusky, sensual, tempting, Dominique. She was looking back, intently. She is beautiful, admitted Christian, and probably dangerous. But what is she doing here? "The Cuban Revolution is a classic. The purest revolution in the history of conflict."

Christian did not want to continue the painful history of revolutions. The Russian Revolution became too messy and the various factions wasted energy fighting amongst themselves, at a time when Russia was weakened by war and depravation, and, given the Russian penchant for self-destruction, they ended up killing off the intellectual class that created the rebellion and gave it direction. Without the elite and the intellectuals the Russians would have dissolved into tribal warfare long before the Bolsheviks. And may still. The French Revolution, though it succeeded, was out of control from the beginning. The reasons were the same but again, too many intellectuals and bureaucrats died along with the nobles. Once the peasants tasted the blood of their perceived oppressors the appetite for murder was insatiable. It took years for France to recover a bureaucracy and an economy. What saved France was her location and resources. A poor country on the fringe of world society cannot quickly rebuild a nation torn by civil war and slaughter. He decided to skip that part.

"Castro plans to take control of Cuba's economy and return it to the people. The American mob money is not enough because too little of it trickles down to the people in the provinces. The sugar cane harvest is..."

"Fuck the sugar cane! You sound like an economics professor!"

He did. He was also sounding pompous. He was light headed and that made him talk faster just to stay on his feet. The room began to move. The noise faded, replaced by the ringing in his head. The pressure building, like the night before, as the wild summer storm approached the harbour. The edges blurred. He might have climbed the loft ladder with help, he wasn't sure. Someone undressed him. Just before he went out he focused on Dominique, her lovely face framed by a halo of dope smoke...

When Christian woke he was on cool silk sheets, on a mattress and he wasn't alone. Dominique, a warm arm across his bare chest, breathed softly in his ear. One bare leg touching his. It was very hot. He was cold. The spells were like that. He wanted to move closer to the heat of Dominique's body but this was all wrong. She was Jean-Pierre's woman.

Dominique opened her green eyes, lips moist, very red, which highlighted the texture and tiny lines, the ones that gave her such a perfect pout. Her mascara was perfect. The long lashes curled and even. The liner deepened the effect of her dark eyes. He was falling into them. She smelled very nice, spicy, especially her breath, like cloves on an Easter turkey, with the glaze and the roasted pineapple rings. There were dark brown rings around her pink nipples. He felt as though he would pass out again. Intoxicated. "Hi," he said rather stupidly, embarrassed, compromised, even afraid.

"Hi yourself. Feel better?"

"Pretty good, I guess. Did we, ah, you know?..."

"Do you want to?"

What should he say? Of course the idea had crossed his mind about a thousand times since he first saw her perfectly tanned form descend the loft ladder; was it only yesterday? "It's just that, you're involved."

She drew her long fingers with the perfect red nails across his bare chest, electrifying the soft blond hairs. Would he ever have real chest hair he wondered? "Christian, I'm not bourgeois, nor am I anyone's bitch," she said firmly but softly. Soft enough to cause Christian to ease closer until his thighs were touching hers. He felt for her moist patch. Her fingers trailed down his side to his belly, then teased his curly pubic hair. Of course it was happening. How could it not? She held him like the handle of a hoe; the beautiful peasant princess of the Ukraine tending a golden field of wheat on the Steppes, red babushka bobbing to the task. Work, work, work, comrades, for the glory of Mother Russia. Caress, caress, caress, "...to sooth the weary hero of the glorious revolution, home tired from the front, rising like the sun to a new day, dedicated to the cause of world communism..." he said aloud. He remembered that first morning, in Cuba, when he woke from a spell, and Esy, who he did not know formally, was cuddled beside him, caressing, as Dominique was doing now, but Renée was on the other side, also touching and caressing. Oh my God! "Where's Jean-Pierre?" Jean-Pierre who had guns and blew up banks. He imagined Jean-Pierre mounting the ladder as he was about to mount his woman, gun drawn, or maybe a knife. Broken wine bottle at least, but even that did not discourage his erection. Oh God!...

"Jean's gone off with Henri and his mob to cause trouble at some new office building."

"They're going to blow it up?"

"No, no. Demonstrate. It's an Anglais bank. Royal Canada."

"Is Jean-Pierre a propagandist or an agitator?"

"Pardon? You're asking me a question, at a time like this?"

Where had that come from, and indeed, at a time like this? He was losing his mind. Or maybe he really was just scared. "Ah, the propagandist creates many ideas, but not many of his followers understand the ideas. The agitator takes one or more of the ideas and makes them understandable to the masses, unifies, a theme, a slogan..."

"Christian, you're delirious. Maybe we should wait."

"Okay, but, Lenin...Only revolutionary intellectuals can save the working man from bourgeois influences and lead him to pure Socialism..."

"Lenin? You're quoting Lenin to me when I'm about to offer myself to you in all my youthful exuberance?"

"You sound like a propagandist. Offering many things. What should I do?"

"Are you crazy?"

"Maybe we should wait. Mathieu's dilemma. Sartre gives his

middle-aged protagonist two choices. The lovely but pregnant Marcel and an honourable but stifling existence, or the tantalizingly youthful but distant Ivich, always a gesture away, retreating further from his grasp..."

"I'm not retreating! I'm lying here holding your cock. What are you going to do, besides talk nonsense?"

He really didn't know. Wait? Abstain. So many images poured in and out of his brain. Images of Renée on the beach at Andros. Esy boarding the army truck for Pinar del Rio. Saying goodbye at the convent door. Juanita, like a large brown tree in the forest, falling on him, naked...what would Lenin do? Lenin was an ideologue, but also a pragmatist. He dealt with situations as they arose. "I shall arise to the occasion."

"You've already risen, now what are you going to do with it?"

Wait, he decided. "I've taken a vow of celibacy." This sounds too much like Renée, the stage director, the logician, the field commander in the battle of the sexes. But, Renée excited him, like Dominique. Dominator. What could he do? Wait. He fell asleep with her still holding him.

Later, when Christian slipped away, Dominique did not awake. She slept, easily, peacefully; achingly lovely in the diffused light of candles. Her makeup still perfect because she had not let him kiss her. He awoke confused because he was still excited, or beyond tired. But he was hungry. The large room was quiet and the night sounds of Montreal distant. A siren far away on the mountain was echoed by a boat whistle down river. He peered over the edge of the loft. There were two cats, one sleeping on each arm of the sofa, with a body in between. It was Vince.

Christian dressed quickly in shorts and T-shirt, his only wardrobe, noting the musty smell of clothes worn too long. He regretted the loss of his change of clothes in the knapsack more than the loss of his money, and Jocinto's guitar. Easing down the ladder so as not to wake Vince, maybe he was already dead, he limped around the kitchen space looking for something to eat. He was also exhausted from tension, lack of sleep and hunger, not to mention the thrill of being shot at by high powered rifles and white water adventures at the helm of a runaway steam-tug and almost making love to the most beautiful creature he had seen since, well, Rosameralda at Jocinto's funeral. But it was Esameralda he had fallen in love with, maybe, while he still longed for Renée, who was also in love with Esy...just find something to eat! Sex is too complicated. Celibacy would be a good idea. Vince startled Christian.

"Food's in that box." Vince pointed to a cardboard box beside the chair.

"God, I thought you were dead." He dropped into the chair opposite Vince.

"Me too. They gave me blood. Police asked a lot of questions then I left the hospital. Escaped through kitchen an' grabbed some food on the way out."

"Are you okay?"

"Okay. Fine. Alphonse is a good shot. Always goes for the arm or the leg. Never killed anybody. But, still, you don't want being shot too much."

"No kidding. So, what was it about? Alphonse, didn't want you dealing with Jacques?"

"Not so much. Goes way back. Alphonse is Iroquois. Wacky Gilles is Huron. I'm a Mohawk Warrior. We don't always get along."

"A tribal thing?"

"Yeah. My partner will sell the dope to Wacky Gilles anyway. Then he'll take it north to trade with the Cree up on James Bay. Cree don't use dope. They might trade it to some Eskimaw over to Labrador who'll trade it to the Americans at the air base near Goose Bay for gasoline and booze. Americans fly it to their home base down south somewhere. Florida maybe. Like the old trade routes, before Europeans like you come here to spoil our land."

"Whoa! Wait. Not all whites. I mean, my generation was born here. My parents came from Ireland. I didn't have a choice."

"You should go back. Find your roots. Live in your natural space."

"I think we're from East Dublin and I doubt there's much natural about the slums."

"Maybe not, but a man must dwell within his own ground to understand the earth from which he springs."

"True, I guess. Where are you from?"

"Brantford, Ontario. Woodlands tribes. Good fighters. Fierce. Resourceful."

"I can see that. You escaped from the police and gathered food."

"Yeah." Vince laughed. "First things first. Warriors have to eat to run, in either direction."

It was Christian's turn to laugh. "An army moves on its stomach, as well as its feet."

"True."

"But why do you still fight? Surely the old tribal wars don't happen now?"

"Sometimes it's necessary for young men to show they're strong and can protect their women."

"This is the nineteen sixties, not the eighteen hundreds."

"Doesn't matter. It could be sixteen-sixty, or the time before time. A warrior still has to prove he can protect his village, even if the village is a mission in downtown Montreal and the battlefield is Dorchester Street. And the fights aren't meant to kill, just to fight. Otherwise, Alphonse and I would be dead, an' Wacky Gilles would be alone in his church steeple."

"I see, I think."

Dominique was awake. "Christian? Who's there?"

"Just Vince."

"Who's Vince?"

"Friend. The guy we pulled out of the river."

"Pulled along the river," said Vince, exploding with laughter.

Christian laughed too, remembering Vince on the end of his tether, like a water skier who couldn't get up.

"Christian, come back up here."

"Your woman's the boss of you?"

"Ah, no, we're just getting acquainted."

"Your chief said that the French once owned our land from the St. Lawrence to the Mississippi. Now the English own it. They never owned the land. Just trespass on us."

"You still think you can get the English out of the Great Lakes Basin and the French out of the St. Lawrence Valley?"

"No. We just want the treaties. But if they want a fight, we'll fight. Indians were the first Socialists you know?"

"Never thought of it that way."

"Lived together in villages, shared long houses, shared food women. Dogs. Shared raising kids. Once upon a time we had North America very organized. You could get anything from anywhere. Copper from Lake Superior. Sea shells from Florida. Silica from Labrador or the mid-west. Depended on who was trading an' who was fighting."

"Indians traded sand? Silica's sand, right?"

"Yes an' no. Silica's a rock for making tools. Tools are very important. Like weapons made from the flint. Traded all over North America. They find Labrador silica tools in the St. Lawrence Valley all the time. How'd it get here? Traded. Same as Wacky Gilles'll probably trade the hashish to James Bay Cree, and on to Labrador. Trade routes all over the place for thousands of years."

"I see. You're right of course. Trade routes spread civilization. Except the Europeans didn't think of the Indians as, well, very civilized."

"More civilized than Europeans! When Europeans still hiding in caves we were trading things all over. Silica traded ten thousand years ago. When Europeans were still throwing rocks an' using clubs, Indians were trading fluted points, you know...arrow heads and spears an' knives. Made them out of rocks like chert, jasper, quarts, obsidian. Obsidian's a volcanic glass and very brittle. Very sharp when made thin an' pointed, but not as strong as chert. Mostly used on the West Coast, but some made it to the Great Lakes from Wyoming. Ten thousand years ago. You tell me what they were doing in Europe then? Hiding in caves an' daubing mud on the walls. Creep out from time to time to club food. We traded."

"Wow, you know a lot about your history. Was this passed down to you by the Elders or something?"

"No, I spend time in libraries an' go to free lectures at the university when it's cold, to get off the streets."

"Oh. That's too bad, about the cold I mean. I think it's great that you study your culture."

"We've got culture, boy, have we got culture. The Jews an' Arabs have culture too. But you don't have much culture. Europeans just had ships an' diseases an' capitalists. Borrowed culture, or stole it."

"You should read Marx and Lenin sometime."

"I did. Didn't care for it. The Communists got it all wrong. An' that man in Cuba, this Castro, he's going to get it wrong too."

"I think you're right. I have a theory..."

"Don't tell me no theories! Fuck theories! Everybody's got a theory. Indians didn't have theories. We just had culture but we still got no theories, nor treaties neither, 'cause the one's with theories too busy thinking up new theories to listen to us. Fuck theories an' fuck you! If I didn't have this shot up shoulder I'd beat the piss out'a you!"

"Whoa, wait, Vince. I pulled you out of the river this morning. Twice. I'm just along for the ride."

"I heard you talking about Castro an' that new socialists junk. We are the original socialists. You should listen to what we have to say about getting along."

"Then why were there so many Indian wars and so many tribes fighting?"

"Because, necessary, like I said, Indian man has to prove himself. Wars were just for show, until the White Man come along with guns an' whiskey. Then things got mean."

"Can't argue that..."

"Christian, what are you two arguing about?"

"You know, the usual." Just the usual, he thought. Life reduced again to communism and revolutions and Dominique, like Renée, ordering him back to the loft. He was hungry. "What's to eat, Vince?"

"White man's food'll kill you quick. Go up the mountain an' snare rabbits."

Christian rummaged hopefully in the box, rustling through waxed paper, coming up with a wrapped sandwich. White bread and processed meat slices. Stale. Dry and green around the edges. Besides the meager, uneaten fish, his most recent meal had been a dried out cheese sandwich on the train. Days ago. One day, actually, but it seemed a long time. "Ah, thanks, but I'll wait."

"Get a rabbit an' boil it for a few hours with lots of salt an' some wild parsley. Boil it down to a gravy, then suck the bones an' then put in some potatoes an' anything else, like turnip or carrots. Sweet potato's good. Works with rats too. Don't eat the fish out of the river. Too much poison."

"How did you get back here?"

"Gerard come to hospital, Hotel Dieu. Nuns make you pray. His brother drives a taxi."

"Where's Gerard now?"

"Don't know."

"Yes you do."

"Don't tell him I told you. He's uptown at the Haitian restaurant. Creole. Café Caraibes. Back alley near Rue St. Denis. He takes me there sometmes. He has friends who hide him from the cops. He's wanted for murder, you know?"

170

"No, I didn't know."

"Ton ton agent was sent to Montreal to kill Gerard's brother."

"He told me that much."

"Gerard found out and waited outside restaurant for the man in his brother's taxi. It was a cold night. Windows all clouded up. Gerard kept a little patch open, motor running like he's waiting for a fare. The man shows up, an' gets in the taxi. Gerard drives him to east end, docks, down by the refineries? Sunoco I think."

"Funny name for dirty oil, don't you think?"

"Don't know. Gerard breaks fucker like a stick, an' drags 'im to river, dumps body so brother not involved, you see? But there's a witness, a worker up on one of the towers. Gets the number of the taxi an' what Gerard looks like. Not many Haitians in Montreal so Gerard is marked, by the cops an' the Ton ton. Very bad people. Ton ton I mean. You stay away from them fuckers."

"Thanks for the tip."

"You want to go to a voodoo sacrifice? Good fun."

"Don't think so."

"They only sacrifice chickens now, sometimes. Maybe your cock." Vince grinned broadly, missing teeth like crenellations in a wrecked castle. "This woman Gerard knows, beautiful, does the ceremony. Catholic mass and voodoo sacrifice. Very interesting. Good sex too if you want. Costs extra, but very professional."

He could only think of Juanita and her Santaria shrine in the cave. It too was a mixture of Catholic icons and African dolls. Beads and candles seem to be a common denominator of most religions. Africans have a curious tolerance for mixing religions, the way Montrealers used to tolerate races. Voodoo must be in the same league. Maybe he'd try it out for the experience.

"Christian," said Dominique descending the ladder in the summer dress that barely covered her exquisite derriere. She knew it of course. He regretted his inability to seize the moment. She turned and smiled, taunting him. "I'm hungry. Since you don't want to fuck let's at least go out for dinner."

"Ah, I don't have any money."

"Of course not. My treat."

Jean-Pierre said Dominique came from privilege, straying from Outremont to annoy her parents, but they wouldn't let her go without means. He had doubts about that story. He thought of Renée, the money and the diplomatic passport. Privilege is the preserve and the purpose of the wealthy. Handy at times, but what of freedom? Doesn't privilege come with a price? But he was too hungry to protest. "Vince, would you like to eat with us?" He felt uncomfortable including Vince on Dominique's dime.

"Yes, do come, Vince," she said easily but sincerely.

"Naw, that's a'right. I've got a bottle."

"You sure?"

"Yeah, I'm a'right. You be careful. Very bad people in these parts."

"It's just Montreal, Vince, not the wild west," Christian said, hopefully.

They walked arm in arm west along Rue de la Commune through Vieux Port; comfortably worn and shabby Old Montreal's industrial waterfront with its cheap cafés for the working classes and sailors from foreign lands. Drunks. The outcasts and the homeless. It was late and the streets were quiet, darkly luminous and misty from the rain. Almost deserted but for the odd figure shuffling through the gritty heat, looking for a place to sleep. It was humid again after the storm, the clear air was only a short respite from the oppressive funk of summer in the city. The smells were interesting though, a blend of humanity and nature, the sounds and smells of birds swooping about the dockside elevators and the rats snuffling for hidden kernels, the night crawlers pissing in alleys. Coal smoke from idling steam engines, yellow smog, blotting out the tops of the unfinished office towers of Place Ville-Marie and the banks. Jean-Pierre and Henri were leading their intense mob of freedom fighters against les Anglais, perhaps planning to blow up the new tower, a symbol of English capitalism in Québec.

"Why would Jean demonstrate at night?"

"Strategy. At night the television cameras are more available and the crowds look larger. You can create more confusion, and escape easier."

"Clever."

"Besides, the English are at home watching it happen on television. He says it's no use to yell at glass doors when the real enemy is forty floors up and can see only Westmount."

"You don't approve?"

"I'm not political. My protest is against my parents. I'm in front of cameras enough to suit me. I don't look good in bad lighting."

"You look great at any time."

"You're so sweet. Lets go back to the loft."

"And you're incredible, but I really need something to eat."

"I'm not nourishing enough?" She actually pouted.

There was a group of toughs lounging on the corner. Christian steered Dominique north on Boulevard St. Laurant toward St. Paul. Some of the boys called out and whistled. "I think we should take a cab."

"Okay, where?"

"Café Caraibes? Vince mentioned it."

"It's not your type of place."

"I want to find Gerard, that's all."

"Okay, so you think Gerard can protect us?"

"We don't need protection. I'm thinking of, well, the way you look tonight." He wished he hadn't said that. Straight off the WABC play list.

"You are sweet."

A yellow and green cab turned the corner at St. Urbain, going east on St. Paul. The gang turned the same corner to intercept, jiving toward them, calling rude things to Dominique. Christian stepped onto the road to make sure the cab stopped. The driver was black. Thank God, Christian whispered as they scrambled into the back seat. A bottle whistled overhead and smashed against a building.

"Friends of yours, mawn?" the Jamaican driver asked, accelerating away, tires howling. His perfect white teeth flashed in the mirror. Christian relaxed in the warm comfort of the Islands.

"We were about to get acquainted."

"Should know better than to come down here with a beautiful woman, mawn."

"Yeah, right. We started out down here. Anywhere else is up."

"Where you want to go now?"

"Do you know the Café Caraibes?"

"Oh, mawn, are you crazy?"

"I just want to see a friend."

"Okay, but if you have friends at the Caraibes..." He let the inference hang.

"He's a good guy. Gerard Désulmé. Know him?"

A long pause. "No, mawn." The driver's expression changed from open to cool and guarded.

"His brother's a cab driver..."

"No. Never heard of them."

Christian sensed their driver knew the story. The cab crawled slowly from light to light up Rue St. Denis, the driver not in a hurry to venture into Haitian territory. Traffic was sparse but there were people on the streets, or sitting on apartment steps and balconies with wrought iron railings, wandering in and out of bars and restaurants, or lounging against parked cars in an attempt to escape the heat. Island music swelled from transistor radios and there was electricity in the heavy air, the crowd swaying like a slow moving carnival. Dominique took Christian's hand and put it on her cool thigh then moved it to the warm side. She could feel his racing pulse.

"So, you read Sartre," she said, and moved his hand higher until it caressed the edge of her soft summer dress.

An unusual question, he thought, given the circumstances. "Yes, a little."

"You don't seem the type."

"Why is that? What type reads philosophy?"

"You don't read him for the philosophy. You're not the type. You read Sartre because he's 'in', with the pseudo-intellectuals."

"I'm not..."

"I know. What's your fascination with Castro? Why did you go to Cuba?" She drew his sweating hand into her crotch and held his fingers against her soft cotton panties until he could feel her wetness.

"I can't answer questions if you're going to do that."

"Sure you can. Concentrate." She spread her legs and pressed his fingers into her, manipulating, massaging the spot. The driver was watching them in the mirror. "Eyes on the road please. There. Just there. Now you do it and tell me about Castro."

She undid the button of Christian's shorts and worked the zipper free. Faces drifted by the windows at intersections. Dominique waved her free hand at the boys.

"Dominique..."

"Did you go to Cuba because you believed in the Revolution?"

"Would you folks like a hotel instead?"

"Just drive, please. Rub. Come on, Christian, tell me, please. Oh...oh...yes...!"

The cab turned into a narrow, dark side street, as narrow as an ally. "Café Caraibes," he said in a chirpy, sing-song imitation of a tour guide.

"Oh, too bad. Later, about Castro, I mean," she said playfully and laughed.

Dominique's too cool, he thought, buttoning up. She had been to the Café Caraibes and had to know the timing, damn...

The Café Caraibes wasn't much for style. An orange-sherbet

painted street level door was sandwiched between a lime green hair salon and a peeling mud-brown pawnshop. They climbed the worn wooden stairs towards spirited Latin music pulsing from an over-heated room on the upper level with bad lighting, a few small tables and a high bar with the usual array of bottles and colourful signs. A narrow hallway lead to the kitchen and a back door and beyond was the roof deck. What gave the place some distinction, besides the handsome men without shirts leaning over gorgeous ladies in dark places, with only candles glowing on high cheekbones and shimmering breasts in low cut dresses, was the voodoo shrine beside the bar packed with candles and icons. All the Caraibes lacked was Juanita, thought Christian. Someone turned down the record player and everyone stopped talking, gazing at Christian and Dominique. Mostly Dominique. Christian had spent two years in the Islands with Blacks but he was intimidated by the Haitians on their home ground, the intensity of the focus, as if he was being dissected and labeled.

"Turn the music up, my man," said a tall, very black man at the bar. He was lean and hard muscled, the white undershirt only intensified the effect. He moved beside Dominique in one fluid motion. "Dance with me, my beauty," he said, his arm already around her waist, stepping out even before the music returned, loud and brassy, Tito Puente, hot Latin jazz.. He flung her away, kept her hand and reeled her in. Christian was mesmerized. Why can't I do that, he wondered? Dominique whirled and shook her shoulders, and stomped her high heels as if she had done this before. She pushed the man back and then jumped at him, legs spread, shivering as he advanced, driving her backward over a table. She forced the man back and spun away with a screech of triumph. The man laughed and attacked again, this time his legs surrounded her so she could not escape. She grabbed his neck, jumped into the air and clasped him around the waist with her long legs. The tall man twirled Dominique about like a ballet master. Dominique shrieked with delight, landed on her feet and shook some more. All she lacked was ruffles and a fruit basket on her head. Carman Miranda!

The music was intoxicating, and the entertainment fascinating, but he was standing alone in the middle of a Haitian bar feeling conspicuous while his gorgeous girl made Mambo shake-shake with the local stud. He needed a drink. It was the first time he had ever felt that alcohol was necessary to fill an awkward gap. "May I have a beer?" he asked the bartender; herself stunning, so sophisticated and polished, as if she had just stepped out of a Parisian fashion magazine.

"What kind of beer, white boy?" The 'white boy' was said with a flashing smile that delivered messages.

"Any kind, Miss, ah, Mam, as long as it's cold."

"I'm no Miss nor Mam. I'm a woman. An' you wan' watch that Mister François. He steal that woman. He can dance, but that's not all, if you know what I mean?"

"I get it. He's got, 'it', right?"

"You can believe me, honey." She placed a dripping beer on the bar and put a smooth dark hand on Christian's when he reached for the bottle. Long fingers and long nails with incredibly red nail polish to match her lipstick. "Firs' one's free, suga'. Drink one beer an' two-three more, 'cause you gonna need all the help you can get." She laughed and tilted her gorgeous dark head towards Dominique. "You know François?"

Christian gulped his beer, comparing the dark beauty behind the bar to Juanita who was almost the opposite in stature. Though taller, she was half the size of Juanita but had the same worldly-wise demeanor. This one's slim and beautiful, but still Juanita. "No. I'm looking for a friend...Gerard?"

Her bright face was suddenly a mask. "Gerard, huh? An' you think I know this Gerard."

"He comes here, I'm told."

"Which Gerard are we talkin' 'bout, honey?"

"Is there more than one Gerard?"

"More questions. You're too young for a cop."

"No, I'm just a friend. Gerard and I made a little trip together last night."

"Oh, that Gerard."

"Then there's more than one?"

"No, sonny, long as you can tell me the nature of this trip."

"Sorry, I can't tell you that."

"An' you should not. Never tell nothin'."

"Thanks for the beer."

"That's okay. You want anythin' from the back room, suga'?" She wasn't offering the special from the limited menu.

Tempting, another day, in another life. "Ah, no, thank you. I'll just wait for her...well, she's not exactly *my* woman."

"I know. She's Jean-Pierre's woman an' you playin' dangerous games."

"Oh, you know Jean-Pierre?"

"I know some Jeans. You know Vince?"

"I know Vince," he answered. "Small town."

"Crazy good Indian. He comes in, we go straight to back room, for the specialty of the house." She raised perfect dark eyebrows in that way. The music ended. The tall Haitian delivered Dominique to the bar, glistening and almost out of breath.

"She can dance, that one," said François flashing a broad grin. "You want to get around that lady good. Three beers, momma."

She put three cold Canadian beers on the bar. No money changed hands. The tall Haitian offered a beer to Dominique and slid one across to Christian. "We'll drink to the dance and beautiful women," François said, nodding his beer to both Dominique and the bar tender.

"To beautiful women," agreed Christian, trying to decide which one would take first prize.

And Dominique said, "To Tito Puente!"

"Who?"

"The Latin jazz music. You've been to The Islands and Cuba

and you don't know Tito Puente the Mambo King?"

"I was only in Havana a few days, before the Revolution."

"So, you fight with Castro too." François said, as if he knew the story.

"Not exactly with," Christian answered, hoping the man would not press for details. "And not on purpose," he said cautiously as the bar tender whispered in the man's ear.

"So, why you want to find Gerard?" asked François. His expression changed subtly and he rose from the barstool towering threateningly over Christian, or so he imagined.

"We're friends. Gerard Déslumé is just a connection to Cuba." He was feeling uncomfortable, vulnerable and regretted leaving the island. Regretted not going to Paris with Renée. Dominique was not a replacement. And there was something not right about her slumming with the anarchists. So, why didn't he leave them all, including Gerard?

The bartender intervened. "Gerard's out back," she pointed down the narrow hall. "Meeting. Maybe not want to be disturbed."

"That's okay. If you could just tell him we're here."

"But if you was with Gerard night las'...We'll entertain your woman."

"I'm with him," Dominique said.

They negotiated the darkened hallway past the back rooms that gave off a strong, sweet odour of burning vegetation. And there were more candles. Candles in this heat?

The roof deck was contained by a grey, wood-planked fence and a spreading beech tree, but it was a little cooler in the open. Tito Puente's Island music dripped in tinny notes from a cheap speaker. The city throbbed as an undertone to the music. Lights of the business towers cast a soft blue glow on the fog that hung like low clouds. Gerard, at a corner table set apart from other guests, was talking with three men. Candles in glass bulbs showed the tension on their faces. Gerard looked up, smiled, and motioned to Christian and Dominique.

"Ah, my friends. Come. Sit." Gerard took Dominique's hand. The move was natural, but there was something more in the easy familiarity. They had slept together, he decided. "Christian. Dominique." The other men rose as Dominique sat down. "Philippo. Rudy. Doctor André." The men bowed to Dominique, shook hands with Christian and then sat down in the order they were introduced. A young boy brought Christian a chair. There was an awkward silence as they adjusted to the dynamics of a table only large enough for four. Dominique was the first to speak.

"How are you, Gerard? Christian told me about the police..."

"Oh, the police never close. Gerard slips away like a zombie before sunrise." He laughed and the other men nodded or grinned. The men were an odd assortment. Rudy, probably Haitian, holding a damp handkerchief, was fleshy and short, with a crinkle of hair, dressed in a dark, rumpled suit, obviously suffering from the heat, as was the other short man, Dr. André. Uncomfortable in an ill-fitting jacket, he had broad shoulders, muscular arms and scars on his textured face. Christian guessed the doctor was an ex-boxer or Mafia. Anything was possible in this odd group. The third man, Philippo, a European, was lean and tall, like Gerard, but older and more guarded, withdrawing from the light of the candle. Only a monk's hood could have shielded him better than his long, undefined hair with much grey and experience, and the beginning of a salt and pepper beard looked like a disguise. He was also dressed in black, including a long sleeved shirt with the collar buttoned. Tattoos of snakes curled out from under the cuffs of the shirt, which was silk and well tailored. Christian pegged him as Eastern European, probably Russian, and in this company, a drug lord or an assassin. Dark thoughts, but then the mood had become dark. Now that he had found Gerard and intruded on the meeting he felt completely out of his element.

The awkward silence tightened. A police siren wailed in the distance, punctuating the dilemma. The men looked uncomfortable. Only dishonest or desperate men react to sirens, Christian said to himself. Gerard signaled to the wait-boy who nodded and went inside. "For tonight we want rum with ice. My friends and I starting early. Only thing to keep down the heat. It was never like this in Haiti. Hot, oh, my beautiful Jesus, yes! An' the salt air get into your skin, but mawn, we never have fog like this, this palpable presence always overhead, a sulfur cloud like to drop down any moment to choke out life like a snake strangles a monkey."

Christian had often tried to describe Montreal summers to his Island friends, but nothing came close to Gerard's analogy. People coughed more in summer than winter. There was more sickness and more domestic incidents on sweat-heavy nights. The police siren could mean an enraged man pummeling his terrified wife with closed fists because the heat made him crazy and his mother had never taught him respect for women; herself a victim of humidity and perpetual poverty.

"You met François," said Gerard. "My brother." Christian made the connection. "He's come from New York. These men have joined our cause. Philippo," he indicated the tall man, "has certain interests in Haiti and Cuba. Rudy is a survivor of Papa Doc's assassins. His family died because he writes poems. André is a doctor, like my brother, but he cannot practice in Port au Prince or anywhere on the island because the Ton ton Macoute is after him. You know about this brutal army of Duvalier? The Ton tons are here in Montreal to kill those of us who oppose Papa Doc in exile."

Dr. André, who looked like his practice was back alley abortions on the run, nodded gravely. "Gerard is a marked man since he killed one of them bastards."

"But Vince said they know this place."

"Those men in the bar? All good Haitian fighters. Exiles. Smell Ton ton. Ton ton man walk in here an' he be dead, like that." Gerard snapped his fingers, like the sound of breaking bones.

"What do these Ton ton look like?" Christian asked, feeling a new danger lurking beyond the fence.

"Like any Haitian, except for the eyes. They look guilty."

"So, you have to get pretty close to tell. That's dangerous, isn't it?"

Gerard shrugged. "It's the way we do things. Danger is our way of life here and at home. Here we must first overthrow the government of Québec, weaken the Federal Government so they have to negotiate and then we can bring our people here to establish a new Haiti in exile. We work to get funds and then return to our home and wipe Duvalier and his Ton tons from the face of the earth!"

"Don't forget Jean-Claude, that fat little Baby Doc. Like father, like son," intoned Rudy.

"Amen."

"This heat makes them crazy," said Philippo to Dominique.

"Is Castro crazy with the heat?" asked Rudy as if he also knew Christian's story.

The heat, like the rhetoric, pressed Christian into his chair. It would be better in the fall when the air clears and the crisp breezes come from the lakes and spruce forests, thought Christian.

"It will be better in the fall," said Gerard, as if reading Christian's mind. "I even look forward to winter. But summer is much better for revolution. Make plans in the snow. Make rebellions when everyone is hot an' angry. Revolutions seldom work in winter."

"The Russian Revolution," said the Russian.

"Well, the Russians didn't have a choice," laughed Gerard.

The tension eased a degree and the drinks arrived: dark rum with soda and confectioner's sugar, with ice. So much ice it was hard to tell if it was a drink or a snow cone, but the rum held up even as the ice melted. Later it was just rum and sugar with water running down the sides of the glass making puddles on the table. The boy came often to wipe away the water, empty the ashtray and bring more drinks. Christian was falling behind. The talk weaved in and out of politics and revolutions, with Haiti the main topic and references to France and Montreal; they called it the Québec Situation. Christian wondered why he was allowed to hear the discussion.

Christian also began to whither under the effects of the close heat, the lack of food and fatigue. Soon to follow would be the sounds, the pressure and the peripheral haloes, as the night began to close in. Please, not now...

"Christian? You don't look well," Dominique said, putting her cool hand on his arm.

"Maybe the drinks?" offered Gerard.

"It's the heat," said Dr. André, dabbing at his own face.

"The weather's changing," said Christian, as if to reassure the man that his own suffering would soon be over. "High pressure system coming by morning. Fine weather, for Montreal."

"You can read the weather?" asked Dr. André.

"I know when it's going to change."

"What else?"

"Ringing sensation, the ears seem to fill up. Hearing dull, distorted."

"Yes, I thought so. Do you experience the vertigo?"

"What's that?"

"Extreme dizziness, often with nausea."

"Sometimes." He meant to say, too often lately.

"We should have a talk. Back home there's a woman who has the symptoms. She goes into a trance and falls down. Brings up bile. Has visions and voices in her head. Could be in a trance-like state for days. Some say she's possessed. There's a clinical explanation."

"A doctor told me it was just the drugs, you know, I had a little problem. Let's not spoil the party. I'll be okay, in a day or so."

"Yes, I see...when the high or low pressure passes."

"Something like that." Christian didn't want anything more to drink; alcohol repulsed him when he was beginning a session, but he held up his water glass in a weak attempt at a toast. "To better weather."

"Amen."

"Amen, and none too soon," said Rudy.

Gerard made a sign to their waiter. The waiter nodded and went inside and returned shortly with platters heaped with Island food: roasted fish with peppers and garlic, beans and mangoes, pork in a thick, blood-red hot sauce, a melting steamed chicken with raisins and bananas and a seafood platter on rice and sweet potatoes, heavy on the shrimp. All spicy. All hot. Not the kind of food most Haitians enjoyed at home, except in dreams. Christian tried to eat. Only the chicken and rice would go down with some ice water. Dominique picked at the chicken while the four men talked politics and helped themselves to the rich repast.

Christian tuned out the rest of the conversation and seemed distracted by sounds from the outside world. Dominique was watching him, curious or concerned. There would be no Castro inquisition or anything else that night. Gerard and the men continued their discussion about the coming revolution. For them anarchy in the streets of Montreal was only a matter of time. Dominique's attention wavered from Christian's condition to her own immediate concerns.

The taxi ride back down to the river was a sharp contrast to the trip uptown to The Caraibes. The sidewalks were almost empty. Few taxis crawled along sweating streets. Escapees from stifling flats lingered on balconies and in doorways, the carnival atmosphere replaced by a damp, heat-heavy lethargy. Dominique, on the far side of the seat, was distant so Christian tried to put the evening, the day and night before, into perspective. He was alone in a strange land, an outcast, a self-induced estrangement, and he regretted the distance.

The yellow and green Chevy cab was descending Rue St. Denis at a leisurely pace approaching Avenue Viger. The driver, by his photo and badge, was a French Canadian from Montreal

East. "This is my own cab. I could take you to the Mount, half price. Drive around a bit. Mount Royal. The park's cooler." A young couple late at night was a bonus. "I've been robbed three times this month, but I can't take fares during the day." Dominique reached across the seat and took Christian's hand. "Driver, take me to Place d'Armes station, please."

"Oui, Mademoiselle, as you wish." The polite response did not mask his disappointment.

"Place d'Armes? The Metro?" Christian asked, knowing the answer.

"I'm going home."

"Oh, I see."

"You can take the cab to the Market Basin. I'll pay in advance."

"No, I'll walk. Driver, please pull over here."

"Oui, Monsieur."

The driver pulled to the curb at the intersection of Viger and Rue St. Denis. The light was green but there was no other traffic.

"Christian, I'm sorry, about tonight, and tomorrow."

"Why tomorrow?"

"And the next day. Because I can't see you again like this."

"I understand. Jean-Pierre..."

"No, not Jean-Pierre. He means very little to me. A lunatic idealist and a waste of my time. Yours too."

"This isn't exactly an ideal life style. I mean..."

"Anarchy doesn't happen in wood paneled libraries."

"Montreal Harbour?"

"It's more, but I can't explain. I'll get in touch."

"Okay, when?"

"Please get out."

Christian crossed Viger against the red. The driver had to wait for the green to turn onto Avenue Viger. Christian didn't look back and had only a slight twinge of regret for being ushered out of her life. Who or what, is Dominique, he wondered?

A Montreal Summer

High summer passed in a humid haze, like the film of ancient dirt on the windows of the warehouse that Christian called home, with Jean-Pierre and the cats and the ever-changing mob. Dominique returned less often to the loft, and when she did there were arguments about money. The heat continued in moist waves of brown-tinged mist, the new term was smog, between sudden summer storms and brief clear days. The ever-changing river glowed bright with promise or turned iron gray with anger, then placid and lead-heavy. A steady stream of earnest young rebels paraded in and out of the squalid meeting place. The Cuban Revolution, the unrest in Latin America, and the rising Red Tide from China opened the taps of restless angst among the young people beginning to test the waters of freedom fuelled by rock and roll, drugs and communist ideology, in the name of freedom, as long as it spoke of dissent, the freedom to be young, confused and irreverent. Some were just curious students on a break from university who wanted to taste anarchy. They talked about bombs and terrorism in the abstract. Others, hardened reactionaries searching for the vehicle to enlightenment, but finding Jean-Pierre's angst-ridden mob too steeped in ideology, drifted away. Planning bank robberies and committing misdemeanors did not count as total anarchy. In a desperate attempt to gain supporters Jean-Pierre lectured about race and religion and about tearing down churches as well the government. Henri, the president, was more concerned about overthrowing the government than in breaking windows and smearing paint on synagogues. Anarchy just for the hell of it was more a recreation than an issue. The arguments became as heated as the Montreal summer air.

Christian, who was tolerated but seldom consulted about political theories, began distancing himself from the inner circle. His status as a Castro fighter, a role he stopped denying, meant he had a following of young women who would have given their all to

Ché but settled for the handsome Anglais who seemed perpetually at sea searching for an island refuge.

There was the question of survival. A group of young people interested in a socialist agenda and not employment had to forage, borrow or steal the necessities of life but wine and narcotics arrived daily in sufficient quantities. It allowed them to focus on the other evils of the world; capitalism, capitalist thinking and cronyism. The best example was Batista's run of greed in Cuba. The world was awash with fat men in suits sucking the lifeblood of their people. Closer to home it was the English establishment; the hated foreign money mongers of the towers. There was much talk of bringing down the new Capitalist tower under construction, Place Ville-Marie.

"The trains run right under Ville-Marie! And we know who is building that monolith to money, les Anglais!" roared Jean-Pierre in a typical drunken rage. "I say blow it right over Westmount to Pointe Claire!! And the Church of Christ with it!" Finally, a strategy for violence to satisfy the hunger and the train to Central Station was the perfect delivery system for explosives carried by revolutionaries dressed as Anglican priests on a pilgrimage to their own cathedral. Who would volunteer to set off the explosion? Who would volunteer for anything? "Where would we get that much explosives?" some wondered. And it went on for many wine soaked hours while the anarchists once more became frustrated with the ideologues. The strategists remained fixed in the crumbling furniture as the details were worked out and discarded item by item until dawn.

Near the end of July, Jean-Pierre announced that it was time to begin planning seriously for their first bank robbery. Money was the issue. Money had not arrived with Dominique since the night of the Caraibes meeting and the New York cash had disappeared with François and the beautiful bartender. The Russian lost interest in Québec politics because he said Québec was more complex than Mother Russia. The Haitians, Dr. André and Rudy, left for Miami. That left liberating cash from banks.

There was growing tension between Dominique and Jean-Pierre. Dominique was also cool and distant with Christian until one night Jean-Pierre steered her toward the ladder to the loft. Her eyes sought out Christian's in the candlelight. She was dressed for the heat and Christian could not help his emotions. Was she entreating him to confront Jean-Pierre and challenge the leader for the prize of the pack? Wow, what a concept, he said to himself as he watched Dominique manage the ladder like a queen ascending her throne. Damn, if only...

Solace for failing to act was a good bottle of Bordeaux. The rest of the group smoked dope and argued about the revolution. The bank robbery was on hold for lack of guns. Instead the talk went around and around until it was decided that another run to Caughnawaga was the only answer. The Mission: to acquire guns and explosives in exchange for a few pounds of marijuana. Hashish was out of the question as economics forced them to lower their sights. Christian voiced his doubts but was told that this was a military operation and the Political Provo should not interfere. He must, however, go along since he had river experience, in case they had to come home the 'chute route'. Henri said he would enlist Vince who had returned to the village because Wacky Gilles was on a mission to the south and it was safe for Vince to contact the suppliers.

Christian drank his Bordeaux, pondering how to avoid the next river run. Fun was fun, but he had no desire for another cruise up the famous St. Lawrence Seaway or down the infamous Lachine Rapids.

Maartyn and Paulo

The argument had been going on for days as they made their way up the coast. "Christian's in Montreal," Maartyn said with conviction.

"I don't give a good god-damn!" Paulo answered as usual. But it was Maartyn's boat. "Y'all can do what ever the hell ya want. I'm goin' to Montreal. And that's the best route," he said, stabbing the Michelin road map that doubled as their chart. It covered the east coast of North America from Newfoundland to the Great Lakes Basin.

The St. Lawrence Seaway is an elaborate and expensive ditch connecting the Atlantic Ocean to the interior of North America. There is also the winding Mississippi River route to the Great Lakes. Hudson Bay is another way into the heartland of North America, but Maartyn was only interested in the one that led to Montreal.

Maartyn limped the *Bayou Queen* north, moving with the Gulf Stream, listening to AM radio stations, jiving to the latest rock'n'roll. They dumped their rotting cargo of marijuana after Paulo tried to dry it on deck, in the salt air, arguing they should head to the sunshine of the Bahamas, but it was too late to turn back, the twelve bails of expensive weed were a mouldy mess, and the Mexicans and the FBI were still looking for them.

In a Georgia bayou, where the battered *Queen* was hiding, they were told that a Louisiana shrimper called the *Bayou Queen*, wanted by the Coast Guard, was last seen heading into a hurricane near Miami. *Be on the lookout*. Crew desperate and probably armed. They laughed.

The boat was in bad shape, and they were short of cash so Maartyn did what he knew best; they dragged for shrimp. The *Bayou Queen* was not licensed but there are buyers in the backwaters. The coasts of Georgia and South Carolina, like the Gulf Coast, are a myriad of creeks and salt marsh harbours where markets are available and few questions asked. Maartyn was determined to go straight, not counting selling illegal shrimp, because he had a plan.

The shrimping was good, so even with a leaky boat, busted

up gear and nets more holes than mesh, they managed to sell enough crustaceans to bankroll repairs. In July they ran the *Queen* ashore in a creek off St. Helena Sound, close to Charleston. They licked their wounds, repaired the leaks and made plans to shrimp their way up the coast to Canada, Maartyn insisted.

It took Maartyn and Paulo weeks to patch up and paint the *Bayou Queen*, rejuvenate the motor, and cut in a registration number lifted off a wrecked shrimper. Her new name was *Delta Queen* and she was a pretty shade of light blue. The owner of the wreck swore that he had never sold the number before. Maartyn was in no position to argue. The paper work was easy enough, for a small fee and Maartyn's prize possession. How he hated to part with Lucille, but Christian had assured him that there was no need for guns in Canada.

Maartyn had no idea what the trip would involve, but he was determined: Christian was in Montreal. Paulo desperately wanted to get home to his Basque enclave, regroup and restart his career.

There was one item on the itinerary that gave them pause. Christian often talked about life in Canada, mainly the weather: relentlessly cold, months of snow, freezing rain, fog, hail and sleet. Maartyn imagined polar bears or moose on Main Street even though he had only a vague notion what a polar bear was and the only moose he had experienced was the truncated head above Juanita's bar, but Paulo believed him and said it was a reason not to go. Although Maartyn was skeptical he argued that Christian meant only in the wintertime. It was summer. In Montreal, Christian had said, it was hot, like the islands. But the fall was lovely. They would shrimp their way to Montreal and settle down for the winter. A piece of cake. The Gulf of St. Lawrence and the river was just another waterway on a big chart of North America, the one that they found during the refit under the skipper's bunk in the big cabin behind the wheelhouse. "We'll leave tonight." 'Tonight's the Night'...Shirelles.

The *Delta Queen*, né *Bayou Queen*, sailed from St. Helena Sound about the time Jean-Pierre's gang was planning the latest abortive gun run to Caughnawaga. Maartyn intended to cruise the coast, shrimping as far as Chesapeake Bay, and New York City, then maybe jig some cod in the Gulf of St. Lawrence. Juanita had salt cod from Newfoundland and they had to pass the cod island on the way to the St. Lawrence River.

The shrimp ran out before they reached New York City but they had enough cash to keep going, fishing to eat, riding the Stream and the tides, nursing the old boat along. Off the coasts of Maine and Nova Scotia they ran into thick fog and had anxious hours getting beyond Sable Island. Paulo, eternally pessimistic about their chances, had heard the stories of shipwrecks from Basque fishermen. By the end of the first week in September they were in the Gulf, turning the corner for Cape North and the estuary. The fall gales were about to descend on the St. Lawrence.

On a beastly day of wind and sleet in mid September, a day that kept the Gulf ferries in North Sidney and Port au Basques, the *Delta Queen* was hammering north reaching for the lee of Anticosti Island to escape the worst of the Nor'wester. Their big chart showed only Port Menier as a possible refuge. Ten miles from the harbour Maartyn spotted a small boat making bad weather in the Strait and he immediately changed course. The old shrimper strained and complained, taking the seas broadside to close with the odd looking vessel.

"It looks like it was blown all the way from France," said Paulo.

"They ain't goin' much further looks like. Their mast's broken an' she's low in the water."

Maartyn put the boat in his lee and eased alongside the floundering replica. It was dangerous work but a good show of seamanship. A small, terrified woman bailing for her life, huddled under a canvas sail in the bilges of the bateau. She began waving frantically but the man at the helm sat stone faced and rigid, clutching the useless tiller, refusing to acknowledge the presence of a rescuer.

"Do y'all need help?"

Finding Breeze O'Keefe

Christian was determined to change course as well.

"We can't admit you without paying tuition, even if you are a former student," said the interesting looking young woman behind the registration table. She had beautiful sea green eyes and wore large black-rimmed glasses. "I'm sorry," she said as if she meant it. Her nametag said, 'Hi, I'm Bridged'. She was dressed in a green velvet jumper over a severe white linen blouse, long black stockings and sandals. A mass of unruly red hair was pulled back and held by a green bow, in dubious submission, ready to spring out at the first opportunity. She had musician's fingers and a million freckles but her face had that high cheek-boned strength that reminded Christian of the Mediterranean, at least somewhere well south of Ireland. A proud mouth and full lips in a perpetual smile set off slightly over lapping front teeth. Christian was in love the moment she spoke. His reply was an invitation for a walk.

It was a perfect Montreal late summer day. "Mind if I take my socks and sandals off?" They walked on the grass beside the path to Mount Royal. Bridged curled her long bare toes deliciously in the grass. "My family name's O'Keefe. You don't get much more Irish Catholic in Montreal.

"*Bridged*? An unusual spelling, isn't it?"

"I'm called after my grandmother, Brigid. We came here from Newfoundland. Béhathook Cove. No one's ever heard of it. A tiny fishing village on a small island, out in the ocean. Mother brought me to Montreal when I was just a baby. We came on a big boat from St. John's and when the customs officer asked for names she said mine's Brigid, but he wrote down *Bridged*. So it was, and so I am."

"It means bridge, literally? Like the Jacques Cartier Bridge?"

She laughed easily. "Mother told me my grandmother was a grand woman. But that was not exactly true, except that she was grand, huge, I mean."

"And who are you?"

"Me? I'm just a shy Newfy girl from the wrong side of the mountain."

"You seem to do fine on this side."

"We adapt well. Grandmother was in love with a sea captain named Sean O'Keefe who died at sea and she became an invalid to compensate because her other lover, my mother's real father, wouldn't leave his wife. I've said too much. I don't know why I'd run off like that, you're a perfect stranger."

"That's okay...go on."

"You actually want to hear about my family?"

"I'm fascinated."

"Mom had to look after Gran night and day. Her own lover, Lliam Dwyer, who thought he was my father, had gone to Boston to become a writer and she longed for him but Lliam's brothers got to her first, just before Lliam returned apparently. One of them, a brother see, is my real father. I don't know which one yet. I think Garret. Mother won't say, but I'll eventually find out. There's a journal written by Lliam. I've read some of it. Don't want to bore you with more of the sordid details of my family, since I'm not supposed to know the truth. I think it would break her heart. She's been mourning one of her lovers at least, since she left Fogo Island with me in her arms. But enough then. I'm in the classical music program."

"Oh," he said, still hanging on the edge of her story. "Do you play an instrument?" he asked. What a stupid question. Her eyes were even deeper green under the trees, and in the dark depths was a story. A past steeped in some kind of Newfoundland Irish mystery. "Sorry, dumb question." Why was he so nervous?

"No, no. Not at all. We also study theory and composition. I want to be a great conductor. Females don't get to conduct."

"Like there's no great woman chefs?"

"Funny, huh? Women are supposed to be in the kitchen, just not in those fawncy restaurants." The word sounded nicely funny through her teeth. She also had a bit of a lisp. He was more in love. "Don't you think that's unfair?"

"Yes," he said. "Women should do what they want to do."

"Exactly!"

"So what do you play?"

"Cello." She made a double passé and blushed deeply between her freckles. "What's your major, if you get in?"

He was imagining her standing before an orchestra; tall, self-assured, but vulnerably pretty. Pretty? Not good enough. Actually, she reminded him of Olive Oil, but he wasn't Popeye the Sailorman. And what did looks have to do with anything? She wasn't beautiful in the Hollywood style, more peasant handsome with those high, proud cheek bones and full lips; the Mediterranean connection. But she was also enough Irish with her red main tossing about in the wind and there was definitely a story. He thought of Renée, Esameralda, Rosa and Dominique, all beautiful and interesting in their own way. Bridged was different. The green jumper didn't reveal much...He found that extremely attractive. Nice hips though. Long legs...Good strong legs and ankles. She moved with an easy grace, like a cat, as if conserving herself for a leap. He found the pace of their walk relaxing. Just idling along toward the mountain, the promise of fall in the air. A weather shift from the Canadian Shield where the Northern forests would be turning yellow and gold. He imagined her red hair and green dress against a bed of golden leaves...

"My mother loves music. She sings about a wild woman called Grace O'Malley, the Pirate Queen of Ireland? I'm not sure if Grace O'Malley's real, but some day I hope to find out. Hi? Am

I boring you?"

"No! Sorry, I was just thinking about...something." It was Christian's turn to blush. Then she took his hand.

"You're very nice, but something's troubling you."

Christian felt his face burning. Dizzy, off balance, but not from the usual cause. "Did I tell you my name?"

"It was on your application. Christian James Joyce."

"Oh, yeah. I forgot..."

"I asked what your major is."

"Haven't decided. What's your full name?"

"You'll laugh. Bridged Mary Pearly-Moon Ortiz, after my gran. They call me Briddie because I don't like Bridged. Who would?"

He wondered about the Ortiz, the Mediterranean connection. Maybe Spain or the Balearic Islands "Bridge, as in crossing over. Briddie? That's better?" He was transiting a deep sea.

"I don't like Briddie, either."

"Oh, okay. What should I call you then?"

"Breeze, after my mother. What's your choice?"

"That's perfect. Bridge over troubled waters is good, but Breeze of wind in your sails is better."

"I wish. Do you sail?"

"No. I know almost nothing about boats, but they seem to keep protruding into my life. It's just that, well, my situation is a little…complex."

"I know." She squeezed his hand. "You're searching. Conflicted by something. You want to enroll, but don't have the money. There was no address, but you are from Montreal."

"How do you know all that?"

"Your accent. It's mixed up. You can't decide if you're from Ireland, France, Québec or the Caribbean, but, yes, Montreal. What's your story?"

Rats! Couldn't they just walk into the sunset holding hands forever? He didn't want to bare his soul, but he decided to tell her everything. Well, almost everything. Everything except about Sartre and Renée. But, he would have to tell her about Renée..."Okay, but first, tell me what you most want to do, besides conduct an orchestra."

"Some day I want to sail to Ireland," she said assuredly, "and be a pirate like Grace O'Malley." They both laughed.

Later: Story told, and in a quiet interval, they were lying under the stars in the shadow of the Cross on the Mount, the evening strollers indulgently ignoring the couple sprawled on the grass. It was one of those clear, fragrant, late summer nights he tried to explain to his Cuban friends. Bridged, Breeze, was tucked into his arm, her body warm and close. "Well, Christian James Joyce, that's quite a tale. And now you're here with me, and we've known each other for, oh, hours and hours and I feel I've known you all my life." She turned and kissed him on the lips.

He felt that excruciating pain of happiness, then suddenly and without warning, fear. Why had he told her so much? A personality disorder since childhood. The diagnosis...an unstable person, fumbling along the highway of early adulthood, without the adult along for the ride. And was it going too fast? "Wow, that was nice." Nice? It was amazing. "You're amazing."

"You don't know much about me. I could be a pathological liar with a husband and kids at home."

"No, I don't think so. Your fingers."

"Oh, those. You have them too. From that guitar, the Cuban jazz master, Old Jocinto?" She touched his cheek with her calloused fingertips. Electricity shot through him. Face on fire again. "And I'd love to meet Juanita. A tragedy about Rosameralda. But Esameralda sounds very, interesting. Are you unhappy because she's a nun?"

"No, not really," he answered honestly. At least he wouldn't have to keep bringing Bridged, Breeze, up to date. She knew all the characters in the Cuban story. Already had him down, like a music score. Could play him by ear, fine tuning the relationship. Whoa. Slow down. This isn't a relationship. "Where are you from?" he asked to move the narrative in her direction.

"Montreal West. Like you, but further out. St. Charles, the Irish ghetto. Mother's husband's family settled in St. Charles about eighteen fifty-five, just escaped Dublin in time."

"My family's from Dublin too. I don't know much about my history, except that I have uncles in the IRA."

"Me too. We have much in common, Christian Joyce."

"I'm not sure that's a great thing. The IRA connection, I mean. They're not a thing to brag about."

She laughed with a lilt not that far removed from the Green Isle, by way of Newfoundland. "I suppose not. But with your background in rebellions and all, aren't you a little sympathetic?"

"I don't know. Ireland's so complex and tragic. I'd like to go to Ireland to trace the family though. Montreal isn't home," he said sadly because he knew it was true.

"Okay. Let's go. First to Fogo Island so I can find my New-foundland ancestors and then to Ireland to see what they're rebel-ling about. Mom said she used to stand on the shore and pretend she was sailing over the ocean. There was an old schooner on her beach that she wanted to fix up, then her lover, Lliam, began building his own, to escape she suspected. He never did until lured away by the IRA and the schooner unfinished. Dreams. Well, I'm going to do it! Want to come along?"

"Sure...why not." That seemed to be settled. "Going home." He was going home, with Breeze. He didn't like the boat idea, however. He had a different plan.

"I'd take you home tonight, but my step father...you know. Mother would probably love you, but she's stricken with grief. Has been since I was born. Some day she may recover. Hey, I know! We could take her to Ireland with us. She'd love that!" She laughed again. "What will you do, tonight I mean?"

"I'm staying with Jean-Pierre, temporarily."

"Avoid Dominique. She's trouble. I've an idea. There's a friend on the student paper, The Harbinger. They're very political but they pay. You'd be perfect."

And that was settled too. Breeze set her red hair free. He wanted it to be perfect. "Have you read Sartre?"

"No, not yet."

"Good. I advise against it."

"But I have a minor in philosophy. We're doing Hegel and Kierkegaard this term."

"Oh, does it stop there?" he asked, hopefully.

"Next term we do Nietzsche and Sartre."

"Then we have a few months grace."

"What do you have against Sartre?"

"Nothing, really, everything..."

They kissed, deeply, and he could feel her body trembling. He thought of Mathieu and Marcelle...Go away Mathieu, Marcelle and Sartre. This is not the same thing.

Baby Sean or Muirgheal (Muriel)

Love has a compelling momentum of its own and once set in motion there is no stopping or going back: "I think I'm pregnant," she said without warning or drama. They were sitting in a coffee shop near the University, holding hands across the small table. Bridged had a new glow under her freckles.

"Breeze...?" The news caused an avalanche of emotions in Christian though. "Are you sure?"

"No, I said, 'I think's I'm pregnant, my dear,'" she answered easily, slipping into Newfoundland inflexions with a smile.

"Yes, you did say..."

"It was probably that first time on the mountain. What was a poor lass to do? My mom got pregnant on a hill overlooking the ocean. One of Lliam's brothers, just before Lliam returned to the cove. Garret I suspect. There were icebergs in the distance and a cold wind off the sea, but it was warm on the juniper mat, in the sun and she thought she could see Ireland. It's in the journal. Lliam's part in the affair, where he thinks he did it."

"Oh, wow! Isn't it weird to read about yourself being conceived? By whoever. Jesus Christ," he whispered. His brain was doing loops. "Do you mind, being pregnant?"

"Christian, you *are* funny. One doesn't mind or not. It's a case of being pregnant and getting on like."

"But, are you okay with it?"

"Well, it will make playing the cello some problematic."

"I suppose it will," he said vaguely, amazed by her calmness. He laughed self-consciously. She was smiling through those perplexing eyes with the mystery yet to be revealed. Lovely, deep pools of green, like the ocean near the shore, and he wanted to make love...

"I'll call him Sean. That's very Irish. Or Michael, after Michael Collins. Or maybe after Garret, who I think is my father. Or Grace after Grace O'Malley or Muirgheal, means 'bright as the sea', Mom says."

Suddenly he wondered what he would do with Maartyn.

The Dilemma: Friends and Poseurs

The *Delta Queen*, bearing Maartyn and Paulo, arrived in Victoria Basin out of the blue, with the Poseurs in tow. Then Breeze announced she was pregnant. Then Mathieu was back. *When Marcelle told Mathieu about the baby, Mathieu saw his last chance for freedom fly into the bleak Paris night.* And Christian, like Mathieu, was earth-rooted, a dumb tree. Christian wasn't sure freedom was the problem. He had to experience a place of confinement before he could suffer the need to flee. He was confined in his own body by circumstances. Renée would quote Sartre and say he must learn to live with his earthly burden and make the best of it. Leaving the loft was just logistics, and the complication of money. Maartyn was a complication too. The return of the Princess and Gargoire were complications, as weird coincidences often are. Jean-Pierre, Gerard and his job at the student paper were also complications. And there was the complication of Dominique who tried to seduce Christian when she suspected he had a lover. Although Bridged had been kept a secret, women have infallible intuitions to match their instinct to protect what they claim. Dominique's response was to attack Sprudence just to distract him, so he thought. The fight was savage enough. Tall Dominique on top of small but powerful Sprudence. The shrieking and scratching. Hair flew.

It all began the week before with the sudden arrival of Maartyn, Paulo and the *Delta Queen*, né *Bayou Queen*. Christian watched the familiar shrimp boat approach the Market Basin from the loft windows. The colour was different, light blue instead of dirty, rusty white, but the shape was unmistakable. There was not a vessel like her for thousands of miles. Probably one had never been seen on the River especially towing a replica bateau. And there was Paulo at the bow with a dock line, and Gargoire standing beside him, refusing to help, not surprisingly. Then Christian realized Gargoire was not helping because his hands were tied. It was a surreal tableau and Christian's early warning chills returned.

Christian and Maartyn had much to talk about: the details of the trip from Florida, the rescue of Sprudence and Gargoire, or their capture, and what to do with the escapees. Jean-Pierre wanted to shoot them on the spot and throw them in the river. Paulo, recognizing a kindred spirit, and vowing to never set foot on a boat again, introduced himself to Jean-Pierre and convinced him to retire to someplace safe and get stoned.

Later, Paulo, sufficiently drugged and exhausted from the trip, was asleep on the mouldering couch near the spool table. Gargoire was installed on a chair tied to one of the posts holding up the loft so that his hands were free to feed himself. Princess Sprudence cringed in a corner, sobbing, still clutching the case as if her life depended on the bogus guitar.

"We should kill them both," said Jean-Pierre when he recovered from his introduction to Paulo. "Traitors! Thieves!"

"Whoa, they only took my guitar and some money."

"They stole my block of hash. They stole the fucking boat! Anti-revolutionary actions that require strong measures to deter enemies of the movement from further treachery!"

Jean-Pierre had become a raging tyrant since his last fight with Dominique over money and loyalty. The dwindling cash from Outremount was not sufficient to buy the explosives they needed to bring down Place Ville-Marie before the construction was finished; the mission they had finally agreed upon as the ultimate statement, and there was no money from New York. He was suspicious of everyone's commitment to the cause, especially since the second river run failed. At St. Lambert Lock a dockhand tipped off Jacques that 'they' were waiting for him at Caughnawaga. Didn't say who 'they' were. The summer revolution sputtered with the declining revolutionary zeal, especially after the beginning of the university fall term. He snapped at Christian when his Political Provo advocated more politics and less violence. But by this time Christian had met Bridged, and he was in a quandary as to how to extricate himself from the group. One moment Jean-Pierre would threaten to kill him if he left and then threatened to kill him if he didn't. Then he would lecture about the Political Provo's job: be political, turn over his stash and shut up about the bombing plans. Jean-Pierre seemed in danger of imploding from angst and confusion. And, after a screaming argument, Henri left Jean-Pierre's chaotic cadre to form his own group, the Front de Libération du Québec.

Now Jean-Pierre and Henri were rivals. Comrade against comrade competing for followers. The English capitalists forgotten for the moment in bitter enmity. Dominique encouraged the rivalry by threatening to align with Henri, and sleep with him as well as finance his cause. This would send Jean-Pierre into fits of rage or silent depression. Christian tried to mediate and at the same time, figure out what Dominique was up to.

To add to the confusion, Christian was pressured by the college newspaper to do an exposé on the underground groups and create a detailed file on each member. They would pay for his research. Christian wondered why, but did as he was asked, writing good articles about anarchy in Québec but reporting only sketchy details about the clumsy attempts at sabotage and bank robberies without actually naming the members involved. So he felt guilty for doing his job without revealing vital details. But most of all he hated his disorderly, dirty, dangerous home in the warehouse.

Bridged, he only thought of her as Breeze now, was a haven of grace in a swamp of ugliness. Each morning he retreated from the warehouse to Bridged's embrace. They could walk and talk or be securely silent. In good weather they made love in the dry autumn leaves on the Mount. On cool, wet days they would sit in the coffee shop and dream about far away places like green, uncomplicated Ireland. Or talk about Fogo Island and the mystery of Bridged's ancestry or the whereabouts of his own family. And there was the promise of warm Cuba with some good memories. Bridged held Christian up like a lifeguard in a sea of sharks. And there was the baby.

They hadn't actually talked about their own future. Nor had Christian whispered a word about Bridged to his warehouse friends; did not want her brought down to the level of the slovenly anarchists. Nor could he tell suspicious Dominique who became increasing enigmatic. For Christian it was not the problem of the eternal triangle. He loved Bridged. He did not trust Dominique, realizing early on that one pursues a Dominique at one's peril or is possessed by her fatally. But the other eternal problem for a young man is raw physical attraction and Dominique, unquestionably attractive in the animal sense, made it clear that she was willing to mate with the strongest male of the pack but she was the Alpha female.

The dilemma for Christian was advanced by a suggestion.

"Let's get an apartment," said Bridged one night as they strolled the streets of Montreal. The weather was cool and damp. Fall threatening to crash into that difficult period known as pre-Montreal-winter, the time before Indian Summer. Bridged was avoiding the long bus ride back to St. Charles alone but was worried about Christian's fragile existence with the anarchists.

"That would be great," agreed Christian, "but we can't afford it." It was unlike Christian to consider the material aspects of life.

"I have my scholarship."

"No, you need that next semester."

"I could get a job too."

"I have a job, but the newspaper hasn't paid me anything yet."

"Then demand your money."

Christian sensed a turning point. His situation in the group of anarchists was a problem, not a solution to being. He had fallen in with Jean-Pierre by accident. There was nothing about manifest destiny in the meeting. Or was there? What had pulled him down to the river that day? Fate? He didn't believe in fate or otherworldly forces. Then what was his meeting with Bridged? Luck. He willed himself to the University that day to register so he had a choice. Meeting Bridged was only a consequence of the process. Really? Their attraction was so compelling that Christian felt no such freedom of choice, wondering what force of nature draws two people together like electromagnets, complete with sparks? The moment he looked into Bridged's eyes he was captivated, but not trapped. No Existential bullcrap allowed to mess with their spirits. He was not like Sartre's Mathieu, constantly analyzing his impossible relationship with Marcelle, and his imagined loss of freedom. It was just situational, a problem of logistics.

He had to leave the group but Jean-Pierre, suspicious of everyone's actions, would ask questions. Dominique could also be a problem. She continued to torment Christian with her beauty. And Jean-Pierre began to threaten them both. The trap for Christian was the thin security of the group. The Provos received 'expense money', supplied by Dominique. Christian survived day to day on stipends. The job on the student paper was still a promise dangled like a carrot on a stick. He worked hard on his writing as a diversion, to put in time while waiting to meet with Bridged. The Harbinger paid his tuition, which made him obliged to the paper, but he received no actual money. It was always about to happen, until the day he announced, on Bridged's urgings, that he could no longer work without expenses. Suddenly there was cash in his hand. It made the apartment decision easier but then Maartyn would be adrift again, or worse, move in with them. For better or worse Paulo had disappeared one night, and though somewhat relieved, Christian felt responsible for him too. Then there was Gargoire, still a captive in the loft, making threats of his own. He was a menace, difficult to bear but too unstable to set free. And Jean-Pierre brandished a handgun, threatening to kill Gargoire so often Christian began to wonder. His sense of the ethical treatment of humans no matter their crimes caused him guilt feelings. They were holding the man hostage, against his will. And, as an accessory, Sprudence, a blubbering annoyance, tormented them all by playing the guitar and wailing between fits of self-pity. Her mental state had deteriorated even further. Unfortunately Christian had not bothered to reclaim the guitar, perhaps out of sympathy for the lost soul. Nor had he demanded his money which he assumed was still in the guitar case. He did mention it to Maartyn one morning before the others were awake.

"It was Paulo. Ya know, I recognized your guitar and knew something was up. But Paulo took the money, man," Maartyn said. "That funny old Canadian stuff was in your knapsack. He

204

went through everything an' that's how we knew for sure it was yours, the little book you write in?"

"He did give me the book. No mention of money."

"I was busy just getting them and the boats up the river. Man, how did I know Paulo was such a lousy friend?"

"That's okay. You didn't know."

"I'm really sorry, man."

"I said it's okay. I never felt comfortable with Juanita's money anyway. I plan to repay her someday."

"You will."

He felt safer with Maartyn in the gang but Maartyn was having his own problems. Jean-Pierre befriended Maartyn because he wanted his boat. Petit Jacques had shifted *Elloise* downriver to Québec City after the last botched run to Caughnawaga. Vince was dead. Shot on the Reserve they said, just an internal feud. People seemed to go in and out of Christian's life in chaotic, disorderly ways. Christian missed Gerard who had vanished into the Haitian community. He worried that Gerard would be caught by the police or worse, the Ton ton Macoute. Maybe he followed his brother François to New York. There was a rumour on the street; the cabbies hinted that Gerard lead a group of exiles into New York State through Caughnawaga and were caught in the gunfight that killed Vince. The old gang was breaking up. He had to laugh at that.

Sunday: Christian was looking forward to meeting Bridged at the University, but Maartyn had a plan of his own.

"I'm splittin', man," Maartyn announced that morning after a frenzied Saturday night session of anarchist infighting. Dangerous looking recruits with guns had stood behind Jean-Pierre who ranted more than lectured; the rhetoric running to the demand for increased violence until Christian wondered if he and Maartyn should shift to Henri's FLQ for safety. Henri's bunch seemed more focused, were occupying a house in suburban Longueuil and had better financing. But they were still anarchists determined to change Québec by violent means. "This shit's just too crazy. I'm checking out."

"I know. I want out too."

"An' it's gettin' cold, man. Come south with me."

"Can't leave." He knew Maartyn deserved the full story. "There's a girl, and a baby."

Maartyn's eyes went wide, then he frowned "A girl? A baby? Yours?" A slow, wide smile brightened his face. "I get it, *daddyo*. An obligation. You taught me that word."

"It's okay. I'm fine with it. I just need a place for us."

"The *Queen's* yours."

"No thanks! What would I do with your boat?"

"I'm not taking her down river this time of year. She just needs someone to look after her, while I'm gone, like."

Christian didn't have an answer for Maartyn's dilemma. "Where will you go?"

"Maybe back to Cuba an' look up Rosa."

"Maartyn, I have to tell you something…"

"I know, man, she's too much woman for this ol' Louisiana boy. She's probably got that machine gun guy." Maartyn blinked and shrugged.

"It's not that. Rosameralda's…Rosa died in a gun battle near Havana. Miguel said she mentioned you. Sent her love." It was a lie, he never lied, but what harm would it do to say it? "I'm sorry, Maartyn, I know how you feel."

"Oh, man! Not Rosa! She…" Maartyn looked away.

"I shouldn't have told you, but I didn't want you to go looking for her, thinking anything."

"Then I'm just goin' home. The Delta. Take my chances with the FBI. Couldn't be worse than this fuck up."

There was a finality to the announcement. It was the first time in his life he realized he might be closing the book on a relationship. Friends were forever, weren't they? "I'm sorry, Maartyn, things didn't work out. It was a long trip for nothing."

"Hey, man, it's okay. I didn't have anything else goin', ya know?"

"You're a good friend."

"I don't know. I'm supposed to give you something, from Renée." He took a tattered envelope out of his pocket and offered it to Christian. "I wasn't sure if I should, you know. I knew you was broken up about her."

"What's this?" Christian asked, hoping it wasn't money.

"Kind'a one of them John Deere letters. She gave it to me before she left Havana with that guy, Ramon. Said if I every saw you again…"

"You didn't come all this way just to deliver a letter?"

"Sure. Why not? First class service, huh punk." He punched Christian on the shoulder and turned away to give him privacy.

Christian turned to the dusty light of window to read Renée's saltwater stained letter written in her flowing, private school script.

The Letter

Bayou Queen. Havana. January 12, 1959

My Dearest Christian:

Forgive me for leaving you like this. Cuba and our lives here have become surreal and yet too real. One cannot live through what we have just experienced without being touched deeply, forever. I found great friends in you and the girls. Esy and I said goodbye that night at the Ché Hospital and I promised to see her again. Say goodbye to Rosameralda for me. Rosa is special, but distant. I could not get as close. I love Esy so much and miss her dearly. There was much to love about Los Espiritos and Cuba, but with the war and everything, it could never be the same.

Today, here on the deck of Maartyn's boat, I am the pure Ex-

istentialist. This place, this boat defines my existence, has brought me to this reality, and yet I recoil from that reality, and choose to see it as non-existence. I have seen enough to know despair but do not feel it. I will pass through one day and perhaps know life, but never joy. Dostoevsky said, 'suffering is the origin of conscious-ness'. But Sartre says, 'that life begins on the other side of des-pair'. And I say, despair is the daughter of love. It is too late for joy and yet, and yet I accept, as Sartre says, the despair of life. And love as it happens, as it was for us. Do you remember our talks on the beach at Andros? You were very angry with me about philosophers and I said 'Philosophers need to ask the questions that open our eyes to possibilities'. I didn't say they were always right. And you said you think philosophers ask too many ques-tions; questions that don't need to be asked and give answers that don't add much to our understanding. Then you said, 'If we make love and you feel the experience do we need Sartre to explain why my body enters yours or how you know it's me?' I couldn't an-swer you then, and I'm only a little closer now, Christian my rambunctious young goat, stay with Sartre, and one day he will reveal all.

I don't know if we can ever be the same again but I do love you in a large part of me. But, Christian, as you know there are other parts of me yet to open. We have had a very interesting journey and of all the boys I could have shared it with I am so glad I shared it with you. You have a quality that, even though you are very young and confused, and need to mature, will get you through and I hope will keep you well. Your innocence is en-riching, especially when I feel at times so overly used and know too much about the world and the people I meet, even before I meet them. But you, Christian, were always a nice surprise.

Ramon means nothing to me. A diversion. He wants to show me his New York and I'll show him my Paris, we'll fuck of course, and then I'll kiss him goodbye with no regrets. I hope you can un-derstand.

Please come to me in Paris in the spring, or the fall. Isle St. Louis is magic at any time. The Left Bank and Monmartre only steps away. We'll walk to the footbridge and see Notre Dame at night, as we planned...

My love always...RJ

He wondered if the salty marks were her tears. When he turned from the window, a misty veil over his eyes, Maartyn was gone. Maartyn could do that; marine training, his style to just vanish without a sound, or arrive the same way. He put the letter in his pocket, remembering a passage from Sartre. *'You do not put your past in your pocket. You have to have a house.'* Maybe he understood that one. You need a place to store up your experiences, the collection of memories, not material goods. He had nothing but allusions to places and people. The footbridge? He had crossed it once, before Renée. That was the summer after he entered McGill, the first time. He had hopped on a tramp freighter in Montreal Harbour and worked a passage to Rotterdam and hitched rides to Paris. Tried to work into the Paris jazz scene but he was too young, too unhip, and came home disillusioned but vowed to return. Then he tried Chicago. Then the Islands and found Renée. They had talked about Notre Dame and the footbridge so often on those warm, soft Andros nights. She said her own island in the Seine was the center of the Universe. It was a dream shared. But now there is Bridged and the baby, and a future as ethereal as morning mist.

He wandered down to the Market Basin hoping to find Maartyn. The *Delta Queen* was there, with her own cargo of memories, taking the space left by the *Elloise*, looking quite dead in her peeling blue paint; like a ruined drag queen coming apart after the cabaret riot. And tied alongside was the bateau, broken stump of a mast defiantly poking up like the finger salute. "Well, fuck you too," he said to no one in particular. Sartre lurked...Bridges, Bridged, 'Saint Brigid, pray for me'.

Then he drifted further west along Rue de la Commune and dropped down to the service road along the industrial quays. The grain boats were silent. Even the harbour was very quiet except for an obscenely large American yacht poking along the far shore, heading home to Toledo, a rich Great Lakes Steel Port.

But it was Sunday in October, his time in Montreal. Air crisp and clear. He wandered out on Quay Jacques Cartier, the quay his boat left from on his first journey to the Old World, and the same he returned to after the summer of disappointments in Europe. He felt empty, then as now. He read Renée's letter again, waiting for some sign or feeling. There was perhaps the beginning of a dull ache that told him almost nothing. What is the reason for the nothing? Does there have to be a reason? Oh, shit! Sartre again. He had to warn Bridged. "Don't do it!" he screamed at a seagull cruising by the grain elevators. "Should set Renée's letter adrift in the current. Send it back to France, or Cuba." The current swirling around the knuckle of the quay was repulsive and the dark water offered nothing so the letter stayed in his pocket. He decided to tell Bridged about the letter. Bridged would understand about Renée.

Later that day: Bridged didn't understand; she was furious. They were taking the last of the good sun, lying on a bed of crimson and yellow leaves. It was Indian Summer-warm. She, hormones boiling, wanted to make love. He, weighed down by the letter, wanted to draw her closer to his world. A perfect day in a perfect universe and he was stupid enough to show her the letter.

She read it quickly, turning as red as the leaves, crumpled it and threw it down the slope. "I don't want to know anything more about your French pastry, that eternal cherry-less tart! I don't care if she was reading the Kama Sutra at eight years old and lost her virginity to the gardener's son at twelve. Don't care! Don't give a flying fig!"

Christian retreated into silence. Had he misjudged Bridged's big hearted understanding of his complex life in progress? What did he expect would be her reaction? A big wet kiss on the forehead?

The sun was going down through the bare trees behind the Mount, painting the eastern shore of the river from Chateaugay to Sorel, shades of gold and orange, with green and silver accents, and dabs of cadmium red roofs. The light was intensely clear. The Sunday homecoming traffic crawling along the Autoroute toward the bridges sounded close. Bridged turned away and fumed silently while he pouted, until, finally...

"I'm sorry, Christian. My hormones are a little riled today. Breakfast wasn't much fun. I threw up and had to tell a lie. Church was excruciating. Mother hates going but her husband's family are so religious they might as well be Orthodox. I'd kill for a coffee."

Christian put his hand gently on her tummy. "That's okay. I understand."

"Really? And how many times have you been pregnant?" Her green eyes sparkled and there was a hint of a laugh in her voice. He was forgiven.

"How many times for you?" he asked with a sigh of relief.

"Six. Drowned them all like kittens."

"Sure. So, your parents don't know yet?"

"If they did my stepdad would be standing over you with his blunderbuss."

"Great. Does he actually have one?"

"Oh, yes. His father brought it from the Old Country. Said it was just the thing for close-in work. Street gangs, you see? Gran'father and some other men would go up to Belfast to torment the Ulster boys. It was a time the English wouldn't allow the born Irish Catholics to have guns, so the 'blunder' was carried in a blanket, like a baby. It was short, but awful, if you know what I mean?"

"I get it."

He didn't like to hear his Breeze talk about guns and killing. There should be no violence in their perfect world. Three important women in his life had been forced to bear arms and one was dead. So far away from his new world, here on the Mount, in his city, beside a woman he loved, and yet, the violence was just a decision away. At the warehouse and in other underground enclaves, death and destruction were being plotted by intense young Québécois who felt it was their time to revenge the shame of defeat and assimilation. Breeze was right. He did feel some kinship with the Irish as well as Jean-Pierre and Henri. There are many wrongs in a sad world that need to be set right. The downtrodden need a future and there must be leaders, and there would be bloodshed, but Jean-Pierre was too dangerous and his story could only end in tragedy. Christian, once again near the center of a revolutionary storm, wanted to flee to safety with Breeze but he felt in his heart there was no real escape...the inevitability of life on the run, but not fate. Their parting that night was long and tearful.

He woke some time after three a.m. and crept to the loft area. The others were sleeping or unconscious from substance abuse. Gargoire was dozing, slumped in his chair, still bound hand and foot, allowed only bathroom privileges under guard. Jean-Pierre insisted that the traitor remain a captive in this classic way, like a prisoner chained to a post in a town square. Pilloried. Even the repulsive Gargoire didn't deserve being humiliated, Christian rationalized.

Christian had argued with Jean-Pierre about the treatment of the couple regardless of their crimes. Jean-Pierre flew into the usual rage, threatening everyone in sight with the handgun until Christian believed he would shoot Gargoire, or someone, eventually. Gargoire appeared defiant but his dark eyes showed real fear.

Christian felt sorry for the pathetic poseur who tried so hard to keep up the hard front, desperately trying not to show the gut wrenching paranoia. He stirred at Christian's approach. "Gargoire? I'm going to..."

"Leave me alone. I don't need you."

"*Shhh*. Don't talk. I'm just going to cut your ropes," whispered Christian. "Leave quietly. Just go and keep going." He used his utility knife to slice through the thick hemp rope. It took time. He felt threatened by Gargoire, knowing that the man could turn on him in a moment. Gargoire said nothing when the job was done, just stood up and began to ransack the kitchen area. Typical, thought Christian, but they are survivors. He couldn't imagine them surviving well, just scrounging and stealing their way through life. Gargoire, the name, sounded like gargoyle. Gargoire, the young man, looked like a gargoyle. The pinched face of an old man tortured by rage and resentment. The image forever etched in Christian's vision of one of life's odd and destructive encounters. History and the future would not be kind to Gargoire who left without bothering to wake his mate.

Christian woke the Princess. "You can go, now. Quietly. Take the guitar, it's yours."

When they had gone Christian shut the door carefully, but defiantly left it unlocked, and then shuffled back to his chair passing the couch where Maartyn had slept the night before. Gargoire was out of his life for good, he hoped, but with Maartyn gone he felt vulnerable again. He lay awake until dawn thinking about Dominique asleep in the loft above, Renée in Paris, Esmeralda in a Cuban convent, and longed to be with Breeze so he could sleep with his hand on her smooth growing belly.

The Decision Made

They were walking aimlessly east on Boulevard de Maisonneuve to Rue St. Denis, enjoying the sunny, cool weather. They stopped at a Jewish deli market to get a lunch. "I want to see where you live," said Breeze as they picked through the interesting offerings in the deli. The shop was small but the ethnic choice was good. An old man with a mane of white hair like Albert Einstein, wearing a clean white apron over his dark suit, waited patiently for them to make their selections, nodding approval when Breeze pointed to the pastrami. He was proud of his smoked meat section. He puffed a cigar slowly and had the air of a man who was indifferent about life, as if he had eternity on his side. It was dark in the store and he stood in front of a small side window so that the smoke blurred his silhouette. Although the deli was clean the smoke reminded Christian of his dirty, smoke filled loft.

"No, Breeze, you don't want to see where I live."

"I do. And I want to meet your friends."

"You definitely don't want to meet my so called friends."

"Are you ashamed of them?"

"You know everything about them, you tell me."

"Ahh, you don't want me to see Dominique. Is she that beautiful?"

"She's...interesting."

"That's evasive enough." Breeze selected plump bagels and ordered pastrami and kosher beef, sliced thin. "Pickles please. Big ones." Pointing to the jar on the shelf. "The garlic ones. Yes, those. Three, no, four. And mayonnaise. I've had this craving lately. Never liked pickled things usually. My mom tried to get me to eat salt herring. *Yuk.*"

"Try the gefilte fish, my dear. Or herring and sour cream, eh? Or mayo, delicious," offered the old Jew. "Don't tell the rabbi but..."

"Now I think I could eat herring. Put enough mayo on I'll eat anything, even salt cod."

"That's your Newfoundland heritage showing," Christian said.

"No, that's my tummy showing. Have you ever had salt fish?"

"Actually I have, in Cuba. An old dried cod that was out of water about twenty years. A gift from Juanita. It's all we had to eat for days."

"Then Fogo won't be a surprise, my dear," she said with a definite accent.

"Hot mustard? Make it myself with a little horseradish, for a kick. That's my joke for the day."

She laughed. "Yes, please," said Breeze, "and lots of butter." The old gentleman buttered the bagels with a spatula from a tub he kept aside, carefully covered the butter with the dark mustard with whole mustard seeds, then wrapped them separate from the meat, slipping in two big soft pretzels with a wink at Christian. "Thank you." Christian dug into his jeans for the last of his change.

"Now, we need wine to go with this," said Breeze surveying the small collection on the shelves behind the counter. The dusty bottles were stored on their side: vintage wines of good breeding. "But my goodness...!" she exclaimed scanning the labels. "Oh, it's all so expensive."

"Should you drink wine?" Christian noted that the wines were of surprisingly good vintage and not all that expensive given their age and quality.

The old gentleman bent down below the counter and came up with a whiskey bottle of red wine. There was a screw top and no label. "This I also make myself. Grow the grapes in the yard. It's on the sweet side, like your liqueur, but. My wife always had a small glass with Sunday dinner. We raised seven kids. All healthy."

"Oh, then it should be okay. How much?" she asked counting change.

"A gift. My wife died not long after our last child."

"I'm sorry. Thank you for the wine. We'll do all our shopping here. Are there any apartments for rent in this area?"

"My child, my child, you are expecting a baby? No, no, no. You would not want to winter in anything you could afford in this area. A walk-down, eh? Too damp."

"You're right. I never want to live in a basement."

"If you don't find anything, come back. I'll rent you half of my flat. It's right above." He pointed up with a crooked finger. "I'm alone now and live small."

"Thank you," she said. "You're very generous. What's your name?"

"Haim. Haim Goldman. Goldie, eh? My wife was a Liebermann. We're from Austria, before that Poland, and so on, but... we came here before the war. Rebecca, my wife, may her soul rest with Him, her parents knew something was going to happen, the Germans, yes? They begged us to emigrate. They were supposed to join us, but...my own parents too, and three brothers. All gone, to work camps. We're the lucky ones, eh? Three of our children were born in Austria, and one on the boat?" He's in the Navy. The old gentleman smiled sadly.

They walked on with their deli goods and a blessing from Goldie, looking for a place to eat. The weakening sun was doing its best to warm Montreal's side streets.

"The old man's very lonely," sighed Breeze.

"Yeah. He misses his wife and family."

"What if we don't find anything not damp, should we...?"

"Yes, we have an offer from Haim. Where would you like to eat?" asked Christian, hoping she would want to stop at a bench in the good sun.

"By the river. After we visit your place."

"Believe me, you don't want to see the warehouse." The mood had deepened since leaving the deli. "He sees people everyday, but it's not the same thing."

"I wonder what's become of his children?"

"Grown up and moved away. Professionals or failures. You know, living well, or ashamed. Too busy to visit dad." He felt a pang of guilt. He should find his own family. His only family is Bridged, or Breeze, and a baby, but is it safe to think of her in that way? They had talked about the future in vague terms. Marriage was not mentioned. What could he offer a woman like Breeze? She doesn't need him as much as he needs her, he admitted. But there is the baby and obligations. They walked in their own thoughts for a few blocks, always descending toward the Market Basin.

Breeze studied the imposing, shabby mass of the warehouse. "You're right, I don't want to visit that. Let's find some grass near the river."

Christian was relieved. "There isn't much grass. Just concrete and dirt, mostly. But there is a boat."

"Your friend's boat?"

"The *Bayou Queen*. But she's not much better than the loft."

The *Delta Queen*, né *Bayou Queen*, was a mess. The hard voyage from Louisiana had left the *Queen* looking like a royal wreck, the remnants of a palace coup. Even to a landlubber's eye she seemed unfit to travel.

Christian noted with relief that the bateau was no longer tied alongside the *Queen*. But with the odd couple went Jocinto's guitar and another connection to Cuba. He helped Breeze over the rail and handed her the paper bag. "Not much to look at."

Breeze surveyed the cluttered wooden deck, appraising, as if they had been shown a shoddy house by a real estate agent who had vanished, embarrassed by the fraud. Breeze put down the bag and kicked a stanchion, causing a loud but dull *thud*.

"Breeze? What are you thinking about?"

She kicked another stanchion. There was another resistant

thud. She went about kicking stanchions and tugging on gear. "She's sound. Like a neglected but well crafted cello."

"How can you tell just from kicking things?"

"Same as testing an instrument. You tap it and listen. The quality of the reverberations will tell you. And she is still afloat."

Christian climbed aboard with some misgivings. Breeze opened the wheelhouse door stepping carefully over the high sill. He followed, reluctantly, stepping over junk scattered about. Maartyn would never leave his boat in this condition, he said to himself. Vandals had scoured the boat for loot and there was evidence of drunks and drug users. Breeze was out the other door heading forward. She opened the fore hatch and climbed down into the stifling galley, a shambles like the wheelhouse, with the addition of mouldy smells. She cleared a space on the grimy table and set the paper bag down, then she was off further forward to the crew cabin. A darker, mustier space, with two tiers of bunks; another disaster of scattered clothing and soggy matrasses. There was a separate toilet room, inexplicably called the 'head', so said the sign on the door; also unspeakably filthy.

"Why don't we just eat on deck in the sun?"

"I want to see the rest of your boat." And she was off again, up the ladder, leaving their lunch behind. "Come on. What's back there?" she asked, kicking things as she went.

"Breeze? It's just a filthy old boat that even Maartyn gave up on." And it was a vessel too crowded with memories, even though his time aboard the *Queen* was restricted to a few minutes one evening helping Maartyn load the bodies of the Cubans into the skiff. That time he would have gladly remained on board and sent the Cubans adrift to find their own final resting place. He remembered the smell, not much worse than the present odour. He felt sick but grabbed the paper bag and pursued Breeze up the ladder.

She was down another ladder into the engine room but Breeze was at bay, momentarily, confronted with the great silent engine and all the attendant wires, pipes and gauges. Breeze shrugged. "I don't know about any of this stuff. This is your department."

"My department? What? Why...?"

"You said your friend gave you this boat."

"Ah, well...he asked if I wanted it."

"Same thing."

"So? I said no."

"So? It's a gift. You only have to make something out of it."

"Like what?"

"A home!"

Christian stared at Breeze, hoping she was joking. "Are you...? No, you're not. Yes you are."

"Christian, sweetie, it's just clutter. We can clean it up."

"But...yeah, then what?"

"We can live here, free!"

Christian's heart fluttered. "I was afraid you'd say that."

"It's our chance, Christian, to be independent. Make this into our place! It's perfect."

"It's not perfect. It's a pig sty!"

Breeze seemed to not hear. She was looking around the engine room, appraising. The engine room, despite the oilcans and rags and tools scattered about, was the least messy part of the boat, so it was good. And Maartyn had spent hours on the engine, making it run perfectly and painting the monster an unusual shade of light green. He had even stopped cursing the foreign object because it proved to be strong and dependable, 'almost as good as a Jimmie', he had said. Maartyn had some weird affection for diesel engines and Christian was not surprised that the big green Bota stood out like a polished jewel in a cinder bucket.

"Does this motor actually work?"

"Probably. Maartyn's a good mechanic...why?" he asked, experiencing a new fear.

"Because! If the motor works we can drive this old boat to Newfoundland!" And she was climbing the ladder again.

"Are you crazy? What about the baby?"

"Babies are less trouble than you."

"Fine. Can we eat now?"

"You can be the engineer *and* the cook."

"Right. Perfect..."

They sat in the sun, backs against the wheelhouse savouring Haim's bagels and smoked meat. The McAllister tug was blessedly silent. The watchman, having a smoke on the after deck, waved at them. All of Montreal seemed to be taking a break and it was pleasant to sit and pretend it was spring coming instead of winter. Pleasant as it was, Christian had dark, cold thoughts. Mostly he was concerned that possibly Breeze *was* crazy.

"You're serious about this boat thing?"

"Oh, absolutely. Mom always told me that if someone gives you a gift you make something of it. A silk purse out of a sow's ear for instance, or a floating home out of an old fishing boat."

"What if it sinks? Maartyn said the old girl was..."

"She's floating now isn't she?"

"Yes, but for how long?"

"I guess boats float as long as you keep the water out."

"Maartyn told me about the hurricane. He said the *Queen* twisted and moaned like a dying person. Afraid she was going to come apart any moment."

"My dear boy, he didn't have much faith, now, did he?"

It was funny how Breeze's speech reverted to Newfoundland inflections as she talked about the boat. "You can take a Newfy off the Island but you can't take the Island out of a Newfy," he said.

Breeze laughed. "Mom, bless her heart, often says that. She's Newfy through and through, but she always told me I was to talk mainland. Not that she isn't proud, she's just pragmatic. In Montreal it pays to assimilate, she says."

"Don't tell Jean-Pierre that. He has a gun and wants to use it on assimilators."

"Christian, you have to get away from that mob. If what you tell me's true they're headed for a tragic confrontation."

"It's what they want, complete with bombs."

"Why do you stay?"

"I don't know? The job. Lack of a home..."

"Well, that's solved. We can stay with Haim until we get this mess cleaned up. But about this job? You're hired to write, true?"

"I'm hired to do research as well. Compile records of people in the underground movements."

"Why would a student newspaper want that kind of information?"

"A question I ask myself. None of the insiders are actually students." He was quiet for a moment, thinking about an incident the week before.

"There's a dark trouble spot, right there." She touched his forehead gently. It was Breeze's code for 'something's bothering you, tell me'.

"Week ago, Monday, I went to the paper to get my press pass for the Communist rally. It was early. I saw Dominique in the office talking to the publisher and the editor."

"That woman's spying on the group."

"I don't know. Maybe they're just friends. The editor used to hang around the Socialist League."

"Hang around? No, Christian, it's more than that. Listen, my friend on the paper told me to warn you. The RCMP are on campus asking questions. He has a friend who was interrogated for five hours about who he knows in the underground. They threatened to cut off his scholarship."

"Maybe you're right. Dominique's a puzzle and there definitely is something odd about this newspaper thing. I wasn't going to complain as long as they paid me. In fact if I do complain, about anything, they just give me more money and tell me to keep the files coming. I'm the one who's spying on my friends."

"Jean-Pierre's not your friend. What do you owe him?"

"He was a friend when I needed one."

"And now it's time to get out."

"It's not that easy."

"Let's drink our wine and get to work."

Christian didn't like the sound of that but he opened the wine. "Let me try it first." He guessed what the work would involve. He took a sip. The wine was thick and sweet, cloying, like a liqueur. "Whoa! Not what I expected. Powerful. Maybe you shouldn't."

"Okay, you drink some then kiss me."

Confrontation and Consequences

"Look, Jean, I'm not selling out. I'm just moving out."

"What's wrong with this place?"

"Nothing. Everything. I'll come to meetings..."

"You have a woman."

"Well, yeah, I was going to tell you, at the right time."

"You should have told me first thing! I had to find out from Dominique. Can she be trusted, this new woman? Who is she? What does she do?"

"She's a student. Music school...we just met..."

"Lie! You met in September. What did you tell her about us?"

This was a full out interrogation. Where would it lead, Christian wondered? The two bodyguards were asleep but he had to be careful, be honest. "Not that much. No more than anyone knows about the student radical groups in Montreal."

"This isn't some pansy fucking student movement, Christian. This is the future of Québec. The Movement Québécois will yank our state out of Canada and kill those fucking pigs in the National Assembly who collaborate with les Anglais."

Jean-Pierre was on his feet, leaning across the spool table, eyes darting, nostrils flaring in anger. The ever present handgun waving in Christian's face. Christian had faced Maartyn's revolver many times but he never felt as threatened. It was time to get out. He stood up slowly, never taking his eyes off Jean-Pierre's. "I'm just leaving, okay."

"You won't be welcomed back."

"I don't want to come back."

"I know what you do at that fucking rag."

"The Harbinger supports what you're trying to do."

"English bullcrap! It's a front for the cops and you're playing right into their game. You think I don't know these things? Dominique's with them too. Everyone is selling us out!"

"No, Dominique, wouldn't..." Then he realized it might be true. Why else would she be meeting with the publisher? A new fear crept in. Anarchy in the streets was one thing, the expected actions of hot young Québécois aching for the chance to shake up the complacent rich, to rattle the office doors of the establishment, by espousing socialism at its deepest roots; Marx and Engels and the boys, but this was conspiracy. For one brief, painful moment he wondered about Breeze. Who was she working for? Don't be ridiculous. We met by accident and Breeze's carrying our child. Or is she? He had many doubts and no proof of anything.

"Well, what about this woman? Can she be trusted?"

"Breeze is the one thing in my life that *is* real."

"This is real!" shouted Jean-Pierre, pointing the gun at Christian. The bodyguards were on their feet. They drew their guns and circled Christian.

"Okay, you know something, I'm tired of people pointing guns at me. I'm getting out of here. Good luck to you and the movement."

Christian picked up his knapsack and walked to the door, opened it and was face to face with Dominique.

"Christian...Hi."

Obviously Dominique had been listening. "Maybe you should have a talk with your boyfriend and tell him the truth," he said quickly, and at the same time trying to warn her.

"Why don't you tell him?" she said, too easily, pushing past. "You know as much as I do. Maybe more."

"I don't think so."

Jean-Pierre grabbed Dominique. "What about the money?"

Breeze looked at Christian intently, waiting for him to continue. "It was ugly," he said sadly. "He hit her. I couldn't do a thing. The bodyguards, holding me back, forcing me to watch."

"Don't feel badly, Christian. Those people thrive on violence."

"But, it was Dominique. Jean said he would beat her until she told him everything." They were in the reading room of the library. Christian was looking out the big window: an expensive donation by a wealthy alumnus, he recognized the name. A heavy, substantial, window, blown glass framed by stained glass. Students lounged on the benches in the peaceful courtyard, a temple of learning and higher pursuits. Sunshine filtered between the bare trees making mosaics on the cobblestone walk. The air was clear but there were threatening fall clouds over the mountain. Beyond the courtyard students and professors moved about their business. Order and security ruled. But he knew that given the right circumstances and enough anger, the peaceful campus could be turned into a battleground. The window could be shattered and security with it. Soon the windows would be protected by steel mesh and the scene distorted. Breeze put her arms around him. "They let me see enough blood then the bully boys threw me out. I don't know what happened to Dominique. Maybe I should have called the cops."

"They'd know instantly it was you. So, if she is working for the RCMP she can look after herself. You have to disappear and we're going together."

"Breeze, I don't want you mixed up in this."

"Seems I am, my dear."

Christian had to stand back and try to put his life into perspective. There was no longer a shred of youth or innocence left. And no excuses. No thought of languorous nights on tropical beaches, dulled by cheap rum or scalding tequila with beer chasers, and always the numbing dope to mellow out the rough spots in the morning, which became indolent afternoons and the endless discussions about permissive philosophies. Do what you want to do, now, because life is a promise of despair and tomorrow is only a distant possibility. Facing death and having friends disappear has a way of forcing one to become more introspective; climbing the ladder of self-awareness one rung at a time. He began the process as they walked to Uncle Haim's deli.

Later Christian began composing the next entry in his journal. *'I'm walking on this street called Boul. Maisonneuve. Maisonneuve was a French soldier who, along with a devout nun, Jeanne Mance, not unlike Esameralda perhaps, founded Montreal in 1642, on faith, and faith alone, that the wilderness could be made to kneel before the rule of France and Christ; in that order. And what did the soldier and the nun do in the wilderness of New France for recreation? Don't try to inject cynicism. The mission collapsed because the natives didn't catch the fever of European progress, just the flu and small pox, and the French were only there for the beaver pelts. And how was it that by 1759 the militia in Québec City gave it up to Wolfe, the English general who turned a tip about a path to the river Laundromat into a decisive rout on the Plains of Abraham?'*

'The occasion was the central episode in the French-English story; European cultures wrapped around each other like two vines, each trying to outdo the other, until right now, my friends are plotting to blow up English buildings because on that day in 1759 the English general was bold and the French general was merely brave. If the English had miscalculated or one soldier tripped and fell on the steep path from the river, or Montcalm had chosen to fight inside the walls, it would have been all off and the

225

French may have held out and got their supplies and survived the winter and the English been forced to retreat and run for England, and maybe the Brits would have demurred. Or, what if, over breakfast, the English king decided to have peace and give the troublesome, cold colony, to the French in trade for say, Martinique?'

How different would be his life at that moment? Simply walking to Haim's with Breeze who used to be called Bridged and only two months before wasn't pregnant, but was just going to spend her scholarship on becoming a conductor, maybe the first to lead the Montreal Symphony in Offenbach, Ravel, Debussy... *'It would be so good to just play classical jazz on the sax, make a recording, become the premier jazz impressionist: small combo, sax, piano, bass, with Jocinto on guitar, doing Debussy. International acclaim. Paris, opening night, lights go down, blue smoke rises through the spotlights, I step forward ready to play, and there's Renée at a table near the stage, adoring eyes, fondling her date under the table...damn! Not much progress.'*

He should have gone to Spain and died at Madrid, but he was too young, not actually fully formed when it all started, but there were other wars. Too young for the Korean War, so automatically he could do nothing about the fall of Hong Kong to the Japs either. There were rumours about South East Asia. The French were having some problems in a jungle country, one of their colonies called Indo-China or Vietnam and the commies were making threats all over the place. And the English writer Graham Greene had written a tidy little story about the failure of the French in Indo-China and warning the Americans to go easy, or stay home. What about Hungary? What about the tanks? He could have gone there, but there wasn't time to organize the brigades and no one was writing poetry about the Prague Spring. It didn't have the caché or the momentum of Spain. It wasn't sunny, nor did the Mediterranean lap its shores, nor the mountains reek with grapes in bloom or hang with scented dust at noon and purple mist at sunset.

It was just a quick takeover, and weren't the commies also socialists, and weren't the Socialists the darlings and heroes of Madrid?
He and Renée did have Cuba. Castro was about to declare for Socialism. It was all so confusing. And wasn't life just so confusing,
and weren't they running to Uncle Haim in time of need? The
Irish running to the Jews for shelter. And where were the Irish in
'42? Neutral, and giving shelter to the Germans, who were gas-
sing the Jews and killing the English who were crumbling under
the jack boots and dive bombers and facing invasion of their tight
little island. And only a brave soldier, well, a portly, cigar waving
politician, to stand in their way until the Americans stopped trading with the Japs and the Germans and sent their boys to die
alongside the boys from the colonies with Stalin as an ally. On
VE Day the gleeful English held parades all over the Empire and
the English and the Scots of Montreal made a huge show to em-
barrass the reluctant French and the ungrateful Irish and, oh my,
what a mess, and it was still a European mess, left over from colonialism for the most part, with the Asians making trouble, and
the Muslims in the Middle East waiting to explode, but there were
bombs to place in Montreal office towers so that the French Canadian kids could make their desires known to les Anglais...

"Christian, you're shaking. What's the matter?" Breeze waited for him to catch up. She put her arms around him.

Haim beamed with pleasure when they returned and accepted his
offer. "Yes, my dear children, stay. With my blessings. We'll dis-
cuss the rent later."

"Thank you, Uncle Haim," said Breeze, giving Haim a hug.
"We'll try not to be any trouble."

Haim blushed. "I know, I know. But what is wrong with your
man? He seems ill?"

"He just needs to rest. May we go up?"

"Of course. The door is always open. Use the back stairs.
You'll know which room. Go."

Breeze guided Christian to the back of the deli and the door that opened on the alley. The narrow alley was another world, a rough playground, a confined chaos with children and dogs gamboling about. Washing hung overhead from wall to wall. A back yard mechanic worked on a leaky Chevy pickup truck, feet protruding from under the front bumper. The mechanic waved a wrench. Iron stairs rose to a vine-covered balcony. Breeze guided Christian up the stairs. He needed her strength, as if he had lost the will to move, remembering the family apartment on Sherbrooke West and sanctuary in his mother's arms. A temporary truce with his sister, both safe until their father returned from work, drunk and angry. He remembered the smells. His mother always baking, even in the summer, and the dry heat of the woodstove was better than the wet heat of Montreal. He should try to find his mother...

The back door opened on an airy sunroom. Breeze imagined nursing the baby and putting him down in the afternoon sun. But that was in a world of calm and order. She didn't see the future in those terms. Another door opened to Uncle Haim's kitchen, also bright, and tidy and purposeful. Uncle Haim was either fastidious in his preparations or he did not take meals in his own home. Perhaps he lived on meat and bagels in the deli. "We'll have to see about some food. Can't live on shaved beef. Are you hungry, my darling?"

Are you hungry, my darling? He wanted to die in her arms. "No. Yes. I don't know. Just want to lay down."

The kitchen, large for an apartment, was the focus of the flat. Breeze imagined a big family gathered for sedas, or shushed to seriousness by Haim at morning prayers wearing the cap and a shawl. Maybe she was being too sentimental. A narrow hallway lead to a tiny parlour overlooking the street. In between were four doors, two on each side of the hall. Three were bedrooms. One would be a bathroom. Compact. Efficient. But seven children? It must have been crowded. One door was open, Haim's room. She chose the last door on the right. The door creaked as though it hadn't been opened for some time. The room was small but the bed large. It was also stifling, airless, but there was a window overlooking the side street, above Haim's watching window in the shop below. Haim would be sitting there listening to their footsteps, memories flying back to the days of his family. The boys stomping around and the girls giggling about boys. Did he admonish and shush them or absorb them?

She eased Christian onto the bed, made him comfortable and opened the window. There was dust in the drapes. She would shake them out later. She saw a boy's room and Christian recognized the wallpaper. Mounted Police and Indians, horses and canoes. How strange in the present reality. The RCMP may be looking for Christian's friends. There were three chests of drawers, one for each boy. A closet with suits for occasions and shoes, arranged, waiting for the sons to come home. The drawers...the same. Underwear, socks, undershirts, dress shirts. Plaid everyday shirts and patched denims with plaid lining. Very practical for Montreal winters. On the wall were the usual school certificates, awards for achievements, ribbons for sports, but more for academics. And on embroidered runners, photographs in cardboard standup frames sagging with age and marked by fly specs. The fading photos showed their progress from childhood to adolescence to high school graduation, then, no further record. Some were from the Old Country by the dress. Maybe in Haim's room there were photos of their extended families, daughters married, and more children, as the clan grew and moved away. Breeze wanted to look... "This is so sad." She wanted to satisfy herself that Uncle Haim had a family that still adored him and visited on Sabbath, or Hanukkah at least. But there was no evidence that the sons returned. What about the daughters? She might investigate their room, accidentally, when searching for the bathroom.

The fresh wind blew the curtains shedding dust and Christian turned on his side. She worried about the dust. "You must be cold, my dear." There was a blanket on a box at the end of the bed. "Maybe there's something interesting in the box," she said as she picked up the blanket. "No, you will not open that box, Bridged O'Keefe."

Christian was asleep before Breeze drew the wool blanket over him gently and sat on the edge of the bed facing the window. She was cold also, and would lay with Christian to get warm soon. "So, this is home. It's fine." She went to find the bathroom.

Breeze settled in and cleaned their rooms to her satisfaction while Christian rested and wrote notes for his reports. Uncle Haim was very quiet, tip toing about during the evening, staying in the store during the day to give them privacy, reading in the parlour at night or talking about the Old Country. He seemed to enjoy having the young people share his home.

"We have to get going on the boat soon, before I get too big."

They were sitting in the kitchen of Uncle Haim's flat, finishing their morning coffee and toasted bagels. Haim had taken a cup of coffee and a bagel with canned herring and gone down to open the deli. The lingering smell of the canned fish made Breeze nauseous.

"Imagine, Uncle Haim has all that food to choose from and he eats canned herring."

"Breeze, I don't think it's a great idea."

"It's just temporary. Haim's so kind, and lonely."

"No, I mean the whole boat thing."

"Can't leave that mess, it'll only get worse, and the watchman on the tugboat says that every night some louts try to get aboard of her. He sends them packing but it's not his job. We'll do some tonight after class and on the weekends."

"Are you sure you're up to it?"

"What about yourself? You gave me quite a fright, you did, with sleeping for three days. I was going to call a doctor. You sweated so, and rolled about, moaning."

"I'm sorry...I caused you trouble."

"No, my dear, only saying that name gave me pause. I was so tempted to give you a good smack."

"What name?"

"The Parisienne whore. I know...I know...she's a special girl from your past, but, I'm Irish, I'm special too. I have red hair, and the temper to go with it." She grabbed his ear and twisted, then planted a wonderfully wet kiss on his lips. "That should send her packing."

It did. Christian felt a thrill race through him. This extraordinary woman was always a surprise. But Renée had said that about him too, and wasn't there a dull ache of anger or regret? If he was still angry with Renée it meant something but this wild Irish girl was slowly pushing Renée into the distance. Then what about Esa? Problems. He could not think about Esameralda Diez without feeling guilty because Esa had entered his psyche deeply. Was there room for all of them? Awake, half awake, dreaming, the girls circled his emotional ground, as if his exposed heart were an iconic statue and the dancing figures pagan love goddesses waiting to spring upon him. Where would the spirit go? Into the Alpha female and one of them would devour his heart as the Iroquois warriors did when they killed the Jesuit missionaries.

Paulo Again

Breeze fed Christian her best Irish stew and love in large doses until he was feeling strong enough to work. Haim made them both a wonderful chicken soup they could take with them to work on the boat. On a cold, sunny day in late November they dumped the last load of rubbish into the harbour as the McAllister Tug watchman said to do. Everybody did it he assured them. They were in the galley trying to get the hulking cook stove to work when Paulo showed up.

"There must be some kind of gas supply," Christian said, tapping the fuel tank strapped to the bulkhead above the stove. "There's a line from somewhere to the tank." He wiggled the valve below the tank. "Probably empty. Maartyn would laugh at me. Where is he, I'd like to know?"

"Too bad he didn't tell you how this boat worked before he left so abruptly," Breeze said sarcastically, wiping the grime off her hands with a rag. She was dressed in her stepfather's blue coveralls, the bulge in her tummy now showing.

"I did refuse the gift and he wasn't too happy."

"And then we accepted it, posthumously. Sorry, poor choice of words. De facto..."

A jarringly familiar voice called from the dock. "Christian! Hey, are you aboard? Chris!" The French-Basque accent was unmistakable.

"That's Paulo."

"Your personal drug dealer?"

The sound of footsteps on the deck and a shadow at the gangway announced the arrival of his nemesis. Christian was conflicted; relieved that Paulo was alive, but distressed that he was alive and still in Montreal. "Paulo, I thought you'd left for France."

"You would not believe, man..." Paulo descended the ladder backwards and turned to face Christian. "...this fucking place! This so called cosmopolitan city! What a rat hole!"

It was the same old Paulo, always complaining of personal disaster, but Christian would not have recognized his odd friend on the street. His black leather jacket was torn and dirty, and he was even thinner than Christian remembered. His face, once handsome and chiseled, was pulpy and disfigured with scar tissue. But most obvious, the grey eyes were dull and lifeless.

"Jesus. What happened to you?"

"Long story. Not worth telling." Paulo almost collapsed on the bench in the eating space that resembled a cheesy diner booth, complete with well worn red leatherette. A match for the chrome chairs in Jean-Pierre's lair, but Breeze had succeeded in getting it clean.

"Are you hungry?" asked Christian. Why was he always concerned about Paulo's well being? "We've been trying to get this stove working to heat up soup."

"Famished. Beyond hungry." Paulo looked at Breeze for the first time. "And who are you, my beauty?"

"Ah, Paulo, this is Bridged, or Breeze. Breeze, Paulo."

"Hello," said Breeze, extending her warm hand. "Christian's told me so much about you."

"Really. I can imagine." He looked at Breeze's swelling belly. "And, let me guess, you're pregnant? No need to ask about the relationship. Renée will be thrilled."

Breeze stiffened and turned back to the stove.

"Ah, Paulo, let's not be quite so open, okay? The past is history."

"Still the brilliant raconteur. *The past is history.* What the fuck else could it be?"

"Okay, look, you're here. You know this boat. How does the stove work?"

"You light a match."

"Tried that."

"Did you turn it on?"

"Did that."

"Before that you open that valve."

"Okay, let's stop being clever. Is there fuel somewhere?"

"There's a pump in the engine room. Don't know. Seldom went down there. Hate the stinking mess."

"You two get acquainted," Christian climbing the ladder to the deck.

"No thanks," replied Paulo, yawning loudly, slumping on the bench, eyes closed.

Breeze looked dubious. "We're going to Newfoundland in the spring, after the baby's born."

"I'm ecstatic for you," he said, one eye opened to emphasize his delight.

"I can see that," shot back Breeze. She could also see that Paulo was a hard nut to crack. He would come around or not but she continued just to torment him. "The timing's just right, see, after the winter, when the ice has cleared off. My mother told me all about the ice around Fogo in the spring. She said it was a wonderful sight to see the ice right to the horizon for months at a time and then one morning you could look out and the ocean would be so blue it would hurt your eyes...the wind, see?"

Paulo did not see, or care. He was asleep. The galley was cold and damp so Breeze put a coat over him and went back to cleaning.

Christian flipped switches on the electrical panel beside the ladder. A tiny light came on over the engine. Nothing happened so he turned it off. On the bulkhead separating the engine room from the galley there was a red cylinder with a wooden handle in the center. "Okay, that's probably a pump." Above the pump was a hand lettered sign, 'Galley Tank. Twenty-five strokes'. He tested the handle. It moved one way and then back the other way twice as far. "Must be a stroke." He tentatively moved the handle back and forth and was rewarded with gurgling sounds. "Right. Maybe that was four." Twenty more strokes and the gurgling stopped.

Breeze found wooden matches in a tobacco can. The stove resembled an old-time kitchen wood stove, but smaller. She lifted the miniature manhole cover and peered into the firebox. The smell of diesel fuel made her nauseous and she headed for the deck to be sick.

Christian shook Paulo awake. "Hey, Paulo, how do you light this thing?"

"Drop in match." He yawned and stretched. He looked like a street drunk waking in a mission. "Light match first."

"Very funny." The third damp match flared to life. He held

the burning match over the hole but was afraid to let go. When the flame burned his fingers he dropped the match. Nothing happened. "Ah. Paulo, it isn't working. Paulo?"

"That never worked. Wax things, in drawer." He pointed.

Christian opened the drawer. In the jumble of marine junk he found the bundle of tapers. He recognized the candle lighting tapers from his days as an alter boy. He lit one and gingerly prodded into the darkness of the firebox. A moment later there was a feint whoosh, a flare of light and a black cloud of smoke filling the galley. He dropped the lid and stood back. Smoke continued to waft up around the edges of the lid. "Paulo...now what?"

Paulo was face down on his arms. "Is it smoking? Turn down the fuel."

"Okay, how?"

He pointed. Near the bottom of the stove was a black box with an indicator knob and a plate so worn only the letter H showed. The indicator pointer was in between H and something else then Off. Christian chose the 'something else'. Nothing much changed. The smoke kept coming out and the galley remained shrouded in a haze of black particles. Breeze appeared at the gangway and immediately turned away. "Oh, God. Please turn that off."

"Paulo? It's still smoking."

"Huh? Smoke. Yes, of course. Can't use blower due kill battery. Wait, it'll warm up."

They had been using the single light in the galley while they were working, but the light had been steadily dimming. Breeze said it was the battery going off. Christian thought she meant it was rotting and smelled. He had much to learn about marine things. As Paulo predicted, the smoke diminished as the stove heated up. The air gradually cleared and Breeze was able to come back down and put on the soup from Uncle Haim's. There were stale crusty buns and a chunk of dried out salami. Breeze and Christian agreed they liked it better that way. Haim said they could have all the dried out meats they wanted because he only fed it to the neighbourhood dogs. Paulo refused to eat the stale buns or the salami. Uncle Haim's excellent soup, he agreed, was okay.

"You're rather picky for a starving man," Breeze said, clearing away the remains of the meal. The light bulb was going dim again so she turned it off and lit candles.

"I have my limits. Some day I'll have servants and never eat left overs."

"In the meantime, care to tell us what you've been doing for the last month?" asked Christian.

"Making contacts. Business."

"By the looks of it you haven't been staying at the Windsor Arms."

"This fucking place, man! No class. I met this guy, you know..."

Christian was constructing the scenario. Paulo meets a guy, hooks up with guy, meets another guy, falls for second guy, etc. Ends up in triangle or quadrangle or pentangle. "Yeah, you met a guy. You do drugs. Guy beats you up in gratitude."

"That's about it."

"Figures."

"Not the first one. He was sweet."

"Was it only drugs?"

"Not at first."

"Okay, we don't need details."

"Third was your friend, Henri. You know him. Very heavy into the revolution. That's how I knew where to find you."

"Henri? FLQ Henri?"

"Yeah, some outfit like that. In Spain they have ETA. Everywhere they have these fucking groups with initials. FLN, IRA, ANC. All the same, man, rhetoric up the bung hole. Talk, talk, talk. Sometimes, kill, kill, kill. But this Henri, he's something else. Very intense and very committed. And he knows about everything in Montreal. He said you should stop messing with crazy Jean-Pierre and clear out. The Federal police, what you call...RCMP, another initial bunch, and the Surité are out to get Jean-Pierre and he's out to get you because you betrayed him. What the hell have you been up to since I left?"

Breeze stiffened and took Christian's hand. "Do they know Christian's here?"

"No, they think he's gone with some girl, that would be you, to some other part of Montreal. I'm telling you, Jean-Pierre's on the run but if he finds you it's big trouble. Henri's taking out a contract on Jean-Pierre because he's such a loose cannon. Dangerous to everybody. He killed his girlfriend, you know the woman, Dominique..."

A bolt of lightning shot through Christian. "Oh, God! no...sweet Jesus!"

They stayed on board that night, afraid to leave the boat for the streets and they couldn't go to Uncle Haim's. It was impossible to know who was watching. Cab drivers are the equivalent of Petit Jacques' observers. They know everything about the mean streets between the waterfront and the suburbs, are mobile and they have radios. Your best friend or your worst enemy. They have issues and affiliations and, as immigration increases the numbers of politically motivated refugees with few opportunities, they are tenacious about their turf. Anybody who threatens their community is the enemy. The anarchists straddle the line. Gerard was an emissary between the Haitian community and the anarchists and Gerard was back.

Later that night Gerard's tall figure boarded the *Bayou Queen* silently, waiting in the shadow of the wheelhouse before approaching the fore hatch. Christian and Breeze were sitting at the galley table with one candle burning, talking about the future. Paulo was sprawled in exhausted sleep on a bunk in the fo'c'sle.

"*Shhh*. Someone's on deck," Breeze breathed.

Christian blew out the candle but light leaked from the top of the diesel stove and cast a damning circle of orange light on the ceiling. It didn't matter, the heat and odour from the stove would give them away. The hatch rose slowly showing a rectangle of night sky, then a silhouette. They froze in fear.

"Chris? Mawn, it's Gerard," he whispered.

"Gerard. Oh, my gosh! Wait, I'll light the candle."

"No! Ton ton's looking for me."

"Come down."

"I have news."

They remained seated in the dark talking quietly while Breeze made coffee. Gerard was strangely reluctant to share his news after the first flush of greetings.

"Gerard? Is something wrong, I mean besides everything?"

"I hear breathing."

"Paulo. He's a friend, from Cuba. Came on the boat with Maartyn."

"Yeah, I remember Paulo, Chris. He's trouble, mawn. That one tried the drug scene. Made some bad enemies in a short time. If they find him...an' he's with you an' your woman?" He shrugged, the message clear.

"He only said he'd been involved with some dealer and Henri's group."

"Bad enough, but Henri's not about to kill him. Jean-Pierre maybe. The drug lords for sure. You heard about Dominique?"

"Yes. I can't believe it. I might be responsible."

"No, no. The cops don't know yet. The body disappeared. They'll be looking for her soon, then you be implicated." He let that information sink in. Christian was numb. "Look, we know what you're doin' at the newspaper. That's harmless. Cops know about the movements an' the leaders, an' about the disciples. Most of them just kids who run back to momma first sign of trouble. We let you do your little thing an' gave you much false information. But, Dominique, she was in deep with the police."

"We suspected that."

"They supplied Dominique the money for Jean-Pierre's mob, just enough to keep it goin' an' tried to get the movement to step out of line. Then the police have excuse to move in an' smash the leaders. That whole story about wealthy parents in Outremont?...just a cover, mawn. She used everybody. You understand me?"

"The quintessential agent provocateur."

"Whatever, mawn. She was supposed to deliver Jean-Pierre an' Henri to the cops, an' she was the one who pushed for the Place Ville-Marie business, but never delivered enough to actually carry it off. A dangerous game but Jean-Pierre would do it. Henri thought so too. He split off to get distance, but hear me, mawn, one day Henri an' his bunch will kill somebody. Petit Jacques thinks so too. It's why he moved down to Québec City. He likes smuggling, dope an' pornography. Dealing prostitutes. Everything illegal to make money, but he didn't want to get innocent people killed."

"And what about you? Why are you back?"

"I went to New York with François to see some people. I'm back to help organize my community, to make sure they get a decent deal. Montreal's a tough place for Haitians. New York's tough too, but there's more jobs. We can disappear better into the Hispanic scene. Here the language is easy, but you got to eat. It's a hard choice, dig?" Christian nodded. He understood too well the hard choices his friends had made in Cuba, and suffered. "We got to go where blacks are tolerated, as long as we stay in line. It's my hope to become a force. I thought Jean-Pierre and the Movement Québécois might be a way to get control, you know, but I was naive. The government's not going to turn against les Anglais, no matter what they say. This Lesage guy is another federal ass kisser. Keep peace and take the crumbs from the Master. Dig?"

"No. I'm confused. You bring people here, then take them to New York. Why not just come in from the Gulf of Mexico."

"Not so easy. Americans're totally paranoid about Hispanics. An' now with this Castro business, it's even harder to get in. Florida is closed. Canada? No problem. I could bring the population of Port-aux-Prince in here, but the problem is jobs. I say that in twenty years we will be a force here too, but we don't want to be part of a revolution. If the movements fail it will be hard on the little people. Not as bad as Haiti but we have no voice in Haiti. We have only tyrants like Papa Doc and we have poverty. No education? No chance. In New York we have a chance, but they don't make it easy. Know what I mean?"

"Are the police after you too?"

"Yes, the police too. I have no papers."

"By the way, I didn't mention you to the paper, reports."

"I know. We have a person on the inside."

"I can't believe what's happening. I left Cuba thinking...what? I don't know. But I do have Breeze and the baby."

"Then you have everything. Listen, Jean-Pierre put the word out for you downtown. Never thought you'd be on the river. You got to get away from here."

"Where? We don't have enough money to just run forever. Maybe we should go back to the islands, or find Maartyn."

"Okay...here's the news about Maartyn. Didn't want to tell you, mawn, 'cause I don't know what you might do."

"What? Tell me what?" Christian had that chill of fear.

"He's okay, sort of. The FBI is holding him in a place called Champlain, in Upper New York, near the lake. Same name."

"How do you know all this?"

"He was arrested with some of my people. We have people who see things, like Jacques, eh? It pays to know."

"How did he get caught?"

"Trying to cross the border. No papers. Maartyn's a good friend, Christian. He said he didn't want to cause you any trouble an' better to go home. So, I told him ways to get into the States. He was with the group that night Vince was killed. The plan was good but somebody tipped the police. I took my people by road to a place called Ile aux Noix to meet the boat. Look here..." Gerard produced a worn roadmap of Québec and the North Eastern United-ed States. "See this river, the Richelieu. It runs from here," point-ing to Sorel on the St. Lawrence River, between Montreal and Trois-Rivières, "...straight south, an' then Lake Champlain, an' still straight south to the Hudson River, an' right into downtown New York. It was perfect, mawn. The Feds never suspected. I run many groups down that way. You can get on the river in many places. Ile aux Noix was perfect. They grabbed them at a place called Rouses Point, just over the border. Three fast boats with searchlights were waiting. A tip off for sure. Me an' François got away an' made it to New York. Vince was killed. Too bad about Vince. He was just going for the ride because he wanted to see New York City."

"What about Maartyn?"

"That Maartyn, mawn. He actually stole one of the Fed's boats while the fight was on an' made it to Plattsburg before he run out of gas. They brought him back to Champlain because they think he's a Canadian. They're holding him in a motel with the others until they decide what to do with them. If they find out who he really is, your boy's in serious trouble."

"Yeah, he had some kind of run in with the law even before I met him."

"Mawn, he told me the whole story."

"Really? He never would tell me the details. What did he do?"

"No time for that shit."

"Then, what do *we* do? Can't leave him for the Feds."

There was a difficult gap in the conversation. The three of them sitting in the pale flicker of the diesel stove, contemplating their options. Breeze only wanted to go to Newfoundland. Gerard was on the run for all the usual reasons and Christian was about to be on the run but his friend was in trouble. Breeze spoke first. "You have to go and get him."

"From the Feds?"

"I don't know, but he's your friend. Think of something."

"Oh, right, we just drive up to the front door of the motel waving a Canadian flag and say, give us Maartyn's liberty or give us death."

"Very funny. Here's the choices," began Breeze. "If we stay with Uncle Haim we risk his business. The police are looking for you too, so we can't stay at the University. Somebody's looking for Paulo to kill him. We can't stay here on the boat because someone will eventually find out, am I right, Gerard?"

"Yes, Miss. The cabbies know. The watchman. Everybody know except Jean-Pierre and the RCMP and they will know soon."

"Then we have to leave Montreal. We'll take the boat," she said simply. "But right now I have to sleep."

Breeze kissed Christian and climbed the ladder.

Gerard waited until Breeze closed the hatch. "That's some woman. You better hold on to that one."

Christian nodded. "I know."

"But, I have something else to tell you. On the road to Ile aux Noix, Maartyn told me about your French woman."

Gerard could have hit him in the stomach. "Oh, Renée, she's...well, you know...in the past."

"No need to explain, but Maartyn sent Mademoiselle Renée a letter that she should come to Montreal immediately."

"Oh, my God, Renée. I tried to tell him about Breeze."

"Now you really are in trouble. Police an' terrorists is one thing, but an angry woman, mawn. An' you about to have two of them on your hands." Gerard whistled and laughed.

"It's not funny."

"Oh, mawn, I got to see how this works out. But seriously, Chris, you have to get clear of us. Your French woman can help?"

"Renée...Maybe she didn't get Maartyn's letter. Maybe the

world will stop turning...Oh, Jesus, I feel sick." Numb was how he felt, but still, the most urgent thought, besides getting Breeze away from the tragi-comedy called 'Times with Christian', was what to do about Maartyn? "Breeze's right, we can't just leave him to the Feds."

"Listen, this is a long shot but...you remember that night at the Caraibes? Philippo? The Russian?"

Christian stiffened. The alarm bells were going off again. Maartyn, the Russian, Cold War, Revolution. The FBI. He stared blankly at Gerard. "This Philippo?...What's he got to do with any-thing?" Christian wished he hadn't asked.

"Philippo gets things done, mawn. I won't go into details but, if I call Philippo, an' tell him a friend of yours is being held by the FBI?"

"What will he do?" Christian asked, dazed by the further complication. "Why would he help Maartyn?"

"He'd help *you* because I ask him." Christian looked more confused. "Okay, details then. Philippo hates the FBI. Listen, af-ter the war he tried to defect to the Americans with his family. Philippo was an agrona-something at Texas A an' M., into sci-ence an' plants. Made a fortune on some discovery to do with plants an' frogs, an' things to make plants not freeze in Siberia. He went back to Mother Russia to revolutionize agriculture. An' do you know what them bastards did? The Soviet government forced him to do research on some kind of killer plant seeds to in-fect American farms. Understand me? The KGB has a plan to de-stroy the Americans by starvation. All this atomic bomb an' submarine an' missile bullshit is just a decoy, mawn. Hear me?"

"Okay, yes, but I don't get..."

"Philippo ran with his family. First by boat to the Mediterra-nean an' Malta. The British helped him defect to the USA. He took a huge risk by contacting the CIA, but once back in the States he's arrested by the FBI who are still holding a file on him from Texas A an' M an' the FBI are not told by the CIA that he's a defector. The FBI take his family an' hide them but he escapes. Then the CIA denied they ever heard of him an' he's on the run. Christian, all that man has is money, lots of it. He can buy his way around. But all he wants is his family, an' if he has to destroy every FBI agent to find them he will."

Christian felt weak. "This is too ridiculous...I can't handle this."

"Yes you can. I'll make a call. I'll arrange it. Here's the plan..."

Later that night Christian crawled into the bunk beside Breeze exhausted but unable to sleep. It was all going too fast. Out of control. Renée may be winging her way to Montreal direct from Paris. Maartyn was going to be rescued by a crazed one man Russian commando unit. Dominique's dead and Jean-Pierre's a psycho murderer. Vince's also dead. Breeze is keen on the rescue of Maartyn then going to Newfoundland and having a baby, then it's off to Ireland. Montreal is a nest of terrorists and all they have is a rotting shrimp boat.

The Plan

They sipped hot black coffee out of chipped mugs, huddling like conspirators in the close, damp warmth of the galley, contemplating the sudden turn in their lives. The strong coffee at least smelled better than the diesel stove fumes but no one felt like eating. During the cold night in the skipper's cabin Breeze had lost her glow. Christian was tired from lack of sleep, his mind racing ahead from one possible disaster to the next and laying beside Breeze and feeling the baby move under his hand he was tormented by the need to make decisions. Paulo, who looked as though death had come close in the night, was propped up in the booth, eyes shut, while Christian tried to explain to Breeze how the plan would work.

"Gerard's coming with a cab. We'll go to Uncle Haim's to get our things."

"He's going to be very disappointed," sighed Breeze, thinking of Uncle Haim's feelings despite their own predicament.

"I know. But, Breeze, you're not known in this mess, you don't have to go. And, and what about school? Your music. The scholarship."

"They'll keep, but life won't. And there's your friend Maartyn in some kind of trouble."

"We don't know. Gerard couldn't be sure he's still in Champlain. We're messing with the FBI."

"I'll take my cello and I need some clothes."

Paulo opened one eye. "A cello to amuse the FBI? You *are* all crazy."

"You don't have to go with us, Paulo."

"What would I do in Montreal? I can't sleep in the streets."

Christian stared at his troublesome friend for a long moment as if replaying their history. "Paulo, is there any money left?"

Paulo opened the other eye then looked away. "What money?"

"The money you took out of my knapsack when you rescued those two mistakes of evolution."

"That mouthy bastard Maartyn!" Paulo had a rare twinge of conscience. "All right. I have the god-damned money, but only because I couldn't spend it."

"How much is left?"

"About a thousand dollars. Why? What good is it?"

"We can change it at the bank. Gerard says we may need cash to bribe the guards holding Maartyn if Philippo doesn't come through."

"I don't like that part of the plan," said Breeze. "The Russian's involvement is bad enough, but bribery?"

"Gerard said not to worry."

Paulo was fully awake. "You are so naive, man. What do you

think the Russian will do, put big fluffy pillows over the guards to keep them quiet?"

"I don't know, Paulo, it's beyond me. Gerard's making the arrangements. We just have to get the boat up the Richelieu River. The Russian will grab Maartyn and meet us at some location, then we go to New York. Gerard will make it look like Maartyn escaped back to Montreal. And no, I can't explain how that will work either. It's all so crazy."

"Yeah, sure, and your woman can play the cello to distract the police."

"And maybe she will! It's none of your damned business!"

"Okay, boys. Easy. We need plans, not fights."

At ten o'clock Gerard arrived with a cab for the trip to town leaving Paulo to guard the boat. First to a bank to change the old bills and withdraw Breeze's scholarship money. There were questions but Breeze handled the negotiations, telling the manager that the old, singed money had been hoarded by her sainted Irish grandmother in the backyard after the fire. The manager said it was not uncommon. Immigrants were cautious. The address checked out and all she had to do was sign a few forms. When asked why she wanted her scholarship in American funds she said she had a chance to study for a semester at the Julliard School in New York. A call to her music faculty established that she was a student in good standing. Now, two thousand dollars richer, they scrambled back into the cab for the trip to the St. Charles district to get her clothes and the precious cello.

On the way across Montreal Gerard revealed more details of the plan. "You rendezvous with Petit Jacques at Sorel. He has everything on board *Elloise* to fix your boat."

"Petit Jacques doesn't even like me. Why would he do that?"

"He loves you. Wishes you were his son. You steered his boat safely down the Lachine Rapids."

"*Phew*, that was just luck."

"He knows that, but the point is you did it, an' as far as Petit Jacques is concerned you are a real river rat."

"Thanks. Rat sounds more like it."

"No, no. That's good, mawn. River rats run the river. Know everything."

"Wait..." interrupted Breeze. "Gerard, you said, *you* are supposed to meet this Jacques. Does that mean you aren't coming with us?"

"Correct, Miss. I'm needed here. This is absolutely secret. We're going to take out Jean-Pierre. He's become too dangerous."

"You mean, kill him?" Breeze asked in shock.

Gerard looked at them in the mirror, a strange, tense smile on his broad, dark face.

"Jesus, I feel sick," sighed Christian.

"Me too," admitted Gerard. "He used to be a friend."

Christian could see the sadness in Gerard's expressive eyes. Gerard had an honest, open face. When he said something it was meant to happen, but this new information further worried Christian. Without Gerard the trip and the rescue mission were doomed to failure. What did he know about running a boat? "I never wanted to be the leader. That's how I grew up. At the back of the class. At the back of the pack. Paulo at least spent time on the boat with Maartyn," he said hopefully, knowing that Paulo was even less dependable.

"Paulo's a prissy girl, mawn. No offence, Miss. You are a real woman. You way better than that shifty motha'fucker...sorry. It's just that, I seen too many like him. I never liked that mawn the moment I set eyes on him, an' what I know of his time in Montreal, well, I like him even worse. He should have gone down river with those other two strange people. They'd have made a great threesome. An' maybe this time they'd all drown in the Gulf. Ha! Some people."

"Well, Gerard, for better or worse, Paulo *is* my friend."

"That's okay with me. Just don't expect him to be there when you need him, that's all I'm saying. An' as far as the boat's concerned, Maartyn told me about their trip up from Florida. He said the old boat had heart but wanted more than once to make fish bait out of that bastard Paulo."

Christian, who could seldom find it in his heart to dislike anybody, no matter what his or her crimes, wondered why Gerard was so vehement in his condemnation of Paulo. Sure, Paulo had problems and issues, but what was it that Gerard knew?

Breeze and Breeze Sr.

Christian was as nervous as a high school boy picking up his date for the prom. "Mom, this is Christian."

The woman whose hand Christian was holding was a shorter, broader version of Breeze, minus the freckles and the red hair. The mother's hair, once raven black, had the same wild untamed mass ready to fly about at the first provocation. Her large, expressive eyes were dark and deep while Breeze had sea green eyes and now he could see the Portuguese genes under the Irish mantel. Despite the lines of grief and sorrow, the woman was handsome, and like Breeze, high cheek-boned and proud. And he could imagine those full lips singing songs of poetry around ritual fires. Or kissing a man with passion or a child with tenderness. Christian was entranced.

"Hello, Mrs. O'Keefe. It's so nice to meet you."

"Breeze. Please, call me Breeze." Breeze Senior did not let go of his hand. Christian almost panicked. What should he do? He wisely chose to keep a firm grip, returning the feeling, whatever it meant, and he also wisely kept his eyes gazing into hers. He was being pulled closer for inspection, and she kept reeling him in until Breeze Senior had him in an embrace. She held his shoulders and placed a kiss on each cheek then gently released him. His mouth was dry and he felt incapable of uttering a word. "So,

Christian, my daughter's pregnant with your baby."

He nodded. Fortunately it was neither a question nor an accusation.

"I told you he was good looking as well as very nice," interjected Breeze.

"Bridged never had time for boys. Music and school was all. What makes you so special?"

The abrupt question was more difficult to answer than the interrogation by the psychotic Cuban policeman, Justo Carnero.

"Could we come in, Mom? Can't stay long, our cab's waiting."

"Of course, come in. Come. Where are you going in such a rush?"

"Newfoundland."

Breeze Senior took Breeze's hands. "Newfoundland is it? Just like that. And what has occasioned this bit of mad cap adventure in the middle of the school term?"

"Long story, Mom. I'm taking my cello so I can practice."

"I see. And what, pray tell, will sustain you in your travels?"

Breeze suddenly headed for the stairway. "We're going to Béhathook. We'll stay with relatives and have the baby there. Want to come along?" She was halfway up the stairs. "We're going by boat. It'll be fun."

She turned to Christian. "Did she say by boat?"

"Yes...Mrs. O'Keefe, Breeze." Now that the issue was out in the open he felt very calm in her steady, penetrating gaze. He also stopped wondering if *his* Breeze was crazy, realizing that she had the spirit of this woman, her mother, and maybe everything would turn out okay. Just a fleeting hope. More fervent wish than probable outcome because, well, there's Renée, and other things, like murder and terrorists, cops and Russians. Then he was once again at the bottom of a very steep cliff. He couldn't flee from the danger, he had to climb the cliff. And in the presence of Breeze Senior he wanted desperately to measure up.

"At this time of year?"

"Well, we're not going directly to Newfoundland, I don't think," he stammered. "Ah, the plan is to go south, New York, by river, and, ah, to pick up a friend along the way and, then..."

"You have no idea what your doing, do you?"

"Ah, no, Ma'am, not really."

"Then who, pray tell, is concocting your plans?"

Christian drew in his breath. The gods of chaos probably, if only it were that simple. "That would be Gerard, the one driving the cab?"

"A cab driver?" Breeze Senior looked beyond Christian to the taxi in her driveway. Gerard smiled and waved. "A cab driver's making the plans to take my babies to Newfoundland, by boat. What kind of boat would this be? The ferry from North Sidney to Port aux Basques?" she asked hopefully

"No, Ma'am...Mrs. O'Keefe, I know it sounds crazy, but my friend, the one we're picking up in New York, gave me his fishing boat, and we were cleaning it up to live on and Breeze thought it would be a good idea, to go, like." He stopped explaining because it sounded like an even dumber idea when put to words. However, stupid idea or not he had to run. He just wished Breeze had not insisted on tagging along. Well, there's another stupid concept. Breeze was dragging him by the nose, not just to Newfoundland but all the way to Ireland possibly. He wondered if Breeze Senior had any notion of that plan? Might as well get it all out in the open. "Did you know that Breeze wants to go to Ireland?"

"Why are you calling her Breeze?"

"Ah, she sort of gave me the choice of Bridged or Breeze, and I liked it. So does she."

"I know. She's always been mad at me for naming her after my own mother. She chose my name as a child because the kids teased her awful about being a bridge and it was harder to make fun of the wind. Of course they tried but sometimes your name is your strength. You're named after an Irish writer? What good will that do you?"

"I'm not sure."

"You don't seem sure of very much."

"I'm sure I love Breeze."

"Good enough. Obviously she's having you whether I approve or not. Only time will tell. Christian, sit down. There's some things you should know."

Christian sat close to Breeze Senior on the couch in the small, tidy living room. There was little to distinguish the modest house except for the many photographs on the wall; generations of stern-faced, haunted looking fishermen, their wives and children. Tintypes taken by itinerant photographers working the outports long before Confederation annexed the Island to Upper Canada, prowling Newfoundland's coasts, capturing for posterity a rare race of people unknown to the outside world. The solid mothers and determined fathers and their multitudinous progeny. Two families existed side by side. He assumed hers and her husbands', Breeze's stepfather. But the stepfather was a labourer and had no connection with Newfoundland according to Breeze. His family had emigrated straight from Ireland to Montreal. But all these people looked like they had sprung from the rocks of Ireland, another country of rugged coastlines. He had a lot to learn about Ireland, but his assumption was correct. Breeze Senior, taking his hand in hers, saw the direction of his gaze. "That's what I want to tell you, 'bout our families. You see..." At that moment a bundle sailed down the stairs and landed in the hallway. Breeze followed, *thumping* down the stairs in leather work boots, lugging her precious cello in its black case.

"There, I'm packed." She was dressed in overalls and plaid shirt, loose and practical, sporting a peaked cap, the ubiquitous costume for dock workers and labourers of Northern Europe and fishermen in the Maritimes.

"Another time, perhaps. But I will just tell you there's a old journal. Bridged doesn't know I know she's read it. It's probably in that bundle, by the sounds of it." Breeze Senior patted Christian's hand and stood up to embrace her daughter. "What will you do for money?"

"Oh, I withdrew my scholarship. Christian has some money. What have we to eat?"

"I made bread." She headed to the kitchen calling, "There's a stew. I'll put some up in jars."

"You'll love Mom's stew. It's the best."

"Breeze," Christian said, getting to his feet, his head reeling. "We're not going to summer camp."

"I know. Doesn't mean we have to start out hungry."

"Daughter," Breeze Senior called from the kitchen, "I don't know what you're about, but please be careful, especially with the baby. And when you get to the Cove, look up Garret, if he's still alive. I've not heard a thing for years. Terrible how families can drift apart."

They studied the photographs in awkward silence until Breeze Senior returned with a heavy sailor's duffel bag. "This was Garret's sea bag."

Christian accepted the bag and felt compelled to ask, "Is Garret your brother, Mrs. O'Keefe?"

Breeze Junior made a sudden gesture that meant stop, don't ask. Breeze Senior indicated a photograph on the wall. Christian turned to look. There was a picture in a simple frame, set apart from the others. A young man, by the build and posture, but the face was gnarled and disfigured, like a lunatic in an old world asylum. In certain times the distorted freaks of nature were closeted away in institutions but this wizened monster of a human was held out to view, without shame.

"Yes, that's Garret. Some lovely isn't he? But don't judge that man by his face, Christian my dear. If you ever learn anything in life, it's that. Never was a better man born to woman. He should be a saint, that one. My son, what he suffered, and if he's alive, suffers still. I never should have left him, to my ever lasting regret."

The cab's horn sounded sharp and urgent. "Sorry, Mom, we got to go."

Breeze Senior was crying silently. She embraced Christian and then her daughter. "You take care of that little one. Call me the moment you gets to Fogo. Many has phones now."

The ride back to the Old City was subdued. Christian and Breeze held hands in the back seat. The cello rode up front with Gerard.

"Gerard, can we go in along Sherbrooke?" Christian asked.

Gerard headed east to connect with Sherbrooke Street. When they turned on Sherbrooke Christian became distracted, looking at the storefronts on the left as they approached Westmount. "There. Pull over, please."

Gerard stopped in a bus lane across from a row of old storefronts with apartments above. There was nothing unusual about the area: commercial and residential mix, working class. Every big city has block after block of two story buildings that grow with a city to house the multitudes of immigrants, the first wave; Europeans first then later the refugees from the Middle East and Asia. There was the grocery store on the corner with the usual signs for soft drinks and cigarettes, beer and wine. "I want to see if they know anything about my mom."

Christian crossed the street and stopped at the apartment door beside the vegetable stand, the meager show of produce agreeing with the season. He tried the handle but it was locked so he entered the grocery store.

"Is your family still in Haiti," Breeze asked Gerard, to fill the time.

"Yes, Miss, what's left of my brothers, except for my brother, in New York. My mother died of heartbreak five years ago. My father's missing. We don't know what happened to him."

Breeze didn't know what else to say. Fathers are not supposed to just disappear. She watched the grocery store until Christian came out, looked up at a window above the store then crossed to the cab.

"The store owners don't know. They recently arrived from Pakistan. She says the woman, a Mrs. Joyce, lived alone and moved back to Ireland."

"Was that your mom, do you think?"

"Has to be. I've only been gone three years." Those three years suddenly meant great loss. His family was gone as if the Joyce's never existed in Montreal.

"Then we've another reason to go to Ireland."

The cab moved back into traffic. Gerard was respectfully silent, although by his eyes Christian could tell he wanted to talk.

Last stop was Haim's deli. Gerard parked in the alley and waited in the cab. If Uncle Haim was devastated by the news he held it inside, but blessed them and pressed money into Christian's hand when Breeze went up to the apartment to pack their few belongings. "For the baby," he said. "Be safe and look after your family, yes?"

"I will. Thank you for everything."

"You weren't here long enough for everything." Haim turned away to his window, fumbling to relight his cigar. "It's going to be a long time before the grapes are ready. A winter. A summer, but...Will you be back by then?"

"Uncle Haim, I have no idea if we'll be back, but we'll remember you. I'm sorry..."

Breeze entered the back of the deli with a bundle. "We hope you see your family soon..." said Breeze with a kiss on both cheeks, sensing the sadness in the old man. With so little time and so brief a history shared there wasn't much to say, other than goodbyes and promises to return, someday.

When they arrived at the Market Basin a taxi was pulling away from the dock area. Renée was standing on the deck of the *Bayou*

Queen dressed as if she were embarking on a luxury cruise. For Christian it was a moment he would not soon forget, possibly because the emotions he felt were burned into his senses so deeply, but he was never able to explain the feelings coursing through his body from brain cortex to extremities. Breeze sensed his distress, not just because his grip tightened; it was in his eyes when he looked from Renée to Breeze and back again to the gorgeous young woman out of context on the bow of the old fishing boat with the shabby port scene as a backdrop. What Breeze saw, beyond Renée's poise and confidence, was a threat. "That's Renée?"

Christian had to swallow hard before he could answer, and he knew the answer better be honest. "Yes, that's Renée. My former lover, as you know, companion in difficult times, my trusted confidant and hopefully, still good friend. Don't be put off by her superior ways. And don't be shy. The best thing you can do is take her in your arms, like I am going to do. By the way, Maartyn couldn't have warned her about you so this will be interesting."

"Well, that's blunt enough."

"This will definitely be interesting," said Gerard sarcastically. "Sorry, I can't stay to watch. Good luck, mawn. You too, Miss."

Christian and Renée embraced and shared their special feeling, briefly, due to certain constraints. "You're not Dominique," Renée said to Breeze awkwardly waiting to be introduced. Maartyn's letter had been emphatic. *Christian was in trouble.* But who is this woman with the wild red hair dressed like a British dockworker? Renée had just arrived from Paris and, no longer into Beatnik-Bohemian mode, was turned out in a chic travelling ensemble: suede boots with unusually thick heels, long shearling coat with fur trim and a jaunty suede tam to match, all in natural tones, but with a garish purple and orange silk scarf, oddly out of sync, framing her face. Christian remembered it was Esameralda's scarf, the one that held back her fabulous black main the night Escobar brought the Diez sisters to Christian's villa. The same Esameralda who was lying beside him by morning as Renée feigned sleep. Oh, god, how complicated life can be! That caused Christian another small crisis of conscience. And then the other oddities came into view when she took off the scarf. Renée's blonde hair was shoulder length and flipped. He missed her long braid. And she was wearing make up, more European chic even than Christian remembered. But in Cuba she was slumming in Bohemia; now, just stepping off a jet from Paris, into the industrial dock scene, she was a stunning beacon among the industrial marine clutter.

Then Christian remembered there were certain elements of his hometown who might be out to kill them all, for various reasons. "Breeze, this is Renée. Renée, this is Breeze. We're pregnant, but let's get down below."

Breeze, dragging the cello, lead the way to the fore hatch and Christian carried Renée's heavy luggage. Luggage?

The Explanation

To Renée's eternal credit she made no sign that the small, austere but almost clean galley was a problem. She peeled off the suede coat and flung it on a bunk above the still sleeping Paulo. Maartyn *had* warned her that Paulo was part of the equation so she accepted his presence as inevitable and probably part of the reason Christian was in trouble. He was just a complication from their recent history. But she did have a comment about the abrupt confrontation with Breeze, and the news. "Well, a tropical rain storm could not have flattened me any better," she said in French not realizing Breeze was fluent in her language.

"Sorry, there was no time for formalities. Visibility is a problem."

"I think the baby is a great idea, but you really are in trouble according to Maartyn's brief letter."

"Much. Except that the baby wasn't an *idea* and as for

256

Breeze, she insists on being part of this madness," he continued in English to include Breeze who was visibly annoyed.

Breeze wanted to hold some part of Christian but Renée had taken control. Breeze and Christian were side by side in the booth, but Renée and Christian were holding hands across the table, both hands. Renée was too sophisticated to show any outward resentment toward Breeze. Breeze, despite Christian's urgings, was shrinking in her presence. What to do? It was difficult enough trying to bring Renée up to date quickly, he also had to balance the chemistry. It was merely problematic until Paulo rallied and joined them. Suddenly Christian was in a double quandary. Renée and Paulo had been lovers and companions, sharing much of the Cuban episode, so what would the dynamic be?

"Renée," he said, sliding into the booth beside her, casually as if they had never been separated.

"Hello, Paulo. How have you been, or should I ask?"

"Oh, you know me, up and down...That was a joke."

"This isn't a cabaret. You look awful."

"Thanks. Montreal doesn't agree with me. So, you're mixed up in this crazy shit too?"

"Apparently. Perhaps we could begin with an explanation. I'm dying to know what has been going on to cause Maartyn such anxiety."

"Poor choice of words, Renée," said Christian, letting go of her hands in a pretext of pouring coffee so as not to put Breeze in the roll of servant. It was going to be difficult enough to reconcile his love life but he had to keep the girls on even terms. He knew that Breeze could hold her own in certain quarters, and if Renée could spin down from her natural Parisienne arrogance, there was some hope. In Cuba Renée had been haughty with Rosameralda and Esameralda at first, but he knew that Renée was trying hard not to be intimidated by the supremely gorgeous, confident and intense Rosa. The next day the girls went swimming and returned to the villa arm in arm, talking about girl things that are incomprehensible to young men. But in the hills above Los Espiritos the girls had bonded. What was their secret? He had no idea, so perhaps it was best left to the girls. Maartyn had been smitten by Rosa and suffered badly. Christian did not have time to see the effect the news of Rosa's death had on him, the leaving was so abrupt, but he guessed the hardcore marine-fugitive had a few bad moments. And that reminded him that Maartyn was also in trouble and he better explain the other issues. Whether the two girls liked each other, loved each other or ended up rolling on the deck in a dragged-out catfight, was beyond his abilities to control.

"Renée, I have to give you the facts. Things may happen that force us to leave in a hurry, on this boat, apparently."

"Why? If it's that serious we can just fly out. I've come prepared."

"No, it's much too complicated. It's Maartyn..."

"Where is Maartyn?"

"Well, that's one of the complications."

"He's in trouble too?"

"Seems like."

"How much trouble? Jail?"

"The FBI. He was caught trying to cross the border, with a group of Haitians and no papers. Our cab driver's trying to arrange getting Maartyn out of their hands so we can pick him up, by boat."

"From the FBI? Are you all crazy?"

"Yes, certifiably," interjected Paulo.

"Is there at least a plan?" she asked sarcastically.

"Gerard's looking after the details..."

"Your cab driver," she said flatly but there was no mistaking the tone.

"He's not just a cab driver. He's a Haitian freedom fighter. Fought with Castro. Leader of the local resistance, in Haiti I mean, against Papa Doc."

"Wait. Maartyn said you were involved with a revolutionary

group plotting the overthrow of the government. How did you get mixed up with Haitians?"

"Coincidental. Gerard's a friend of Jean-Pierre...I don't know. I arrived in town and met this guy, Jean-Pierre."

"Yes, Jean-Pierre. Maartyn said I was to definitely get you away from him, and this Dominique woman. Fine. I'm here to do that. But now Maartyn's held by the FBI. You want to cause an international incident?"

"No, it's, complicated I know, but people are after us, me and Paulo, including the police, and since we have to go anyway, and Maartyn gave me his boat, and Breeze wants to go to Fogo Island..."

"Where?"

"East Coast. Newfoundland. Remember the dry fish Juanita gave us?"

"Ugh! Remember? The smell never stopped and this shrimp boat! My God, it still smells."

"It's all we have."

"No, it isn't. I have tickets for tonight's flight, extra tickets in case. We'll be in Paris for breakfast, lunch actually."

"I suppose you made reservations at your favourite bistro."

"Don't be sarcastic, darling, it's not like you. But I did get tickets for a Sartre lecture. As a surprise."

"Oh, God, Renée..."

"Well obviously I should have reserved three tickets, but then no one warned me, did they? And while I'm on the subject, when *were* you going to write?" Renée asked, the colour rising in her cheeks.

Christian realized it was not going well, and he still had to tell her about Rosameralda. "Okay, look, I appreciate you coming all this way, to...do what exactly?"

"My plan is, what father calls, a surgical strike. Rescue my former lover and still friend, from terrorists!"

"Ouch. Sorry, I asked for that one. Look, you do not want to get mixed up in this. I would understand if you got back in a cab. Gerard could drive you..."

"Don't be silly. I'm not leaving without you."

"I have no idea what happens in the next hour, tonight or to-morrow, or any time after that, except that Gerard's coming back tonight with supplies for the trip to New York, I guess."

"Tonight? Is there a decent restaurant at least?"

Christian watched them walking along the dock, Renée and Breeze, heading out on the town. Breeze, thinking they were just going to Newfoundland, had not packed downtown clothes so Renée gave her the choice of a nice dress or a tailored suit. Breeze being two inches taller than Renée, chose the dress. A better fit; a dark burgundy, not a great match with her hair, but understated, at least with her black running shoes and green parka. It was either those or the work boots. Christian had to laugh but whatever the outcome of their afternoon on-the-town, life was about to become even more complicated.

Breeze touched Renée's arm to signal stop, even though they had a green light. She saw the car coming against the red, but had a feeling it would turn without stopping, despite pedestrians. "Walking in Montreal is an adventure."

"And Paris. Athens is worse," said Renée. "Milan's almost as bad as Athens. The Greeks don't have roads or brains, just cars. At least, thank God, they don't make them. Italians on the other hand, because they create classics they think there are no laws that apply."

"You've travelled a lot."

"Maybe too much. The world seems small and delicate. Always in trouble."

"We can cross now."

They wandered west on Rue Notre-Dame to Boul. St. Laurent, far enough from the industrial docks to have good restaurants.

Sitting side by side at a small table over a reasonably good lunch of French onion soup, roast chicken and a passable avocado salad, Renée briefed Breeze on her life and travels, not dwelling on Cuba. Breeze said it must be wonderful to travel so freely, remembering what Christian had told her of the Bohemian experiments. "Yes, I suppose. A consequence of being raised by a diplomat. My father is with the Foreign Service. New York mostly, but it seems when I was a child there was always a problem somewhere in the world that we either caused or had to settle, so the family travelled a lot. I believed the world was just normally in chaos and that the real danger was on the streets of large cities. The traffic, ah! European cities are not meant to be driven in, except on bicycles and donkey carts. Now, even walking is a risk. Paris was at least given a chance by Haussmann. He demolished old Paris to provide these great wide parking lots called boulevards, all leading to traffic circles where you can go round and round as if life is a carnival ride. Jump on, jump off. If you can survive traffic circles you can survive anything. Cuba was nothing and Montreal's a *breeze*." She nudged Breeze with her arm.

Breeze laughed and took Renée's hand. Renée kissed her red curls. Christian was right. "Then coming to Montreal was not such a scary thing?"

"Not really. The scary thing is that Christian's in trouble again. He's such a nice boy, but so naive and trusting. Easily loved and easily hurt. You are just what he needs, Breeze. I sense you're the strong one. I would gladly have taken him away to Paris, but I can see he's in love with you, so you must be the one to guide him through this latest crisis. You can explain it to me over desert. Have to feed la bebé. Then we're going shopping."

The girls returned to the Market Basin loaded down with, what Renée considered, a few essentials for the voyage, walking arm in arm toward the *Bayou Queen*, a heavy shopping bag in each free hand, chatting like old friends catching up. Christian was in the wheelhouse continuing the cleanup and when he saw the girls, backed by the setting sun, he was reminded of that day in Cuba, the brief few hours of peace before the chaos. The three girls, Esa, Renée and Rosa, returning from the hills, arm in arm, laughing, like innocent beauties in Paradise. Nothing is he also reminded himself.

It took several shuttles to empty the cab of essentials: mattresses and blankets, sensible sea boots, down parkas for everyone, on Breeze's assurance that Newfoundland was near the Arctic Circle. Cases of good wine and brandy, on Renée's assurance that they were necessary to sustain life. Renée refused to travel without some luxuries and boxes and boxes of food in case Gerard's supplies did not include smoked oysters, sun dried tomatoes, olive oil, spices, fresh garlic, cheeses to match the wines and rings of sausage, French and Italian bread and, in case the supply ran out, flour to make more. Fresh vegetables for salads and chocolate truffles for what, celebrations? Comfort? Renée left little to chance, including stocking up on bandages and flashlights, a consequence of her time as nurse Renée, comandanté of the rebel cave with a nine-millimeter pistol strapped to her hip.

The girls chirped and chatted in French, juaol and patois with the Haitian cab driver about the logistics of getting the supplies aboard and stowed in proper places. Christian, worried about the cabbie's suspicions, followed Breeze or Renée as directed, but was more concerned about being obvious. The Market Basin was visible from the warehouse although hardly anyone but Christian bothered to look out the grimy windows. Jean-Pierre may be on the run but his spies could be watching. The boat keeper on the McAllister tug *was* watching, fascinated, as two beautiful women loaded supplies on the old fish boat, and at one point asked Christian, enviously, if they were planning an expedition to the Arctic. Christian answered that they were going to winter in the south.

"Good plan," he said enviously. Paulo for his part commandeered a mattress and retreated to his bunk.

Darkness arrived finally, but not soon enough for Christian. It had been a tense day, despite the pleasant chirping of the girls and their sporadic laughter. What had they talked about all afternoon? he wondered. Whatever it was the chemistry worked. One less worry. But where was Gerard? And what was known about their plans, now that the obvious activity would be reported all over Montreal by cab drivers? Christian occupied himself in the engine room, staring at the big green Bota engine. He pumped up the diesel stove tank, ten strokes. Less than half a tank in twenty-four hours. He wondered how much fuel there might be in the big hulking storage tanks? He identified the shaft that drives the propeller, noting that there was a steady trickle of water coming in around a big nut, just where the shaft vanished into the stern wood. It had been doing that since Maartyn left and there seemed to be a lot of black water in the bilge. How long could it do that before the boat sank? There must be some kind of pump he reasoned.

The electrical panel was a confusion of switches, buttons, gauges and coloured lights. One small light glowed red. It had been doing that also since Maartyn left. Christian rationalized, correctly, that the electricity was leaving the boat at the same time the water was coming in, advancing his thinking to, 'should probably reverse that process'. There was one green button that seemed to dominate the panel. He wondered what would happen if he pushed it. Normally he would shy away from experiments that involved things attached to any kind of power source, but, on this occasion a new feeling came over him. Maybe it was the need to do something on his own. It was, after all, 'his' boat.

Like mankind reaching out to touch the hand of God, Christian's finger approached the green button, and pushed tentatively. Nothing happened. He pushed it again, harder. Grinding noises issued from the engine, then, Armageddon sounding as if all the hounds of hell were loosed. He whirled to face the beast as The Great God Bota rumbled to life. The noise, to a novice, was incredible. The boat shook and rattled. Many parts of the engine moved and whirled. Christian plastered himself against the ladder waiting for the explosion that must be the inevitable result of such a catastrophic eruption.

Footsteps thumped across the deck. Breeze was at the gangway. "Christian!?"

"I don't know!"

Then Renée was beside Breeze. "Voila! She sounds even better! Maartyn has been at work."

Christian climbed out of the engine room and slammed the door. On deck the world was different. The boat had a purposeful vibration. The hull seemed alive and the mutter from the exhaust stack very business-like. "You mean that's the way it's supposed to sound?"

"But of course. That Maartyn."

Of course, indeed, Renée made the voyage to Havana with Maartyn, and Ramon! "But how do I shut it off?"

Paulo appeared on the scene, looking very annoyed.

"I don't know," said Renée, looking at Paulo. "Maartyn did something in the wheelhouse. Paulo, shut it off!"

Only Paulo could be annoyed about progress. "Fucking amateurs." He entered the wheelhouse and a moment later the engine died. The silence was broken by a siren somewhere in the city. Then another.

"At least we know she still functions," said Renée.

"She? You call that monstrosity, she?"

"It's what Maartyn calls it, her, because it, she, was cantankerous, bitchy, and short tempered. His words. But I don't remember that motor looking or sounding that good."

That night the four of them sat in the galley sharing a bottle of good French wine to celebrate the awakening of Bota. The galley was almost cozy with the stove flickering, candles burning and the remnants of a good meal evidently well eaten.

"Should we be showing lights?" asked Breeze.

"Doesn't matter now. The whole world knows we're here," said Christian. "Gerard should be here by now."

"So, where's this Gerard you keep talking about? If the situation's so grim, shouldn't we be getting away from this part of the harbor at least?" reasoned Renée.

"You can't trust fucking Haitians," offered Paulo, in case the wine had taken the edge off their fears.

Candles burned down and were replaced. The heat of the stove increased until they had to open the hatch to breath. Breeze dozed on Christian's shoulder, and then burrowed down into his lap and slept. She had some problems tucking up, making room for the baby. Paulo retreated to his bunk in the fo'c'sle.

"I wonder how Esy is? I wrote to her many times." Renée's eyes were edged with tears, or it may have been just the diesel fumes.

"Don't forget, Renée, Esy could barely read or write."

"I know. Oh, Christian, I feel terrible. In my second letter I almost demanded to hear from her or Miguel. How insensitive of me. I sent her my telephone number, but then, I wasn't home that much and the staff had no instructions about personal calls. I spent most of my time at the chateau with my mother."

At the chateau? Not sleeping with an army of student radicals on Ile St. Louis? Christian mused silently. "Renée, I'm sorry, in all this I didn't ask about your father. Is he...did he?"

"No, no. It was a miracle. After I returned home and formally renounced my errant Bohemian ways he seemed to get better and then he went to Switzerland to see a famous doctor who sent him to South Africa. I went with him, as he and mother are not on the best of terms. Frankly, I think she has a lover, finally. Father was very good about it. How could he not be, considering? But that's so much history. I talked to both of them about the new world thinking and you know, they seemed to agree, however, unfortunately that did not bring them closer. Some things go beyond free thinking. Someday the children will be adults. However, father...had an operation in Johannesburg and now he's back at the ministry."

"That's great news."

"Yes, and who knows, maybe he'll live long enough to reconcile with mother. But you know, it would be better if he did not live too long, for his own peace of mind. He loves his country but things aren't good in France. There's so much unrest in Paris...the communist theories wash into the Seine like rainwater, but the streets are more clogged with theories than ever. It's like here. Breeze has explained it well. Young people are dissatisfied, angry. They have no direction but you know, it will build and become its own movement for no other reason than momentum. And it will be hard on men like my father. He's very much the old guard who can deal with world affairs and wars, but are unable to understand the ungrateful young they sired, who, no matter what their parents do for them, will resent everything and demand change. Since the war the Socialists and the Communists are very active in Europe. The universities are full of them now. I tell my father to make his compatriots aware that while they look beyond France for solutions to our problems, the real problem is with the students on the streets. It's happening all over Europe. Do you know why? I don't. The wars are history and the scars healing. We should be looking forward to peace and prosperity. Listen to me, I sound like the worst kind of bourgeois bitch."

"You do sound older, but not bitchy. What happened?"

"Cuba. We were so young and stupid then. Before the Revolution it was just beaches, rum and fucking. I don't regret it. I think we deserved that, don't you?"

Christian looked down at his sleeping Breeze and stroked her hair. Deserved? Maybe it was nothing more than opportunity and hormones, and an endless supply of rum and dope. That was over and the present reality bleak. Somehow, he knew, he would have to navigate them through this crisis but lacked the knowledge and experience. "I think it does have a lot to do with the legacy of the wars. And what does father say about the Cold War?"

"Many in government dismiss the Cold War as a distraction, living in the glory of the triumph over the Germans. Our parents think we should be grateful for their sacrifices. We grew up too secure, and take our freedom for granted, so we can be stupid and irresponsible, because, well, they made it easy."

"During the Depression, here in North America at least, when the bums tramped around looking for work, they never thought of just wandering aimlessly for recreation, like we did."

"Yes, that's all it was. I thought we were out there for experience, an education, and that once acquired we would settle down and use that experience to make a better world. To build on what our parents started. The war must have left very deep scars, not to mention a whole generation killed off. Can you imagine what that will be like?"

"Yeah. I think about it."

"The artists, writers and philosophers gone too young. We've lost much. Yes, and don't forget the genes," said Renée. "They send always the best young men. By the laws of evolution the strong survive, but in the new wars there is no time to survive. Just suppose the ones who might have made a difference were killed, and those left, like us, aren't up to the task. Did we sacrifice our future Einsteins, Descartes, Rembrandts, Dalis, Mozarts? Can the new of us fill that void?"

"Depressing, but think about the possibilities," said Christian, trying not to sound pedantic. "The world has always been at war, or just recovering, or about to go to war. For thousands of years the ranks, the foot soldiers, have been the young, the potential geniuses. Yet we still have Renoir and Debussy, even some decent politicians like Churchill, so we will never know what we missed."

"I suppose, but I still worry that if we keep on like this, as we progress and find more ways to kill each other, that some day we'll be reduced to crawling about in the gutters like rats, so weakened, so unable to survive."

"Rats are survivors but you can thank the self-serving religion-obsessed leaders if that becomes true."

"*Phew*, no one will be thanking anyone. The religious fanatics will be too busy making accusations to accept any responsibility."

Christian looked at Renée's watch. "I'm worried about Gerard."

"Back to our own reality, yes? Speaking of survival, our plane has left for Paris."

What if they had got on the plane, he wondered? "I should put Breeze to bed."

Neither of them moved. They were both thinking what they would be doing now, if not for Breeze and certain other realities? Their hands moved across the table and entwined. Christian kissed hers, and Renée his. Sometimes, when two people have shared emotions, faced danger, loved deeply, words are not necessary. Nor is it always possible to know what the message unspoken means.

"Breeze," he whispered, "bedtime, baby. Bed."

Breeze mumbled in the affirmative and burrowed deeper. She had been in a warm, protected sleep, trusting that Christian and Renée would look after her. Not time to worry yet...

Christian tucked Breeze into the skipper's bunk. "I'll be right back."

He checked around the boat and watched for movement on shore. The harbour was very quiet and the night unusually mild for December. There was a heavy mist in the air. Dirty yellow clouds hung like rags over the muffled city. Everything could be seen in the reflected glow but with blurred edges, and nothing could hide. The McAllister tug was silent and dark. Christian stood near the bow thinking of the 'calm before the storm'. It was just too quiet. Too still. Only one boat moved on the Seaway down bound, in a hurry. The saltwater boats were fleeing Canada before winter locked the Continent in a freezer. The only other movement seemed to be the Lachine Rapids and the swaying green buoy near Ste. Hélèna Island. He could hear the rush of water around its base, like a pulse, as if the thing were swimming upstream, forever breasting the river, and that reminded him that they were committed to a voyage. Suddenly he was anxious to get going, less afraid of the river, more threatened by the heavy silence of the city. Montreal no longer felt like home.

Breeze was still awake when Christian slid into the bunk, savouring the warmth of her smooth body. "Hello, sailor. What were you doing so long?"

Was there a hint of suspicion? No. Just Breeze being funny. "Checking the boat. Looking at the city. Can't sleep?"

"I was so gone before, and now I'm awake."

"You should try to sleep. We have to leave early even if Gerard isn't back."

"But then we won't know what to do."

"I know. But I don't like just sitting here knowing people are out there looking for us. This is so wrong, Breeze."

"*Shhh*, Gerard will be here soon."

"You have that feeling too?"

"Funny, eh? He seems solid. Has it together. What if Haiti had a leader like Gerard instead of those awful people, like Papa Doc?"

"Yeah, funny. Or just twisted sick logic. Life isn't fair." He was quiet, absently stroking her anarchy of red curls.

"You're thinking about *her*."

"Sorry, Breeze. Renée means a lot to me. I guess. I'm not sure. Renée always confuses me. Am I being too honest or too complicated?"

269

"You're only a clean slate once, before you experience your first love. And that's why you never forget. And after that, little pieces of every lost love stick to your heart and leave marks. But when the real love of your life comes along, you know, that love has to erase all the other marks, except for the first one, which is indelible, and that's how you know it's real."

"Wow. Why does everyone but me understand love? Remember Miguel? I hate to use the term houseboy. He told me about love one day as we drifted along the shore in the skiff. That was just before all hell broke loose in Los Espiritos. I was on my way to meet Ernesto Escobar. He ended up being shot by a firing squad, Escobar did."

"I know. You told me."

"Yes, I did. You already know a lot about me, the Cuba part at least. Seems so long ago. Funny, Miguel was talking about Renée too."

"You still love her?"

"I don't...know. I never know about Renée. I have feelings."

"You love her."

"No, it's not like that now. Once you have experienced things as we did it's hard to stop having feelings, completely. Like what you said about the pieces sticking."

"But if she is your first love then I'm just one of the pieces."

"No, no! You're not. Not a piece. The whole. Everything. The first and last real love of my life."

"How would you know that? You haven't lived your whole life."

Christian had to admit it was a tough argument. He was tempted to say, maybe he was lucky to have survived Cuba and maybe his luck had run out, and Breeze would be his only true love. "We're different Breeze, you and me. I don't mean from each other. I mean we come together from different reference points, from what Renée and I had. Young, footloose, on the road, no responsibilities. It grew, yes, into something more than just a fling. I don't know what. We're just different, you and me, now."

"Should I be afraid of that difference? What if life with her is what you really want? She obviously still loves you." Breeze turned away so Christian could not see the hot, silent tears. But he could sense them.

"Breeze, don't be afraid of her. Renée never wants to commit to love. She plays these little games to keep her distance, regardless of what she actually feels. You read her letter. It's a philosophy that she believes in. So I learned to be somewhat withdrawn, defensive, to protect myself. But I don't have to do that with you. From the first moment..."

"What if she changes her mind? Will you run to her?"

Oh, the anguish of being honest. He knew he should answer immediately. The slightest hesitancy...too late. Please, please, wait...don't assume anything.

"Christian?..."

She's giving me the chance, he said to himself. Answer her, honestly. "Breeze, I can't answer that, yet."

"Yes you can. You're deciding right now, so you might as well tell me."

She's being so fair..."You're asking me to be honest about something that might happen in the future, over which I have no control."

"Honesty is what I need right now. Do you know...can you honestly say that you wouldn't run to her if she summoned you?"

"You mean into bed?" He needed time. A change of course. Anything..."No, it's not that base. Bed...sex. Means nothing compared to the love you cannot deny in your heart, even in the deepest place love might hide until someone strips off the covers."

"No, not just a writer's words, I need honesty."

"In that case I can only say, I don't know, honestly. I guess we'll just have to go along and see what happens."

"And that's life, isn't it."

"Yes, that's life," he sighed, wishing it wasn't true.

Breeze held Christian's hand to her lips. He could feel the hot tears; the silent tears, the deepest, hardest kind. But she moved her whole body closer to him. Then she said, "Thank you for telling the truth."

"Breeze, it would have been easier to lie, to protect you."

"I know. I also knew you wouldn't. She told me."

Renée was still there, in the conversation. What had they talked about? he wondered.

Christian awoke suddenly. Was it a noise on deck? He waited, listening, hearing whispers, muffled sounds...he assumed it was Paulo moving around, or perhaps the wind, but the Basin was dead still. Then a car drove away from the docks, slowly, tires crunching the wet gravel. It was just the night watchman arriving, he decided. He drifted into a light sleep.

Breeze was asleep. It was a good sleep, secure in the arms of her man who had been honest about their relationship. Breeze was pragmatic, like her mother. Hard lessons learned and passed on. Parents make mistakes too, she had said often, usually in the impetuosity of youth, if there is no one to guide them through the shoals of adolescence. Breeze Senior had made the mistake of love. Not the loving, but letting love cloud reason. What good is reason if avoiding love leaves a spiritual void? Better to suffer the consequences than to go through life empty, being self-possessed. Missing the one thing that drives human nature: the absurd idea that giving will be rewarded with life-ever-after happiness. Breeze Senior could write the book, Breeze had said. Her lover, Lliam Dwyer, did write the book, the journal, and Breeze Junior carried that book aboard the *Bayou Queen*. Christian about to have life revealed from the perspective of two tragic people he only knew briefly, suffering destruction of the spirit in a microcosm of the greater human tragedy. Why tragic? Christian was becoming aware that tragedy stalks anyone with passion. Anyone foolish enough to think that a strong will alone can defend against the forces of darkness.

He was still awake listening to Breeze breathing, going over the story again and again, his and hers, and what he knew about her mother and Fogo Island. The details yet to be revealed but promised, once they had solved their immediate problems...

The jarring sound of tires on the dock beside the *Bayou Queen* announced a new crisis. He whispered, "Breeze...get dressed."

Three taxicabs were spilling people; many people lugging bundles and carrying boxes, onto the dock area, trying to be quiet but not succeeding. Gerard was directing the lead group. They talked in harsh whispers, gesturing at the *Bayou Queen*, arms flailing in protest. Obviously Christian's boat was not what they had expected. Gerard drove them forward in a dark wave. There were at least fifteen young males and females, speaking a mixture of Spanish, French and Creole patois. Haitians, Christian knew. Except for two boys carrying bundles, urging the people forward. They looked lighter, perhaps Latin American. Gerard sent the cabs away and joined the boys pushing the people aboard.

"Gerard...what's going on?"

"No time to explain, mawn, but these people coming with us. The police looking for us an' you. Word's out that you murdered Dominique..."

"No!..."

Gerard jumped aboard, untied the bow lines, flinging them overboard, then pushed his way into the milling mob to the wheelhouse. He ordered a Haitian to get the stern lines. "Go, Chris! You run the boat. I'll see to the engine. We got to go, now!"

"Jesus!..."

"Señor, Christ!!..."

A body came flying through the air. "Oh, my God! Miguel? What?..."

"Señor, Christ...yes, it's me. This man said nothing...this boat, Maartyn's boat. I had no idea it was you."

"Where did you come from?"

The Bota engine rumbled to life. The *Bayou Queen* was drifting away from the dock, helped by the new guests who, accepting that the old boat was their only hope, were in a hurry to put distance between themselves and the authorities. The collective urgency caused them to all talk at once. 'Go! Go!' Explanations would have to wait. Christian pried himself loose from Miguel and ran into Breeze.

"Christian, what's happening?"

"Apparently it's time to go, and they're coming with us."

"Señor Christ, can I help?"

"Yes. Get these people off the bow. Make them go aft, back there."

"Aye, aye, Señor Christ."

"And stop calling me Christ!" Christian pushed Breeze ahead of him into the wheelhouse. "Okay, what makes this thing go?"

On the dash, to the right of the big wooden wheel, there were two chrome handles. Each handle had a coloured knob. One was black and the other red. Since there was nothing else that seemed likely to affect the engine he pushed on the red handle. The engine began to race and vibrate. Too loud. He pulled the handle back. The engine idled. "Okay, then this one makes it go forward, maybe."

"Christian, you have no idea how to run this boat."

"No, I've been telling you."

"If we want to go backwards try pulling that handle."

"Do we want to go backwards?"

Renée appeared on the fore deck, followed by Paulo. Christian waved them into the wheelhouse for the reunion of Miguel and Renée. For once Paulo was of some use, preventing Renée and Miguel from crashing over the rail in the crush of greetings. The fluid refugees who Miguel had herded to the stern were returning to retrieve belongings. The decks around the wheelhouse became a whirl of Haitians chattering as if it was a picnic excursion on the Meriposa Belle.

"Señor Christ, Señorita Renée, this is like Christmas and fiesta!"

"Miguel, how did you get here?" asked an incredulous Renée.

"Jésus and I had to leave Cuba..."

"Look, everybody, I'd like to know the story, but we've got to get moving, and I can't see!"

The wayward *Bayou Queen* was nuzzling the McAllister tug. The night watchman, in his pajamas, was gesturing from the bridge. "Hey, Rookie, get that floating junk off my boat! And bon voyage!" As if the battered *Bayou Queen* was a threat to the steel work tug. Gerard joined the growing crowd in the wheelhouse. "Go astern, Christian, and soon."

"Okay, I know." Christian pulled the black handle and turned the wheel lock to lock until he was reasonably sure the rudder was at least straight. He had learned something from the river run adventure. The *Queen* began to move, backing nicely away from the McAllister tug, aiming somewhat down the middle of the Market Basin. Gerard was at the wheelhouse door watching their progress, but he kept throwing worried glances at the dock area. What did Gerard mean by, 'he was accused of murder'? Dominique?

"Christian! You're going too far to port!"

"Port? What the hell?..."

"Go ahead and then come again, mawn. Steer a little to starboard."

"Go ahead. Port. Starboard..." Renée was asking Miguel about Esy and Rosa. Christian suddenly realized with dread that he had not told Renée about Rosa. He meant to tell her at the right time. This was not the time. "Miguel! Go to the stern, immediately, and tell those people to shut up and sit down!"

"Yes, Señor Christ. Immediately. You are the boss."

There was more than a little hurt in Miguel's voice, but he went, saying, "I have something to tell you about Rosa, Señorita Renée. Very sad."

"Christian? What's he saying? What about Rosa?"

Breeze stepped in and took Renée's arm, gently pulling her to the back of the wheelhouse. "Renée, I know it's not my place, but...well, Christian told me that your friend Rosa, died..."

One crisis resolved. Twice more Christian had to back and fill to exit the Market Basin. The last time he experienced this tactic he was a puzzled passenger on the *Elloise*, watching in awe as Petit Jacques manoeuvred his steam tug by backing into the Lachine Rapids. The current! The *Queen* was gathering speed astern.

"Now what?"

"Go ahead, mawn, an' turn to port!"

He pushed the shifter forward, too fast. There was a startling *thump* from the transmission as the propeller kicked over. "Okay, now what?"

"Next time shift to neutral first, then ease into gear."

He had no idea what Gerard was talking about. "Okay, but nothing's happening." They were still going backwards and the bow was dropping away. In a moment they were broadside to the current, rocking in the waves. "Did I break something?"

"No, mawn. Just give her power, now."

"Power? You mean, this thing?"

"Yes, that *thing*, would be a good thing to push, but do it easy, mawn. That is a very big engine and you should do nothing sudden, or you *will* break things. Dig?"

"Okay, right, got it." He eased the throttle ahead. The *Queen* began to move, but now she was heading for Ste-Hélèna Island. The green buoy startled Christian as it flashed too close to the bow. The number M199 was burned into his brain, like a song that won't go away.

"Christian, turn the wheel, to port, very soon."

"Right. Port. That's left?"

"Yes, mawn. Left."

"Why don't you do it?"

"She's your baby."

Breeze and his *baby*, and Renée and Rosa... "Renée, I'm sorry I didn't tell you sooner." He turned the wheel and the *Bayou Queen* curved away from the shore, putting the millrace on her stern. The world of chaos suddenly went quiet but the boat was racing downstream. "Maybe I should slow down a little."

"Yes, skipper, we don't want to attract attention."

"Okay, Gerard, can you tell me now what the hell is with all these people? Especially my houseboy?"

"Houseboy? You mean the one who never stops talking? Miguel? All I know is they got off a ship last week from Port-au-Prince with my people. The little buggers hustled food and clothes for them. Did everything for those people. He's some character."

"And this group? Is it what I think it is?"

"I figured, mawn, since we were goin' down to New York anyway, it would be a good time. I lost money on the last ones. You see, when you don't deliver you don't get paid. And some of them were with Maartyn's group, so they are a little nervous. I didn't tell them we were going by boat. They thought we were goin' to the border in those cabs."

"I see. Since we're already in trouble, running illegal immigrants won't matter much, especially since I'm wanted for murder. How the hell?"

"Dominique's been reported missing by her family. Police asking questions. Jean-Pierre set you up...his boys told the police you two had a big fight, then you went into hiding...watch where you're goin'! See that buoy, there. The green one? You just stay this side."

They scraped by buoy M195. The light blinked at them and then it was dark again. Even the lights of the city seemed to fade away.

"It's so dark..." He was thinking of the big storm that almost overwhelmed the tug that first night on the river.

"Goin' to rain, mawn. Then it's goin' to snow."

"What do we do with our guests?"

"Cargo hold?"

"Yeah, I guess so. Smells pretty bad."

"Okay, then, you just keep going that way, stay close to the greens, then you'll see M193, it's where Jacques turns to go up the canal, but you go on to the next light. That one, the red, flashing faster. Go on past that red and stay in between the reds and the greens. That's the east shore, stay closer to the greens. You'll be okay."

"Really? And what if a big boat comes?"

"Call me, and don't hit anything."

Christian looked down river on a maze of lights: red and green and white, flashing, blinking, in no particular order. Gerard left the wheelhouse.

At M193, green, he headed for the quick flashing red. So far so good. Then new lights appeared out of the darkness; a Great Lakes freighter heading upstream. Which side should he choose? Then he heard a scream. Then another. There was a surge of refugees toward the cargo hold. Then the whole mob sent up a rolling wave of shrieks and wails, running away from the hold. Renée and Breeze grabbed flashlights to investigate.

"Now what?" asked Paulo, grumpy with sleep. "Those Haitians...get excited about nothing."

"Maybe somebody fell overboard. Jesus! Paulo, go see what happened," Christian ordered.

Christian steered, remembering the feeling of helplessness watching Vince floundering in the rapids. He throttled down and put the engine into neutral. Waiting, waiting...then...

Breeze returned, looking ill. "Christian, there's a body in the hold."

The *Bayou Queen*, left on her own, was carried past the red flashing buoy at the tip of Ile Sainte-Hélène. The crew and passengers stood around the open hatch looking at the naked female body lying as if in sleep on the grey boards of the cargo hold. The flash-lights played tricks. She could be asleep and breathing. Dominique who was so darkly beautiful in life, seemed so trans-lucent and fragile in death. The Haitians huddled together, whis-pering, speaking of curses and omens.

The warning wail of the freighter started them screaming again. Christian ran for the wheelhouse, Gerard close behind. The *Bayou Queen* was pointing at the eastern shore. "Go that way!" shouted Gerard. It would be close. They were almost under the bow of the upbound freighter when the *Queen* gathered way, plodding for the holding area near the Longueil Yacht Club Basin, passing over the wreck of the *Honour France Villard*.

They continued down stream in shocked silence allowing the new crisis to settle.

"Shouldn't we call the police?" asked Christian.

"No, mawn, too dangerous. Petit Jacques' goin' to meet us at Sorel. Jacques will have fuel, supplies for my people, an' he will take care of the body."

"That sounds so cold," said Breeze.

"Christian, was she your girlfriend too?" asked Renée.

"No, she...we, it's complicated."

"Señor Christ always has some complication with his women. No disrespect, Señor, but it's true."

"Miguel, this would not be a good time..."

"I know many things your new woman would be interested to hear."

"Miguel! No. Some day write a book, okay?"

"Okay, but it seems a shame to waste all these stories, espe-cially since you have a new woman who may want to know what she's in for."

"For your information, I already told Breeze everything."

"Everything?" asked Renée, eyebrows raised.

"Almost. Look, this isn't the time. I wanted Breeze to know.

No surprises. I had no idea you would all end up in our life."

"You aren't happy to see me?" pouted Renée in her special way.

"Please, Renée, don't make it more difficult."

"I'm sorry. You're right. There are more important things."

"There *is* a body, yes," said Gerard.

"I hate to be indelicate," said Renée, "but isn't it, she...? You know?" It took time for the implications of a body and time to sink in. "Well, what should we do?"

"Wait, there's bags of salt in the hold," said Christian. "Remember the dried cod?"

"Too well," said Renée.

"Juanita would be proud," said Miguel.

"I'll see to it," said Gerard. "Let's get moving. Just keep heading down river and stay close to the green buoys."

"Outside?"

"Inside, to the left. Come on, Miguel."

They placed Dominique on a tarp, packed her slender body with salt and wrapped the canvas tightly to make a neat bundle, tying it with rope. With help from Paulo and Jésus they moved the body from the hold and placed it right aft against the transom covered with fish nets. Gerard's eulogy was brief.

Then it began to rain. Gerard herded his people into the hold, assuring them that the salt had exorcised the spirits, he said to convince himself. The illegal immigrants settled reluctantly on the floorboards of the stinking cargo hold and lit candles, made signs, but the spirit of Dominique lingered. They prayed, chanted and lit more candles. Gerard and Miguel replaced the hatch cover boards leaving one ajar for ventilation. "No other lights," warned Gerard.

"What about food?" asked Miguel, who was used to comforting and victualing people in strange, even dangerous situations.

"They won't eat near dead spirits."

The flashing blue light of a Harbour Patrol boat curved out from the city shore to intercept the *Queen.*

"Oh, Jesus! Now what?" sighed Christian, almost to himself.

"You four just be cool," said Gerard calmly. "You're on a party cruise. Slow down. Drink wine or something. Smoke dope. They'll understand that. If they ask, say you will be docking at the Longueuil Yacht Club for the winter. Miguel and I will be in the engine room."

Paulo, to his credit, understood the situation perfectly. He dodged down the fore hatch and returned with two bottles of wine and his hash kit. Breeze was reduced to stunned silence by the turn of events, and chose to be inconspicuous at the back of the wheelhouse. Renée, schooled in crisis, and who had made Christmas dinner in a Cuban cave while Batista's army tried to bomb and burn them out, opened the wine. Paulo lit his hash pipe. Christian steered. The fast patrol boat circled the *Bayou Queen,* sweeping in from astern throwing spray over their rail.

"Stop your boat!" an officer shouted through a bullhorn.

Christian throttled right back and shifted into neutral, but the *Queen* was still ranging ahead. The Harbour Patrol kept pace, easing alongside. When the two boats touched, the young officer sprang aboard. "Hi. Bon nuit," Christian offered.

"Interesting vessel. From the south I see," he said in French, appraising the battered Louisiana shrimper. "This your boat, Skipper?" he asked Christian.

"Yes, sir," answered Christian promptly, consummating the relationship with a slug of wine. "Former shrimp boat. Ah, now she's a yacht. Or will be. We're fixing her up." He was talking too much.

"I see. You've got some work ahead."

"Yeah. We're just out for a cruise. Last party of the season, before...winter, eh?"

"Don't get many boaters this time of year. You're brave ones." The officer sniffed the smoke and looked at the wine bottles on the dash. He also noted that the boaters were four normal looking Caucasians doing the usual illegal things on the water. "You were docked at the Market Basin for a few weeks."

"Ah, just temporary, waiting for a place at the Longueuil, the Yacht Club."

"You wouldn't be running immigrants or contraband?" Christian was beginning to sweat. "Ah, no sir. Just a cruise. Last one...I guess. Cold."

"Right. Snow tomorrow the Met says."

"That would do it, yes."

"Okay, Skipper, did you know that you aren't showing your running lights?"

"Running lights? Oh, yeah." What the hell are running lights? wondered Christian. "Forgot, I guess. Thank you."

"Stoned perhaps?"

"No, no...I never touch the stuff, when I'm driving." He would give anything to be drugged into oblivion at that moment. A good hit and soon all would be gone in a golden haze...

"Okay, let's see those lights."

"Right. Lights..." he stalled for time.

Paulo stepped forward and offered the glowing hash pipe. "I didn't see that," said the officer. "And I still don't see your running lights."

Paulo casually reached above the officer's head and flipped a switch on the electrical panel. "There. Those damned lights...you know, we all forget," he said in street French.

Renée was beside the harbour cop, hand on his arm. "No excuses officer. We were having such a good party. It's my friend's birthday."

The officer seemed intoxicated by Renée. "We'll let it go this time. Have a nice night. Next time remember your lights. And don't forget to report in when you enter Longueuil."

"Yes. Thank you."

"Do you have to go so soon?" asked Renée, almost purring.

She followed the officer to the railing. Don't push it, thought Christian.

The officer hesitated, sighed and dropped into the patrol boat, waving as the craft peeled away. Renée shut the door and exhaled deeply. Breeze, hands over her face, slid slowly down the bulkhead to the wet deck, trying not to cry.

"Breeze? Are you all right?"

"Uh-huh. I'm not used to being so...illegal."

"I'll make coffee," said Renée.

The coffee helped. Gerard drank his at the bow keeping watch for channel markers. Breeze stood beside Christian massaging his neck, hovering protectively. Renée and Miguel sat on the chart table talking softly about Cuba. Paulo opted to smoke hash in the galley, sulking about his ever-declining lot in life.

The *Bayou Queen* cleared the commercial part of Montreal Harbour at Longue Pointe but not passing out of the glare of the shore lights reflecting off the low rain clouds sliding in from the new front. With Gerard's help Christian was becoming familiar with the buoyage system, sticking to the greens, as they say, trying not to think about the past or the immediate future, fantasizing that, if they survived the trip down river, life might become normal, but the reality was Dominique's body and the last vision he had of her being attacked by Jean-Pierre. He also realized the guilt would not go away for a long time, if ever.

Then the rain came in sheets, pattering on the cabin top like thrown gravel, streaming down the wheelhouse windows. Visibility was poor even with the help of the refineries of Montreal East, whose flares were throwing a deathly pall on the low clouds between squalls. Christian sent Miguel to check on the passengers.

"We can't continue in this," said Gerard at the wheelhouse door. The rain drifted in around him and the air was colder. "Petit Jacques showed me a good place to anchor below Boucherville, near Varennes. Many islands to hide behind, but difficult to go in

283

there at night."

Christian, hearing Gerard but not comprehending, was staring straight ahead, a tight grip on the wheel.

"Christian?" Breeze felt his body going ridged. "Christian, are you all right?"

"No, I need...lie down." He lost his grip on the wheel and staggered back. Breeze caught him. Renée was there. "Get him to bed, now," she ordered.

Gerard and Breeze supported Christian out of the wheelhouse and into the captain's cabin. Renée took the wheel. She had been waiting for this to happen because she knew Christian better than anyone, the spells, and her heart ached.

"Can you steer?" asked Gerard.

"Yes, of course," she said defensively.

"I'll be at the bow. Watch for my signals. Steer close to the green lights but keep them always on your starboard side. Right. That's..."

"I know what starboard is."

Renée concentrated on the flashing green lights smeared across her vision like tiny bolts of lightning. One flashed along-side and filled the wheelhouse with garish green colour. The buoys came up too fast. The current was two knots and the wind was still from the Southwest, behind them. It would go to the Northeast, then North during the night. She tried to focus only on the lights while assessing their situation. Christian was down again. They had a hold full of illegal immigrants and a body on the stern. If the police had been tipped off by Jean-Pierre they would soon be looking for the *Bayou Queen*. Their anonymity could not last. At least the weather was a blessing. Some blessing. She missed Paris, the rain was softer. Breeze was beside her. "In Paris, on a night like this, the river is still beautiful."

"Renée, what's wrong with Christian?"

"Is he sleeping?"

"He seems unconscious. It happened once before..."

"Sleeping. Keep him warm, feed him hot broth when he wakes and comfort him." She was thinking of that first night with Esa. Christian had been delirious for three days. She nursed him with all her powers, including chicken broth. Then Esameralda and Rosameralda arrived. She wanted to make love with Esameralda. It was a very odd situation, and the relationship remained unusual to the point that Christian was jealous of Renée's affection for Esameralda. Esa returned the feeling for each in different ways. She made warm Latin love with Christian and drew Renée deep into her soul. That became a problem for Renée. She wanted to hold Esa in high esteem, but at the same time longed to lay with her in the heat of Cuban nights...a buoy, dead ahead, flashed and startled Renée but she reacted immediately. Gerard was waving frantically. The *Queen* scraped along the floatation tank. The light flashed accusingly and was gone astern and Gerard was still yelling about female drivers. But he was also laughing, wet and glistening, looking exotic in the glow of the running lights. Something stirred in her, a residual urge from thinking about Esa and Christian and the old Island magic still at play. Gerard was very attractive, yes, and she was visualizing. In the Islands pursuing the native boys had been a fantasy, something erotic to tease Christian. Now in their present situation the rules had changed. What rules? she wondered.

"Sorry." Maybe if it stopped raining he would come inside. She could reach behind her and...

"But what's wrong with Christian?" Breeze asked, interrupting her erotic reverie.

"There's nothing wrong with Christian," she said too strongly. "He just needs a little more time...the drugs said a doctor. He never eats properly!"

Breeze was taken aback by Renée's tone. That afternoon the two girls had established a rapport. Now Renée was different: arrogant and defensive. They were all tense. It was understandable, but there was more. "Are you still in love with Christian?"

"Love? What's that? What makes you so sure I was ever in love with him? We're friends and we had a good time."

"He showed me a letter." Breeze instantly regretted saying it. She had betrayed a trust but she had been angry with Christian and that made Breeze insecure, not a condition she was used to. Her mother breathed self-confidence into her daughter from birth. There was only one way to survive in a Newfoundland outport, or the world at large: be stronger than the rocks and sea, but never tempt fate by being foolish. Was she being foolish or was she being bold? Renée had grown up in comfort and security. There was dangerous magic in being able to summon your lover to Paris to share a river of dreams. Not a river like this one, of death and danger. Fugitives in the night. Not fair. How could Christian resist a summons from this beautiful European woman when she was just a fisherman's progeny from a down at heels northern ocean outport?

"Yes, my well read letter."

"Do you?"

"Do *you* love him?"

"I'm having his baby...in love." She thought that more important than romantic river walks in the City of Lights.

"Have you read Sartre?" Renée asked.

"Christian asked me that same question but advised me to avoid the man like the plague."

"He sympathizes with Mathieu, you know, Christian does. When Marcelle becomes pregnant he sees it as a net over Mathieu's spirit. He calls her a caster of nets, in a biblical way." She laughed at the remembered joke. "Marcelle was a soft, pink weight holding him down in a soft pink haze. Mathieu was rooted to Paris but fled to Madrid in his mind because he could not accept the idea that he was losing his freedom. It's all nonsense of course...freedom's an illusion."

"Yes, I suppose it is," agreed Breeze, "and yet, those poor people in the hold, they think they're running to freedom. They'll probably never know a moment's peace, if they make it, but New York's their Holy Grail."

"Holy Grail? Come, Breeze, freedom's just a flag waved to stir up the peasants as they march always to their deaths. Some even run to it. We survived a revolution, Christian and me. We weren't fighting for freedom but we came out less free than we went in, because we became captives of reality. Since then I have had to look at my life differently. I must be less of Renée the International Tramp, and more Renée Jalobert, respected daughter of destiny...probably become just what Papa had in mind. Why? Because it is what I know best, politics of the powerful. But, the first time, before that could happen I ran."

"You actually ran away from home?"

"I ran away to be bad. I was bad enough, but all I learned is that, once you have privilege it's hard to live without it. Those who reject privilege do so because they have no chance of ever being free. I don't pity those refugees. Refugees are just doing what they have to do, and are better for it."

"Better for being victims? The could die on the run."

"We all die of something, Cheri. Some horribly and some of soft living. A refugee who survives gains something, perhaps character or strength, and when the time is right, will fight. Some may even become what they are fleeing from. Sad, but true. Desperation makes iron. Iron makes war. Ergo, war kills or hardens."

Breeze was repelled by Renée's logic. "Ergo, war is good for evolution. That's nothing more than survival of the fittest."

"It does get reduced to that. Not very uplifting."

"I'm worried about Christian."

"Why?"

"Because he's, so...vulnerable."

"Because you're afraid he's weak? Don't worry, Christian has qualities he's not aware of. If he survives this he will continue to gain strength."

Breeze resented Renée's assessment. The cool Parisienne had

shared love and danger with her man. Renée is right but she is also wrong, thought Breeze. She is not dependent on him for her future.

Renée tried to concentrate on the next green buoy. How, she wondered, had her life become narrowed to green buoys? Wait, they were no longer in a row and Gerard was waving frantically again, now running toward the wheelhouse, pointing. They had been making a long gentle curve to starboard after passing Longue Pointe. Renée, mesmerized by the night, confused by the refinery lights of Montreal East, and talking philosophy, had lost the next green buoy in the flashing white lights of an anchorage.

"Go left!" shouted Gerard.

"Oops...sorry." Renée spun the big wheel. The *Bayou Queen* obediently turned away from the mud bank and re-entered the channel.

"Women cannot drive and talk at the same time," he chastised, but not severely. "It's why they don't let you drive taxi cabs in Montreal. You like to visit too much."

She hoped they could anchor soon. She was going to take this good looking Haitian to bed and dead bodies, police and refugees be damned. Life was short. Life must be lived where it lies, not in perfection. Not in some hazy future. She hadn't lost all her Bohemian instincts.

The wind gusted up and the rain turned to ice pellets. Gerard, cold and shivering, hunched lower in the bow using hand signals. Renée felt guilty. The ice pellets became thick, heavy flakes that tumbled down and vanished on the black river. Little bombs of frozen water splatting against the window and running down, coagulating until the window was almost covered. The wind increased to a steady gale and Gerard had to stand in the doorway shouting steering directions.

"Not far now. Just keep on." And later... "A little more right. See the white lights in a row?"

"Yes. I think so. Flashing?" The world was a tormented *blur* of blinking lights and coloured snowflakes. Gerard was a dark presence and she could feel his closeness, smell his power.

"That's right, my lady." My lady? Chivalry in adversity. This slight woman is strong and confident, he said to himself. Poised under pressure, polished in elegant casual clothes. He couldn't help admire her lovely face, delicate profile, shining blond hair in the flash of the marker buoys. "The flashing ones. We go on along by those to Pointe Trembles. I was down here with Petit Jacques. We anchored in the traverse just between two channels. Boats on one channel think you are a boat on the other channel. We hide out there." And maybe get to know one another, he was thinking.

"Okay, tell me when." None too soon for her plans.

"You'll see the church at Pointe Trembles." Yes, the church with the spire like an erection pointing to heaven and bliss. "Pilots used it in old days. Put the church on your stern and go between two markers." He could imagine her nicely rounded derriere above those long legs. "They aren't lights so I'll show you." And show you more in time...

It was as Gerard said. Even with the snow and wind, the church and the markers appeared and they turned into the traverse. The *Queen* drifted with the current until Gerard let the rusted anchor go. The chain rattling out the hawse pipe frightened the passengers waiting in the darkness of the hold. Although safely at anchor in the deep cut between Iles de Boucherville and Iles de Varennes, the passengers would require convincing. That was Miguel's job.

Gerard shut down the engine and turned off the lights. He and Renée went below where Miguel brooded in his bunk. Miguel wanted to talk but Renée convinced him his duty lay with the passengers. Paulo was asleep at the galley table, a bottle of wine clutched to his chest. When Miguel left the cabin Renée undressed Gerard slowly, deliberately. They folded into a bunk almost too tired to make love, but...when young...

Miguel's Story

The wind shrieked and howled through the rigging and around the cabin eaves. "I tried to join Fidel," he babbled to Christian and Breeze who were also trying to make a kind of comfort love. "They laughed at me in Havana. Just a humble boy from the Pinar del Rio province. What did I know about running a country? I told them I'd been hustling since I was seven and what was the difference between being a pimp and being a politician? Unless the politician is the whore. That was after Rosa was killed and when they found out who I was they tried to put me in jail, but I ran away and took Jésus with me. There's nothing to do in Los Espiritos with Juanita out of business so we travelled by the train to Santiago and then on a coastal boat to Haiti. We joined some people who were escaping Papa Doc going on a boat to Canada. Juanita told me stories about Canada. She made them up of course, but then I remembered you were from this Montreal in Canada and I decided to come and find you."

"Did you have any idea how big Canada is?"

"Yes. No. I knew Montreal is your home and figured you'd come here and I'd find you because you are a famous jazz musician. All I'd have to do is hang out in the jazz places, like Juanita's, maybe hustle some tables and keep my ears and eyes open. But instead, I'm on my way to New York City, like it was a dream. Remember, Rosa wanted to be a lawyer in New York? So I thought, I'll first go to New York and hustle the jazz places and some day you'd show up and we'd get together and by that time I'll own the joint and hire you to be my personal musician. Just like the old days except you'd be working for me, Señor Christ, and I wouldn't have to call you señor, but you'd call me boss, okay?"

"Sure. When you get your own club, I'd be honoured. The first night will be free, then after that you'd pay me scale for a month and then I'd want a grand a week. And after the first album sells a million, I'll buy you out and you can be my body guard."

"Okay, by that time I'll be big and mean."

"Don't get mean, Miguel. Esameralda wouldn't approve."

"Okay, maybe I'll become a priest instead."

"Your family adapts to career changes very easily."

"We're famous for being two or three things at once."

"I know. How is Esa?"

"Not seen her since Rosa's funeral. It wasn't a funeral like Jocinto's. That was special. Rosa's funeral was very sad. Fidel's men were already looking for her. You don't know what happened after we left Los Espiritos. Rosa's funeral was in Havana, in secret. Her lover, the one with the machine gun, was captured and shot by Fidel's army because they said he was an accomplice of Rosa and Ernesto. That also was tragic. He was loyal to Castro, but there was so much confusion it wasn't safe to be anybody but Ché or Raul, and even then...You were lucky you stayed in Los Espiritos with Esameralda. Juanita was able to pay off some people with her money in the Havana Bank and being a friend of Major Marti. But later Marti was put in jail because they said he was working too close to Batista. He's till there. His trial is soon. You should go back and be a witness for Major Marti. No, that is not a good idea. I hear that your friend Maartyn is on a list and that Fidel's agents are waiting for him to come back with American spies on this boat. They think he is a big time agent for the CIA and because he worked for Escobar and knows the water, he is dangerous. That makes you a suspect too, because you fought with him in the hills and with Rosa..."

"We were fighting Batista's army."

"I know that. You and Maartyn know that. But things are very strange and violent in Cuba since you left. Everyone suspects everyone else of being an American agent."

"What about Esa? And your parents?"

"My parents have nothing left except your old fishing boat

that my father uses to go out for a few bonitos. They live in a shack of tin on the beach but aren't suspected of anything. Esa's safe in the convent hospital, because she was connected with the Ché Guevera Hospital."

"But that was Escobar's villa."

"I know, but it was considered honourable to serve Fidel and she was praised by a Fidel agent who was in the hospital, posing as a wounded Batista soldier to test everyone's sympathies."

"She passed the test."

"She passed. But she had to fuck the agent to convince the man that Los Espiritos was not a traitor's camp of Escobar's followers."

Christian experienced a surge of pain. "Was this going on while I was still in Pinar del Rio?"

"Yes, Señor Christ, Esa felt badly, but you know her ways. She did what she had to do, always has. She misses Señorita Renée."

Breeze could not follow the conversation but the names and the tone were unmistakable. Christian translated the jist of Miguel's report. She wasn't jealous of Esa, but still not sure of her feelings for Renée.

"So, what troubles you the most?" asked Breeze, when Miguel finally fell asleep on the cabin floor. "Esa sleeping with that agent or Renée down below taking the measure of Gerard?"

"That's an odd question."

"No it's not. It's a very important question right now. Who do you love the most? I'm sorry. Don't answer..."

A sharper wind gust ripped across the anchorage. The *Bayou Queen* staggered back, turned sideways to the current and snapped her rusted anchor chain like a dry twig. The report of the broken chain was lost in the gale but Gerard knew. On deck the snow swirled and the church spire at Pointe aux Trembles was visible only in snatches.

"I'll start the engine! Steer that way!" shouted Gerard as he bolted down the companionway to the engine room. The current and the wind were pushing the *Bayou Queen* sideways along the traverse toward the small craft channel. Breeze was beside Christian who was revived by the emergency. "What's happening?" asked Renée entering the wheelhouse, pale and out of context in the dim light. They had been through bad situations and he depended on her strength, but she had on only her short leather coat and looked vulnerable. He wanted to tell her to go below. Gerard was calling from the engine room. "Go, mawn! Go. She's running!"

If the future flowed through our lives like a river all one would have to do is wait downstream for life to arrive. Christian didn't believe in fate, but in this case he knew his future was between the anchorage and the Port of Sorel where Petit Jacques might relieve them of their cargo, or more likely at the small boarder town called Champlain, where they may or may not die rescuing Maartyn, but definitely the Harbour of New York City. Things happen in New York. So he assumed New York was their destination.

The Lower St. Lawrence River between Montreal and Lac St. Pierre is a maze of islands and channels. Locals with knowledge of the channels and hiding places, whether they are poaching or running from the law, can stay lost for weeks.

"Where? Which way?"

"That way, mawn. Between that red light and that green light," Gerard said calmly.

"Too many lights!" Coloured lights blinking and disappearing in the squalls, whirling in the wind, the boat turning in the current. Christian spun the wheel.

"No! That way!" said Renée who did not need to shout. Christian could feel her warm breath on his neck.

"Okay...okay. I got it."

Renée pushed the throttle herself. The engine vibrated then got down to business.

The *Queen* straightened out and approached the lights Gerard indicated, but the boat was still moving sideways across the traverse toward a mud bank. Renée increased the throttle as Christian corrected the angle.

"Be ready to turn to port on that red buoy," ordered Gerard, but the red buoy suddenly disappeared, blanked out by a squall and did not reappear. "What? Where is it?"

"Wait. Hold steady."

The squall blew away. "There? Is that the one?"

"Don't know, mawn."

"That's the one," said Breeze calmly.

"How can you be sure?" asked Renée.

"I never took my eyes off the spot and it's flashing faster than the others."

"The boat was moving sideways, miss, are you sure?"

"I compensated," she assured Gerard who simply nodded. The boat was being run by a committee but it worked.

"Okay," breathed Christian. "That one then."

The tension in the wheelhouse was as thick as the intermittent squalls.

"I'm freezing," said Renée.

"I'll get your things," offered Miguel, opening the wheelhouse door to another blast of snow-laden wind.

"Hey, next time use the lee door," said Gerard, but without reproach. "An' you'd better check on our guests."

The quick-flashing red buoy was coming up too fast. Christian reached for the throttle. "Only half," said Gerard. "Otherwise the wind got you." The *Queen* slowed forcing Christian to guess at the next angle. The red buoy, closing very quickly, flashed at him like a malevolent eye. He anticipated the turn and began the correction.

"Very good, skipper," said Gerard. "I believe you got the feel of 'er now. I guess I'll go below with the nice French lady and get us warm."

"No!" shouted Christian. "No, I need you both."

Breeze felt a sudden chill of alienation. She thought she knew what he meant but reproached herself for over reacting.

"Just kidding, mawn. This is a tricky part ahead."

The *Queen* cleared the buoy and swung into the small craft channel. He lined up the bow between the red and green lights. The small craft channel looked very narrow after the main channel.

"Look," said Breeze. She was pointing behind them across the traverse. "That blue light."

"The patrol boat!" exclaimed Gerard flicking off the running lights.

The flashing blue light of a harbour police boat was moving erratically down the main channel like a lost spirit.

"Looking for us I suppose," sighed Gerard. "This bad weather is our friend." They stood in silence, listening to the shrieks of the wind, the pulse of the engine, the splash of water along the hull, holding on as the *Queen* rocked to each new blast. "Better slow down now, or we'll meet them at the end of the island. Just keep enough power to steer."

Christian adjusted the throttle and tested the wheel. The *Queen* was sluggish but held her course. They passed a green buoy on their right; afraid the flash might give them away. Christian turned his attention to the next red. "How deep is the water here?"

"Deep enough, in the channel. Not much outside. If we go on the mud we'll just have to wait until they go away."

"And how are we supposed to stay hidden?" asked Renée.

"The Harbour Police can only go as far as Cap St-Michel. This channel crosses the main channel below Varrenes and goes behind more islands. If we keep the islands between us 'til they get below, we can cross into the western channel before they turn at Cap St-Michel."

"And what if they don't behave?" asked Renée, moving into

Gerard for warmth.

Christian sensed Renée's motion. He wanted Breeze, or was it Renée? How could base physical needs be important at a time like this, he wondered? They were now fugitives from the law, with a body on the stern and illegal immigrants in the hold. He could see Jean-Pierre attacking Dominique. Dominique's tormented face hovered on the periphery of the darkness. Concentrate, he said. No time for guilt or self-recriminations. Gerard gathered Renée into his large frame. "Then we have the big islands between us. And my guess is they won't go below Vercheres."

"What if that young officer's only after Renée?" said Breeze to relieve the tension.

"Then we have to sacrifice this one," said Gerard with a laugh.

"That's not funny." Renée did her best to storm out of the wheelhouse by the windward door, but could not force it open. She kicked the door and retreated to the lee side. Gerard patted her bare derriere as she squeezed through colliding with Miguel returning from his errand. She grabbed her clothes and disappeared.

"What has upset the Señorita?"

Their slow passage down the small craft channel was an agony of building tension and quick decisions. Christian worried about the sound of the big diesel engine. They were entering a wide spot in the channel when the lights of the patrol boat reappeared over the low end of Ile aux Fermiers, the last of the Varennes group of islands. Gerard reached for the throttle, this time to slow the *Queen*. Renée reentered the crowded wheelhouse now dressed for the conditions, taking station between Gerard and Christian, adjusting to the dark, with no words spoken. Breeze, having so far kept to the back of wheelhouse, moved closer to Christian as the patrol boat slid across their view at an oblique angle, agonizingly slow.

The *Queen* slewed to the right. "Gerard?"

"You've got some water here. Don't worry about going off the channel now."

"Can we turn around?"

"No. Jus' keep on best you can. They can't see us, yet."

Ahead and to each side, lights blinked and flashed through blowing snow. Two dozen light buoys vied for Christian's attention. "I can't see much either, other than too many lights."

"Find one green buoy that flashes faster than the rest."

Christian scanned the lights. "Damn! They don't stay on long enough!"

"Find the quick-flashing one."

"There. On the left," said Breeze.

"Okay...I see it. Gone again!"

"That's all right. It's back."

"But, why do they do that? Why can't they just be there?"

"They have to have character, like names. Now, fix that light in your mind. See, there, again. Steer toward that light. Never mind the others."

"Okay. But..."

"The water's good until just before the main channel. Now find the red that flashes like the green."

"One thing at a time!"

"Steady, mawn. When you get to that green you got to know where is that red, 'cause you're crossing the main channel there. Dig?"

"No, I don't dig! Why don't you steer! Why do I always have to steer at the worst time?"

Breeze put her arms around Christian's waist and pressed her swelling breasts into his back, breathing on his neck. Lips caressing. He could feel her delicious mass of red curls stroking his prickling skin. Strong arms holding him together. He began to calm down, wanting her. Breeze like an opiate, like the first sweet rush of heroine... "You can do it," she whispered and pressed her lips to his ear. He couldn't do it without her, or Renée. Either or? Red...green. Both? Damn!

Breeze was being possessive but Renée was ever present. Like she-wolves claiming their territory. Miguel was watching with interest, knowing the history of his affairs. Christian whispered, "Breeze, please...not now..." Breeze giggled. "Okay," she said. "Better concentrate."

"More left," said Gerard.

"Okay, left," she squeezed and giggled again.

"Breeze...*sssh!*"

The Patrol Boat seemed to be stationary but it was just an optical illusion. When the *Queen* was opposite the lights of Varennes the patrol boat was approaching Cap St-Michel so the angle was such that the blue light of the patrol seemed directly ahead.

"They're almost at St-Michel. They'll turn back at Seaway calling in point, twenty-four. If only we had a radio that worked."

They didn't have a radio or much else that worked. They had no anchor but the steering gear was functioning. The galley stove worked but smoked badly. The compass was of little use without charts. They had to depend on Gerard's knowledge of the river and Maartyn's engine. "I wish Maartyn was here." Crazy, steady, confident Maartyn.

At that moment Maartyn St. Jacques, Louisiana waterman, and fugitive, was making a bid to escape from the FBI in Champlain New York. It was dark. There were gunshots.

They crossed the main shipping channel and slipped into the small craft channel again. The patrol boat turned below Cap St-Michel as the *Queen* vanished behind Ile Deslauriers and Gerard shut down the engine. "Steer between those two green buoys and put her aground." Christian let the *Queen* drift off the channel until the bow nudged the soft mud. The patrol boat passed upstream with the narrow island hiding the *Bayou Queen*. The group in the wheelhouse huddled in silence, barely breathing, until the patrol boat was opposite Pointe aux Trembles.

Safely on the mud the old boat seemed to relax while the fugitives began to take stock and think about a plan. "What if the cops are looking for us all the way down the river?" asked Christian, feeling the burden of responsibility shifting to his slight shoulders.

"We'll travel at night. There's plenty islands between here an' Sorel where we meet Jacques."

"Then what do we do?" asked Renée.

"Don't know, Miss. Stay invisible 'til Jacques come."

"We could cut brush," offered Miguel.

"Brush?"

"Yes, to hide the boat like the army hides tanks. You remember, Señor Christ. When Batista's tanks came we could not see them at first because they were covered with palmettoes. I think the soldiers got as many wounds from the sharp points as they did from our guns, especially yours, since you refused to shoot at them. But Señor Maartyn, he was like a movie hero..."

"Okay, no need to remind me."

"Miguel has a point," said Renée. "I mean about the camouflage."

Christian remembered too vividly the last battle for Los Espiritos. Renée had been strong, Rosameralda inspiring as the commander and Maartyn in his glory blasting away until their ammunition was gone. Even Wolf the dog could have been decorated for valour. Christian had fired his rifle until his fingers bled but never aimed at a moving target, satisfied just to make noise and survive the ordeal. Then he thought of their young companions in the cave, just children of war. Not old enough to vote, but trained to kill like universal soldiers and dying horrible deaths in foreign campaigns...Breeze snuggled against Christian. She was tired and no longer interested in the game. Newfoundland seemed far away. Montreal and Mother Breeze still tantalizingly close. She wasn't a fugitive from anything, only pregnant and cold, and her back ached and her feet were sore.

"You should get some sleep," he said gently. They held each other close, the warmth brief and tempting. Cuba faded too. "Okay," she said. "I wish you could."

Gerard went below to restart the engine.

Christian backed the *Queen* off the mud and aimed the bow downstream, searching for the lights on his highway to the future. How did I get here? he wondered. After the chaos of Cuba he returned to Montreal to see if life had waited for him, perhaps to test the waters of his birth. Instead he was drifting down this dark channel away from danger and into more danger and life's only horizon, the next light buoy. There was no grand purpose or a master plan. No guiding hand from a supreme being pushing him along or tipping him into further danger; nor protecting him, he mused. He wasn't smug enough to believe that Christ, the Virgin Mary, or a single saint, would intercede for him in any special way. His small presence in the dark peril of the first winter night of 1960 was of no consequence to anyone outside the circle of friends on his boat. His boat. His island. His refuge. Well, his lifeboat was in peril and so were his people. And what of the hopeful Haitians? Was he responsible for them as well? "They're Gerard's people," he said aloud.

"What did you say, Señor Christ?"

"Miguel, here's a question. Those people you travelled with from Haiti. What are their hopes?"

"To get to New York of course."

"And who should get them there?"

"You, Boss."

"That's just the point! I'm not a boss of anything!"

"Señor Gerard says this is your boat now and you're the captain. So that makes you the Boss Man. An' those people believe in you because you're all they got in this world right now."

"Jesus," he whispered, remembering how vulnerable he felt in Cuba. There were many people guiding his life then also and they were not as concerned with his safety. He was only a bit player in a tragi-comedy. Maartyn was a natural leader but had his own issues. Escobar, the would-be king of Cuba, had other plans. Major Marti had a Cuban agenda. Even Carnero, who held his life at the point of a gun, was too crazed with getting power to worry about a foreigner. But the women seemed to be in control; Juanita, his seductress, benefactor and landlady, lured him into the revolution. Rosameralda, the militant but deceitful rebel, drew him deeper into the plot, but Renée, his friend and sexual guide, rescued him. And Esameralda? She possessed his heart...

"Señor, Christ!"

He looked up in time to avoid the buoy. A snow squall swept across the water and the next light was an apparition. It's mate, the flashing red, which suddenly defined his world, was a burst of colour, like an explosion. He steered between the green apparition and the colour of blood, returning to his reverie, taking stock as he often did in tense situations.

Homeless Caucasian male of Irish decent, age twenty-three: Number of friends or acquaintances already dead? Five. Depth of water? Twenty feet at buoy number MS69. Number of friends under his care? Five. Six, counting Maartyn. Number of refugees under his command? Fifteen, including Miguel. Different categories. Distance from Montreal? Thirteen point three statute miles, but Christian was not aware that they were still within the Montreal Harbour limit. Why did the patrol boat turn back? Twenty-five point three nautical miles to Sorel and the meeting with Petit Jacques. Petit Jacques? Two hundred and thirty-three pounds. One hundred and five point seven kilos, rounded. Which he was. Number of revolutions on the propeller? Three hundred. Half speed ahead. Months since the Castro Revolution? Twenty-four. Number of dead bodies on his boat? One. Number of bodies on the *Bayou Queen* in total: that he knew about? Four, counting

Dominique. He had seen them all. Near death experiences? Seven, not counting drug overdoses...

"Señor, Christ? Are you alright?" Miguel was touching his arm. He realized how cold he was.

"Yes..." No, he admitted.

"Concentrate, Señor Christ."

"All the lights are the same and some I can't even see for snow."

"How do people live in this awful country? I'm dying of the cold. In Cuba we only have a hurricane about every ten years and the rest of the time it's fine."

"Then what are you doing here?"

"Looking for you, Boss."

"Great. Shouldn't you be counting refugees or something?"

"Señor Gerard sealed the hatch, to keep them warm. But there are still fifteen, counting Jésus and me. Not counting the dead woman at the stern. One of the women is pregnant and could drop a little one at any moment. That would change the score, like a squeeze bunt in the late innings of a baseball game." Miguel laughed at his own joke. "Look, there! Another light."

"Okay, I got it." Buoy number MS65. Three lights bunched together. The channel was turning to starboard. One half-turn on the wheel. No, only a quarter turn. His existence reduced to numbers. What would Sartre think? Who cares what Sartre or anybody thinks? "What time is it, Miguel?" Christian had never owned a watch. "We have to find a place to hide before dawn."

"Don't know, Señor Christ. I'll find Gerard."

"Engine room. Ask him to come up." Miguel dodged out the lee door. The temperature drop was imperceptible because it was as cold inside as out. Wondered if Breeze was warm enough in the cabin. And the baby? The engine hesitated, dropped revolutions, then resumed beats. It had been doing that for the past hour. Funny how the noise of the engine almost disappears from consciousness until it changes. But why the sudden change?

Gerard crunched into the wheelhouse and was thrown against the door jam when the *Queen* heeled to a gust of wind. "Watch your course, mawn." Gerard peered at the lights.

"What's with the engine?"

"Doin' fine now, but the bitch she has some voodoo into her. Might be water or dirt in the filters. Gettin' close to the bottom of the tanks. If she quits try to find a soft spot."

"Sure. I'll just close my eyes and pray." He almost never prayed.

"Pray for mud."

"Dust to dust..."

"Chris, mawn...see there...?"

The squall had passed and the low clouds diffused available light. In the distance, among the mechanical flashing buoys there was a flickering orange glow. "Yeah...a fire?"

"Looks like boat burnin', mawn."

"Now what?"

"We soon know. Better get some people on deck."

Christian throttled the *Queen* down even though they were more than a mile from whatever was burning. The pace was too slow and the *Queen* sluggish on the helm. He increased revolutions, not because he wanted to arrive at the scene sooner. He had a bad feeling about the next episode. People milled about on deck. Renée, better dressed for the occasion, was trailing Miguel behind her with extra clothes in case there were people involved. Paulo was unhappy about being disturbed. Gerard was peering into the darkness appraising the situation. "Boat on fire. Sure of it. See the silhouettes. Two at least."

There were two black objects, silhouettes rigid against the dancing fire, the flames leaping up and dying down as if the fuel supply was running out. The boat was tied to buoy MS52. Breeze was suddenly beside him.

"What is it, Chris?"

"Boat on fire."

"Oh, no!" She was bundled up in a down parka, coveralls and boots, wearing a soft cap with ear lugs, peak pulled down to her thick, black-rimmed glasses. She looked like a studious New-foundland seal hunter waiting to go over on the ice. They were close enough now for the flames to dance on her lenses so that her eyes were on fire..."Oh, sweet Jesus! It's them," he whispered.

"Who?"

"The Bateau People. The Gypsies. Thought we were rid of them for good."

"Maybe you are. They aren't moving."

No one on deck spoke. The gap between the *Queen* and the bateau closed slowly as Christian rehearsed his manoeuvre to come as close as possible. The burning hulk was low in the water, gunnels burned away amidships. The Princess was poised in the bow as if ready to leap over the side. The Poseur sat upright in the stern, arm still draped over the tiller, steering to nowhere in hell. Everything in the middle of the boat was burning and the mast had gone over the side. He could see the probable cause of the fire, a small steel drum used as a brazier. The fire may have got out of control as they headed down river to Nirvana. Christian eased alongside.

Then the awful smell rose up to them, swirling into their nos-es and eyes as the gust back-winded in the lee of the large shrimp boat. The stench was both sweet and sour: frying flesh and burn-ing hair. Skin on distorted faces bubbled through blackened crusts like fish held to a cooking fire on planks of wood. Clothing flak-ing off, grey-black ash, layer by layer, carried away by the wind. Christian thought it was a fitting symbol even if they were just city folk pretending to be natives. It is not right to criticize anoth-er's symbolism. Do not mock epithets carved on graves because it's the last word of the former living and their final testimony. Be charitable in death, if not in life. Forgive harms. Let the poor bas-tards have their last ritual, their death pyre, like Vikings, East In-dians or unfortunate Christians.

Renée turned away in shock. She had seen much in her young life but the scene was too gruesome to behold for longer than it takes to commit it to memory. Breeze too, repulsed by the sight of the Princess, cried softly on Christian's arm. Gerard stood in the wheelhouse door, blocking the sight.

The *Queen* drifted away as if she also was appalled by the sight of another vessel in distress. Miguel threw a grappling hook and crouched behind the gunnel to escape the heat. There was a hammering and calling from the refugees in the hold. "Don't let them out," ordered Christian. He stood watching the bizarre ritual death scene.

"What you want to do?" asked Gerard.

"Bring them aboard. If Petit Jacques won't take them we'll have to. Can't leave them like this."

"Yes, Skipper."

Christian turned the bow of the *Queen* to bring her closer to the bateau, risking setting his own boat on fire. Gerard was the first to reach aboard the burning bateau to grasp the Princess. Miguel was beside him. In his young life Miguel had experienced so much death also, Christian realized. This was just another episode. But he also knew that Miguel was blessed with an irrepressible spirit protected by youth.

The Princess came over the rail stiff and grotesque, like overdone liver. They laid her gently on the deck. Renée had a blanket ready and covered the small body. Paulo was sick to his stomach over the windward rail and suffered for it. Miguel rescued the guitar and Christian's knapsack as the two boats drifted apart. When Christian tried to bring the stern of the *Queen* close to reach The Poseur the bateau's bow line parted from the buoy and the burning wreck drifted down wind, out of the channel and across the shallows, to fetch up on the mud bank of Ile Dansereau. Without a small boat they could do nothing except watch the flickering light dissolve into another squall with the charred vision still sitting erect and alone.

Left to the elements the bateau burned until only the flat bottom remained squatting on the wet mud to be slowly hidden from sight by winter. The body became a pile of bones and bits of clothing slumped in the bilge water, still clinging to the stump of a tiller. The local poachers and contraband runners told the story for years but did not report the body to the authorities. The Poseur vanished from the world he disdained. The spring ice carried the remains of Gargoire downstream like a cremated Viking on a shield. Deaths of people close to Christian? Seven. Numbers of dead on board the *Bayou Queen* since Christian met Maartyn? Now five.

Ile de Grace Rondévous

The *Bayou Queen* had her nose on the beach with her stern in deep water. "You must cover the deck so the airplanes cannot see," said Miguel.

Camouflage, right. Christian put Miguel in charge of camouflaging the *Bayou Queen*. Miguel enlisted Jésus and five of the refugees to cut brush on Ile de Grace. He took the job of supervisor seriously, striding busily up and down the beach exhorting his workers who hacked at the dry scrub poplars with small machetes. It was then that Christian realized his passengers were well armed.

Dawn came late with sleet and a biting wind from the Northwest but daylight found them in a safe haven behind Ile de Grace at the edge of Lac St. Pierre, below the Port of Sorel.

"How do we find Petit Jacques?" Christian asked Gerard wearily as he sipped hot coffee in the wheelhouse. He was exhausted from the long, tense night of navigating and being invisible, finally slipping past Sorel with an hour to spare before first light amazed that Gerard found the spot in the dark. Two Coast Guard boats had gone down river in the main shipping channel. Looking for them, Christian was certain.

"Jacques will find us. He showed me this place one time when we were running cigarettes and booze for the Americans. We come down river like we did tonight and hide in these islands."

"Better get some sleep," he said. He imagined Gerard's naked muscular body, sliding into the bunk beside the smooth whiteness of Renée...

"Sure, mawn, but first we should pull the boat sideways to the beach, so she look part of the island."

"Right." Damn! Why hadn't I thought of that? he breathed.

Christian took a bottle of wine from the galley and shut himself up in the engine room, sitting with his back to the big diesel. The engine was still warm but he was shaking with tension and the smells from the bilges didn't help his mood. The engine room reeked of diesel fuel and hot oil and the bilges were like a cesspool; black and dank. Maartyn would not approve.

Breeze dozed in the captain's cabin. He should be with her but his emotions were in confusion. Renée would understand his problem, but Renée was cuddled up with Gerard in the fo'c'sle. He could hear the sounds of the work party chattering on the shore, *clomping* around on deck. Branches were thrown over the glass of the skylight, already so dirty the morning light was a diffused grey fog. The portholes had long ago been boarded over; the glass shot out by Batista's navy during a blockade run. Always running from the law, he muttered, the good ship *Bayou Queen*; international fugitive. He took a long drink of the heavy wine. He should not be cowering in the stinking bowels of a Louisiana shrimp boat, hiding from the RCMP, he reasoned. If he had stayed in Chicago he might be merely dead, or still waking up in a sweat-soaked bed, delirious for a hit of narcotics to take away the pain. If he had stayed in Pinar del Rio he might be waking up in the arms of Esameralda, in a convent. Not likely. If he had gone to Paris with Renée they might be lunching at a small café across the Seine from her flat on Ile St. Louis with the afternoon to fill. Maybe a gallery and a jazz club later that night. Or the theatre.

Maybe...in Montreal he could have been having breakfast in the small diner, in Rue Tremont, with Dominique. Dominique?...But he could be lying with Breeze, holding her and the baby, and dream of not being afraid of everything. Would he have gone to Spain to fight the Fascists? So many young men had joined the brigades to fight for the cause in a foreign country. World socialism had no strong single voice, but a discordant chorus wailing in the darkness about the rights of the working class. He was an intellectual who had escaped from the working class and it was the intellectuals who led the charge, but the Brigades were made up of the unemployed or disillusioned who had nothing better to do than go on an adventure to sunny Spain. They knew no more about their chances in Spain than he did about the coming night on the river. He heard the sound of a low flying plane just before he took another drink of wine and shut his eyes.

Breeze was awake and hungry. "Where's Christian?"

"Don't know, Miss. Thought he was with you," answered Gerard, absently watching the dark, silent river from the wheelhouse door.

Breeze found him in the engine room, asleep in the arms of fuel lines and exhaust pipes. The half empty wine bottle nestled in his crotch. "Chris, baby? What's wrong?"

"Huh? Oh, nothing. Checking engine..."

"Why didn't you come to me? I'd understand."

"I know. It's just, I didn't want to worry you."

She sat on the engine bed and took him in her arms. He melted into her warmth, could die there. "Well, I was more scared when I couldn't find you. The natives are restless. They don't like the bodies."

"Gerard says Jacques'll be here tonight."

"How will he find us?"

"Petit Jacques knows everything on the river. Look, I'm sorry...about this."

"No, *shhh*. We've been through that. Gerard says no matter what Jacques does we should just go on, down river."

"And what of Maartyn?"

"Going to New York is the worst thing we could do. I'm very pregnant. Think of it. If we get arrested trying to help Maartyn, with a stolen boat, bodies, illegal immigrants, carrying drugs and users like your friend, the dealer."

"You mean Paulo."

"Yes, I mean Paulo. I found him unconscious in the galley. Renée's trying to revive him. She said he'd overdosed. Narcotics. Why would Paulo do such a stupid thing?"

Christian sat up searching for the comfort of her sea-green eyes. "There's something else I need to tell you about me...before Cuba."

"I guessed. It's history, isn't it? Come to bed."

Petit Jacques found them just after midnight. He could have found them at anytime he chose. The *Elloise* eased alongside the *Bayou Queen* like a stealthy living creature; breathing, pulsing and throbbing with hot life. Except for the telltale oil smoke from her stack, the steam tug was the perfect contraband runner. She could move as silent as a ghost under Jacques' command and slip into dark anchorages with no lights showing. She was already tied up alongside the *Bayou Queen* when Miguel shook Christian awake.

"Señor, Christ! The fat man's here. He says you are a lousy skipper to let him sneak up like this. He could take you without a shot."

"What the hell. Are we pirates now?" Christian slipped out of the bunk and started to dress. Breeze reached out and pulled the sleeping bag closer. "Petit Jacques' here," he whispered. "You sleep." Christian kissed her gently and stepped on deck.

"I can't sleep." She got up to dress and join the meeting.

Jacques got quickly to the business. "Your friend may already be dead," he said flatly. The galley was crammed and stifling. Whiskey was the drink of choice and Petit Jacques had plenty to share. The table was heavy with a half dozen bottles of good quality booze.

"Not Maartyn. He's too tough," declared Christian.

"I'm not certain he's dead. I'm told the American tried to escape. Ran toward the lake and the Feds were shooting at anything that moved. Two Haitians died. Four or five wounded. The Russian was captured. There's going to be a big political fuss so you can't go down to New York with this boat."

"Then, what about our refugees?" He put his arm around Miguel.

"I'll take them on *Elloise*. There's many places to put them ashore safely."

"I could stay with you, Señor, Christ."

"Thanks, Miguel, you go with Renée and look for Maartyn."

"I've got a legitimate tow for New York," continued Jacques, pausing for a gulp of the whiskey. "Big motor yacht went aground coming up from Tadoussac. Those crazy Americans, they pile up million dollar boats an' fly home. Message said, 'deliver boat to City Island Yacht Club by Christmas. Price no object'. Can you believe some people? The god-damned boat is hull down with good Canadian liquor, an' they weren't even smuggling. Freezers full of food. And the wine? Mother of God! These people must own a vineyard."

"What about the bodies?" asked Breeze.

"*Phew*...no can do. Oh, fuck, dump'em in the river, or bury them on the island."

Christian shivered. Jacques was too matter of fact, even heartless, but practical. He thought of Dominique and her spoiled beauty united with the disfigured Princess. The mud flats of Ile de Grace seemed an unfitting resting place, even if the name had promise.

"Couldn't you put them in the freezer of your motor yacht?"

310

He was grasping at straws but freezing was a normal solution to troublesome bodies in Christian's recent history.

"Then what? Declare them to Customs when we enter New York State an' say, oh would you mind looking after these poor bastards?"

He thought about the implications for a few moments. "Okay, we'll deal with them," said Christian, resigned to the task. He looked at Breeze who shrugged and sipped her Scotch.

Jacques took another big drink. "But I'm not taking that son of a Sacrament!" He pointed to Paulo semi-conscious in the bunk forward. "I don't want no fucked up druggies on my boat. These Haitians are one thing. They can be terrified into being good. An' they pay. What's he good for?"

Renée bristled. "I'll look after Paulo, and *pay* for him." Christian could see the spots of temper in her cheeks. It was rare, but if she got her French fire up Petit Jacques would hear something. He realized how much he knew about Renée. His stomach did an interesting turn, or maybe it was his heart. She was going with Gerard of course, so he was losing her again, and to New York, again! She had come to rescue him and he was letting her slip away. It would be so easy to sink the *Queen* and melt into the crew of the *Elloise*, with Renée and Miguel, heading for New York, and from there...Breeze would not hear of scuttling their boat. To her the dilapidated old *Queen* was their refuge, a gift of circumstances. How often, she had reasoned, did someone make such an offer? And didn't he have some responsibility to his friend? His reply? Maartyn had abandoned the *Queen*. "She's not even his boat. He sort of stole her from the Cubans. They were dead, but still..." And Breeze countered, "He nursed and badgered the *Queen* on a three thousand mile voyage to reach Montreal looking for you."

Breeze pressed her argument well. Could he honestly just abandon the poor thing when all she needed was a good hand and a refit. A costly refit; thousands of dollars they did not have, he countered. In Newfoundland, her mother had assured her, there were relatives who could fix anything. "What, they just walk into the woods and get things for boats?" he had asked, rhetorically. "Yes, I suppose," she replied. Mother told her stories of Béhathook Cove. When they needed a boat, a house or a coffin, they made them. Christian was skeptical. Breeze often talked late at night about the ways of the islands; things that mainlanders could not dream of doing, they do routinely. "All we have to do is get to Fogo Island."

"And where exactly is Fogo Island?" Christian wondered. "On the far side of the moon?"

"No, just on the other side of the Big Island. There..." On the chart of Eastern North America, she traced the route. A thousand miles of deadly waters, he assumed. Fogo was a tiny spot of rock off the northeast coast of Newfoundland, pushed out into the Atlantic Ocean with nothing but a blue void between it and Ireland. He was more skeptical...

Jacques refilled their glasses. "You know the woman was working for the cops," Jacques continued.

"Yes, I know." The deception had disappointed him, but had not diminished her mystique. Montreal seemed so far away and the politics of the fledgling revolution that would become the FLQ crisis, just another saga in the chaotic struggle of two cultures.

"Oh, an' Gerard told you they killed Jean-Pierre?"

"He said they would...who?"

"Henri's new group? FLQ they call themselves. But the cops're still looking for Dominique."

"And we've got Dominique."

"Cops suspect that too. Word's out."

They drank to Dominique. Dead acquaintances? Eight.

It may have been the booze but cops and dead friends retreated to the abstract. The river and the voyage were more immediate concerns. He wasn't afraid of the river, he told himself. He actually looked forward to the journey, setting off with Breeze, but moving away from Renée was a symbolic break. The dark river and the unknown seemed less of a danger. Don't be a fool! He loved Breeze from the moment he saw her and that was his one reality. His mind was made up. He was taking Breeze home, on his boat. Hope returned, then paled in an instant. Damn!

Petit Jacques' deckhand filled the *Bayou Queen's* tanks with diesel fuel and installed a VHF radio. Jacques presented Christian with charts of the river and the estuary as far as Sept Isles. "You go to the office of the Labrador Iron Ore Company. Ask for Madame Trembley. Nice woman. Likes her sailors aggressive. She'll provide charts. Give'er a bottle of good wine. After Sept Isle you're on the Gulf."

"Okay, then what?"

"There's plenty good ports on the North Shore, all the way to Blanc Sablon. You run the Straits from Point Amore. Bad tides, maybe ice. Be careful rounding Cape Bauld. She's a bitch this time of year. Currents, fog, snow. Once around Cape Bauld you're home free for Twillingate. I worked on the coastal boats out there. Beautiful country. Beautiful people, but hard coast." Petit Jacques doubted Christian and Breeze would survive the journey. The boat definitely not, but it wasn't his concern.

Jacques finished his whiskey and said, "I left the American yacht in the basin at Sorel. The Coast Guard will be asking questions."

Christian offered to pour another round but Jacques put a broad, hairy hand over his glass. "Be very careful crossing Lac St. Pierre. Bad waves an' not much water off the channel. After Trois Rivières you shouldn't have too much trouble, but watch the Richelieu Rapids, just here." He pointed to one of the charts spread out on the galley table. "Best thing is to pass down at high tide, then ride the tide down to Québec City."

"How do we know about the tides?"

"Call the Coast Guard. Channel sixteen. Just say you're an American yacht out of Tadoussac, make up a name. Say you're at Ile Coudre...here. Ask for high tides at Québec City, Portneuf and Richelieu Rapids, in that order. They'll think you're going upriver."

"An' mawn, watch out for the big freighters," offered Gerard.

"Okay, but it sounds so complicated."

"One problem at a time. Survive the first few days an' get out of the river. Cops won't be looking for you out there. Only a fool would..." He stopped to laugh.

"Only a fool would be out there in December, right?"

"No, some fishermen are out in any weather. Yachters not. It's easier out on the big water, except for the gales this time of year. I doubt this old bitch'll stand a chance in a proper Gulf gale. Been in a few myself. Ugly water."

"Thanks for the warning. What do we do if there's a storm then?"

"Listen to the weather reports. If they give gale warnings get off the water."

"Any port?"

"Not all ports. Some you couldn't get into without a pilot."

"And how do we know that?" Christian had further doubts.

"The pilot book. But you have to know where you are, so if you see a fishing boat, call. Speak French. Talk like a fisherman. If you ask in English they ignore you, then the Coast Guard gets nosy. What's a dumb tourist on a yacht doing heading out into the Gulf?"

"Exactly. What *are* we doing?" He caught Breeze's glare.

"An' watch for new ice in the Straits. Can't see it. Not like bergs. New ice is dark an' low in water. Hard. Cut this old wooden hull in half like a machete. We have to go," said Petit Jacques abruptly. "An' remember, cops are maybe looking for you with planes. Best travel at night."

They filed up the ladder to the deck. Miguel and Jésus practically carried Paulo aboard *Elloise*. Renée and Christian held back to say their goodbyes. "Take care of your woman," Renée said as they embraced.

"I will. Take care of yourself, and Maartyn, if you find him."

"You've changed, Cheri. For the good. I'll do my best to find Maartyn."

They kissed briefly, like brother and sister, each wanting to say more. Gerard was watching the interplay.

Miguel was waiting at the rail to say goodbye to his boss, promising to meet again, too shy to embrace his Canadian friend but he couldn't deny the tears.

"You want the woman, mawn," Gerard said as they waited on deck for the deckhand to disconnect the fuel hose. The long black rubber hose snaking up from *Elloise's* engine room made Christian think of Gerard's black dick. About ten times larger than mine, he digressed. But for Renée just another erotic experience..."It's all over your face, Christian. You in love with that woman, no doubt."

"I don't...know, no…we're friends."

"I see how you look at each other. An' she told me about before."

"I'm with Breeze now."

"An' miss Renée can look after herself. She's got style an' money. Your woman's got your baby."

"I know." It was a simple fact. Renée didn't need him. It was a truth that still gnawed at Christian's heart. Renée was far ahead of him in life's progress and the affairs of the heart. His naiveté made him feel superior at times, but at times like these, confronted by Gerard's brutal logic, and his own imagination, he felt inadequate. Worse, he felt like Mathieu...*Do the right thing and be a martyr for love, not love...Lust, the curse of the weak.* Shut up Sartre! And he wasn't sure how much Breeze needed him either.

The grumbling Haitian refugees were packed into *Elloise's* dank, dark forepeak. It would be a cold uncomfortable trip but Jacques could not allow them to luxuriate on the yacht heading up the Richelieu and into New York State. Renée and Miguel waved forlornly from the bow as the old tug backed away, turned on her heel and churned up the mud of the narrow channel. Christian and Breeze stood together at the rail, surrounded by Miguel's camouflage, watching the *Elloise* chug out of sight into the twilight.

The wind was sharp and damp. Dark grey clouds crowded the Northwest quadrant like a malevolent hand sweeping in to clear the untidy world of debris. They were alone except for the wrapped bodies on the stern. The lumpy, graceless form of the howling Princess united in death with the beautiful, but deceitful, Dominique. What cruel twist of nature could create two humans so different and then entwine them so closely in death? The equalizer was Ile de Grace and the name too ironic. In the wheelhouse Christian entered his thoughts in the recovered journal and began the log entries. He looked back at the blank pages, vowing to fill them in, sometime...

"Christian?"

"I know. I'll get the engine."

"Hey, Skipper, we're going to be fine."

They entered the main channel at Quick Flashing S114, heading north and east. "That next green light should be S111," she said with confidence. "It's flashing faster than the rest. The chart shows a turn."

"We passed some between Montreal and Ile de Grace."

"That's right. What does it mean?"

"Change of course, Gerard said, but..."

"Wait...yes, it seems to do that every time the channel changes direction."

"Okay. There's a pencil. Mark them off."

"There's nothing beyond S111."

"Nothing? What?..."

"No land I mean. Lots of lights."

"Lac St.-Pierre."

The waves were already building to steep ragged crests even though the wind was from the northwest and the shore only two miles away. The long, narrow lake was shallow beyond the dredged channel and notorious for killing small boats. Christian had to brace himself to counter the sharp roll. Breeze, feeling sick to her stomach, hung on to the chart table and checked off buoys.

The black night was filled with the usual problems: steering from light to light, constantly checking the chart, doubts about position until the number could be verified and crossed off. The wind increased to gale force with sleet and then snow. Ragged hags of Miguel's camouflage blew past the windows, tearing at the rigging. Waves smashed the port side with insistent angry blows. Spray running down the windows and freezing made every navigation mark a question mark. The currents were tricky also, not following the channel, and the *Queen* constantly slewed to starboard trying for a final resting spot on a mud bank. Christian wheeled and worried. Would the engine run or stop, or the steering fail? Breeze only took her eyes from the flashing channel marks long enough to scan the chart with the red flashlight and go to the starboard door and check the buoy number. But now, at least, they were alone, together, piloting their way through a strange marine landscape. But as the night wore on and the *Queen* continued to respond, Christian became more confident. And as the snow and wind diminished the lights were more defined and the channel a moving highway to some destination too obscure to intrude on the immediate concerns. Breeze called off the marks and Christian bore down on the next green. The distant reds to port were only a reference to keep them in the channel. Then suddenly, "What the hell's that?"

A city had sprung up in the middle of the wild lake.

"Jesus Murphy! A big ship," said Breeze in awe.

"We're on the wrong side."

Christian froze, undecided which way to steer. The ship towered above the lake like an apartment block, lights blazing from a tall white superstructure. Masthead lights, deck lights. Bright lights defining the length of the black hull.

"The running lights."

"Lights?"

"We don't have the running lights on."

"Jacques said not to."

"They can't see us."

"Wouldn't matter. What the hell should I do?" The wind was pushing the *Queen* toward the big freighter. The distance seemed to be closing quickly. "How deep is the water off the channel?"

"Six feet. Enough if you don't go too far."

"Should I go left or right?

"Wait!" said Breeze. "That ship's not moving. It's anchored. There's a big wide spot off the channel, just there." She stabbed the chart.

Christian could see the buoys again so he knew they were still in the channel. The freighter was not. Neither spoke as they motored past the steel wall so close a boat hook could have scrapped the barnacle encrusted hull and their own exhaust noise tumbled back at them as if mocking their little boat. The wheelhouse of the big ship was so far above them they could not see the watch officer on the bridge wing gesturing wildly. The freighter had been up bound, dumping ballast, preparing to take on a cargo in the Port of Montreal when the captain, unfamiliar with the Seaway, and despite the orders of the pilot, had chosen to anchor fore and aft in the exposed anchorage to ride out the gale. The watch officer saw the *Queen* coming down river only as a blip on the radar. He was tempted to report the miscreant to the authorities but his English was imprecise and the French-Canadian traffic operators can be surly at night, annoyed at having to speak English with foreign officers. He decided to forget it and just yell a warning. His reluctance to report the odd vessel may have been due to the contraband in oil drums lashed to the deck.

They left the Bangkok-registered vessel and the cursing officer behind, concentrating on the buoys. Lac St.-Pierre continued to hammer on them with a nasty chop. Spray froze on everything like a crystal veneer. "I wish we were anchored too." Breeze sagged away from the chart table and put her arms around Christian's waist.

"We don't have an anchor. Are you okay?"

"I'm fine. A little tired. We have to find a place to hide."

Of course she's tired, he said to himself. But she says nothing. Never complains. "We'll stop soon. But where?"

"Yes, must remember we're fugitives from justice."

"What time is it?"

Breeze rummaged in her heavy coat for the pocket watch; an ancient engraved timepiece that once belonged to her grandfather, the sailor. Besides a box compass, a few well-worn British Admiralty charts, and an outdated pilot book of the coast of Newfoundland and Labrador, it was his most reliable navigation instrument in the old days. The days of sail and hard knocks on the Atlantic now given way to modern technology but the crew of the *Bayou Queen* had only one other piece of equipment; Jacques' VHF radio. It glowered at them from its perch on the deck head, like a malevolent bird of prey, crackling and cackling like a domesticated crow.

"Almost nine o'clock."

"Okay. At least we know when the sun comes up."

She hugged him tighter, pressing her rounding belly into the small of his back. The heat and the pressure felt good. Three people locked together by the strength of a good woman's arms. Christian tried to relax. He felt many things, summed up by the fear of just about everything. The symbolic distance growing between he and Renée as two boats moved through the night in opposite directions. He felt closer to Breeze than at any time in their brief, intense but chaotic relationship. "This is a miserable trip for

319

you."

"It's a wonderful voyage. We're going home."

Home. A strange concept, he thought. "I've never had a real home and you've never been to Newfoundland."

"Ireland, I mean. Home isn't always where you live you know. It's a state of mind. Where would you like to live?"

"I had a great villa in Cuba. White stonewalls. A terrace overlooking the beach. Islands. Blue water. All I had to do was sleep with the landlady once in awhile."

"You didn't!"

"Once, reluctantly. She got me drunk."

"You easy sleaze!" She punched him playfully on the back.

"I thought Cuba could be home; before Batista's army shot it up and burned the entire village. It wasn't the same after the Revolution."

"That was the time with Esameralda, after Renée left?"

"You already know most of this stuff."

"Not about how you felt about your home. Maybe not about how you feel now about Renée."

"What's the next buoy number?" He wished he hadn't asked. She would let go and return to being the navigator. He preferred the warmth.

"I don't remember."

"I need to know how long to Trois-Rivières."

Breeze turned back to the chart table. A single tear fell on the green buoy. "The next buoy should be S41." She used the dividers that Jacques had given them with the charts. Her musician's fingers and her mathematical mind adapted quickly, walking the divider legs along the charted channel to a point abeam the city of Trois-Rivières. "About twelve miles. How fast do you think we're going?"

"Three or four miles per hour, maybe. Gerard called them knots." He had failed to take into account the current hustling them along.

"Three hours."

"We should be there about midnight." It would be sooner.

"There's a big dock all along the waterfront."

"We'd look funny at sunrise with our floating forest, what's left of it. Better keep going. What's after Trois-Rivières?"

Breeze spent a lot of time studying the chart, searching for place names. The symbols, the numbers and the little arrows with the feathers were beginning to make sense. "Christian, I think there's a current." She went from chart to chart. The lower river was nothing like the island-rich stretch between Montreal and Lac St.-Pierre. The shoreline of the great river became a mass of shallow water and rocks.

"Current, of course. I've seen enough of that on the *Elloise*. My first experience steering a boat and it was down the rapids. It was wild."

"Jacques mentioned rapids ahead."

"But big ships take those so it should be okay. Find a place like Ile de Grace, with enough water to park this thing on a beach."

"We're going faster than we thought. It might be only two hours to Trois-Rivières. There's an island about the same distance below the city, as we are from the city now."

"Can we get in behind?"

"You look."

Breeze took the wheel, adjusted her glasses and aimed for the next green buoy. Christian studied the chart. "If those numbers mean feet, we should be able to get into a channel by going around...Battures de Gentily."

"That's what I thought. We'd be there by two o'clock, or so."

"Two o'clock. But that means wasting four hours on the river." He peeled away the charts, scanning the river for islands or harbours, anything of refuge. "There doesn't seem to be any place to stop between Gentily and Québec City."

"That's what I thought too, except for a place called Portneuf. That's just a long dock stuck way out in the river."

"Too far. And Jacques says there's problem tides to run. Do these charts say anything about tides?"

"There's a little box...Tidal Information, but it only says how high or low."

"I see it. Jacques said to be at the rapids only at high tide. We better stop at Gentily. Besides, you need the rest."

"I'm okay if you want to go on."

"No, look here, there's a distance box." It took Christian a few minutes to figure out the distances to places between Montreal and Québec City. "It's about eighty nautical miles from here to Québec City. That's further than miles. It's about ninety regular miles. And there's the rapids in between."

Christian took the wheel and slowed the *Queen* down. They were still going four knots. The wind was dropping steadily and the lake backed off from its insistent harassment. Breeze returned to studying the chart and the puzzling marine world, all the while humming a Stravinsky piece; *Summer*, from the Four Seasons suite. "When we stop I'm going to play."

That was the most optimistic news Christian had heard for weeks. He eased by buoy number S31 and noted that ahead was a flashing green which signified a change in the direction of the channel, a long curve to starboard. He could see the lights, reds and greens, flashing and quick flashing, stringing out to the loom of Trois-Rivières. The sky had cleared. Visibility was good. Maartyn's engine almost purred under their feet, warming the deck boards. She thought of Maartyn on the run. "I wonder what's happening to Maartyn? He's not dead," she said.

"You read my mind. It took me a long time to figure him out. Maartyn, the tough guy, beat your brains in for a laugh, tough guy. And he *is* tough, but so insecure."

"Transparently insecure."

"He had a difficult childhood, and not much of a legacy. Oh, he bragged about the Delta, and how he survived the marines, the fights, all that stuff, but you know, I think he wanted something better out of life when he saw the other side."

"Did knowing Renée have something to do with that?"

"Renée really confused him. I mean, she has everything, and always talked about throwing it over, being so Bohemian. It drove Maartyn crazy. You couldn't grow up much poorer. He could never get over the gap in our lives, and yet, we shared something in the Islands. We were friends. Even Paulo. Man, he's a case."

"But, what is it you see in Maartyn?"

"I don't know. After awhile, when I got used to him threatening me with guns and stuff, I learned to trust him. He was there when I needed him. Never asked for much in return, just that I be his friend."

"That's all you can ask, with friends, I mean. The trust thing."

"The guy was brilliant too."

"Was? You think he's dead?"

"No, not Maartyn. Listen to that engine. He's a genius with mechanical things. What could he have been with an education? A brain surgeon, inventor, engineer, anything he turned his hand to, if he had a choice. How did you choose to be a musician?"

"Mom encouraged me. We were poor but she worked hard, so I did it for her."

"Do you think she's disappointed, about this trip?"

"Not disappointed...worried. But she came up poor and strong. When she left Béhathook Cove she had nothing but me and her free spirit. What good was I? A gawky, mewing burden with a tit in my mouth and a loaded diaper. Poor Mom. But I think she's happy that I up and left on this voyage. She wants me to be tough and independent."

"Breeze, your Mom has no idea you're a fugitive."

"Neither did I. It's just what we make of it now."

They crept past Trois-Rivières in darkness, keeping to the far side of the channel, looking like a floating island of untidy shrubs.

"What's that awful smell? Like rotten eggs," asked Breeze in a whisper. The wind was from the town's industrial site.

"Paper mill. I hitch hiked through here a few years ago. You can feel the rumble of the machinery blocks away. The old section's nice, but I felt sorry for the people who had to live close to the mill. The noise. The smell? Man."

"People have to live in strange circumstances."

If it had been daylight they would have seen the tea-brown effluent pouring out of the Saint-Maurice River, the brown foam like small ice flows whirling downstream, and fishermen angling in the murky water. Christian would have been reminded of the gaunt young man lying beside the river, angling. They had a momentary start when a police car sped along the wharf, lights flashing and siren wailing, on a mission of civil order. And another when they saw the dormant Coast Guard cutter lying at the dock in the shadow of the warehouses.

Below the mouth of the Saint-Maurice River they passed Cap de la Madeleine and the big church with its floodlit spire, beckoning the faithful. What a normal life the good people on that shore must lead, he thought, and here we are, running under the cover of night, guilty by association, carrying the bodies as evidence. If we get caught...Breeze was still humming Stravinsky, making bowing and fingering motions with her long arms and delicate fingers. He wanted those arms around him. Christian felt guilty. She could have been so normal if he hadn't approached her table on registration day. There were other tables, he remembered. There was one with a girl who was really pretty, in a Westmount way but he had been drawn to Breeze by a power stronger than any known force of nature.

The black river strung out ahead of them defined by domestic lights on the shore; tidy riverside homes where honest people slept and prepared for another day while the ghostly mariners, adrift as if in a dream punctuated by little emergencies, were checking off the buoy numbers, an inventory of a passage into middle earth, following the River Styx rather than crossing it to perdition. The worst of their trials were still in the distance but each would remember the voyage in different ways. Christian could not shake the feeling that he was running from his past, his undiscovered family, his fears and failures, guilty of deaths by omission, pursued by images more dangerous than the faceless authorities in boats or airplanes. Breeze was on a voyage of discovery, going home with confidence, or at least the blessing of not knowing enough about what lay ahead to be afraid. Christian now regretted leaving Montreal as much as he feared the unknown of the future; the next minute, the next day...accompanied by the steady mutter of the diesel engine and the throb of the propeller relentlessly drawing in and pushing out water, forcing them onward, conspiring with the current, indifferent to their peril or survival. The thrill of leaving Ile de Grace for the voyage had been replaced by the dull, aching reality that they had no experience for the task ahead. Their vehicle to freedom, the *Bayou Queen,* was just a tool: a means of escape, with a cargo of the living and the dead, and the history of work and tragedy, used for the best and worst reasons in the employ of men. Christian tried not to personify the dumb instrument of their escape, but could not shake the feeling that Maartyn was present in the wheelhouse or standing guard over his engine, and that was some comfort.

They found Ile Gentily by counting buoys and felt their way around the point into a back channel, with Breeze standing on the bow holding the big electric torch to pick out landmarks, showing Christian the mud verge, shouting distances off and guessing at the entrance to the anchorage. They were doing reasonably well until Breeze saw the black shape of another vessel ahead of them; a much larger ship that appeared to be blocking the narrow channel. She crept back to the wheelhouse, afraid to make another sound.

"Chris..." she whispered.

"I see it. Too late. They'd hear the engine."

"Maybe it's one of those smugglers Gerard told us about."

The wind had fallen off with the passing of the gale and the *Queen* was just making way against the current curling through the channel from the main river. The vessel ahead was ominously quiet, not a light showed.

"We can't back out."

They approached the big vessel as if drawn by a magnet, their noisy exhaust rumbling back at them. Christian shut off the engine and they continued to range ahead in the lee. The night was creepy silent. Breeze got up the courage to shine her torch on the wheelhouse of the old goélette, an ancient coastal trader like the *Honor France Villard.*

"It's on a funny angle."

"I think it's stuck on the shore."

The silent hulk was lying across the channel with its bow wedged in the mud. "It's a wreck," she whispered.

They drifted to within a few feet of the derelict and the *Bayou Queen* came to a stop as if reluctant to approach the stranger. Christian ran forward, gathered up the grappling hook and pitched it, tangles and all, over the rail. He dragged the line back until the hook caught on the cap rail. He and Breeze pulled the *Queen* forward until her rail touched the wooden hull. They spent a few minutes securing fore and aft to their host, then, with chills of apprehension they crept over the rail of the goélette. Cautiously at first, they poked about, looking into open doors until satisfied that the ship was deserted.

"Well, this is a break," she whispered.

"No need to whisper, Breeze."

"Right. What is this old thing?"

"Cargo boat of some sort. That's the hold." They peered into the cavernous cargo space that took up the forward part of the vessel. "She's old. Been here some time. Look the hold's got water and there's nothing left, except some garbage." There was evidence of previous visitors: broken windows, beer bottles and food tins in the scuppers. The only piece of equipment not hauled away by scavengers was a big rusted anchor with its fluke defiantly caught over the rail of the raised fo'c'sle. Probably left behind because it was too heavy for the skiffs used by latter day salvors. In the old days of serious wreckers the anchor would be a prize.

The goélettes of their time were ubiquitous in the backwaters of Québec and the Maritime Provinces. Marine dump trucks of the coastal economy carrying cargoes from pulpwood to cattle, plying every available creek and harbour from Montreal to the Gulf of St. Lawrence. Rough built but strong, with a shabby grace that showed some breeding, like their ancestors in the sailing trade, but were given a unique flat bottom below the turn of the bilge because they spent half their lives sitting on the mud at low tide. Their goélette was called the *Roche Noir* and they would remember that name as prophetic.

Secured to the rotting *Roche Noir*, protected from gales and assured that they could not be seen from the North Shore, they decided to stay a day and regroup, forgetting for a few hours that they carried a sensitive cargo of their own. Their first task was to boil water and have a good wash, scrubbing each other, paying attention to areas that may be of special interest later. Breeze even managed to wash her hair, luxuriating in the warmth of falling water as Christian poured, allowing the rinse to run into the bilge. They didn't know that the soapy, luxuriant fresh water mingled with brackish river water seeping in through a broken garboard plank that had been working since the hurricane. Maartyn just pumped her out regularly, but since Christian had refused to take responsibility he failed to mention the details. The bilge was filling up slowly but steadily.

It was nearing four in the morning when they settled exhausted into the captain's cabin. It was also colder. Neither could sleep. They held each other close, shedding their clothes again under the blankets until they lay skin to skin. Christian rubbed Breezes belly, kissing her breasts, gently, tasting the large brown nipples, savouring the round firmness of life, then let his fingers search for the soft red patch and the wetness of her anticipation and gentled and rubbed her until she inhaled in short spasms and then breathed out in an ecstasy of relief. He was satisfied that she was satisfied but she insisted on reciprocating in inventive ways. Alone for the first time since escaping from Montreal they were for the moment, content, and then they slept, deep and long.

They slept like the dead through dawn while the river world came to life around them. A distant ship's whistle woke them around seven. They both thought of the bodies on the stern. "We have to do something with them," she said sadly.

"I know," he replied, trying to hold the feeling of the night before, alarmed by the shrill cry of seagulls swooping by to investigate this new presence in the channel, puzzled perhaps by the forest of shrubs. An airplane droned overhead and passed on. They both wondered if the police were still looking for them.

"I hope there's enough camouflage left."

"I'm not getting out of this bed to cut more."

"Some backwoods husband you'd make."

Neither wanted to approach the subject and so snuggled and fondled each other to distraction. They drifted back into warm, protected sleep and drowsed a while longer.

"Do you realize what day this is?" she asked as they stretched into the sunlight pouring through the porthole. They could see their breath.

"It's a day off," he said.

"Christmas Eve, dummy. Where have you been?"

"On some bizarre trip I guess, and wasn't paying attention to dates, just my own warm pregnant person."

"How should we celebrate?" asked Breeze, throwing back the covers.

"Celebrate? You still think this is a pleasure cruise to Paradise."

"Well, we have to do something special. Something romantic and frivolous."

"Okay, let's give ourselves the gift of that anchor."

"Wow, that's really special."

"You're welcome. Sarcasm becomes you."

"Speaking of thank you...thank you, if I forgot to."

"You didn't forget. And thank you too."

"And you thanked me twice, remember?"

Breeze made a special breakfast: Brie and caviar for openers, on crusty baguettes broken and buttered, then stovetop-browned, the butter running off, bubbling and sizzling like bacon. Smoked salmon as the entré and coffee made with fresh ground beans followed. Renée had insisted on buying a small hand grinder and dark Cuban beans. The aroma of the raw oils intoxicating, even over the smell of diesel fuel. The grinder whirled and the dark brown powder was dumped into cold water in an enamel kettle, and slowly brought to the verge of a boil. Her mother had taught her how to make real coffee. It seemed excessive but Renée had insisted that brandy and coffee were de rigueur for the finalé, deserved by any one forced to live rough.

While Breeze was doing domestic things Christian climbed aboard the *Roche Noir* and descended into the dank fo'c'sle to investigate the anchor chain, knowing Breeze would have been just as happy to mess about with the chain. In the light of the torch Christian found a mounded pile of rust but under the rust was enough solid chain to hold the *Bayou Queen*: half the length and a tenth of the weight of the goélette. But all that weight was a challenge.

The *Bayou Queen* had derricks for lifting nets. The goélette had a cargo mast forward with a boom drooping wearily over the port rail. All the goélette's lifting gear was gone of course, but the *Queen* had spare blocks and coils of line in her own fo'c'sle.

Christian spent a half hour lugging the gear to the deck and untangling lines, vaguely aware of the physics of pulley blocks and ropes. His only reference was randomly attended physics classes.

"It's a mess," he said over breakfast. "I need your help."

"Good. First you can do up the dishes, while I make the captain's bed "

The weak, but optimistic sunshine of the early morning was replaced by low clouds and wet, indecisive snow, flung fitfully about by a rising wind. After breakfast they lingered in the warmth of the galley sketching the plan on the back of a grocery bill. "I wonder how Uncle Haim's doing?" Breeze asked wistfully. "I really hated to leave him."

"I know. He seemed so lonely."

"We would have been his family."

Christian experienced a rush of regret. He had made only a half-hearted attempt to find his own family in Montreal. He wondered if it was because he was still angry with his father, or because he was ashamed of what had happened when he left Montreal the first time. He blamed himself for the breakup, but not then. Then he had lashed out in his embarrassment at his broken family, hurting, but not yet fractured beyond repair. He should have been more understanding. That comes with knowledge. Knowledge comes with experience. He had been selfish, thinking only of his own pain and limited, but damaging, experiences.

The downward spiral had been swift, but subtle. He was into the drug scene with Howie's help, out of university and out of Montreal bound for Paris and then Chicago, too fast to figure out what went wrong. The months in Chicago, awash in a blur of narcotics and music allowed no room for introspection until the day he came face to face with his own mortality. And then the answer was to run, again. This time to the Islands. The recovery was slow, but there was Renée and Maartyn and a revolution and more running, but this time back to Montreal with the intention of starting over. Making amends. Where had he gone wrong, again? Was it meeting Jean-Pierre and the squalor of mind as well as body, and another revolution driven by desperate people and no one to trust? The Poseurs were an example of life at the bottom where it would have been easy to dwell. But never in control of his own life, he sacrificed his naiveté to chance. And he was once again on the run with one of the Poseurs frozen stiff on the stern, the other a ruin of charred bones, slumped in final obscurity in the poisoned mud of a septic river, a tragic end to a worthless life, but who's to say? He could be no better given the circumstances. It comes down to survival; who survives well and who steals survival? Is the end experience corruption of self? But..."I have you and the baby..."

"You do," she said simply to counter his gloomy thoughts.

"That's important. You are goodness."

"And you as well."

"Let's do good and liberate that anchor."

The heavy anchor finally yielded to physics and ingenuity. Christian and Breeze, using a block and tackle, pulled the chain yard by yard out of the *Roche Noir* in a cloud of dust and fed it into the *Queen*, then using the derricks, swung the anchor from the rail of the goélette to the bow of the shrimp boat. The persistent snow made any movement difficult and dangerous, but much was learned by their mistakes and recovery. It took hours.

After a lunch that was a lot like breakfast, but with wine to celebrate the feat of the anchor, Christian summoned the courage to use the VHF radio. Jacques had given them a perfunctory lesson in radio etiquette: lift the microphone, press the button, identify with false name, call the Seaway Montreal operator, lie about their destination and request information about tides as if they were some blundering American yachters heading home to New York. Some of the names they came up with over wine were: Drunken Naifs. Swiggers. Spirit of Bourbon Street. "Hello? Ah, Seaway...Montreal? This is the yacht Happy Hearts...we're, ah, goin' home...New York..." Breeze giggling in the background was not helpful. The blundering part was easy, but miraculously the Seaway operator asked no questions and gave them tide times that night for Québec City, Portneuf and The Richelieu Rapids and wished them a good voyage home, hoping to get the Americans safely out of his sector.

In the afternoon they crawled into a bunk forward of the warm galley to wait for nightfall. Christian imagined he could smell Renée's perfume on the pillow and he dozed holding Breeze with conflicted emotions. The snow cleared off while they were sleeping and the temperature plunged leaving the two vessels coated with crystal ice, like a gleaming wedding cake; a distraction from the real bride and groom, unfavoured by nature, disguised by accessories of the special day.

That evening they dined on smoked meat and toasted baguettes, avoiding wine or brandy because it was time to go. Using their new-found skills with ropes and tackles, Breeze swung Christian ashore and together they turned the *Queen* by hand. He had to slog through the snow and mud hauling on lines. Breeze used a boathook to break the skim of black ice forming around the hulls. It was dark by five thirty and there was no sunset. At seven that night they crept carefully out of their refuge, crunching through new ice along the Gentilly channel and like a furtive spirit the *Bayou Queen* entered the main channel at quick flashing buoy C3. It was twenty miles to the rapids. High tide was at eleven thirty-three the operator had assured them. Breeze calculated it would take about five hours to get there for midnight in the Richelieu Rapids, and with luck they would be clear of Québec City by Christmas morning.

"Merry Christmas."

"I love the anchor.

"Thought you might."

"I love you, too."

Their narrow marinescape had changed since they took refuge at Gentily beside the old *Roche Noir*. Heavy snow blanketed the valley and by the loom of lights they could easily see the shoreline and fields around the villages. The voyage went reasonably well for the first two hours of the passage to the Rapids, the new epicenter of their narrow rushing water universe. The Richelieu had that certain significance that new place names have when one is travelling: a milestone, a destination, a goal or an obstacle to be avoided or surmounted. Jacques had warned them to be at the rapids for high tide when the current is slack. Still water only lasts for a few minutes, he said. And mariners traversing the Seaway keep watch for the Richelieu. Coming upstream at low water a big freighter would have to buffet the wind and a five to six-knot current and slog its way up the ladder wasting fuel. Some older ships could barely move ahead. Engine or steering problems assured disaster. They would wait below the rapids at anchor, or hover in the current opposite Portneuf Wharf. Going down stream with the current meant a rush of speed so terrifying to a big boat captain used to the open ocean that most pilots choose to hang back, anchoring in Mouillage Batiscan or Grondines. Jacques had failed to mention what would happen if they arrive too soon.

Innocent, although apprehensive, of the danger ahead, they took turns steering. More confident now, they neglected to check off each buoy. Breeze even descended to the galley to make strong coffee two hours into what they still believed was a five-hour run at half speed. Confidence can be as dangerous as overconfidence. While drinking hot coffee and relaxing they lost track of their location. The engine purred reassuringly. A hypnotic calm set in. Breeze played air cello and hummed Stravinsky. The lights strung out ahead to left and right and they cruised as if on a suburban parkway: young lovers out for a night in the old jalopy. The riverbanks closed in but only seemed to add to the cozy atmosphere. Time and distance should have put them at a point somewhere between Cap Levrard and Cap Charles. They noted the quick flashing reds and greens, they seemed to be close together, followed the turns and had many lights to define their highway. Buoys slipped by and prominent landmarks came and went until Breeze checked the chart.

"There's a white light," said Breeze suddenly. It should be green. Where's the green?"

"There's a red, to port. Check the number." He eased the *Queen* across the channel so that Breeze could pick out the number. She had to force her way on deck against a northeast wind that had risen since they left Gentily. It was a shock and bitterly cold, and Breeze had to wait for Christian to get close enough. She came back into the wheelhouse chilled through.

"D4. That's not right." She poked her glasses higher on her nose and focused on the chart, tracing the route with shaking fingers. "Chris, its only ten thirty. We shouldn't be at D4 already."

"Too fast! The current. Damn!"

"The rapids! Right there!" She stabbed the chart angrily.

The St. Lawrence River was pouring through a narrow gap at five knots against the wind and incoming tide. The *Queen*, making ten knots, hurled herself into the caldron. Riding the current in the dark would have been problem enough for an experienced wheelsman. Christian did have experience steering the *Elloise* down the Lachine Rapids but the Lachine route was a single-minded torrent. The Richelieu that night was a mass of jumping, crashing water being pushed back upstream by the wind and the Atlantic tide. Six-foot waves with sides as steep as a wall, leapt and boiled, turning the channel into a run of white water; tide lops, the worst sea a seasoned mariner will experience. Maartyn experienced the worst of the Gulf Stream so the *Queen* was no stranger to waves that jump up and pound boats, buffeting, smashing, tearing at deck fittings, sending spray over the house, blinding, confusing. They were into the run without much warning and the first of the waves rose up and hammered the *Queen* so suddenly that Breeze screamed as their boat lurched to port, heading for the shallows of Batture Simon. Christian, blinded by the freezing spray sliding down the wheelhouse window, could not see a green to starboard. "We're going wrong!"

"Please, God..." Breeze opened the wheelhouse door and risked being thrown over the side but she spotted the next red. "Turn right...more right!"

Christian fought the wheel. The wind shrieked in the rigging and tore away camouflage shrubbery, and as if to mock Breeze's entreaty, the thicker snowsquall swirled around them. The *Queen* rolled down in the trough taking water on deck but slowly answered the helm. Suddenly a green light flashed through the squall. Then again. And again. Breeze pointed, "There!" Christian steadied the bow into the white crested black waves. The *Queen* smashed on, jumping and bucking like a demented thing. Gear crashed about. The derrick they had used that morning and forgot to secure, thrashed and banged until something broke and the derrick slumped to the deck, its wires and ropes snaking around and tangling other deck gear. That was the fortunate event. If the derrick had gone over the side the wires would have fouled the propeller. The crew was too busy to be aware of their good fortune. No, they believed they were doomed. Going faster and faster, again slewing out of control. Too late to turn back.

"That next green should be Q83. The rapids are just ahead."

"There's a red light over there. Wrong side!"

"Where?" Breeze squinted into the scud. "Not blinking." She frantically scanned the chart. "Ignore it, Chris. It's off the channel."

"But, what is it?"

"A dock or something."

The channel straightened and Christian held the course. The wind shrieked louder and the snow flew at them in fat wet bombs that stuck to the wheelhouse windows, congealing with the spray ice. Spray froze to the rigging and the boat became even more sluggish and top heavy. The waves leapt higher and tore at the *Queen's* ancient bow with blows as hard as any hurricane driven seas. Breeze went out again to clear the window, slipping on ice and slush, dangerously close to the dipping rails. Christian was terrified for Breeze but could do nothing. He had to see, he had to steer. What, wondered Christian, would happen if he had one of his spells?

A gust of wind drove a lop wave high into the air and met the *Queen* with a solid blow. The old hull staggered back like a boxer punched in the gut, winded and off balance. And at her vulnerable moment another gust turned her head and she fell into a trough despite Christian's frantic efforts...It is a truism that, in any crisis, if things can only get worse they will. Jacques was generous with his fuel oil but his supply was not the best. Water and dirt had been pumped into the tanks along with the salvaged No. 2 stove oil. It wouldn't bother the *Elloise* and Maartyn had foreseen the problem of bad fuel, installing special filters. But filters can only absorb so much...Now they were into the section where the mighty St. Lawrence River is squeezed down to less than eight hundred feet. The great volume of water speeds up to pass through. The *Bayou Queen*, her cargo and crew, shot through the gap like a pea through a tube. It was at that critical moment, as the *Queen* leapt and then rolled, that the faithful diesel sputtered. The revolutions dropped, then picked up. Christian's heart jumped and almost stopped in response. The engine spluttered again, hesitated, tried and died. The sudden absence of engine noise and vibration was more terrifying to Breeze and Christian than all the banshee wailing of the wind and hammer blows of the confused seas.

Dead and out of control the *Queen* turned broadside to the channel, the current holding her firmly in its grip driving the hull into the waves. Christian rushed down to the engine room and, knee deep in cold black water, tried to restart the engine. It refused. Another fortunate event. If the engine had started they would have run onto the rocks trying to turn against the gale.

When Christian returned from the engine room with the bad new the *Queen* was rolling so badly he and Breeze lay on the wheelhouse deck to avoid injury. Christian wrapped his legs around the pedestal and held on to Breeze as freezing cold water squirted in under the doors and swirled about the wheelhouse. Gear crashed down. The big Christmas anchor on the bow jumped off the rail and skidded across the fore deck like a loose cannon, shattering stanchions and rails. On one trip across it hung up on a stout vent and held, for the moment.

"Are we going to die?" she asked without fear or resentment.

"No. Don't even think that. We'll go aground or something. It's just a river." He didn't believe his own words. He thought of the baby. It would be a shame. They lay without talking for a long time, each with their own thoughts about life and mortality.

"I'm glad I'm with you," she said and held him close.

"Me too." He meant it. They were silent again. The numbness of resignation that comes with helplessness set in.

Breeze pressed the baby closer to Christian. "He doesn't need to know."

"No, she should feel safe. She's safe." A boy for him, a girl for her. It was their gentle joke. The wild ride seemed to go on forever until the forefoot smashed down on a rock and the boat spun back into the channel. Is this how it ends? he wondered. To answer his question the Richelieu spit them out of the giant water chute like a newborn in a hurry. Suddenly it was strangely silent. The *Queen* rocked gently, turning aimlessly in the slack water at the bottom of the rapids. For the moment they were safely in the lee of the north shore ridge above Portneuf.

"We must be through," Christian said in a whisper, as if speech would betray them and break the spell.

"Thank you, God."

They got stiffly up, wet and cold but just as they began congratulating themselves on surviving the rapids they were shocked to see the blaze of lights dead ahead.

"Oh, no! What?"

"A big ship," he whispered in awe.

Without power they could do nothing but hold each other and wait. It was a very long ship; a deep laden Great Lakes freighter coming up from Sept Isles with a load of iron ore. The current was still strong and the gap narrowed quickly.

"They'll run us over."

When nothing happened they realized that the freighter was safely at anchor waiting for the tide. Another officer on watch was puzzled by an image on the radar screen but there were no running lights to be seen ahead in the darkened river. Then the blip disappeared from the radar screen because the *Queen* was right under the big ship's bows, barely missing the anchor chain, glancing off the port side, rubbing and bumping along the vessel's hull. When they came abreast the engine room Christian was again staring at the incredulous face of an engineer standing in his open gangway, wondering what was bumping his boat. The *Queen*, like a ghost ship, silently slipped back into darkness. Christian had to laugh to relieve the tension. "I can't believe this is happening. It's like déja vue and we're still in Montreal."

"You've done this before?"

"First cruise on *Elloise*, with Jacques. Long story." If they had been paying attention to the marine radio traffic they would have heard the ship's officer making a security call saying that he was anchoring below the Richelieu Rapids, one mile south and west of Portneuf wharf, to wait for the right tide. The Seaway Operator answered in the affirmative. Then the Operator radioed another ship up bound and asked if they had heard the transmission. The other vessel had heard. *Thank you. Over...*

"There...another light," said Christian in disbelief, afraid they were about to be run down by a second ship. Breeze looked at the chart. "No, it's blinking...funny though."

"Yeah, different."

"The Portneuf dock. And look, there's two lights right

above...those lights." She traced out two high towers on the far shore. Their identities and height above river level noted. The lights-in-line marker they could have used to steer down the rapids in other circumstances. "They aren't red or green, well, sort of green. See this line...We seem to be heading right for the dock."

They had to land somewhere or anchor. Their big Christmas anchor was for emergencies and this would become an emergency if they missed the Portneuf wharf. The St. Lawrence shoreline from Richelieu to Québec City is a moonscape of shoals and rocky flats that dry out at low tide and are millraces at high tide. And without local knowledge of a tidal creek or a marina to slip into with enough depth to take the *Queen*, Christian and Breeze were as bereft of safe harbours as if they had been in the middle of a panting desert. Portneuf was their best, possibly their only hope.

"We can tie up and figure out the engine."

"Oh, Chris, look, there's another boat." She pointed into the darkness to the east where the river makes a sharp bend for Québec City. Farther down river they could see the lights of a big vessel. This one was definitely moving. In the loom of a buoy the bow wave boiling up looked like a white moustache on Santa and they were drifting in its direction.

They went on deck to make preparations, unaware that a shroud wrapped body kept pace with the *Bayou Queen*. But they were in luck once again. The big ship was working very slowly upstream despite the appearance of movement, the pilot using the easy current to steer, edging slowly up toward Portneuf, treading water like a swimmer. The dead *Queen* was making better time riding the current down and the wind was pushing her out of the main channel toward the Portneuf wharf. The body tagged along.

"Where's the boat hook?" asked Christian.

"I left it on the deck."

"It's gone," he said flatly when he returned from his search.

"Sorry."

"It's okay. We'll use the grappling hook."

The *Queen* was drifting down on Portneuf only visible as a blinking red light until Breeze shone her torch along the face of the wharf. Christian made ready with the grappling hook, this time untangling the line and coiling it down. The black mass of the pier face loomed high above them. It seemed at first as if it would be an easy throw but the current and the wharf conspired to create an eddy. The backwash began to push the *Queen* away. "We're going to miss!"

"Damn! It's a long throw!" Christian heaved the grappling hook. The first try fell short with an impotent splash. He frantically hauled the line in hand over hand hoping the hook did not snag something. The hook *clanged* over the side and he tried again, this time getting extra height. The hook bounced on the top of the wharf and caught on the steel rail. Now they had to fight the current and the weight of the waterlogged *Queen* to drag her back, inch by inch toward the dock. The closer they got the harder the pull. They were both panting and sweating, with fingers bleeding from the rough line. Finally the hull bumped the steel piles. Christian tied off and they went to opposite ends of the deck searching the slime covered pier face for something to put a line on. There was nothing but a steel ladder built into the wall. Christian started up with his dock line. Fear turned his legs to rubber, and his hands almost froze to the metal rungs of the ladder as he forced himself up. What if the line broke and the *Queen* drifted away? What would happen to Breeze? Panic seized him.

"What's the matter?"

"Nothing." What a stupid thing to say. Everything's wrong, he breathed. He forced himself to take the next rungs and then claw his way onto the slippery dock. He nearly tripped over the huge bollard, a dock fitting hefty enough to tie up commercial vessels. He wrapped his line around the bollard throwing in overhand knots, then raced to the bow end. Breeze threw him her line. He tied that off with more knots, ready to collapse with relief.

They were now tied to the land, a strange land, a dock in the middle of a wasteland of blackness between themselves and the snow covered shore. With the current splashing and gurgling along the wharf face it seemed as if they were still on a moving vessel. He became disoriented, afraid to stand up. The lights of Portneuf village in the distance beckoned to a world of warm kitchens and sanity. Hot stoves and coffee. A world where people just eat and sleep and go about life without fear.

He heard…"Christian? You sure you're all right?" Breeze was calling, worried. He was on his knees beside the bollard, still holding on to the bitter end of the frozen line. "Yeah," he answered, ashamed of his weakness.

They fell exhausted into separate bunks in the forward cabin, stopping only long enough to light the galley stove, put on dry clothes and have a drink of brandy. Food and engines would have to wait.

Christian was in a deep but troubled sleep, dreaming of being in front of a firing squad and Renée was holding the sword, ready to give the order, when he felt, then heard, their boat lurch and bump hard against the dock. A wave hit the outboard side of the hull and another lurch and bang sent him into the galley searching blindly for his parka.

On deck it was snowing lightly, a fine dusting, and it was very cold, but there was no wind. And there was no sound of rushing water, nothing to account for the lurching and banging. Christian toured the deck with the torch, stepping over fallen rigging, wondering what to do with the collapsed derrick. Snow covered everything, disguising the worn out old vessel as a sculpture in a water gallery. The remaining derrick and a block still swayed from the previous movements but there was nothing to explain the waves and the crashing about until he picked out the single stern light of the vessel that had passed up stream minutes before. Then Christian noticed that the *Queen's* gunnel was almost level with the top of the long wharf. Something else caught his eye, or rather, what was missing from the scene. There was only one body at the stern and by the size and shape it was Dominique's. He shone the torch around the clutter of the deck, hoping the other was lodged somewhere: hoping it wasn't. "Oh, Sweet Jesus!" he said hoarsely.

"What? What's the matter?"

"Oh...Breeze, the lines. The tide. We forgot about the tide. It's still coming up. Or it's up and about to start going down, I guess."

She dug for her pocket watch and held it up for the flash of the wharf light, squinting to see without her thick glasses. Her image came and went with the blinking light. The snow covered boat went from Arctic white to Hades red every few seconds "It's just after midnight. We've only been asleep for an hour. It must be what they call slack tide."

"Yeah, and what happens when the tide goes down?" He thought she looked beautiful in the red light, with her red hair blowing about, with flecks of red snow.

"The boat goes down too."

"Right. But how far?"

They huddled in the thin protection of the wheelhouse to study charts, both knowing it was going to be a long night. "About fourteen feet according to this," she said, pointing to a small box, near the box with distance information.

"You go to bed. I'll watch the lines," he urged.

"No, I can do it. You have to work on the engine tomorrow."

"Breeze!" he said sharply, "you can't climb up and down that ladder all night. The baby, you're tired." He instantly regretted treating her like a woman. He knew she would resent the patronizing, hoping she didn't use the word.

"No more than you. Besides, I don't have to go up the ladder. You can loop the lines around those things and I can do the lines from the deck. Go to bed."

She *would* think of that. "No, I'm not tired now. I'll see about the engine while you get some sleep. We can't stay at this dock after dawn." She sulked a bit. He felt guilty a bit. Then they kissed and turned to their tasks. "I'll make coffee," she said.

Christian stood in the glare of the engine room light staring at the dumb green Bota. He was the one who was dumb, he said to himself. "What would Maartyn do?" Maartyn, the mechanical maniac, used to ramble on about diesel engines, injectors and linkage when they were drinking. He worked on the *Bayou Queen's* engine for the Cubans. He also went on about balky engines he had fixed and said that when a diesel suddenly quits the problem is just dirt or water in the fuel and vowed that the first thing he would install were proper filters. And he did install filters, obviously. Breeze brought the coffee and sat on the steps watching while Christian sipped the hot black brew with a dash of brandy. "The first thing Maartyn would do is check the filters."

"Good. What's a filter?" she asked innocently.

"I don't have a clue, but he talked about them, often. They'd be between the tanks and the engine, is my guess."

The engine room was a maze of wires, pipes, lines and gauges. In the middle of the space the ailing engine brooded, cold and sullen, waiting for Christian to solve the puzzle. Christian knew how to start it and stop it but hat was the limit of his skill as an engineer. On either side of the engine room there were big steel fuel tanks so he started there, tracing a pipe from the first tank until he encountered a canister. "Shut off the fuel supply, but how?"

"You can do it."

"Are you always this optimistic?"

"Yes. I was never allowed to be negative. Mom calls it being slubby or cross-grained."

They hadn't meant to oversleep, but it had been an exhausting night. Breeze tended the lines and watched Christian learn about filters and fuel lines the hard way. A frustrating, messy session, with much guessing, skinned knuckles and bad language, but after hours of mishaps and much precious fuel spilled into the bilge, Christian found the problem: dirt *and* water. The filters were clogged. Just before a grey, indifferent dawn revealed their presence, the engine turned over, reluctantly at first, then roared to life. Maartyn would have been proud, after some ragging on Christian for not bleeding the air from the lines in the first place.

They should have continued their voyage immediately but talked themselves into a couple hours of sleep...He woke first, his face close to hers, her breath slow and even, grazing his cheeks like a feather. A delicious red curl curved slowly across her cheek as she turned to him, eyes still closed, conscious of his gaze perhaps, yet without waking. He waited for the eyelids to flutter. She looked so different without her glasses but they could not change those sea green pools with the gold flecks. He remembered that first day, and later on the hill, under the trees, the moment he knew they would make love. She knew. She was so composed with him even then, as now, so trusting and offering the same feint smile as he traced her hips and breasts and held her firmly but gently, watching her full lips slightly part, as if she was about to speak. He hoped she would say she loved him, then as now. He needed to hear the words, but drank in her colour; fresh, with a certain radiance, perhaps just the new day, though grey, reflecting off the water. He scanned her freckles, counting the large ones that had shapes and told stories. He wanted to touch each ochre island, trace the borders, name them, give them each a life of their own, as if he was God blessing the stars He had created. He kissed her forehead, her nose, eyes, lips, until she stirred and kissed him back, lips parted, their tongues politely entering with a promise of more. Her eyes opened full on his and the smile showed that her heart was his. They moved together shamelessly, innocently searching as if it was all new, but so familiar, words were not necessary, and they may have made love, not really awake, hovering in that twilight of love only hearts in tune and time can share. Then they slept again.

So, it was almost mid-day when the Québec Provincial Police constable woke them by yelling at the somnolent *Bayou Queen* through a bullhorn, sending chills of fear to rudely chase the warm reverie to a hiding place. The tide was rising again and the *Queen* stood several feet away from the wharf straining to go back up stream. Breeze stumbled up the fo'c'sle ladder, groggy, feeling guilty for letting the tide get ahead of her watchfulness. And she had forgotten to put on her glasses. She squinted at the officer, obviously an authority of some sort by the uniform coat. She could see the police car and the other officer standing further away looking at the stern of their boat, calling to his partner: "Anglais bateau. Americans. Ici, la, South Carolina."

"Madame. Bon matin. Is everything all right?" he asked in English.

She decided to answer in French. "Oh, yes. Thank you..." Think. Think. "We had some problems, ah, with the engine. It's a diesel. Filters and all. Last night...my...husband...fixed it."

The officer eyed the mess of the decks and the slack lines. "This is not a good dock for small boats," he responded in French.

"I, we were watching..." She yawned and shivered. Breeze was in her bare feet, with bare legs and just her big duffle coat pulled around, hugging her belly as if the baby needed protection from intruders. At some point they must have got undressed, washed and cuddled. She remembered making love; was it before or after sleep, or both? Christian climbed out of the hatch dressed for the elements but was disheveled, blond curls awry, looking very red-eyed and tired. If he had had a beard, that too would have added to the ensemble of neglect. The officer nodded knowingly.

"There's a big storm coming. You don't want to be on this dock." He was skeptical if they should be anywhere near the water. "Where are you headed?"

Breeze thought quickly. Too quickly. "New York, City." Just as Jacques proscribed.

"New York? You *are* Americans then?"

It was decided. "Yes." What if they asked for papers?

"You speak French very well for an American."

"I'm, well, actually from Newfoundland, originally. I live in New York, now, and study French at Columbia...University..."

"I see. And why would you study French in New York and not Paris or here in Québec?"

"Ah, music scholarship." Breeze was trying hard not to lie.

"French music?"

"Ah, yes. Columbia has a graduate program in French Baroque music. Very specialized. I have my cello on board. Would you care to hear something? I could get dressed and play."

The other officer approached and said something to the first officer. "Your boat is very interesting. *Delta Queen*. It's a fishing boat? Registered in Charleston, South Carolina?"

Christian did not realize the *Queen* was registered in Charleston or even the name change. Maartyn had not mentioned the change in South Carolina but he decided he had better jump into the conversation before it got too far off course for Breeze to continue the lie. "Yes, that's right, sir. A friend of ours was fishing off the East Coast, last summer and decided to visit us in Newfoundland, but he had to go back to Louisiana, I mean, South Carolina, suddenly, because...his father was killed working on a fishing boat. Delta shrimper, you know the type, like this one? We're just delivering the boat to New York."

"You speak French very well also, but you don't know much about boats, do you."

"Ah, no sir. I guess, well, we had some problems, storm, engine...You know."

"We had a call from the Seaway Authority to be on the look out for some Americans on a yacht heading up river. But the name of the boat was *Happy Hearts*. That's not you? So, there's other Americans crazy enough to be on the river at this time of year?"

"Oh, yes, that could have been us. We were a little drunk when we called the guys, you know, the marine guys...but we weren't driving the boat at the time," he hastened to add. "We were...feeling happy, heart happy, and well, we couldn't actually remember what this boat was called so we...made up a name. *Happy Hearts.* Maybe we should change it..."

"Sir, I'd advise you to get this piece of shit bateau up those rapids on this tide, and out of our area. Once you get to Sorel get off our river and the hell up to Lake Champlain and into the States. You should be safe enough, but be advised, there was some trouble at the boarder the other night, and there might be questions. Can you answer questions?"

"Yes, absolutely."

"Are you the only crew on this boat?"

"Yes, sir."

"Are you carrying illegal immigrants? Weapons?"

"No, sir."

"Are you carrying alcoholic spirits?"

Be honest, Christian. "Ah, yes, actually. But only some French wine, and brandy, we bought," remembering a story he had read about Newfoundland smugglers, "in St. Pierre, the islands? St. Pierre and Miquelon...?"

"I know the islands. I have relatives there. So you stopped at St. Pierre on the way from Newfoundland?"

"Yes," he said, racking his brain for place names. The name Placentia Bay popped into his head. Freud would say...

"Are you an American too?"

The Americans had a naval base at Argentia, Placentia Bay. "Yes. My parents were in the navy, during the war. Stationed at Argentia. He was getting in too deep. He knew he could tell a story if necessary but hated lying. All lies are a trap, especially in other than your native tongue.

"And your parents are still in Argentia?"

"Um, no. They're back home." Well, his mother may be back

home, in Ireland.

"And your home is in America?"

"Ah, yes, I'm from Chicago, or was. I was in Louisiana to work. Met my friend, Maartyn St. Jacques." He suddenly remembered the coincidence. The tale of the two Jacques, or three counting the bridge, but he shouldn't have mentioned Maartyn's name. "The one who owns this boat? Louisiana's very French." And trying to get back on track..."Also studied French and music at McGill University, in Montreal...Québec..."

"We know where Montreal is also. That at least makes some sense. Bon voyage."

Some trouble at the border they said. Jacques and the *Elloise* and the American yacht? What kind of trouble? Refugees. Maartyn on the run or dead. Renée implicated, maybe in jail. Miguel vulnerable. His heart felt like it had been pierced and his gut turned as if a hand reached in and twisted. His friends were in trouble but they had troubles of their own. "Breeze," he whispered, as they watched the patrol car turn on the narrow dock apron, "there's a body missing. I should have told you."

The police officers drove up the wharf toward Portneuf with great doubts about the *Yankees*. They should have impounded the odd looking American boat under suspicion of stupidity but it was no skin off their butts, and it was too damned cold to be messing about on the river with derelicts and morons, especially Anglais imbeciles, though the girl was pretty with nice legs. No, they weren't Coast Guard.

However, come spring, when a Portneuf dog brought home a human leg bone, the police were forced to investigate. They followed the dog to his cache under the Portneuf wharf and found the decomposing body of the Indian Princess wrapped in rotting canvas, lodged under the wharf above the high tide line. There were many questions and some recollections of odd boats and odd behaviour. But lots of strange things go up and down the big river. And about the same time there was the other incident of the *charred bones on a burned out hull*, found further down river near Neuville. The coroner made a connection: season, timing of death and fire, but beyond that and the puzzle of the canvas shroud, there were no signs of foul play and nothing else to be known about the two bodies, other than it was a bizarre coincidence. Their remains went into official storage limbo, labeled 'Male-Female Caucasians. Origin: Unknown'.

"We have to pump out the water again."

"I know."

Time to go. Christian discovered the other hand pump while solving the riddle of the filters and worked until the bilges were clear of oily water. Breeze made sandwiches and coffee for the day. They left the Princess behind to find her own resting place and turned down river towards Québec City bearing their remaining sad cargo. The storm that the police officer warned them about loomed on the eastern horizon and the wind blew fresh by the time they passed Neuville, where the bones of the former Gargoire would go ashore later that spring. The Poseurs had set out on a journey, risking everything. That they disappeared in a foreign country, in oblivion, unmarked and sadly, unmourned, was at least a tribute to their tenacious existence.

"How far's Québec City?"

Breeze counted off the miles with the ancient dividers. "About twenty miles. And there's a current." She traced the charts and the blue and white ribbons of water between the beige strips of fore shore that looked like a rocky wasteland. White means deep water and channels. Blue means, *check the depths*. They had learned recently that the arrows with feathers mean direction of current and speed. It depends whether the tide is rising or falling, whether the water is going upstream or down, whether it's a spring tide or a neap tide, and when it's slack water at either state of rise or fall. The river is under the influence of the Atlantic as far inland as Trois Rivières but tides are not something they had

Surviving Well is the Best Revenge

thought about when contemplating the voyage. There wasn't much planning of any kind and it was not a pleasure cruise. "Looks like about three knots, average."

"And we're doing better than seven? Less than two hours to Québec City. Damn, broad daylight."

"Think they're still looking for us?"

"The cops didn't seem interested. But maybe the Coast Guard. Depends. Maybe nobody cares."

"They wouldn't know we were going to the ocean."

"Who'd be crazy enough?"

The tidal current, now in mid-flight from the land, carried them under the Old Québec Bridge at over ten knots combined speed. There was no turning back or hesitating. They would pass the historic city in full view of anyone watching from the heights, the wharfs or the bridges. But Breeze, while shedding the last of the camouflage, was thinking about a hot bath or a good meal in one of Québec City's charming family inns with greening bronze plaques naming military or missionary heroes who had lived in the quaint stone buildings, as old as French colonialism. Maison Montcalm, convenient to the Plains of Abraham is one she remembered. She had been there on a school excursion. Every Québécois knows the sad story, the debacle of 1756. The bitter taste of defeat lingers, but the owners of Maison Montcalm are pragmatic and serve real French Canadian cuisine to tourists as Old Québec begins to feel the effects of foreign travelers. Climbing the wide stone steps, or lounging with a beer in a paper bag in the church square, one could imagine Lyons or Nice. In winter they compensate with Carnival.

"It would have been nice to stop," she said, with a sigh.

"Not this time. What's after Québec City?"

Piloting great waters by trial and error is never a good idea and there were so many reasons why Christian and Breeze should not have been on an aging Louisiana shrimper, which had suffered more, as yet undiscovered, damage in the rapids, heading for the Gulf of St. Lawrence, which is not hospitable in any season. They were navigating from buoy to buoy while running from the law, afraid to show running lights at night. What would happen when they ran out of buoys? Jacques had said that things would be better on the open water, but how would they know where they were going? The compass did not agree with the charts. Breeze tried to navigate between Neuville and Québec City by matching their compass with the bearings printed on the channels but the readings were not even close, even considering the difference between true compass courses and magnetic headings. "When we can see a point ahead we'll just steer for it and keep on that heading, whatever the compass says, and not what the chart says," he answered, trying to sound convincing.

"Okay, but what do we do when we're out on the ocean and there's no landmarks?" she asked, trying to imagine what the Gulf and the open ocean would be like. If Breeze had greater doubts she didn't express them to Christian. She had instigated this voyage and her mother had taught her to take each day as it dawned, dealing with problems as they arose.

"I don't know. Just follow the coastline, I guess."

Below the great city the river turned east. On the chart two channels offered to take them down river. The first seemed wider and therefore safer so they ran the main channel along the pastoral fields and boarded up cottages of Ile d'Orléans' eastern shore with Québec City on their stern. The low sun struggled through a haze of snow falling under the edge of storm clouds. For a brief moment the shy orb silhouetted the church spires and the Chateau and rays of light shot out dazzling the mariners stealing glances astern. Looking back it was a moment of rare beauty in a sea of anxiety.

When the clouds closed down again like the shutter of a camera briefly open to steal the moment, night came on swiftly and by five o'clock it was dark on the water with only the confusing shore lights and the pin pricks of buoys for guidance. The freezing wind that had nipped at the *Queen's* heels since Portneuf became a gusting, breathing demon, hammering at them first from one direction then another as the storm center passed a few miles ahead. The temperature dropped rapidly and the snow was a fine haze driven across the river in fits and veils. The lights of Québec City were blotted out and the river went from a snarling grey-green to a vicious grey-black, flecked with white caps. The tide had turned. It would be another tide-lop night. This time at least they were prepared. Deck gear and Dominique in her canvas shroud were secured with lines but Christian worried about the fuel filters: at least this time he knew what to do. Trial by mechanical demons seemed to go hand in hand with trial by water, education and experience followed by necessity.

Breeze delivered more coffee and sandwiches to the wheelhouse despite the lurching, rolling conditions. Christian peered into the growing gloom and steered, sipped hot coffee without taking his eyes off the buoys. Green to green. Reds for reference. Another big freighter slogging upstream hogged the middle of the road where the channel curved around the end of Ile d'Orléans, forcing him to steer off line, hoping there was enough water outside the buoys, then turning inward again, meeting the bow wave of the foreign boat. He tried to warn Breeze about the wave bumps. The Salties are always in a hurry to get in or out of heartland Canada before winter sets in and the Seaway closes.

Below Québec City the stream began to broaden and the maritime anarchy was reestablished. They were still navigating in the narrow main shipping channel despite what appeared on the chart to be miles of open water; it was not. Under the surface is a maze of cul-de-sacs and shoals creating a stew of currents and overfalls that even the locals avoid. But the coffee was hot and the thick sandwiches a banquet. Breeze steered while Christian ate standing at the chart table swaying with the motion like an old sea dog, dropping crumbs and mayonnaise on Cap Torment. The river battled the tide, the *Queen* lurched from buoy to buoy like a film strip unspooling. The Pilot Guide warned them to watch out for the channel shift below Cap Torment. The first clue was a down bound freighter that appeared to be on their wrong side, hard under the towering cliffs, but that was an illusion created by the North Shore highlands to add to the confusion of bucking in the current, slammed by the wind coming off the bluffs, wondering why they were so close to shore. The lights of river towns to the east, which seemed tantalizingly close between the squalls of snow, beckoned with safe harbours but the big river is a fraud.

Midnight: Christian, nodding at the wheel, was startled awake when the wash from a passing freighter crashed against the *Bayou Queen*, tossing her aside like a toy. How long had he dozed? And why did he not see the big boat? The storm had blown off heading inland, the night clearing and colder and the buoys farther apart. Green to green. Reds on the left for reference still, but with Breeze asleep on the wheelhouse floor, wrapped in several sleeping bags, Christian had no idea where they were. Breeze had kept track of their location on the charts and he depended on the reassuring updates, as well as her words of encouragement. At first Breeze would unwrap, check off a buoy and curl up again, fighting to stay awake. But sleep had finally won out. She was exhausted from the effort of caring for three souls and keeping their spirits up. Christian throttled down to reduce the noise and vibrations and let her sleep as long as he could see lights ahead. But it seemed to take longer and longer to reach the next green and he missed the running lights of a boat the size of an apartment building. Of course, the tide had turned and they were heading the rush until they were almost at a standstill. There was a quick flashing green buoy ahead. A turn. Time to check numbers but he dare not leave the wheel. Then the warning euphoria swept over him. Senses tuned too fine for too long and hearing too acute, so much so that the engine seemed to be racing. He was tempted to slow down even more, if only to escape from the noise of the engine, the agonizingly tense progression of life on the run and the nightmare of churning in a stream of slime, moving like a snail, falling back, being pulled down. He knew he was only hallucinating again but there was a turn.

"Breeze? Wake up, baby." He was also vulnerable, suspended in the black unknown, swimming against an invisible tide. He felt the nagging fear; not just about the night of dangers, but because he was losing control, experiencing that feeling of helpless retreat after the euphoria. The greens were no longer in focus. Shore lights only pinpricks that could be stars. Then the ringing in the ears returned and the sick feeling in the stomach that comes even without motion. "I need you..."

Breeze unwrapped herself from the sleeping bags, emerging from the warm cocoon, not feeling like a beautiful butterfly, just a tired aching assistant, but she was there beside him. "I'm here. You okay?"

"No. Where are we? There's a turn."

She took the torch and stepped out on the deck into a bitterly cold night. There was no wind and the boat appeared to be dead in the water, yet the sounds of their racing bow wave and thrumming engine should have brought them quickly to the next green buoy. Instead they crawled like a dying water bug whose many legs, endlessly churning as if in glue, could not defeat inertia. Gaining by inches they finally came near the surprisingly large buoy, which seemed to be speeding away from them. Green buoy, K65...Breeze quickly slipped back into the wheelhouse, focused the red light on the chart and discovered their place in the maritime nightmare. Ile aux Coudres. The tide was being squeezed between Ile aux Coudres bank and Cap aux Corbeau. She marked the buoy and turned from the chart table in time to see Christian slumping over the big wheel. Easing him down into the nest of sleeping bags she whispered, "Sleep, my poor darling."

Breeze searched the charts again to be sure of their location, found it and tried to relaxe. Steered and searched the blackness for shore marks. Steered for hours and shivered to keep warm. Steered the maddeningly slow pace until she thought she would go crazy; humming tunes, fingers moving on an imaginary cello, hands waving, conducting Mozart. And it went like that through the hours of darkness until the tide slackened and changed direction. Then they fairly flew down to the sea, like Neptune's Car through a universe filled with blinking, upside-down stars into the false, indifferent dawn, like a monotone snap shot. The purple sun came up briefly over the rounded shoulders of the Notre Dame Mountains before climbing back into the inevitable cloudbank. In winter the weather systems march through the St. Lawrence River valley in an endless parade of cloud systems and gales. A rare good spell is inevitably shunted aside by wind, rain, sleet and snow. The water a perpetual iron grey or sickly green, flecked with white caps. Sea smoke when a really cold front blows over from the interior of Québec and Labrador and the summer-damp fogs are replaced by other problems. The *Bayou Queen*, far from her warm Louisiana waters, with Breeze digging deep into her reserves, plodded on, taking each offering as it came.

Running away down the great river became almost a routine. The hours and the buoys reeled by and Breeze transcended to that zone of wakefulness beyond the need for sleep. The coffee and the cold helped, but it was more to do with drawing on reserves from a deep place she was not aware of, laid down over the centuries as her ancestors toiled on the oceans the way others ploughed the soil. The Celts learned to grapple with the elements and wiggle away a living by nerve and guile, rolling over the seas of plenty, but allowed only enough to survive. The Irish fishermen graduated from the skin curraghs into sailing ships furrowing the seas to foreign homes, to continue the battle, clinging to the rocky foreshores like limpets, tempting the fates and making the sign of the cross in supplication and granted only enough divine protection to endure.

Christian slept and recovered as they came abeam of the big light tower marking Prince Shoal and the entrance to the Saguenay Fjord. It was dark again.

Thinking he had slept for only an hour he crawled out of the warm nest of sleeping bags rubbing his eyes in disbelief. The river scape that met him was a city of lights, blinking and flashing, the effect heightened by two freighters passing through the area, one up, and one down. Breeze, concentrating on steering between them, could not take her eyes away from the freighter close on their starboard side. "What the hell's going on?"

"It's okay. We're between two big boats," she answered calmly, as if she was guiding a perambulator through a summer sunshine park.

"Where are we?"

"Tadoussac."

"Tadoussac? Are you sure?"

"Yes, absolutely sure."

"We can't be! Too soon." He gazed in wonder at the confusion of lights, then studied the chart. The two realities did not explain, confirm or deny each other. "Damn," he whispered. "We forgot the current again."

"No. You've been asleep for twelve hours. We're right about where I calculated we should be."

"Really?" Christian pushed open the wheelhouse door.

"Be careful, my darling. Decks're slippery," she cautioned gently. She had been out several times to check buoy numbers, and to pee, the baby pressing more and more on her bladder. With practice she learned to steer a bit to starboard before leaving the *Queen* on her own, remembering to take a compass bearing. Once she even ventured down to the galley and grabbed bread and cold meats and a bottle of wine. In the twelve hours of Christian's hiatus Breeze learned several tricks of steering and navigation. There had been a close call with the night ferry running between St.

Simeon and Riviére de Loup. Breeze had become used to the pushy freighters, learning to keep to the right, as if on a highway, but did not know what to do when confronted with a big boat crossing her path. She had the right of way, going with the tide, but the ferry pilot took the advantage of size and kept on, forcing Breeze to steer behind him. The rules of engagement are not the same as the rules of the road established by Acts of Parliament. As in the voyage of life, rules in relationships, like Québec ferries, like some friends, are not to be trusted.

Christian stood at the bow taking in the scene. The marine display was the last hurrah of navigational aides before the vast Gulf opened up beyond Tadoussac. They were entering the big water. The St. Lawrence Estuary in turn opening to the embrace of the Atlantic Ocean, the point of no return. He also realized that the air felt warmer and there was little wind. He made his way unsteadily back to the wheelhouse.

"Stop the boat," Christian said.

"What? Why?"

"I've decided. Please, just slow down and put her out of gear."

The *Queen* drifted, rolling easily in the wake of the freighters, now only white stern lights in the distance. The night was unusually quiet and calm for the Lower St. Lawrence Estuary in winter. A brief interlude as if the world had drawn a deep breath. The intervals of white light from the big towers on Prince Shoal and Ile Rouge sped at them over the inky blackness, an insistent code, like a sequenced ballet. The night came closer and was not foreign. And over the mutter of the idling diesel they could hear the exhalations of whales feeding on shrimp in the brackish outflow of the Saguenay River. Soon the whales would head south to their winter breeding grounds leaving the Estuary to the sea birds.

Breeze brought her cello on deck and sat on the cap rail to play for them. J. S. Bach wafted over the dark water. The prelude in D minor...Christian stood near the stern looking sadly at the form of Dominique, so darkly beautiful in life, become grotesque in death; *still life with shroud,* he said to himself. The sad sweet notes spread over the water and entered the domain of the whales. Christian shivered with the thrill of the deep base notes. The whales surfaced nearby, entranced, and lay on the surface, blowing lightly. She played random notes just for the whales and they answered as if in harmony; trumpet runs and deep sonorous moans. *The night of the whales,* she said in tribute. It was a magic moment that Christian would remember for the rest of his life. He wanted it to be Breeze's night, but the reality of what he had to do hung heavy over the thrill of escape on their own terms. He would also carry the burden of knowing where Dominique's body rested and the circumstances of her death. Her family should be informed.

"It's time," he said.

Weight seemed important. He remembered a length of iron pipe in the engine room. Breeze helped him place the weight beside the leg that had so recently, in the warmth of life, tantalized and teased him. Without words they retied the shroud with many turns of line, like a package for delivery. Together they lifted the frozen body onto the stern rail. Christian had to turn away, facing the lights of the distant village where normal people lived normal lives to compose himself for the deed.

"Should one of us say something?" Breeze asked, sensing his distress.

Only the *Bayou Queen* was experienced having bodies dropped over her side. "I didn't know her well, Breeze. She was beautiful. A mystery. One doesn't get to know a person who's an undercover cop, spy, or whatever she actually was. But I think she was a nice person...I feel badly for her parents."

"They may never know what happened."

"They know she's dead."

"When we get to Fogo we can write to the Montreal Police."

"Yes, that would be the right thing to do, except..."

Except that they were still fugitives from justice...

The imperfectly weighted body in its canvas shroud spiraled down leaving a trail of silver bubbles. A pair of minke whales nosed closer to investigate, keeping pace: curious escorts, a funeral cortege spiraling down in sympathy. Satisfied that the canvas-covered body was not of their world they broke away to resume the endless search for food. Down, down, the pressure increasing until no more bubbles marked the descent. A Greenland shark swept in and made a pass but continued on its way towards the Strait of Belle Isle. It too was leaving the estuary, leaving the odd addition from the other world to the shrimp and bottom feeders who came skittering and gliding in to investigate. The body bumped once on the sand, rolled on its side and lay still, never to move far from the spot chosen by Christian as Dominique's final resting place. Small particles of organic debris welled up and tiny silver fish darted in to feed. A snow crab sidled up warily to prod the newcomer. In time the earthly remains of Dominique would dissolve and disperse, nature asserting its dominion over all things great and small. The whales, alerted by the noise of an engine, returned to the surface searching for the sound of the cello but the Louisiana shrimp boat, itself an enigma on the Gulf, had moved away leaving the Estuary cloaked in blackness broken by distant flashes, waiting for the next storm.

The End of Book Two

Book Three: Surviving Well: Fogo Island, continues the travels and trials of Christian and Breeze as they escape the dangerous times and the fledgling FLQ., fleeing the law, running away down the St. Lawrence River. Too late to turn back they begin a dangerous voyage in winter on the Gulf of St. Lawrence, trying to reach the safety of Newfoundland. They are almost broke, have a new baby coming soon and an old boat to complete the journey to Breeze's ancestral home, Fogo Island, searching for Béhathook Cove and the relatives her mother left behind when Breeze was only a baby. It is a circle of life that presents the young couple with an opportunity to start anew, accepting the rigours of a New-foundland Outport or find another avenue, a mist-shrouded journey to Ireland in search of a more distant ancestry. What they find on Fogo Island and how they complete the journey to Ireland will be a grand surprise. The future however, like the winter sea conditions, is a dark cloud on the horizon. The IRA is growing in Ireland but their bloody war reaches across the Atlantic to touch the lives of Christian, Breeze and Grace…That's giving away some information, but only a fragment of the stories to come.

Patric Ryan. The Bruce Peninsula. June 2015